Reginald N Shutte

The Life, Times, and Writings of the Right Rev. Dr. Henry Phillpotts

Lord Bishop of Exeter: Vol. I.

Reginald N Shutte

The Life, Times, and Writings of the Right Rev. Dr. Henry Phillpotts
Lord Bishop of Exeter: Vol. I.

ISBN/EAN: 9783337054847

Printed in Europe, USA, Canada, Australia, Japan

Cover: Foto ©Raphael Reischuk / pixelio.de

More available books at **www.hansebooks.com**

THE

Life, Times, and Writings

OF THE

RIGHT REV. DR. HENRY PHILLPOTTS,

LORD BISHOP OF EXETER.

BY THE REV. REGINALD N. SHUTTE, B.A.,

RECTOR OF S. MARY STEPS, EXETER, AND AUTHOR OF A NEW
CATENA ON S. PAUL'S EPISTLES, LIFE OF
REV. HENRY NEWLAND,
ETC.

VOLUME I.

LONDON:

SAUNDERS, OTLEY, AND CO.

66, BROOK STREET, HANOVER SQUARE.

1863.

PREFACE.

T will perhaps be expected that I fhould fay fomething as to the circumftances which have led to the production of this work. And this is the more neceffary fince fome writers have commented upon my intentions in a way which, if it raifes one's eftimate of their power of invention, fpeaks little for their fenfe of juftice. To none of thefe comments have I thought it needful to reply, but have refrained from ftating my cafe until the appearance of the firft inftalment of my work fhould give me a fuitable opportunity for doing fo.

The circumftances which led to my becoming the biographer of the Bifhop of Exeter are briefly thefe. In the autumn of 1861 I received a letter from my publifhers—to whom I was then an entire ftranger—inviting me to undertake the preparation of a work to be entitled, *The Life, Times, and Writings of the Bifhop of Exeter.* I can truly fay that I was wholly unprepared for this offer. But fuppofing that I had declined it, would the projected work have fallen to the ground? I am not vain enough to believe that it would. So that, in point of fact, I am only doing what fomebody elfe would have done, if he had had the fame opportunity.

But it has been affumed that I have been acting in defiance of the Bifhop's wifhes, and this affumption has furnifhed the text for many a homily at my expenfe. The thought proved too overpowering for moft of my critics, who could not bring themfelves to part with the affumption that was fo groundlefs, and yet fo capable of being made effective.

The facts are fimply thefe. Having collected the neceffary materials, and having done my beft to afcertain that no biography was contemplated by the Bifhop's family, or immediate friends, I wrote to his Lordfhip, announcing the work upon which I was engaged. My letter was courteous and deferential. It is true that, although againft his Lordfhip's wifhes I would not have perfifted in the work, I did not afk for his co-operation in direct terms—for the treatment which I had experienced at his hands in reference to a previous publication forbade it—yet I worded my letter in fuch a way that, while it could convey no offence to a mind however fenfitive, it was impoffible to miftake my meaning.   The Bifhop did *not* miftake it, for he inftructed his chaplain to fay in reply that " he feels that he has no right to object to the undertaking," and, in a fubfequent letter from his Lordfhip to myfelf, he fays, " *you have an* UN-DOUBTED RIGHT *to publifh fuch a work.*" Surely this is explicit enough.   If any objection is veiled under thefe words, I can only lament that I have not been able to difcover it.   The Bifhop admits my " UNDOUBTED RIGHT " to engage in the undertaking ; and if he admits it, who has any reafon to object ? " So far," fays the *Times,** " nothing can be plainer and more fimple than the fubject-matter of the correfpondence."   And this is only doing me juftice.

But now the ingenuity of my critics begins to difplay itfelf.   The *Times* proceeds to affert that I did " not only want to write the Life of the Bifhop of Exeter," but that I wanted " to write it with the Bifhop's advice and affiftance."   It is a pleafant conceit, but, like many other things,

---

* Auguft 22, 1862.

it will not bear examination. So far from my looking for any affiftance from the Bifhop, I told my publifhers, in the very firft letter I ever wrote to them on the fubject, that I was confident that his Lordfhip's co-operation could never be obtained. I went, indeed, a great deal further than this, and in the fame letter added, " *Perfonally fpeaking, I fhould prefer writing independently of any help from him.*" This is repeated in my fubfequent correfpondence with my publifhers and others, and the tone of the Bifhop's reply to my firft letter was not calculated to alter my opinion, and caufe me to feek his aid. The truth is, the Bifhop faid exactly what I wanted him to fay. The utmoft I wifhed was that he fhould not object.

And the reafon is obvious. If the Bifhop had entered heartily into my plan, and had handed me his papers, and otherwife rendered me material affiftance, the value of my work as an independent hiftory would have been gone. It would then have appeared that I was writing at his Lordfhip's dictation, and with the defire of conciliating his regard. To all intents and purpofes it would have been a Life of the Bifhop written by the Bifhop himfelf. However interefting fuch a work might be, it would at leaft be open to the charge of partiality. Now, at all events, my book is beyond fuſpicion.

But I deſired, it may be urged, " to have the benefit of his Lordſhip's judgment on ſome doubtful and difficult points." It is perfectly true that I did expreſs this deſire; but need it therefore be aſſumed—as my critics have ſo eagerly done—that theſe "doubtful and difficult points" were ſo numerous as to neceſſitate a recital by the Biſhop of the changes and chances of his whole life? In other words, when I wrote this ſentence, was I trying to entrap the Biſhop into revealing to me matters of perſonal and private intereſt, which otherwiſe I could not have known? Such a belief could only have been conceived by one who had no knowledge of the Biſhop. I had already aſſured his Lordſhip that my work would relate, almoſt excluſively, to his *public* life, and that all the requiſite materials were entirely within my reach. Whether I ſpoke truly this preſent volume will ſhow. What then did I mean by the "doubtful and difficult points?" On examining the Biſhop's writings, I occaſionally found that ſtatements and facts were capable of more than one inter-pretation. My deſire was to find the *right* one. It would have been ſatisfactory to have learnt this from the Bifhop's own lips. As it is, I have fpared nothing that labour and refearch could effect to arrive at the true refult. I venture to think that even my moft exacting critics will not view this as militating againft my avowed defire of writing an independent hiftory.

And now I come to a deteftable charge—I ufe the word advifedly—that I defigned to publifh certain letters written by the Bifhop, without his confent. The *Times* has directly charged me with having faid nothing about thefe letters in the firft inftance, fo that I might have it in my power hereafter to threaten the Bifhop with their publication, in cafe he refufed to affift me. I can only regret that any one connected with journalifm fhould have fo far degraded himfelf, while meaning to difhonour me.

When my work was announced in the public prints, I received offers of affiftance from various quarters, and, amongft other things, fome letters written by the Bifhop at different periods were fent for my infpection. When I firft wrote to the Bifhop my work had not been advertifed, and I did not receive the letters for more than three months afterwards. This, then, difpofes of the *Times*. Not one of thefe letters was marked "private," and, on perufal of them, I found that there were only a few extracts, relating either to public events, or to theological criticism, which would be likely to interest the general reader. Had it not been for these letters the Bishop would have heard nothing more of me—so little anxious was I for his assistance; but immediately after reading them I did what every honourable man would do under the circumstances, I wrote to his Lordship, saying that I thought it possible that selections from them would be valuable as well as interesting, and offering to wait upon him to submit the extracts, which I proposed to use, for his approval.

I am aware, indeed, that a weekly print has had a great deal to say about the idea of my inviting myself to bed and board at Bishopstowe for an unlimited period, but the writer seems to think that there is no other way of satisfactorily communicating with a bishop except through the medium of a good dinner. In his idea the episcopal heart only expands over a bottle of dry old port. Had he lived in this diocese as long as I have, he would have known better, and would be content to give up the dinner and bed, if he could only command a quiet half-hour of the Bishop's time. And this was really all I wanted—no great thing to ask for, considering

that for eight years and a-half I have been beneficed in his Lordſhip's cathedral city. Had the
Biſhop conſented to ſee me, my buſineſs need not
have detained him many minutes. I ſhould
have read the paſſages I propoſed to uſe, (they
were very few,) and have aſcertained his Lordſhip's pleaſure. If this was not an honeſt courſe,
I know not what would have been. But in
reply to my propoſal the Biſhop wrote to me
ſaying that he " *declined altogether communicating
with me on the matter.*" When he added that on
"ſeeing the letters" he would "tell me whether
he would allow the publication of them or not;"
his Lordſhip failed to give me credit for that ſelf-
reſpect which it is the pride of every right-
minded man to poſſeſs. How was he to ſee
them, if he would not communicate with me ?
Was I to ſend them to his Lordſhip's chaplain or
ſecretary to be dealt with in any way they might
think fit ? Few prudent men would have coun-
ſelled this ſtep, and moſt people would have ad-
viſed me to take the Biſhop at his word, and
attempt no further communication with him.
Had he not been my *Biſhop* I ſhould certainly
have adopted this courſe ; but with an earneſt
deſire to ſhow all deference to his Lordſhip, and
not without a hope that he might be induced to

exprefs himfelf lefs ftrongly towards me, I wrote the following letter. It was only due to myfelf to fet before him a ftatement of the cafe as it affected my pofition with the public. As matters have turned out, it would have been better if in the firft inftance fome fuch letter as this had been written :—

"Exeter, July 18, 1862.

" My Lord,—I beg to acknowledge the receipt of your Lordfhip's letter of the 13th inftant, and to call your Lord-fhip's attention to the following facts :—

" On the 20th of February laft I announced to your Lord-fhip that I had been afked to write your Lordfhip's life, and that I had undertaken to do fo.

" On the 25th of February your Lordfhip replied, through Mr. Barnes, that you offered no objection, but that you de-clined to afford any help.

" Having collected a vaft mafs of materials, and among them many letters of your Lordfhip, I wrote on the 11th of July to offer to fubmit them to your Lordfhip before publi-cation.

" In your Lordfhip's reply of July 13 you decline altogether to communicate with me on the matter.

" Upon the above facts I beg to fubmit to your Lordfhip that it had not occurred to me when I wrote my letter of the 11th inftant that if, on the one hand, I fubmitted to your Lordfhip all letters of your Lordfhip in my poffeffion, but do not receive, on the other, your Lordfhip's affiftance towards fupplying myfelf with reliable matter, I fhall be in a very unfavourable pofition with the public, becaufe it muft appear that I am writing under your Lordfhip's direction, while I am not receiving from your Lordfhip the affiftance which can alone make the book valuable. May I beg your Lordfhip to confider the pofition ? As I am able to look at it, it feems to me plain that if I cannot have your Lordſhip's free aſſiſtance I have no alternative but to fulfil my engagement with the publiſhers in the beſt way I can.

" I have the honour to remain,

" Your Lordſhip's obedient ſervant,

" Reginald N. Shutte.

" The Lord Biſhop of Exeter."

The only anſwer I received to this letter was the copy of a Bill which the Biſhop had filed in Chancery, to reſtrain me from publiſhing any of thoſe letters, or extracts from them, that I never had any intention of publiſhing againſt his wiſhes! Not a word had fallen from me to lead to the ſuppoſition that I meant to uſe this correſpondence without the Biſhop's conſent. In the letter in which I informed his Lordſhip that they were in my poſſeſſion I diſtinctly acknowledged his right to ſay whether any portions of them ſhould be publiſhed or not. All that my laſt letter conveyed was, that if he perſiſted in his determination of not communicating with me, I ſhould not part with the letters, but ſhould go my own way. The truth is that the moment I found that the Biſhop would not communicate wi.h me, I gave up all idea of the letters. They were not in any way eſſential to my work. So that when I told his Lordſhip that I had no alternative but to fulfil my engagement with the publishers in the best way I could, I meant him to understand that no letters, or anything else which he could control, would appear. On reading my letters again I cannot see that they admit of any other sense. A short note addressed to me by the Bishop's chaplain or lawyer would have led me to explain my intentions, if any explanation were wanted. The Bishop, however, preferred to proceed according to process of law, and the energy of his movements induced a portion of the public to believe that I was about to publish certain *private letters* of his—a step which, in common with every upright man, I should reprobate and abhor. I can only emphatically affirm that this book would never have been written had the Bishop objected, and that it was never my intention to give to the world any letters that he might have wished to remain unpublished.

This is the history of the letters. The Bishop (I wish to say it without offence) acted with precipitancy. There was nothing whatever in any of my letters to justify such a step as an appeal to the Court of Chancery, without further explanations. His Lordship ought to have been very clear about my intentions be-

fore he expofed me to the odium of doing that
which every upright man would fhrink from.

I will only fay one word about the ftructure
of this work. It relates exclufively (or nearly
fo), as I told the Bifhop in my firft letter, to his
Lordfhip's *public life*. It never formed any
part of my plan to interfere with the confi-
dences of focial and domeftic intercourfe. This
part of the Bifhop's life I leave to fome other
biographer. A perufal of this volume will
fatisfy any one that I · have faithfully adhered
to my original programme. It was in my power
to have added to the work by the infertion of
jokes, fmart *on dits*, and tales of focial life.
Nothing, however, is given in this book which
need annoy the Bifhop, unlefs, indeed, he be
offended at honeft criticifm of his writings and
public acts. There are weighty confiderations
—certainly not connected with any gain to
myfelf— why this biography fhould appear
whilft the Bifhop is ftill among us. At prefent it would be improper for me to fay what
thefe reafons are. I can only afk my readers,
therefore, to give me credit for acting for the
beft.

One word more. The mifapprehenfion that
prevails refpecting many important events of

the Bifhop's life, makes me confident that this book will not be without confiderable intereft to a large clafs of readers; but at the fame time I do not difguife from myfelf the certainty that it will not confirm the prejudices of others. But however it may be received, this much I can affirm, that with high refpect for the Bifhop it was undertaken, and that it has been written without fear or favour.

R. N. S.

Exeter,
17th *November*, 1862.

CONTENTS.

CHAPTER III.

CHAPTER IV.

CHAPTER V.

CHAPTER VI.

CHAPTER VII.

CHAPTER VIII.

CHAPTER IX.

CHAPTER X.

CHAPTER XI.

CHAPTER XII.

CHAPTER XIII.

CHAPTER XIV.

CHAPTER XV.

CHAPTER XVI.

CHAPTER XVII.

CHAPTER XVIII.

CHAPTER XIX.

CHAPTER XX.

CHAPTER XXI.

CHAPTER XXII.

CHAPTER XXIII.

CHAPTER XXIV.

CHAPTER XXV.

CHAPTER XXVI.

Life of the Bishop of Exeter.

CHAPTER I.

Foundation of the Bishopric of Exeter. Celebrated Bishops of the Diocese. Birth of Henry Phillpotts. Account of his Family. Lived in the same house as George Whitfield. His early Education. Matriculation at Oxford. University Career. Prospect of Advancement. Dr. Martin Routh. Dr. Copleſtone (Biſhop of Llandaff). Interval between B.A. degree and taking Holy Orders. Twice Examiner of Candidates for University Honours. Ordained Deacon and Prieſt. Marriage and Reſignation of Fellowſhip. Offered Principalſhip of Hertford College. His ſubſequent Degrees. Honorary Fellow of Magdalene College. Inſtituted to Vicarage of Kilmerſdon. Preſented to Living of Stainton-le-Street. Nonreſidence. Preferment accounted for. Chaplain to Biſhop Barrington. Controverſy with Dr. Lingard, the Roman Catholic Hiſtorian. Preſented to Living of Biſhop Middleham. Deſcription of the Pariſh. Preſented to Rectory of Gateſhead. Account of the Pariſh. Collated to the Ninth Prebendal Stall in Durham Cathedral. Preſented to Living of S. Margaret's, in Durham. Ill-feeling excited. Character as a Pariſh Prieſt. Preached at Anniverſary of Sons of the Clergy, in S. Paul's Cathedral. Some Account of the Sermon. Collated to the Second Stall in Durham Cathedral.

EXETER is proud of its Biſhops; and with good reaſon, for few Sees can exhibit a roll of more illuſtrious names.

The original ſeat of the Biſhopric was at Crediton, from whence it was removed to Exeter

by Leofric (A. D. 1050), who was solemnly installed in
his new Cathedral by King Edward the Confessor, in
person, and thus became the first Bishop of Exeter,
properly so called. There had, however, been Bishops
of Cornwall and Devonshire for more than a hundred
years previously, but they were only suffragans of the
See of Sherborne.

Among the more celebrated of the Bishops of
Exeter, many of whom were natives of that city, the
following deserve to be mentioned.*

BARTHOLOMEW (A. D. 1161), who was called by
Pope Alexander III. " the luminary of the English
Church," an appellation to which his rare gifts and
profound theological learning fully entitled him. Like
the present occupant of the See, he distinguished himself by an uncompromising opposition to his primate
(Thomas à Becket).

WILLIAM BRIWERE (A. D. 1224), famous for his
saintly life, and the deeds of mercy which he performed
in the Holy Land.

WALTER DE STAPLEDON (A.D. 1308), who founded
Exeter College, and added largely to his Cathedral.
He was brutally murdered by a mob in London.

JOHN DE GRANDISSON (A. D. 1327), renowned for
his princely munificence, and the salutary reforms
which he effected in his diocese.

RICHARD FOX (A. D. 1487), the chief friend and

---

* For a chronological list of the Bishops of Exeter, see
Appendix A.

counsellor of Henry VII, and the founder of Corpus Christi College, Oxford, who united in his single person the characters of statesman, architect, soldier, herald, diplomatist, and prelate : a combination of qualities rare even in those stirring times.

HUGH OLDHAM (A.D. 1504), famed for the splendid encouragement which he gave to literature.

MYLES COVERDALE (A.D. 1551), the translator of the Bible, who was deprived by Queen Mary.

JAMES TURBEVILLE (A.D. 1555), deprived by Queen Elizabeth for refusing to take the Oath of Supremacy.

JOSEPH HALL (A.D. 1627), celebrated for his great literary attainments and theological writings. He was subjected to much ill treatment and persecution.

JOHN GAUDEN (A.D. 1660), the reputed author of the Εἰκὼν Βασιλική, and one of the Divines selected to confer with the Presbyterians at the Savoy.

SETH WARD (A.D. 1662), the celebrated Church-restorer.

JONATHAN TRELAWNEY (A.D. 1688), who was one of the seven Bishops imprisoned by James II.

Many of the Bishops of Exeter are famous for the part which they played in history, and their names are preserved in ancient chronicles as Chancellors of the Kingdom, Ambassadors at Foreign Courts, Tutors and Guardians of Royal Children, and Counsellors of Monarchs. It is true that since the Reformation the See has been shorn of much of its temporal dignity, in consequence of the spoliation of its revenues, and it

has too often been regarded merely as a ftepping-ftone
to other and richer preferment; but ftill the glorious
traditions of the paft remain, and of all the illuftrious
prelates who have ruled the Diocefe of Exeter, it may
be doubted whether any one of them has done more
to merit the homage of the Church than the prefent
occupant of the epifcopal throne—the 60th in fucceffion from Leofric. His name will furvive when
thofe of his contemporaries are forgotten, and the
fervices which he has rendered to religion will be
cherifhed with gratitude, fo long as England retains
her veneration for the Faith which was once delivered
to the Saints.

Among the Bifhops of Exeter, fome may be found
who were of humble origin, and raifed themfelves from
mean ftations to the epifcopal chair by their talents
and learning.   The prefent occupant of it—to his
honour be it recorded—is of their number.

HENRY PHILLPOTTS was born at Bridgwater, an
inconfiderable Somerfetfhire town, lying clofe on the
borders of the bloody field of Sedgmoor, and famous
for its butter and cheefe, on May 6th, 1778, and was
baptized in the parifh church on the 16th of the fame
month.   He was the fecond fon of Mr. John Phillpotts, who carried on the trade of a brickmaker in
that town.   In 1782 his father removed to Gloucefter,
and became the landlord of the "Bell" inn in that
city, a tavern of no great pretenfion.   In former times
none but freemen were allowed to keep inns or hotels
in corporate towns; and when any perfon who was not

a freeman, or a ftranger coming from a diftance, defired to do fo, it was neceffary that he fhould firft be
admitted as a freeman—ufually by the payment of a
fine. Mr. John Phillpotts was admitted as a freeman of Gloucefter, in confideration of a fine, on 28th
September, 1782, and immediately afterwards took
poffeffion of the inn.

It is not a little remarkable that the celebrated Non-
conformift, George Whitfield, was in 1714 born at the
" Bell," at Gloucefter, of which his father was the
hoft.   Unlike his illuftrious predeceffor, however, the
future prelate does not appear to have mingled in the
bufinefs of the houfe, thereby efcaping thofe perils
into which Whitfield fell, when, to ufe his own words,
—" I put on my blue apron and my fnuffers, wafhed
mops, cleaned rooms, and, in one word, became profeffed and common drawer for nigh a year and a-half."
Better things than this were in ftore for the fubject of
this hiftory, for his father fubfequently relinquifhed
the bufinefs of inn-keeping, and became an auctioneer,
and land and timber furveyor.   At this period he refided at Wallfworth, near Gloucefter, and was fortunate
enough to be appointed land agent of the Dean and
Chapter, 30th November, 1799, an introduction which
afterwards led to his eldeft fon becoming chapter
clerk.   He died at Gloucefter, widely and defervedly
refpected, February 22, 1814, aged 70 years; and his
widow, Mrs. Sybella Phillpotts, who lived to fee her
fon afcend the epifcopal throne, alfo died in that city,
December 31, 1833, at the advanced age of 81.

The early education of Henry Phillpotts was received at the College School at Gloucefter, and it fell to the lot of the Rev. Arthur Benoni Evans, a found fcholar as well as a man of fome literary tafte, to mould the youthful intellect of the future prelate. At this time he was remarkable more for his fteady and induftrious habits, than for any brilliancy of mental power, or originality of thought. After pafling through the ufual routine of claffical ftudies, fuch as was then in favour in provincial towns, he proceeded to Oxford, and it is much to his credit that, without any of thofe advantages of education which are infeparable from large public fchools, he was able fuccefsfully to compete for a fcholarfhip.

On November 7, 1791, he was matriculated at Corpus Chrifti College, at an age when moft boys have fcarcely left the nurfery—*thirteen* years. This was the college of Cardinal Pole, Jewel, Hooker, John Hales, and other celebrities. His extreme youth did not prevent him from fecuring fome of the fub-ftantial honours and emoluments of the Univerfity; for, having taken his B.A. degree, 3rd June, 1795, he was in the following month elected a Probationer Fellow of Magdalene College on the Somerfet Foundation. In the fame year alfo he became Univerfity Prizeman, his Effay on " the Influence of a Religious Principle " being adjudged the beft.

And now a fplendid career was opening before him. A ripe fcholar, and a Fellow of a diftinguifhed Houfe, at an age when moft boys are ftill at fchool, it would

have been eafy to predict that the higheft honours of
any profeffion, which he might follow, would await
him. His painftaking habits, joined to indomitable
ftedfaftnefs of purpofe, rendered fuccefs inevitable.
Even his enemies have been compelled to acknowledge that if he had carried his talents and application
to the Bar, he might have rivalled the greateft of
Englifh Chancellors.

It was at this time that he was honoured with the
notice of one, who was deftined to exercife a powerful
and beneficial influence over his future life. In the
fame year that Mr. Phillpotts entered Oxford, Dr.
Martin Routh was elected Prefident of Magdalene
College, and to him it belonged to mould the mind of
the youthful Fellow, and inftil into it thofe found
principles of theology which qualified him- in later
years to become the uncompromifing champion of the
Faith. What Mr. Phillpotts owed to his intercourfe
with this gifted fcholar and divine—the one living
memorial that linked our days to thofe of the Pearfons,
and other giants of theology—it would not be eafy
to fay. To him, above all others, Mr. Phillpotts
feems to have opened the hidden receffes of his foul.
A faithful counfellor in difficulties, a ready reference
in controverfy, a fcholar whofe well-ftored mind was
never at a lofs for an apt quotation, a friend whofe
inftincts foared above all earthly confiderations, Dr.
Routh was the man of all others to win and fafhion
to noble purpofes the ardent fpirit of Mr. Phillpotts.
It is due to both of them to fay that the friendfhip

thus early begun was only terminated by Dr. Routh's death in December, 1854, at a patriarchal age, and that to the very laſt his former pupil was accuſtomed to ſeek his counſel with all the affectionate reſpect of earlier days. Even when the good old Preſident had ſeen him riſe to fame and honours, he ſtill felt towards him as a father, and often was his eye ſeen to brighten when he heard how well he was fighting the good fight, and was laying hold on eternal life.

Another of Mr. Phillpotts' earlieſt friends at Oxford was Mr. Copleſtone, afterwards Provoſt of Oriel, Dean of S. Paul's, and Biſhop of Llandaff. A ſcholar of the higheſt order, and courtier-like in manners, it is probable that this diſtinguiſhed prelate approached, nearer than any man of his day, to Burke's ſtandard of perfection in converſation—" not to play a regular ſonata, but, like the Æolian harp, to await the inſpiration of the paſſing breeze ;" and the charm of his friendſhip will long be a cheriſhed remembrance to all thoſe who were honoured with it.

It was while in daily intercourſe with ſuch men as theſe that Mr. Phillpotts' choice of a path in life was made. The firſt ſtep, however, was taken with much deliberation ; for it was not until ſeven years after his Bachelor's degree that he was admitted to Holy Orders. Meanwhile, the dignified leiſure of a Fellowſhip on the ſplendid foundation of William of Waynflete, gave him all the opportunity that was wanted for cultivating his literary taſtes, aſſociating with the ripeſt ſcholars, and ſtrengthening the foundation of thoſe acquirements which were to be his bulwark in many a ftorm to come.

On the 18th of April, 1798, he proceeded to the degree of M.A., and on the 25th of July, 1800, he was elected Prælector of Moral Philofophy. In 1802 he was appointed one of the firft examiners of candidates for Univerfity honours, jointly with the late Bifhop of Llandaff (Dr. Edward Copleftone), and other diftinguifhed fcholars. On the 13th of June in the fame year he was ordained Deacon by Dr. John Randolph, Bifhop of Oxford. In 1803 he was again appointed one of the examiners of candidates for Univerfity honours. On the 23rd of February, 1804, he was ordained Prieft, at Chefter, by Dr. Henry William Majendie, the bifhop of that diocefe; and on the 27th of October in the fame year he refigned his Fellowfhip, having married Deborah Maria, daughter of William Surtees, Efq., of Bath, and niece of Lady Eldon. On the 5th of November he was felected to preach before the Univerfity on the Gunpowder Treafon.

In the following year (1805) the Principalfhip of Hertford College became vacant by the death of Dr. Hodgfon. This college, under the title of Hert Hall, had been inhabited by ftudents fo early as the reign of Edward I, and in the following reign it was conveyed to Walter de Stapledon, founder of Exeter College. In the early part of the eighteenth century, Dr. Newton, the Principal, obtained from George II. a Royal Charter for converting it into a college, under the title

of Hertford College.   The attempt was unsuccessful,
and the establishment gradually languished for want of
funds.   On the death of Dr. Hodgson the Principal-
ship was offered to Mr. Phillpotts, but, with commendable prudence, he declined it, as there were many
vexatious regulations which he would have been obliged
to swear that he would keep ; and, the time for the
appointment of a Principal having elapsed, the Corporation became extinct.

Before quitting this portion of the subject, it may
be well to notice that Mr. Phillpotts proceeded to the
degrees of Bachelor and Doctor of Divinity on the
28th of June, 1821, and that he was elected an Honorary Fellow of Magdalene College on the 2nd of February, 1862.   This distinction was conferred on him
in consequence of the new ordinance of the University
Commissioners having allowed the College to elect a
certain number of Honorary Fellows, without emolu-
ment, as a mark of honour.   Besides the subject of
this history, the only other Honorary Fellows of Magdalene College are Sir Roundell Palmer and the Earl
of Rosse.

The first benefice held by Mr. Phillpotts was the
vicarage of Kilmersdon, with the chapelry of Ashwick,
near Bath, in the diocese of Bath and Wells, to which
he was presented by the Crown, 1st September, 1804.
The value of this living is 244 *l.* per annum, and the
population at the present time is 2,200.   He continued to hold this benefice until April 1806 ; but it
does not appear that he ever resided there, since all

the entries in the parish register during his incumbency are by Daniel Drape, curate, and there are no traditions preserved of his residence.

On 24th December in the following year (1805) he was instituted to Stainton-le-street, in the diocese of Durham, value 360*l.*; population 150; patron, the Crown. His name does not appear in the parish register, and it is believed that he never resided there. If it should excite surprise that so young a man, as Mr. Phillpotts then was, who had stepped at once from Oxford life into a benefice which would now-a-days be thought a sufficient provision for a parish priest after years of labour, should have been permitted to hold two livings at the same time, without residing upon either of them, it must be pleaded that he was in affinity to Lord Chancellor Eldon.

In 1806 Mr. Phillpotts became chaplain to the Bishop of Durham (Dr. Shute Barrington), that distinguished prelate having been attracted towards him by the fame of his ability and learning—an appointment which he continued to hold until the bishop's death, twenty years afterwards. His studies had early been directed to the Roman Catholic controversy, and an opportunity was soon afforded for testing the depth and solidity of his acquirements. In 1806 Bishop Barrington delivered a charge to the clergy of the diocese of Durham, which was afterwards published at their request, on " the Grounds on which the Church of England separated from the Church of Rome." This was animadverted upon in no very measured

terms by an anonymous writer, who was generally
fuppofed to be Dr. Lingard, the Roman Catholic
hiftorian.   Mr. Phillpotts boldly ftood forward in
defence of his diocefan. Several fmall pamphlets were
written on both fides with confiderable ability, and
Mr. Phillpotts fully eftablifhed his reputation as an
accurate thinker, and a controverfial writer of no mean
order.   The controverfy was renewed feveral years
later with a more ingenuous opponent than Dr. Lingard had proved himfelf to be, when the corruptions
of the Roman Church were moft completely expofed.
It will fave needlefs repetition, therefore, if remarks
on Mr. Phillpotts' conduct in reference to the Roman
Catholic queftion are deferred until his letters to Mr.
Charles Butler come under confideration.

In the fpring of 1806, as has been already ftated,
Mr. Phillpotts refigned the living of Kilmerfdon, and
on June 28th, in the fame year, he was prefented by the
Crown to Bifhop Middleham, in the Diocefe of Durham,
This living was held by him *in commendam* with Stainton,
and as he fixed his refidence here for about two years,
it will be well to give fome account of the parifh.   It
is a village of confiderable fize, irregularly built on
two floping limeftone hills, and in the valley between
them.   The place is poffeffed of antiquarian intereft,
the Caftle of Middleham having been a principal refidence of the Bifhops of Durham from the Conqueft
till the end of the 14th century. Until 1844, the church
was covered with white-wafh, and had been disfigured
at every available point by village craftfmen, modern

fafhes taking the place of lancet windows. It has recently been reftored by Mrs. Surtees, the widow of Robert Surtees, Efq., of Mainsforth, who has a life-rent in fome property in the parifh. A fchool-room, with fmall garden attached, was built by fubfcription in 1770. No traces of Mr. Phillpotts' incumbency remain, beyond fome anecdotes which prove him to have been an active and not always a popular magif-trate. It may, however, be mentioned, that his fecond and third children (a fon and daughter) were chriftened at Bifhop Middleham, the former having been born in the January previous to his inftitution to the living.

The next preferment of Mr. Phillpotts was the large and important Parifh of Gatefhead, to which he was collated by the Bifhop of Durham in 1808.* The value of this living is about 1,050*l.* per annum, and the Rector is alfo *ex officio* mafter of the ancient hofpital of King James in Gatefhead, deriving from it an income of about 250*l.* per annum. The parifh, as it now exifts, contains about 26,000 fouls, but during Mr. Phillpotts' incumbency it was co-extenfive with the borough, which now contains 35,000 inhabit-ants. The Rectory was formerly a good houfe with gardens, and a view towards the river; but it was gradually furrounded by iron works and other factories. The railway company purchafed it, and the fucceffor

---

* The day of the month cannot be given, as the firft fub-fcription book of Bifhop Barrington, relating to the period at which the inftitution of Mr. Phillpotts took place, has been loft.

of Mr. Phillpotts, the Rev. J. Collinfon, removed to a handfome and commodious houfe, nearly a mile to the weft of the parifh church, which is now the rectory. The church is fpacious, and of regular architecture, confifting of a nave, with uniform aifles, weft tower, chancel and tranfept.   The whole of the lights are modern.   There are no details of intereft during the fhort incumbency of Mr. Phillpotts; and the only circumftance to be recorded is that his fecond fon was born in this parifh.

The friendfhip of the Bifhop of Durham was now bearing moft abundant fruit, and in the following year (1809) Mr. Phillpotts was collated to the ninth Pre-bendal Stall* in the Cathedral Church of Chrift and the Bleffed Virgin Mary in Durham.   If a canonry is a poft of dignity, it is, at leaft, no empty honour; and when it is remembered that Mr. Phillpotts, who was now thirty-one years of age, had already held *four* livings, befides a prebendal ftall, it muft be confeffed that he was fortunate in obtaining fuch fpeedy and fubftantial recognition of his merits.

Mr. Phillpotts now refided for a confiderable portion of the year in Durham, and on the Chapelry of S. Margaret in that city becoming vacant, he was prefented to it by the Dean and Chapter, the 28th of September, 1810.   The parifh is an important one, and contains at the prefent time 6,916 inhabitants.   The church was originally one of the four chapels dependent on

---

* Canonry.

the parochial church of S. Ofwald. It ftands on the afcent of the hill, where South Street branches from Croffgate. The value of the Living is about 330*l.* per annum. During the incumbency of Mr. Phillpotts there were no fchools ; but one for boys and another for girls was built in 1860. A parfonage houfe was alfo built in 1849.

Some ill-feeling was caufed by the prefentation of Mr. Phillpotts to this living. The Minor Canons regarded it as a peculiar of their own, and one of their number made no fecret of his difappointment at his fuppofed claim having been difregarded. Mr. Phillpotts is well remembered by the parifhioners as a hard-working and zealous clergyman, gifted with great adminiftrative ability, and fingularly earneft in all the duties of his office. The veftry meetings were not always of the moft harmonious defcription, and the tact and addrefs with which he controlled turbulent fpirits gave evidence of the capacity which he afterwards difplayed in more important pofts, and under more trying circumftances.

In the year 1814 Mr. Phillpotts was felected to preach the fermon at the Anniverfary Meeting of the Sons of the Clergy in S. Paul's Cathedral (May 12). His text was 1 *Tim.* iii. 12 :—" Let the deacons be the hufbands of one wife, ruling their children and their own houfes well." There is nothing remarkable in the fermon, except a paffage relating to the difqualification of a divorced perfon from undertaking any clerical office, which is not altogether inappropriate

to times which have witneſſed a clergyman ſeeking
for relief from the matrimonial bond in the Divorce
Court :—

" The extreme facility with which divorces were effected,
not only among the Greeks and Romans, but alſo under the
Jewiſh law, was more than once remarked on by our Bleſſed
Lord in the courſe of His miniſtry ; and He was pleaſed to
teſtify His reprobation of the practice in the ſtrongeſt terms,
and alſo to eſtabliſh in His new Kingdom an inſtitute, according better with that purity of heart and life which it was
one main object of His miſſion to inculcate.   Since, however, the practice was ſo prevalent, and had hitherto been
deemed ſo innocent, it muſt have happened, in many inſtances, that the new convert to Chriſtianity was already
the huſband of a ſecond wife during the lifetime of one
whom he had divorced.   Now, what had legally been done
before his admiſſion into the Church would not neceſſarily
be annulled even by that law which forbade its followers to
uſe the ſame licence.   The laſt contract would ſtill ſubſiſt ;
nor would baptiſm diſſolve an union which the law of Moſes,
or of the civil government, had ſanctioned.   Yet ſtill as the
precept of the Goſpel was in direct oppoſition to it, and as
the miniſter of Chriſt would have to inculcate this as well
as the other branches of Chriſtian morality, it was obviouſly
unſeemly that he ſhould be living himſelf in a connection
which the pure law of the Goſpel would compel him to denounce in future as adulterous.   It became, therefore, the
ſpirit of a religion, jealous of the character of its miniſters,
to prevent this ſcandal ; and while it did not annul the contract, to exclude thoſe who had engaged in it from being
ordained to any of the holy offices of the Church."

It may be intereſting to notice that in the above
extract Mr. Phillpotts is following cloſely in the ſteps
of S. Auguſtine, who ſays (*De Bono Conjugali*, 18) :—

" On this account the facrament of marriage of our time hath been fo reduced to one man and one wife, as that it is not lawful to ordain any as a fteward of the Church, fave the hufband of one wife. And this they have underftood more acutely who have been of opinion, that neither is he to be ordained, who as a catechumen or as a heathen had a fecond wife. For it is a matter of facrament, not of fin. But on account of the fanctity of the facrament, as a female, although it be as a catechumen that fhe hath fuffered violence, cannot after baptifm be confecrated among the virgins of God; fo there was no abfurdity in fuppofing of him who had exceeded the number of one wife, not that he had committed any fin, but that he had loft a certain prefcript rule of a facrament, neceffary not unto defert of good life, but unto the feal of ecclefiaftical ordination."

The reft of Mr. Phillpotts' fermon is taken up with a confideration of the arguments in favour of a married priefthood; but as our clergy commonly evince little reluctance to enter upon the ftate of matrimony, it will be needlefs to recapitulate them. It was followed by a collection of 914*l.* 10*s.*

Two more children were born to Mr. Phillpotts before he received his next important piece of preferment—the fecond ftall in Durham Cathedral, to which he was collated by the bifhop, December 30, 1815, on the death of Dr. Thomas Zouch. This ftall, although not the richeft in the Cathedral, was confiderably greater in value than the ninth, to which he had already been preferred. He held it for five years, during which time four children were born to him.

And now we approach the period of his literary labours.

CHAPTER II.

Ancient Provision for the Poor. Various Enactments. Vagrancy prevented. The Law of Settlement. Disadvantages of Existing System. Proposals for remedying them. Mr. Sturges Bourne's Motion. Mr. Phillpotts opposed to it. His Letter to Mr. Sturges Bourne. The existing Law not complex. Expense incurred by Parishes in litigation and removals. Debasing effect of Paupers recording that they have acquired a Settlement. Injustice of returning upon Parishes aged Paupers who have lived elsewhere. The real Grievance stated. Danger of drawing Agricultural Labourers into Towns. Removal of Paupers to their legal Settlement, and separation from their friends and connections. Character of Overseers. General Merits of Mr. Phillpotts' Letter to Mr. Sturges Bourne.

N the year 1819 the attention of the country was directed to the Poor Laws, one of the moſt difficult and important queſtions which it has ever fallen to the lot of Parliament to conſider. Previous to the Conqueſt the duty of providing for the maintenance of the poor, who were unable to ſupport themſelves, devolved upon " parſons, rectors, and the pariſhioners, ſo that none of them ſhould die for want of ſuſtenance."* It is ſaid that a fourth part of the tithes was devoted to this purpoſe, and adminiſtered by the

---

incumbent under the direction of the bifhop. After the Conqueft, ecclefiaftical revenues were ftill devoted to the fame purpofe, and monks became the relieving officers, and monafteries the poor-houfes of the land. From that period till the time of Henry VIII. the fame cuftom prevailed, and the wants of the poor were fupplied by the clergy with pious care. It is worthy of remark, as fhowing the fidelity with which this truft was difcharged, that the firft legiflative attempt to provide for the poor was made in the fame year when the property of fo many religious houfes was vefted in the Crown.*

A ftatute for compulfory affeffment for the poor was paffed in the 14th Elizabeth. This was afterwards confirmed by the 43rd of the fame reign (chap. 2), which enacted that a convenient ftock fhould be provided to fet the poor on work, and that this fhould be difpenfed by the overfeers of the parifh. It was thought neceffary to pafs another Act (13 & 14 Charles II. chap. 12), on account of poor people wandering from one parifh to another, where they were likely to find the beft ftock, "and at laft becoming rogues and vagabonds, to the great difcouragement of parifhes to provide ftocks, where they are liable to be devoured by ftrangers." Vagrancy of the kind alluded to was prevented by a certificate from the parochial authorities, which the pauper was com-

* 27 Hen. VIII. c. 28, which contains the firft provifion by which particular diftricts are directed to fupport the poor.

pelled to carry with him when he quitted his parifh ;
failing this, he was liable, within forty days, to be taken
before a juftice of the peace, and fent back to his own
parifh.

It would occupy too much fpace, although it would
be an interefting employment, to defcribe the various
fteps of legiflative enactment in reference to the law
of fettlement.   Suffice it to fay that it was furrounded
and limited by certain rules and reftrictions, which
were relaxed or tightened according to the temper of
the times.   It may fafely be affirmed, however, that
no attempt at legiflation was, upon the whole, fatisfactory, although the general tendency was to difcourage
vagrancy, and give more freedom to the induftrious
poor.

Thus matters remained until the termination of a
long and bloody war left the kingdom free to contend
with one of its greateft domeftic evils.   It was in the
year 1819 that the advocates of amendment of the
Law of Settlement were ftrenuous in urging the dif-
advantages of the exifting fyftem, which they fummed
up under three heads :—

1. The enormous expenfe incurred by parifhes in
profecuting and defending appeals, and in removing
paupers.

2. The injuftice under which parifhes laboured to
which old paupers were fent back, after they had fpent
their youth and ftrength elfewhere.

3. The hardfhip upon the paupers who, having
refided many years and formed connections at a dif-

tance, were fent home to their parifhes, and feparated from all their friends and confolations, to die in a remote poor-houfe.

In order to remove thefe evils, it was propofed that a fettlement fhould be acquired by refidence only, and not, as heretofore, by refidence combined with certain qualifications. The difficulty was, what length of refidence fhould confer a fettlement. One advantage would be gained, in the opinion of the favourers of the fcheme, for if a reafonable period were fixed upon, it would obviate the feparation of an aged pauper from his friends, provided he went before a magiftrate and made oath of his refidence. In cafes of difpute, it was propofed that an appeal fhould lie, not to the Quarter Seffions, but to two magiftrates, and thus avoid all needlefs expenfe.

One of the foremoft advocates of this meafure in the Houfe of Commons was Mr. Sturges Bourne, who, on the 25th of March, 1819, moved for leave to bring in a Bill to regulate the fettlement of the poor. As an active juftice of the peace, Mr. Phillpotts had devoted himfelf to a careful ftudy of all that related to this moft perplexing queftion, and he believed that the propofed amendment of the law would by no means be productive of fuch beneficial refults as were commonly anticipated. He, therefore, addreffed a letter, on the 6th of April, to Mr. Sturges Bourne,* for the purpofe

---

* " A Letter to the Right Hon. William Sturges Bourne, M.P., on a Bill introduced by him into Parliament to amend

of fhowing that the fyftem of the Law of Settlement
then exifting was not fairly open to the charge of
complexity alleged againft it, and that the three evils
already referred to would not be leffened by the propofed amendment. On the firft point he remarks with
much acutenefs :—

 " The moft perfect fimplicity, be it remembered, is very
confiftent with a great number of particulars. A fingle
fweeping provifion will, indeed, neceffarily be fimple ; but
it will not follow that it may not be expofed by its very fimplicity to many of the fame confequences as refult from a
fyftem of extreme intricacy. The main objection to a very
complex law is the difficulty of applying it ; but, furely, this
difficulty may equally be caufed by the extreme fimplicity of
the law, if it meet not with a correfponding fimplicity in the
facts to which it is to be applied."

In reference to the firft of the three evils to be
remedied by the new law,—the enormous expenfe in-
curred by parifhes in litigation and removals,—Mr.
Phillpotts afferts that it amounts to not more than one
twentieth part of the whole fum difburfed on the poor,
or about three-halfpence in the pound on the entire
rental of England. He admits that almoft the whole
of this would ultimately be faved, but adds :—

 " In the earlier ftages of its operation, and for a confiderable length of time, I am greatly miftaken if it would not

---

the laws refpecting the fettlement of the poor, by the Rev.
Henry Phillpotts, M. A., Prebendary of Durham, and one of
his Majefty's Juftices of the Peace for the County Palatine
of Durham."

multiply and aggravate the mifchief in an incalculable degree."

The neceffity for introducing a provifion into the new Bill, empowering every perfon, as foon as he has refided in a parifh long enough to gain a fettlement, to make a record of his having done fo, and thus to arm himfelf with evidence againft the time when he comes to claim parifh relief, draws from Mr. Phillpotts an earneft and eloquent proteft :—

" Nothing can be further from my intention than to fay one word derogatory to the wifdom of the general views of thofe enlightened men who have paffed this Bill. But it is becaufe I have a very high opinion of their wifdom, that my aftonifhment is excited by a provifion which directly contradicts the main principle, which bitter experience has taught us to recognize in the policy of poor laws. Surely the great defideratum of all is to find fome method of reanimating the fpirit of proper independence in the lower orders, of withdrawing their views from the parifh fund, and inducing them to ftruggle hard againft the degradation of being compelled to have recourfe to it. Yet here we find the legiflature itfelf purfuing a directly contrary courfe, and inviting the labourer to familiarize himfelf as early as poffible with the profpect of being a pauper, to connect it with all his plans of induftry or idlenefs—in fhort, to affociate the notion of right, and privilege of triumph over the overfeer, and future gain for himfelf and his family, with that which never ought to be contemplated by a man in health and vigour, but as a difgrace to be fhunned, or a misfortune to be deprecated."

In reference to the fecond evil,—the injuftice to parifhes of returning upon them aged or infirm paupers, whofe youth and ftrength have been fpent elfewhere,—Mr. Phillpotts afferts that it is not a common cafe for aged paupers to be removed to the fcenes of their infancy; and even in cafes where it takes place, he fails to fee the injuftice done to their parifhes. The real grievance, although it is not openly ftated, he declares to be that the poor who refide in towns, particularly the manufacturing poor, are often removed to country parifhes, which would be glad to be excufed from the burden of maintaining any other decayed labourers than their own.

" But let us," fays Mr. Phillpotts, " confider this matter a little more particularly. It will not be denied that a large portion of the natives of every country parifh are provided for by the occupation afforded in towns. Reference to the regifter of all fuch parifhes will fhow that the deaths in them bear no proportion to the births; that there is, therefore, a conftant ftream of population flowing from the country into the towns. Is it then inequitable, as feems to be prefumed, that part of the charge of maintaining thefe fame perfons in their decay or diftrefs fhould fall on the diftricts which gave them birth, but which have been relieved from the burden of finding employment or fupport for them in their earlier years ? "

The danger of perpetually drawing agricultural labourers into towns is very forcibly ftated by Mr. Phillpotts :—

" I prefume to add another confideration, which, obvious as it is, feems to be difregarded : I mean the mifchief of drawing the lower orders of people from the country into towns ; a mifchief of which it is hard to fay whether it be more formidable to the morals and happinefs of the people, or to the peace and fecurity of the ftate. Already the evil is felt and lamented by many of the moft enlightened friends of the poor throughout the land. While the population of the whole ifland is advancing fo rapidly, that according to the fame rate of progreffion it will have doubled itfelf in little more than fifty years, in fome of the ancient agricultural parifhes it is hardly fuftained at its former level; in fome it is even retrograding. Already it is not an uncommon thing for rural labourers to live in the adjacent towns, and never can this take place without injury to thofe charaċteriftic excellencies which were wont to diftinguifh the Englifh peafant."

In reference to the third evil,—the hardfhip which befalls paupers, who having refided many years, and formed connećtions, at a diftance, are fent away to their legal fettlements, and feparated from their friends and acquaintances to die in a remote poor-houfe,—Mr. Phillpotts admits that cafes of this kind occafionally do occur, but denies that they happen fo often as to make them a fit objećt of a remedial law. As a proof of this, he inftances the well-known accommodation between the abfent pauper and his overfeer, which enables him to receive relief without being removed to his parifh. Overfeers, in Mr. Phillpotts' eyes, are models of courtefy and generofity. Harfhnefs is un-known, or only known to be reprobated.

"For one inftance," he affirms, "where a reafonable arrangement is prevented by the obftinacy or inhumanity of the overfeer, I believe that fifty may be found where it takes place moft improperly."

Mr. Phillpotts' experiences have evidently lain in pleafant paftures. He believes that relieving officers are to the poor the fmiling and urbane officials that they appear to him. A few months' work in the lanes and alleys of one of our crowded cities might have undeceived him. The parochial " Bumbles " have not acquired their reputation for nothing.

That these officials have occasionally very trying duties to perform is true enough, but it is equally true that tyranny and rigour are as often seen as pity and discretion. But, after all, the fault does not lie so much with the relieving officers as with their employers —the Poor Law Guardians—whose sole aim appears to be to compress the rates into the smallest possible compass. If a few widows and orphans are crushed in the process, who has any right to complain ? The rates are kept low, and if that is not enough, what more do " liberals " want ? *

But presently Mr. Phillpotts descends from the amenities of overseers, and touches upon the real principle at issue in the removal of aged paupers :—

"I do not see why so great a benefit as gratuitous support at the expense of the public should be thought hardly earned by compliance with a condition, which the good of the public requires. If, even in this age of excessive sensibility, it were attempted to excite our compassion for the unhappy officer, or soldier, whose subsistence is made to depend on a condition often the most painful to his feelings, ' who is torn from his family and connections to die in a remote garrison '

---

* These remarks are not intended to apply in any special sense to the place in which they are written. They are founded on an extended observation, and the writer has much pleasure in testifying to the courteous attention which he has always received from the Secretary of the Corporation of the Poor in Exeter, as well as from the officers under his control.

—few of us, I conceive, would think the complaint worthy of a ferious anfwer. I am myfelf hard-hearted enough to feel as little fympathy in the prefent inftance."

After this avowal, it is needlefs to fay that Mr. Phillpotts is wedded to the exifting order of things.

Some obfervations on the " misjudging tendernefs " in the adminiftration of the Poor Laws bring this letter to a conclufion. It is written with fome ability, and with confiderable knowledge of the fubject from a theoretical point of view. There is, however, an entire abfence of everything that would denote a practical acquaintance with the workings of a moft intricate and difficult law. Mr. Phillpotts profeffes very great refpect for Mr. Sturges Bourne and his companions in philanthropic labour; there is, therefore, no trace of thofe pungent ingredients which give a relifh to moft of his earlier performances. Compared, then, with his other pamphlets, this letter of Mr. Phillpotts muft be defcribed as tame. There is nothing in it to mark the future opponent of Jeffrey, Grey, and Canning. It is the production of a country clergyman, well-fkilled in Quarter Seffions, and gifted with a certain aptitude for making the beft of his cafe ; but it is nothing more.

CHAPTER III.

HE letter to Mr. Sturges Bourne was quickly followed by another on a very different ſubject. And here, for the preſent, Mr. Phillpotts thought fit to withhold his name; but, if he deſired concealment, his wiſh was not deſtined to be gratified, for it ſoon became known, beyond the circle of his friends, that he was the "Clergyman of the Dioceſe of Durham" who had publifhed (30th of June, 1819,) a Letter to Lord Grey on the Roman Catholic queftion.* If all other proofs of the authorfhip were wanting, a convincing one might be found in the way in which the writer addreffes himfelf to his tafk. Firft of all there is lavifh praife, and then there is as liberal blame. And this is the way in which Mr. Phillpotts fpecially delights to deal with opponents. His mode of treatment may be called the lubricating procefs. The oil with which the razor is plentifully fmeared, if it foftens the flefh, only makes the gafh the deeper. Thus, at the commencement of this letter, Lord Grey is, truly enough, defcribed as "eminently diftinguifhed by talents and eloquence, and, above all, by a character for political and private honour, which ftamped an additional value on all his high endowments;" while, at the clofe, Mr. Phillpotts affures him, though "in no invidious fenfe," that he has "yet to learn what the pure fpirit of Chriftianity is," and that it was "neceffary that fome member of the Church of England fhould proteft publicly againft opinions as injurious to the honour of that Church as they are deftitute of all folid foundation."

This letter to Lord Grey was occafioned by an eloquent and animated fpeech delivered by his lordfhip

---

* "A Letter to the Rt. Hon. Earl Grey, occafioned by his Lordfhip's Speech in the Houfe of Lords, on moving the fecond reading of his Bill for Abrogating the Declarations contained in the 25th and 30th of Charles II, commonly called 'the Teft againft Popery.'" This letter is figned, "A Clergyman of the Diocefe of Durham."

in the Houfe of Lords, June the 10th, 1819, on his moving the fecond reading of the Roman Catholic Relief Bill, with fpecial reference to the Teft Act. The motion was rendered remarkable, among thofe which were periodically made on the fame fubject, from its having been feconded by the Bifhop of Norwich (Dr. Bathurft), who refufed, as he faid,

> " To make the fymbol of atoning grace
>   An office key, a pick-lock to a place."

But, in fpite of the epifcopal fanction thus accorded to the Bill, it met with little fympathy in the Houfe, and was lost by a majority of fifty-nine.

That the meafure had been defeated would have been enough for moft men, but in the judgment of Mr. Phillpotts it required a letter to make the victory complete. Within the month, therefore, a letter was forthcoming. It opens, as has been already faid, with fome complimentary remarks on the character and endowments of Lord Grey. The writer then proceeds to fay that, though the Roman Catholic queftion feems to him to be purely *political*, yet, fo many religious topics had been unneceffarily dragged into the difcuffion, and particularly by his lordfhip, that he thinks it not foreign to his office to expofe pofitions which are wholly untenable, and facts which have been greatly mifapprehended.

There can be little doubt that Mr. Phillpotts poffeffed the requifite qualifications for the tafk which he had undertaken, and that he fulfilled it, upon the whole, with judgment and moderation; but how far it is becoming in a clergyman to mingle in a queſtion which he admits is purely political, for the ſake of expoſing the bad theology of a ſtateſman, muſt be determined, to ſome extent, according to the ſpirit and feeling of the times. Now-a-days the attempt would be intolerable, and would be met with cold diſdain. The offending paſtor would be remitted to his pariſh with an unmiſtakeable hint to mind his own buſineſs. But fifty years ago the caſe was different. Clergymen then mingled freely in all the conteſts of a ſtirring age. It was not thought beneath the gravity of their calling to aſſume the part of whippers-in at elections, or of political lampooners. A pamphlet had often led the way to a ſtall. Rich livings had been won by ſtill more queſtionable means. Hence it was that men fitted to ſhine in the world of letters, or ambitious to earn a miniſter's regard, were dragged, however reluctantly, into the whirlpool of political controverſy. The fault was not entirely their own. They might, indeed, have followed the obſcurer life of paſtoral uſe-fulneſs; but, once having quitted it, they were impelled by the neceſſities of an imperious age. And this may help to account for the controverſial tone of the whole of Mr. Phillpotts' writings, up to the time of his elevation to the Epiſcopal Bench. His political ſentiments were keen and well-defined, his temper was ardent, his attachment to his party was ſtrong: what wonder, then, if, in an age which valued and rewarded theſe qualities, he ſhould often be ſeen in the front rank of the battle, ſingling out for combat the moſt giant-like of his opponents?

But to return to the letter. Mr. Phillpotts readily enough admits that there is "a palpable anomaly in exacting from civil officers a much more violent declaration againſt theſe tenets* than is required as a qualification even for admittance into Holy Orders."

The injuſtice of this is manifeſt. But becauſe the Teſt was a hardſhip it did not follow that henceforward there ſhould be *no* ſecurity at all. If, inſtead of ſeeking altogether to repeal the Teſt, Lord Grey had ſuggeſted the adoption of ſome milder form of ſecurity, he would in all probability have carried with him the majority of the thinking men in the country.

But while Mr. Phillpotts admits that the object of the Teſt might be equally well obtained by adopting a leſs offenſive form of ſecurity, yet believing the propoſitions embodied in it to be not only true, but of main importance to the cauſe of pure religion, he feels it his duty to addreſs his lordſhip. And this brings him to the chief ſubject of his letter :—

"One of the moſt ſtriking characteriſtics of your ſpeech," he ſays, "is a readineſs to inculcate the notion that there is, in reality, very little difference of doctrine between the Churches of England and of Rome. The attempt is not a new one. It has long been the uſage of the moſt wary advocates of the latter Church, when defending their cauſe before the Proteſtants both of this country and of France, to ſtate their tenets, and deſcribe their practices, in a manner

---

* Embodied in the Teſt Act.

the leaft offenfive to the principles of thofe whom they addrefs. Such a policy, reftrained within the bounds of truth and fincerity, would merit nothing but commendation. Thefe, however, are not reftraints which the writers of that communion have always thought it neceffary to obferve. From the age of Boffuet to the prefent time there have never been wanting men who will ftrain, or comprefs, the doctrines of their Church to whatever point the interefts of the day may require : and if the more ftaunch and artlefs believers are fometimes fhocked by the latitude in which they indulge, it is feldom difficult to prevent or to palliate the fcandal of an open rupture."

A little further on he fums up what he conceives to be the chief differences in doctrine between the two Churches :—

"If no political bias had influenced your judgment, it would have been impoffible for you to overlook the wide and irremovable barrier which feparates the tenets of your own Church from the corruptions of Rome. You could not have forgotten that the majority of our Articles are framed in direct oppofition to thofe corruptions; that in what relates to the rule of Chriftian Faith—to man's juftification—to the nature of good works, whether they be meritorious—to the Church, its fallibility, and its authority— to the duty of religious worfhip, whether it is to be con- fined to God, or communicated to the Virgin Mary, angels, or faints—to the adoration of images and relics—to Common Prayer in language underftood by all—to the Sacraments, their number, matter, form, and efficacy—to the facrifice of Chrift upon the Crofs, and the perfect propitiation and fatisfaction wrought by it for the fins of men—to His me- diation and interceffion for us with the Father,—that in all and every of thefe particulars, there are irreconcilable differences between the two Churches."

But by far the moſt intereſting part of this letter is that which relates to the correſpondence of Archbiſhop Wake with the Doctors of the Sorbonne. Lord Grey, in the courſe of his ſpeech, had quoted a paſſage from the writings of this diſtinguiſhed prelate, ſetting forth that, in a compariſon between the Church of England and the Church of Rome, " their articles of faith differed very little, their diſcipline ſtill leſs, and that in fundamentals they were nearly the ſame." For the *Church of Rome* evidently ought to be read the *Gallican Church*; and the letter, from which Lord Grey quotes, relates to the ſcheme which the Archbiſhop had formed of reconciling the Anglican and Gallican Churches. If the ſtatement of ſuch a keen controverſialiſt as Archbiſhop Wake were left unexplained, the moſt ſerious miſchief would be likely to enſue; Mr. Phillpotts, therefore, having devoted much time and trouble to the conſideration of this ſubject, and having invoked the aid of one of the greateſt of living ſcholars, proceeds to ſum up the reſult of his reſearches as follows :—

" During the violent proceedings of the Court of Rome againſt that part of the Gallican Church which refuſed to receive the bull ' Unigenitus ' as an eccleſiaſtical law, ſome doctors of the Sorbonne, particularly Du Pin, the ableſt and moſt diſtinguiſhed among them, whether from a ſincere intention of ſhaking off the Papal yoke, which ſeemed to be borne with ſome impatience throughout France, or merely with the hope and purpoſe of terrifying the Vatican into better treatment of themſelves, or perhaps from a mixture of both theſe motives, teſtified their wiſh for a reconciliation with the Church of England. Archbifhop Wake, to whom this intimation was conveyed, anfwered, as became a Chriftian Bifhop, in terms which at once befpoke his anxious defire of peace and union, and his inflexible conftancy in the caufe of truth. In the progrefs of the correfpondence the French Divines began to form a plan of union, and even to ftate the terms on which they were willing to effect it. Du Pin drew up a paper, entitled, '*Commonitorium de Modis ineundæ pacis inter Ecclefias Anglicanam et Gallicanam.*' Without entering largely into the contents of this document (a copy of which is ftill extant among the Wake MSS. in the library of Chrift Church, Oxford), it may be fufficient to fay, that it examined feparately the Articles of the Church of England, fpecifying the extent to which agreement with them could be carried; and that in many important particulars great conceffions were made, efpecially the fufficiency of the Holy Scriptures for falvation, with a flight falvo for tradition, as not exhibiting new Articles of Faith, but only confirming and illuftrating thofe contained in Scripture, juftification by Faith alone, the fallibility even of the Church of Rome, confidered as a particular Church, were freely admitted. Indulgences were limited to relaxations of temporal penances *in this life*, the worfhip of the Crofs, relics, and images, was reduced to an external refpect, and that not of a religious nature; the invocation of faints feems to have been given up; the fitnefs of celebrating Divine Worfhip in the vulgar tongue was not difputed—the Communion in both kinds was held indifferent, and in the article of the fupremacy of the civil magiftrate, fome not inconfiderable points were conceded. Even tranfubftantiation, though the doctrine without the name was affirmed, feems to have been retained only as a fpeculative point, without involving the duties of adoring the Hoft, or thofe other confequences which have made it fo juftly revolting to all confiderate Proteftants. 'In our Liturgy,' fays Wake himfelf, in a letter to his Englifh correſpondent, 'there is nothing but what they allow of, ſave the ſingle rubric relating to the Euchariſt; in theirs nothing but what they agree may be laid aſide, and yet the public offices be never the worſe for it, or more imperfect for want of it.' "

Still, notwithſtanding theſe advances, the Archbiſhop was not very ſanguine in his expectation of a reunion.

" Without the entire excluſion of the papal authority from the Church of France, he deſpaired of an effectual accommodation; with it he hoped for everything. This therefore was the point to which he directed his main efforts; but this, he plainly ſaw, could only be accompliſhed through the co-operation of the Court. Some proſpect of ſuch a co-operation was for a while preſented. The Regent and his miniſter ſhowed themſelves favourable, but the artifices of Rome prevailed; and the attraction of a Cardinal's hat for the infamous Du Bois was ſufficient to extinguiſh the dawn of reformation in France, almoſt as ſoon as it had ariſen. It was after the Archbiſhop's hopes of the aſſiſtance of the Court had proved illuſory, that he wrote to Du Pin the letter from which your Lordſhip's quotation was taken; —and I may now venture to aſk, whether anything more fallacious can be deviſed, than to repreſent the language of Wake addreſſed, under ſuch circumſtances, to Du Pin, as intended to characterize the doctrine and diſcipline of the Church of Rome ? "

The remarks upon tranſubſtantiation which follow merit little notice, except in ſo far as the ſubject affords to Mr. Phillpotts an opportunity of vindicating the doctrine of the Real Preſence. The ſame obſervation applies to his treatment of thoſe portions of the Declaration which relate to the " invocation of ſaints," and " the idolatrous nature of the ſacrifice of the maſs."

Both of thefe topics might well have been omitted altogether, had not the remarks of Lord Grey feemed to Mr. Phillpotts to demand fome notice. This was the more neceffary fince the objeƈt of his lord-fhip had been, for political purpofes, to reprefent the creed and the difcipline of the Church of Rome as nearly in accordance with thofe of the Church of England. He had not calculated, however, upon meeting with an adverfary, like Mr. Phillpotts, who would follow him through all the mazes of a fhifting controverfy with inexorable pertinacity. The accuracy with which he fathomed Lord Grey's theology is fet forth by himfelf with quiet irony fix years later, when he fays of Dr. Milner's *End of Controverfy*, that it " is the grand ftorehoufe from which a main portion of the faƈts and evidence, adduced by the noble Earl, appears to have been drawn ; and a nice obferver might, perhaps, without much difficulty, feleƈt fome fix pages of this work, in which all the theological learning dif-played in that memorable debate would be found to be comprifed."

Having difpofed of the queftion of the Teft, Mr. Phillpotts proceeds to a part of Lord Grey's fpeech, which, as it appears to him to " affeƈt the honour of the Church of which he is a minifter," calls for fpecial notice. His lordfhip appealed to the Epifcopal Bench " whether the 18th Article of the Church of England, or that part of the Liturgy which it had been the well-known wifh of our pious Sovereign to fee withdrawn, are congenial to the pure fpirit of

Chriftianity." It was underftood that the part of the Liturgy referred to was the Athanafian Creed. However high or honoured the name that might be cited againft it, Mr. Phillpotts rightly felt that there was but one courfe open to any minifter who valued confiftency above favour, and that was to profefs his firm conviction that the Creed was not only true in its doctrine, but moft highly ferviceable in its ufe.

" The object of the Creed," he well fays, " is to proclaim belief in thofe great and diftinguifhing doctrines of our religion, the Trinity of Perfons in the Godhead, and the Incarnation of the Blefled Son; doctrines, which they who hold them cannot but efteem of effential importance, for on them depends the honour which is due to our Redeemer and our Sanctifier. It is true, that a fimple profeffion of Faith fufficed for the infant Church; that before the Divinity of the fecond and third Perfons (implied in the Apoftles' Creed) was affailed by heretics, it was not deemed neceffary to depart from the fimple words of Scripture. But when the words of Scripture were ufed in a fenfe which depraved its meaning, and difhonoured the object of Chriftian worfhip, it became neceffary to guard the true faith by an expofition, which the fubtlety of the adverfary could not pervert. The Creed in queftion effects this purpofe; it both ftates plainly what Scripture teaches of each of the Divine Perfons, and alfo introduces diftinctions, which prevent the unwary from being mifled by thofe, who, under the words of Scripture, maintain opinions inconfiftent with its higheft truths. But thefe diftinctions need not be regarded by any who hold the main doctrine."

Every Churchman will be thankful for this manly expofition of the value of the Creed. Mr. Phillpotts then proceeds :—

"The condemning or cautionary clauſes, (call them which you will,) apply to the Catholic Faith generally, and to the doctrines of the Trinity and Incarnation in particular: and he who taxes them as uncharitable, would do well to remember, that as they ſay not leſs, ſo neither do they ſay more, than our Lord Himſelf pronounced of every one ' that believeth not.' The only queſtion which can be ràiſed is about the truth of the doctrine ; for they who admit it to be true, muſt ſee that it is fundamental, that the denial of it muſt come within that denunciation which He, Who is emphatically ſtyled ' Love,' forbore not to make."

More on this ſubject occurs further on. Meanwhile enough has been ſaid to give promiſe of the ability and profound theological learning which Mr. Phillpotts brought to his conteſt with Mr. Charles Butler. This letter to Lord Grey is manly in tone, and, with the exception of ſome few expreſſions towards the end, temperate in diction. The writer is evidently not an entire excluſioniſt; but he is unwilling to remove the Roman Catholic Diſabilities without receiving ſufficient ſecurity for the maintenance of Church and State.

CHAPTER IV.

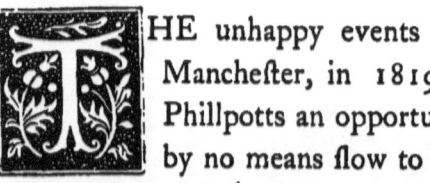

THE unhappy events which occurred at Manchefter, in 1819, afforded to Mr. Phillpotts an opportunity, which he was by no means flow to embrace, of appearing before the public as the champion of Government.

During the fummer large meetings of diftreffed

manufacturers were held at Birmingham, Leeds, and other centres of labour. Matters were carried so far that a " legiflatorial attorney " was elected to represent the people of the former place. On the 9th of August a similar meeting was appointed to be held at Manchefter; but, on the magiftrates declaring that an affembly for fuch a purpofe was illegal, it was abandoned, and another meeting was announced for the 16th of August, for the purpofe of petitioning for a Reform in Parliamentary reprefentation. The fummons was not difregarded, and an immenfe multitude of people, computed by fome at 80,000, affembled in a piece of ground called S. Peter's field. The chief orator was Mr. Hunt, who harangued the affembly from a huftings made of waggons, and furmounted by flags bearing the infcription, " No Corn Laws," " Annual Parliaments," " Univerfal Suffrage," " Vote by Ballot," and other devices dear to popular agitators. While he was fpeaking, and before any breach of the peace had occurred, the Yeomanry Cavalry, fupported by the 15th Huffars, dafhed into the crowd with fabres drawn. No refiftance was offered. Mr. Hunt and others were made prifoners, and, had it not been for the prompt interference of Mr. Nadin, a chief conftable, the yeomanry would have fulfilled their intention of cutting him to pieces. Another charge was then made at the flags, during which numbers of people, including a peace-officer, were fabred and trodden under foot. So little difcrimination was fhown by the excited foldiers that a gentleman who was taking notes for the *Times* was arrested, and carried off to prison. No act of violence had been attempted on the part of the crowd, which was un-armed, until the charge of the yeomanry, and no one present knew that the Riot Act had been read.

Such is an outline of this terrible outrage, in which several defenceless men lost their lives, and others, in-cluding women and children, were seriously injured. There can be no doubt that the magistrates, in the fervour of their loyal zeal, exhibited far too great haste upon this unhappy occasion, and having once directed the yeomanry against the crowd, they were unable to restrain them. Nevertheless, their conduct was ap-proved by Government, the approbation being, as an acute thinker * remarked, " the supposed price of support from the Tories in that part of the country." Three days after the disaster, the Prince Regent wrote to the Home Secretary (Lord Sidmouth), from his yacht at sea, conveying his approbation and high commendation of the conduct of the magistrates and civil authorities at Manchester, as well as of the officers and troops, both regular and yeomanry cavalry, whose firmness and effectual support of the civil power preserved the peace of the town upon that most critical occasion.

The sensation created throughout the country by these events was most profound. It seemed incredible that an act of wanton butchery, such as could be justified

---

* Lord Dudley, Let. 43, to Bp. Copleston.

only by the laſt extremity, ſhould be endorſed by the higheſt powers in the land. Immenſe ſympathy, there-fore, was manifeſted for the ſufferers, and in London and Liverpool it took the ſhape of liberal pecuniary contributions. The excitement reached its height when it became known that ſeveral bills for cutting and wounding, which had been preſented to the Grand Jury at Lancaſter, againſt various members of the yeomanry corps, had been thrown out, and that the magiſtrates had refuſed to commit for charges con-nected with the 16th of Auguſt which had been brought before them.

It was under ſuch circumſtances as theſe that a Common Council of the Lord Mayor, Aldermen, and citizens of London was held on September the 9th, at which a reſpectful addreſs to the Prince Regent was agreed upon, praying him to inſtitute an immediate and effectual inquiry into the outrages that had been committed, and to cauſe the guilty perpetrators thereof to be brought to ſignal and condign puniſhment. His Royal Highneſs returned a reply which ſeverely cen-ſured the conduct of his petitioners, and peremptorily refuſed the inquiry which they ſought.

But the demand for prompt and impartial inveſti-gation was not ſo eaſily to be ſet aſide. The ſpirit of the country was fairly rouſed. People who acknow-ledged no ſympathy with the opinions of the Radical Reformers of Mancheſter felt that an outrage had been committed upon the liberty of the ſubject. Many large cities and towns, therefore, following the example of London, held meetings, and, with more or lefs excitement, adopted fimilar refolutions. Amongft other places, a very influential meeting of the gentry and freeholders of the County of Durham was held on the 21ft of October, in the County Hall, Durham, in confequence of a numeroufly-figned requifition which had been prefented to the High Sheriff, the Hon. W. Keppel Barrington. At eleven o'clock that gentleman, accompanied by Mr. Lambton and Mr. Powlett, members for the county, and others who had figned the requifition, entered the hall. The doors being thrown open, the general public were admitted, and the building was immediately filled with a crowd of well-drefled people, who had for fome time previoufly collected around. After the ufual preliminaries, and fome apologies from the fheriff for his inexperience in public affairs, Dr. Fenwick propofed, and George Baker, Efq., feconded, the following Refolutions, which were carried without one diffentient voice :—

"1. That it is contrary to the principles of the Conftitution, and a dangerous invafion of one of its moft important privileges, forcibly to interrupt and difperfe any meeting of the people, legally affembled, and peaceably held, for the confideration of any matter affecting the public welfare.

"2. That the difperfion of the Meeting held at Manchefter on the 16th of Auguft laft, by a military force, whereby many of his Majefty's fubjects were grievoufly wounded, and fome actually killed, has filled us with anxiety and alarm, and that we have feen with aftonifhment and regret the approbation which his Royal Highnefs the Prince

Regent has, without any fufficient opportunity for inquiry, been advifed to give to thofe perfons concerned in the direction and execution of that meafure.

" 3. That, although nothing has appeared which juftifies the conduct of the Magiftrates and Yeomanry on that occafion, we are unwilling to pronounce a pofitive cenfure upon it, without hearing all that can be alleged in their defence ; but that we feel it to be our duty to demand a ftrict and folemn inveftigation of occurrences, which have proved fo calamitous to fo many of our fellow-fubjects, and which tend to the eftablifhment of a precedent of the utmoft danger to the liberties of the country.

" 4. That while we thus exprefs our opinion, we difclaim any approbation of the political principles of thofe by whom the Meeting at Manchefter was convened, and declare our unalterable attachment to the Conftitution, and firm determination to fupport the authority of the laws againft whoever may violate them.

" 5. That an humble Addrefs be therefore prefented to his Royal Highnefs the Prince Regent, conformable to the tenor of the above Refolutions."

Mr. Phillpotts had refufed to take any part in this Meeting, having previoufly appended his name to a " Declaration " which had been drawn up and figned by fome noblemen, magiftrates, clergy, and others, at the fuggeftion of Lord Sidmouth, who had advifed that " fome of the moft refpectable perfons in the kingdom fhould meet and agree upon fuch a Declaration as the crifis calls for, and, after having publicly announced it, leave copies of it at different houfes of refort for fignature."

The Declaration of " the nobility, gentry, clergy, and freeholders of the County of Durham," com-

mences with a statement, on the part of those who
signed it, that they feel a proper and constitutional
jealousy for the maintenance of their rights and privileges, and that they are determined that no effort shall
be wanting on their part to transmit them unimpaired
to posterity. Having made this unequivocal declaration, they go on to say that they sincerely deplore
the unhappy occurrences which have lately taken place
at Manchester, and they trust, that, in order to allay
the popular ferment, as well as in justice to those who
have so loudly been accused of being the authors of
the troubles, the legal investigation of the whole of
these transactions, which has already been instituted,
may speedily be brought to a close. They next lay it
down, as a fundamental law of the country, that no
one is to be condemned unheard, and continue, " shall
we then suffer the magistrates of the land, and its brave
constitutional defenders, the yeomanry, not only to
be vilified and abused, but even to have sentence
pronounced against them in their absence, and without
having an opportunity of defending themselves?"
They then declare that they will suspend their judgment, and call upon their fellow-countrymen to do
the same. Reference is next made to the agitated
and almost convulsed state of the country, and the
rapid strides which sedition and blasphemy are everywhere making. Firmly impressed with these ideas, the
declarationists express their determination not to attend
any county meeting, to discuss matters connected with
the late transactions at Manchester, and enter their

proteft againft all fuch difcuffions, as not only unne-
ceffary and premature, but as calculated to interfere
with the impartial and difpaffionate judgment of thofe
by whom alone the queftion can be conftitutionally
decided, and to promote the objects of turbulent and
factious men. They conclude by faying, " We folemnly, in the face of our country, declare, that we
will collectively and individually defend, to the utmoft
of our power, the altars of our God, the throne of
our king, and the glorious free conftitution of the
country."

This " Declaration" is dated October 19, 1819, two
days before the county meeting, and bears fixty-feven
fignatures. Copies of it were fubfequently fent for fignature to other places in the county, including Bifhop
Auckland, Darlington, Stockton, Gatefhead, Walfing-
ham, South Shields, Sunderland, Barnard Caftle, Stain-
drop, and Newcaftle.

Mr. Phillpotts having thus vindicated his title to be
confidered one of " the moft refpectable perfons in the
kingdom," in the minifterial acceptation of thofe
words, proceeded to addrefs a letter to the freeholders
of the County of Durham, which appeared October
the 26th, five days after the meeting. His motive for
coming forward is thus given by himfelf :—

" I am one of thofe who have affixed their fignatures to
the 'Declaration' which is now circulating through the
county, and is, I hear, welcomed in every part of it with
ardent approbation. Thofe who fign it are faid to have
been reproached by one of the reprefentatives of the county,

Mr. Lambton, as afraid to come manfully forward and avow their fentiments in the face of thofe who differ from them. To that defiance, I for one, am not unwilling to anfwer. The Declaration itfelf has explained fome of the reafons which kept me from giving my anfwer where it was demanded ; and I cannot hefitate to confefs, that to harangue a meeting, in which an impartial hearing could not be hoped for (even if the fubject had created no objections), would have ill accorded with my perfonal or profeffional feelings. A philofopher of old declined arguing a point with a Roman Emperor, ' I do not difpute,' faid he, ' with a man who has forty legions.' In like manner, the hon. gentleman fhall have his own way, as far as I am concerned, when he has a mob on his fide. But I have not the fame difficulty in meeting him in print ; we are then on terms of equality. The reading public will allow to each of us the due, and only the due, weight of his refpective arguments ; and I cannot affect, what affuredly I do not feel, that there is anything, either in the authority or in the talents of that gentleman, to make an ordinary man backward to cope with him. In truth, backwardnefs at the prefent moment would argue, not fo much diffidence in our abilities, as treachery to our caufe."

Whether it is a fair ufe of terms to defignate a meeting prefided over by the high fheriff, fupported by two county reprefentatives, "a mob," it is fcarcely worth while to inquire ; but whether it was at all neceffary for Mr. Phillpotts to appeal to the public on fuch a matter as this, is a queftion which will be anfwered according as people think on the fubject of political pamphlets being made a ftepping-ftone to ecclefiaftical preferment. If he believed that it was a point of honour to take up the gauntlet thrown down, as he imagined, by thofe who defired inquiry, he had been anticipated in his chivalrous defign, for already there was another clerical champion in the field, in his own diocefe, the Rev. John Davifon, Rector of Wafh-ington, whofe popularity and talents fecured for his pamphlet an extenfive circulation.

But, in truth, while Mr. Phillpotts was endeavour-ing to delude himfelf into the belief that it was needful to defend *himfelf* and his co-declarationifts, he very foon found himfelf writing a letter the manifeft object of which was to defend the *Government*. Accordingly, as his pamphlet proceeds, his natural acutenefs is too great to allow him to be blinded by the plea of felf-vindication.

" It is an unpopular courfe," he fays, " at any time to ftep forward as the advocate of Minifters, on a difputed point. He who undertakes that office is commonly fuppofed to have other motives than a love of juftice."

Thefe two fentences, paving the way for a defence of the Minifters which immediately follows, furnifh the key to the whole of the pamphlet. The minifters are in ill-odour; Parliament is not likely to meet for the prefent; popular frenzy is at its higheft. Anything that may be faid to ftifle inquiry will not be taken amifs when better days come round. But while this is the obvious aim of the letter, it is only juftice to Mr. Phillpotts to give full effect to that part of it which relates efpecially to the county meeting at Durham. Whether fuch a meeting ought to have been held it is immaterial to inquire. That its deliberations were

E

conducted with propriety is allowed by Mr. Phillpotts himfelf, when he fays,—

" I readily admit, that if any fteps were to be taken, it could not be expected that a more moderate courfe would be purfued than is prefented in the Refolutions of the meeting."

It is true that this is qualified, a little further on, by a defcription of the conduct of thofe who attended the meeting, which is, perhaps, more humorous than juft: —

" It amounts, at leaft, to finding a bill of indictment againft the magiftrates, or the military, againft fome of whom, be it remembered, bills were in fact laid before the grand jury of Lancafhire, and by them thrown out. The grand jury at Lancafter were fworn that they would ' diligently inquire and true prefentment make,' and they had witneffes before them, who were fworn to fpeak the truth. Under thefe cir-cumftances, they found it their confcientious duty to reject the bills. The gentlemen in our court at Durham have the advantage of not being fettered in their inquefts by the re-ftraint of an oath, and they have the greater advantage of being able to give as much credit as they pleafe to all the un-authorized ftatements which have iffued from the prefs, under a ftate of public feeling inflamed and agitated beyond exam-ple. Under thefe circumftances they feel it their painful duty to contradict the jurors of Lancafhire, and to pronounce on the bills accordingly."

In difcuffing the proceedings of the meeting, Mr. Phillpotts ftates the cafe thus :—

" The meafure to be defended is this—the pronouncing that there is a *primâ facie* cafe againft the magiftrates and military employed at Manchefter, and that it is neceffary for county meetings to found on this cafe the demand of an in-

veſtigation. Here are two points to be made good in order
to juſtify the proceedings of Thurſday; 1ſt, that there is
ſuch a *primâ facie* caſe as is aſſerted; 2nd, that it is right
to declare that there is, and, in conſequence, to demand an
inveſtigation.

"Now into the firſt queſtion it is not my intention to enter,
further than to remind the gentlemen who have moved the
meaſure, to what point our knowledge of the ſtate of the
caſe, from admitted faċts of an authoritative charaċter, really
extends. It is this; that ſeveral perſons at the head of the
meeting at Mancheſter were apprehended, and detained for
high treaſon, of which that meeting was the alleged overt
aċt; that after their detention for ſeveral days, the charge of
high treaſon was given up, and the parties were held to bail
for a conſpiracy to overturn the Government, and alter the
laws of the land by force; that bills of indiċtment were
preferred againſt certain perſons concerned in diſperſing the
meeting by force; the conſequence of which force was the
loſs of ſeveral lives—and that theſe bills were thrown out.
This, I ſay, is the amount of all that is known from admitted
faċts of an authoritative charaċter; and if it were neceſſary
to come to any concluſion on the ſubjeċt, (which I apprehend
that it is not,) I ſhould contend that the fair preſumption, as
far as it goes, is againſt the legality and the peaceableneſs of
the meeting in queſtion; for there can be no doubt, that if
the meeting was legally held, and peaceably conduċted, all
who were engaged in diſperſing it by force would be guilty
of murder, if the conſequence of that force was the loſs
of lives.

" But it is alleged in one of the Reſolutions that ' nothing
has appeared which juſtifies the conduċt of the magiſtrates
and the yeomanry ;' and it is an obſervation which we hear
continually from well meaning perſons that it is ſtrange that
no attempts ſhould be made by them to diſprove charges
which are reſounded from one end of the kingdom to the
other. Has it never occurred to any of theſe good people

that a profecution is now in progrefs which muft fhow whether there be a juftification or not ?*   Will they take the trouble of reflecting whether it may not be prudent for thefe parties, in refpect to themfelves, to referve the publication of their cafe till it fhall be made known by the proceedings in the Court of Law ?   And even if it be not thus prudent in refpect of themfelves, at leaft that it may be of high importance to the due courfe of juftice in refpect to others ?   Are they to be driven by clamour to make public the evidence which is to pafs on the trial of the alleged confpirators, and fo to defeat all reafonable probability of their conviction ?   The monftrous and palpable injuftice of fuch a demand would make it incredible that fo large a portion of the public fhould fhow it any favour, if experience had not repeatedly proved that no abfurdity is too grofs for the minds of the people, when duly heated to admit it.   The very forbearance from all publication may be, and apparently is, the bounden, but certainly not the pleafing duty of thefe victims of popular delufion; and the rigid manner in which it is difcharged by them may probably be found hereafter to merit the gratitude of every true friend of his country."

Having thus difpofed of the firft of his pofitions, Mr. Phillpotts proceeds :—

" The next confideration is, whether, fuppofing fuch a cafe to exift, it is proper to declare that it exifts; and this involves one of the moft ferious queftions that can be put

---

* Hunt and his affociates were tried at York at the Spring Affizes in 1820.   The trial lafted ten days, and ended in the conviction of nine of their number for holding an unlawful meeting and exciting difcontent.   On the 15th of May following, Hunt was fentenced to two years and fix months' imprifonment, and the reft to one year's imprifonment.

before Englifhmen. It is in fact no lefs than this : whether it is right for popular meetings to announce in this cafe their judgment on the apparent merits of a queftion which is in the courfe of judicial inveftigation. On this fubject fo much has been better faid by others, and, in truth, fo much muft occur to every plain underftanding, that I fhall have no occafion to dwell long upon it. Gentlemen, I will not go the whole length of afferting that it never can be right thus to anticipate the regular courfe of law ; for on political fubjects nothing univerfal can be rationally affirmed ; the beft and moft certain principle muft admit of modifications and exceptions ; and prudence alone can decide (an en-lightened and genuine prudence) when the occafion for thefe exceptions and modifications has actually arifen. But thus much I think will readily be granted to me, that nothing fhort of a great and unequivocal good to be obtained, or a fore and very preffing grievance to be removed can juftify any moderately prudent (I might fay any moderately imprudent) perfons in wifhing to interfere with the procefs of law. A manifeft and moft ferious evil is fure to be in-curred; the benefit fought, therefore, ought to be not only very great, but very certain. The proof of this refts alto-gether upon thofe who propofe the experiment. I have attended to all the arguments reported to have been advanced at our county meeting, and muft frankly confefs that I have rifen from the inquiry more confirmed than before of the extreme unfitnefs of the proceedings of that meeting."

Then follows an examination of the arguments used at the meeting, which offers little intereft at the prefent time. If the letter had ended here, it would have been well. Though it might have added little to the reputation of Mr. Phillpotts as an accurate and profound thinker, and muft affuredly have created fufpicions of his motives, yet it would not have

marked him out as a man eager to give battle to a
political adverſary with weapons of a more queſtionable kind than mere playful ſatire.   Mr. Lambton
(afterwards Earl of Durham) had attended the meeting,
and after the Reſolutions had been propoſed and
ſeconded, it was natural enough, as one of the repreſentatives of the county, that he ſhould ſay a few
words.   However much people may differ from the
political ſentiments of this gentleman, there certainly is
nothing in his ſpeech to juſtify the language applied to
it by Mr. Phillpotts :—" Nothing ſhort of running the
full career of raſhneſs and peril could glut his morbid
avidity of diſtinction."   And then he goes on to ſay, that,
if a verdict of a jury ſhall pronounce Hunt and his com-
rades guilty of the charge laid againſt them, " ſlander
of the moſt miſchievous and gigantic kind will have
been uttered by him, without rational motive, or intelligible excuſe.   I envy him not his feelings on ſuch
a conſummation; ſtill leſs do I envy him, if he ſhall
then have no feelings at all."   He then charges Mr.
Lambton with " playing with the torch of ſedition, and
wantonly toſſing it about amidſt the combuſtible matter
which ſurrounds him," and concludes by ſaying,—

" Theſe are not times when the diſtempered ſpirit of the
multitude ſhould be ſtill further inflamed by men who ought
to exert the influence belonging to their ſtation in allaying
heats and pacifying diſcontents."

All this may be very forcible, but it is ſcarcely the
way in which a clergyman ſhould addreſs a gentleman
of high deſcent and unblemiſhed life, whoſe only

offence upon this occaſion ſeems to have been that he
had the misfortune of differing from Mr. Phillpotts
on an important queſtion which was juſt then occupying the thoughts of the entire country. Such a diſplay of party feeling could only have the effect of
defeating its own end. And ſo it turned out; for, inſtead of helping the cauſe which it was written to
ſerve, this letter created a ·prejudice againſt the ſubſequent writings of Mr. Phillpotts, which has outlived
the memory of this particular event.

It is true that he explained much of this aſperity in
his anſwer to the article in the *Edinburgh Review*,
which next comes under conſideration; but the miſfortune was that many people read his letter who
never ſaw the explanation. Thus, then, friends were
alarmed, enemies were incenſed, and thoſe who were
neither friends nor enemies felt that a great miſtake had
been made, and that a ſpirit of rancour had been
excited by this pamphlet which it might take a lifetime of conciliation to allay.

Many anonymous anſwers quickly iſſued from
the preſs. Amongſt theſe is to be reckoned an
article in the *Edinburgh Review* (No. 64), entitled,
" Neceſſity of Parliamentary Enquiry," which, while
profeſſing to be a review of the pamphlet of Mr.
Phillpotts, was in reality directed againſt himſelf.
The author of it was commonly ſuppoſed to be one
of the moſt diſtinguiſhed of the early contributors
to that journal, who, adding the rank of a ſenator to
the reputation of an orator, was an adverſary that few

men would dare to defpife.   This article was widely
read, and a cheap edition of it (price twopence)
was rapidly diftributed throughout the county of
Durham.

Thefe circumftances induced Mr. Phillpotts to
publifh a ftatement in reply to it,* which appeared in
January, 1820.   And this, it muft be confeffed, is a
moft triumphant expofure ·both of the fhallownefs of
the reviewer's arguments and the feelings which had
guided him in writing.   It was neceffary promptly
to crufh fo powerful an antagonift as Mr. Phillpotts
had fhown himfelf to be, and therefore the veteran
reviewer, armed with malice and mifreprefentation, to
which the power of his cultivated mind lent a double
force, ftepped forth from the ranks to give him battle.
But if Mr. Phillpotts was to blame for the tone of
his pamphlet, the reviewer foon fhowed that he was
incapable of teaching him better manners.   That his
labours fhould have met with fuch a recognition was
in reality an indication of the value attached to them
by his opponents.   A diftinguifhed public character
would not for nothing have remitted his exertions in
a higher fphere to refume thofe of a review, while the
publication of his article in a cheaper form fhowed
the anxiety of his party to make the moft of his
fervices.

---

* " Remarks on an Article in the *Edinburgh Review* (No.
64) entitled, ' Neceffity of Parliamentary Enquiry,' by the
Rev. H. Phillpotts, M.A., Author of a Letter to the Freeholders of Durham, which that Article profeffes to review."

It is needlefs to go through this pamphlet in detail, fince it is merely an expofure of the reviewer's blunders, fophiftry, and malignity. One extract, however, may be commended to the attention of " liberals " of every fhade :—

" To fay the truth, this is not the firft time that I have had occafion to admire the exquifite felicity with which the lovers of free difcuffion and manly inquiry can adjuft their graduated fcale of crimes and punifhments. All who profefs the fame 'liberal fentiments' as themfelves, are at once invefted with an undefined and undefinable privilege. Thefe ' chartered libertines' may fay what they pleafe, abufe whom they pleafe and how they pleafe—they may run to the extreme verge of legal endurance, and even occafionally overftep into the confines of flander or fedition. At the worft it is only a generous indifcretion—while the firft perfon who afks them, why do ye fo ? has the whole fraternity let loofe upon him, unlefs he cuts and fquares his diction to the nice pattern which fuits their felf-complacency."

The whole of this reply is well written, and if the reviewer is fomewhat feverely handled, he richly deferves it. Mr. Phillpotts does not affect to defpife his adverfary; but, while paying a becoming tribute to his talents, he fails not to deplore the manifeftation of " the coarfeft admixture of prejudice and paffion, perverted by party fpirit, and abufed to the worft purpofes of wanton fophiftication, or wilful injuftice."

CHAPTER V.

Further Preferment of Mr. Phillpotts. His Competence, and proper use of it. The Living of Stanhope. Held by Three Prelates in succession. Mr. Phillpotts resigns his Stall in Durham Cathedral. A Description of Stanhope. Mr. Phillpotts builds a Rectory-house. Reminiscences of his Incumbency. Diligence in Parochial Duties. An active Magistrate. His Legal Abilities.

N the year following the publication of Mr. Phillpotts' letter to the freeholders of the county of Durham (1820), he received a splendid mark of his bishop's regard in the shape of a large living. He was already well provided for, but his new benefice eclipsed all his other preferment. In worldly circumstances, then, he was fortunate enough, and at no time of his life could he ever have known what it was to be a needy man. A rare piece of good fortune for one of his profession, when it is remembered that he inherited no patrimonial estates, and was not the representative of an historical name. Many of our great men

" Have been by *need* to full perfection brought;"

but if Mr. Phillpotts never passed through this bitter ordeal, he at least showed himself capable of braving the more feductive accompaniments of affluence. A canonry was no Capua to him ; and if honours and preferment were fhowered upon him, they were not ufed for mean and felfifh ends.

On the 20th of September, 1820, he was collated to the Rectory of Stanhope—one of the moft valuable, if not *the* moft valuable living in England. This princely bene-fice had been held by three prelates in fucceffion, who were the immediate predeceffors of Mr. Phillpotts— Dr. Butler, Bifhop of Briftol, Dr. Keene, Bifhop of Chefter, and Dr. Thurlow, Bifhop of Lincoln. If precedent, therefore, went for anything, it was not hard to predict what his ultimate fate might be. On being prefented to this living he refigned his ftall in Durham Cathedral.

Stanhope, the fcene of Mr. Phillpotts' future paftoral labours, is a town of no great pretenfions on the north bank of the Wear, and is chiefly inhabited by miners. It was raifed to the dignity of a market town in 1421. The church is a plain and ancient fabric, ftanding on rifing ground to the north of the town. At no great diftance ftands an ancient manor-houfe, the feat of the old hiftorical family of Feather-ftonhaugh, the laft of whom was killed at the battle of Hochftadt. In the woods of Stanhope Park the prince-bifhops of Durham ufed to hold their great foreft hunts, the tenants being obliged to furnifh neceffaries for them and their fuite, befides maintain-ing their dogs and huntfmen.

The population of Stanhope, and other circum-

stances of interest connected with the parish, will come
under confideration further on.

One of Mr. Phillpotts' earliest acts after becoming
rector was to commence the erection of a parfonage-
house, as well as a refidence for the curate. It should
be recorded to his credit that he undertook this entirely
at his own private expenfe, without burdening the
living with any charge. The fum expended was about
12,000*l.* The house is very large, and occupied a
confiderable time in building. During this period Mr.
Phillpotts refided in Durham.

His incumbency is well remembered, and he appears
in the main to have conciliated the regard of the
parifhioners. Shortly after his elevation to the Epifcopal
bench an old woman remarked to his fucceffor that he
had fent two of her fons to heaven—a ftrong expreffion,
not to be repeated to fcorners, but intimating, as it was
underftood, that he had diligently and faithfully
attended them till their death, and had been the
inftrument in God's hands of faving their fouls. This
anecdote is enough to show that neither his cathedral
duties at Chefter, nor the theological and political
ftudies in which he was now fo deeply immerfed,
diverted him from the paramount obligation of paftoral
vigilance. The petition of the inhabitants of Stanhope
againft his holding that living *in commendam* with the
See of Exeter will be examined in its proper place.

At this time Mr. Phillpotts was gratifying a tafte for
legal matters, which had early difplayed itfelf, by
difcharging with great regularity the duties of a county

magiftrate. His aptitude for this kind of bufinefs was very remarkable. He became poffeffed by intuition of that which to others was matter of laborious ftudy; and the magiftrate's clerk ufed to aver that Mr. Phillpotts could always tell what would be in an Aƈt of Parliament before it came out.

CHAPTER VI.

*Return of Queen Caroline to England, and the Proceedings con-
sequent upon it. Gave occasion to a Pamphlet by Mr. Phillpotts. Injudicious Conduct of the Ministry. Popular Feeling
excited against them. Meetings held in various parts of
the Country. All Ranks took part in them. The Durham
Meeting. The Speakers. The Address. Reference in it to
Spirit of Discontent existing in the Country. Impropriety of
this. A Counter-Address agreed upon by the Clergy. Their
Justification for taking this step. Mr. Phillpotts the Pro-
poser of it. Hostile Feeling manifested against the Clergy.
Not confined to the Lower Orders. The Northumberland
Meeting at Morpeth. Lord Grey's Speech. His Remarks
upon the Clergy of Durham. Letter from Mr. Phillpotts
to his Lordship. The Peril of coming forward. The
Clergy defended against the Imputation of Underhand Conduct. The Treatment of Mr. Liddell at the Meeting.
Remarks on the Press. Improper Use of the expression,
" The People," exposed. Disingenuous Arts of " Liberal"
Statesmen. Description of Lord Grey's Conduct by Mr.
Phillpotts. His Behaviour in Parliament, in reference to
the Queen's Guilt, compared with his Statements at the
Durham Meeting. What his Conduct ought to have been
had he believed in the Queen's perfect Innocence. An In-
judicious Statement in his Speech. Severe Remarks upon it
by Mr. Phillpotts. An unhappy Quotation of Holy Scrip-
ture by his Lordship. Impression created by the Letter of
Mr. Phillpotts. General Tone of it. Not to be judged by
the Standard of the Present Day. Consultation of Whig
Lawyers to ascertain if it was Libellous. Attack upon the
Clergy by the Durham Chronicle. Action for Libel against
the Publisher. Mr. Brougham's Defence. Its Character.
Conviction of the Defendant.*

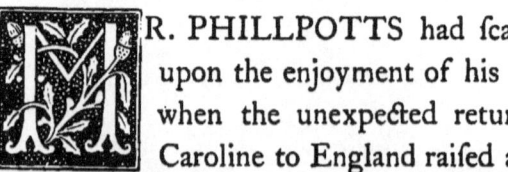R. PHILLPOTTS had scarcely entered
upon the enjoyment of his new benefice,
when the unexpected return of Queen
Caroline to England raised a storm of excitement throughout the country, which soon involved

even the moft diftant towns and villages in its refift-
lefs courfe. It is, happily, no part of this hiftory to
chronicle the misfortunes or crimes of this ill-fated
princefs, or to dwell upon perfecutions which terminated not even with death, but purfued her lifelefs
body to the very confines of the land. It is neceffary,
however, to allude to thefe diftreffing events, fince
they gave occafion to a pamphlet by Mr. Phillpotts,
which created great fenfation at the time, and which
merits fomething more than a paffing notice.

The great perfonal unpopularity of the King, and
the unjuftifiable fyftem of efpionage which had been
fo fuccefsfully practifed upon the Queen, combined to
excite a fympathy in her favour, and to caufe people, if not actually to forget, at leaft to extenuate her
faults. The attempt of the Miniftry, therefore, to
proceed againft her Majefty by a Bill of Pains and
Penalties, which, if carried to its legitimate end, muft
have coft her her life, was about as unpopular and
inconfiderate a ftep as could poffibly have been taken.
In any event it muft terminate in failure. If the bill
fhould pafs into law, the penalty was death, and no
Government would have dared to carry it out, in the
face of the popular excitement which prevailed. If it
was abandoned—as it ultimately was—the Queen's
triumph was complete. The effect of this was that
an almoft univerfal feeling of indignation was excited
againft the conduct of the Minifters. Thus, then,
while the Queen was the idol of the Londoners, and
was followed about everywhere by a fhouting and

triumphant mob, large and influential meetings were held in all parts of the country, and Refolutions were paffed condemnatory of the policy of the Government. Nor were thefe meetings by any means confined to the lower orders, and thofe agitators who find an opportunity for making political capital out of the troubles of the times. Men of all ranks united in reprobating the policy of a Government which could feek to condemn a Royal lady to degradation without a parallel, on evidence which would not have been received againft the moft abandoned criminal in the land.

The gentry of the county of Durham were not backward in declaring their fentiments at this moft critical and painful time. On Wednefday, December the 12th, 1820, a meeting of the freeholders of the county was held in the County Court, Durham, to take into confideration the meafures that had been purfued for the degradation of the Queen, and the propriety of prefenting petitions to both Houfes of Parliament, praying that they would take fuch fteps as might effectually prevent the recurrence of proceedings alike unconftitutional in their nature, and difgufting and pernicious in their tendency. The High Sheriff of the county, the Hon. W. K. Barrington, took the chair; and the numerous attendance of the principal inhabitants of the county, as well as the rank and character of thofe who took a prominent part in the proceedings of the day, ftamped the meeting as, probably, one of the moft important ever held in Durham. John George Lambton, Efq., M.P., propofed, and Samuel Moulton Barnett, Efq., feconded, certain Refolutions, which were embodied in an Addrefs and prefented to the King. The other fpeakers were Mr. Liddell (who expreffed his difapprobation at the proceedings of the meeting), Earl Grey, Dr. Fenwick, Mr. Shafto, and Mr. Powlett, M.P.

Among the topics embraced in thefe Refolutions there was one which was mifchievous and dangerous, and was evidently inferted for party purpofes :—" We humbly venture to ftate to your Majefty," the petitioners fay, " that a general fpirit of difcontent has arifen, which, if not corrected by timely remedies, muft produce the moft difaftrous confequences to the power and tranquillity of this great empire." Now, however true this may have been in fact, it had nothing to do with the requifition, in purfuance of which the meeting had been called. Its infertion, then, was moft fignificant, and could only be regarded as an intelligible hint to the King to change his advifers. The unfairnefs of fuch a proceeding is manifeft. It was, in point of fact, to ufe the Queen's misfortunes for the purpofe of ejecting the Miniftry. Under thefe circumftances fome of the clergy of Durham affembled at the Archdeacon's, and determined upon laying before the King a Counter-Addrefs, declaring their own fentiments, and pointing out what they conceived to be the real dangers of the times. That they were juftified in taking this ftep will be feen when it is remembered that the Refolutions and Addrefs of the Durham meeting went forth to the world under the

name of the nobility, gentry, *clergy*, and freeholders
of the county. As long as the buſineſs of the meeting
was conducted in conformity with the terms of the
requiſition, they would have had nothing to complain
of; and, even if they had not attended, they would
have been bound by the Reſolutions which were agreed
upon : but when topics were introduced of which no
notice had been given, and of which they ſtrongly
diſapproved, no one can blame them for coming forward
and ſtating the grounds of their diſapproval.   Mr.
Phillpotts took an active ſhare in the preparation of
the Addreſs of the Clergy, and it fell to his lot to
propoſe it to the meeting.

As ſoon as it became known that the Addreſs had
been preſented, a ſtrong feeling of hoſtility was manifeſted againſt the clergy.   They were charged with
taking the part of Government againſt the Queen, for
mercenary motives, and were aſſailed, both in public
and private, with epithets of hatred and ſcorn.   Upon
no one did the ſtorm fall heavier than on Mr. Phillpotts.   His conſtitutional energy, and the great and
varied talents which he was able to bring to bear on
every queſtion which he took in hand, ſingled him out
as a favourite object of attack.

Nor were the rancorous feelings againſt the clergy
by any means confined to the lower orders.   An earl
came forward to denounce them under the following
circumſtances.   At the cloſe of December, 1820, a
requiſition was preſented to the High Sheriff of
Northumberland, Wm. Clark, Eſq., deſiring that a

county meeting might be convened to take into confideration the fteps propofed for the degradation of the
Queen. Among the fignatures appear the names of
Lords Tankerville, Grey, and Offulfton, together with
fome of the leading gentry of the county. The high
fheriff courteoufly but firmly refufed to call the meeting. In confequence of this refufal a circular was
fent round (Dec. 26), calling upon the independent
freeholders and inhabitants of the county to attend a
meeting to be held in the Town Hall at Morpeth on
Wednefday, January the 10th, at twelve o'clock, to confider the fteps neceffary to be taken in confequence of
the extraordinary conduct of the fheriff, and for other
purpofes fpecified in the requifition. This was figned—

> GREY,
> JOHN E. SWINBURNE,
> CHARLES MONCK,
> T. W. BEAUMONT,
> C. W. BIGGE,
> JOHN GEORGE LAMBTON,
> GEORGE BAKER.

Notwithftanding the exceeding inclemency of the
weather the meeting was moft numeroufly and refpectably attended. It was feared that Lord Grey would
not be able to be prefent, as he had lately been fuffering from a fevere attack of illnefs. At twelve o'clock the
gates of the Hall were opened, and the preffure to
obtain admiffion was exceffive. Even the noble earl
and the requifitionifts had very great difficulty in pro-
curing their ufual feats upon the bench. The Hall

was denſely filled, and the heat very ſoon became
oppreſſive.

Sir John Swinburne having been called to the chair,
the proceedings commenced.   An Addreſs to the
King and ſome Reſolutions were agreed to, with only
one or two diſſentient voices, the moſt remarkable being
that of Mr. Orde, who came forward and boldly ſtated
(though with much interruption) the reaſons why he
could not concur in the proceedings of the meeting.
Upon this occaſion Lord Grey was the chief ſpeaker,
and his ſpeech was long remembered as one of the
moſt animated which he ever delivered. After touching
upon the buſineſs of the day, he proceeded to enlarge,
with great warmth and energy, upon the conduct of
the clergy of Durham in preſenting their Addreſs to
the King.   This produced (Jan. 19) a letter from
Mr. Phillpotts to the noble Lord, " on certain charges
advanced by his Lordſhip, at the late county meeting
in Northumberland, againſt the clergy of the County
of Durham."   He conceived that the ſpeech of Lord
Grey was a challenge to the clergy, who had joined
in the Addreſs to the King, to avow before the world
the principles which dictated it, and the grounds on
which it was to be juſtified.   Mr. Phillpotts appears
not to have been inſenſible to the perilous nature of
the enterpriſe in which he was engaging :—

" I am not ignorant," he ſays, " that I may poſſibly draw
upon myſelf all the fury of all your adherents, from the
political reviewer, who ſcarcely any longer pretends to regard
truth and juſtice as qualifications for his calling, down to

the miferable mercenary, who eats the bread of proftitution, and panders to the low appetites of thofe who cannot, or who dare not, cater for their own malignity."

He then proceeds to examine that portion of Lord Grey's fpeech which related efpecially to the clergy. His lordfhip had imputed to them underhand conduct, and faid that, inftead of flying into holes and corners and fecret conclaves, they ought to meet thofe from whom they differ face to face. Mr. Phillpotts well remarks upon this :—

" I will not infult your Lordfhip by fuppofing that you made this demand for any other purpofe than to catch the momentary plaudits of your audience. I only admire the perfect gravity with which you make it, and talk of free difcuffion at Durham county meetings as if you were really in earneft. And yet, my Lord, well as you act the part, it is one which by no means becomes you. This petty artifice of daring an adverfary to combat, where you know he cannot meet you on equal terms, ought to be referved for thofe whofe ambition can look no higher than to a fuccefsful difplay on the huftings. You, my Lord, were formed by nature and by difcipline for far better things."

It is worthy of remark, that Mr. Liddell, a gentleman of high family and character, actually did come forward and addrefs the Durham meeting, with a view of fhowing the impropriety of its proceedings ; but he was with the utmoft difficulty enabled to proceed amidft a volley of hiffes, and cries of " fhame," and "turn him out." Whether this ftate of things would have been mended if a clergyman had happened to be the fpeaker it is eafy enough to guefs.

Amongſt other ſtatements calculated to excite popular feeling againſt the clergy, Lord Grey repreſented
them as attributing all the exiſting diſcontent to the
licentiouſneſs of the preſs, and as being advocates for
encroachments on the liberties of the country. To this
Mr. Phillpotts replies :—

"My Lord, we have ſaid no more againſt the licentiouſneſs of the preſs than Mr. Brougham, and others of your
Lordſhip's political friends have often ſaid, and unhappily have
often proved in their place in Parliament. Inſtead of attributing all to the licentiouſneſs of the preſs, we expreſſly attributed 'much to the raſhneſs of headſtrong declaimers,
heedleſs or ignorant of the tendency of their own folly'—
much to 'the apathy of wiſer and better men'—much to
'every evil principle', which can ſhoot forth in rank luxuri-
ance under the general ſupineneſs of the good, and the reſtleſs activity of the wicked. In ſhort, the licentiouſneſs of the
preſs is only one (a moſt powerful and moſt appalling one
indeed, but ſtill only one) of ſeveral cauſes to which we
aſcribed, what we ſee as plainly, and perhaps deplore as ſin-
cerely, as your Lordſhip does,—a too prevailing ſpirit of diſcontent ; we might add, an impatience of all lawful control,
a thirſt for untried, undefined, and undefinable change."

Mr. Phillpotts next defends the Addreſs of the Clergy
againſt the aſſertion of Lord Grey, that it contains
moſt unjuſt and unfounded charges againſt "the people," a ſomewhat ill-defined form of expreſſion which
finds great favour with "liberal" ſtateſmen on the huſt-
ings, and at every criſis of their fate :—

"May I entreat your Lordſhip to produce the paſſages
on which you found theſe aſſertions? Is it the following,
'Widely as the contagious frenzy has ſpread, we cannot
doubt the ſoundneſs of the main body of this great nation.'

Who, my Lord, in your Lordfhip's contemplation, are the people? Not, it feems, ' the main body of the nation'—but fome portions of it—thofe particular portions which the Durham clergy have made the fubject of their accufation—in other words, evil-minded men, who revile and mifreprefent all the meafures of Government, and thofe who are feduced by them to caft off their allegiance—the deluders and the deluded—the vain diffeminators of mifchievous fooleries at public meetings, and thofe whom fuch weak fophiftry can miflead—the teachers and the difciples in the fchools of blafphemy and fedition—the abettors and the accomplices in fecret confpiracies and open rebellion—the Carliles and Woolers, the Thiftlewoods and Brandreths—thefe are ' the people'— thefe are they of whom your Lordfhip proclaims yourfelf the indignant advocate, thefe are they from whofe injured innocence you ' repel the calumnies of us addreffers againft your countrymen.' "

But the part of the Addrefs of the Clergy which gave the greateft offence to Lord Grey, and which he feemed to underftand as applying folely to himfelf, was that which ftated, " We have feen, with feelings which we forbear to exprefs, men of exalted rank and diftinguifhed talents, foftering and ftimulating the difcontents of the multitude, availing themfelves of delufions which they defpife, and of vices which they reprobate, to forward the miferable objects of party ambition." With the utmoft candour Mr. Phillpotts avows, that, when he fubfcribed the addrefs, he *did* confider his lordfhip to be one of thofe to whom the words were juftly applicable; and after this manly declaration, he proceeds to juftify the opinion which he had formed. This was founded chiefly on the difference obfervable in Lord Grey's conduct and statements in relation to the Queen's guilt, when speaking in Parliament, and before the Durham county meeting. The majority who attended that meeting were fully persuaded of the Queen's perfect innocence, and had assembled with the intention of vindicating it.

"Now that you, my Lord," says Mr. Phillpotts, "participated in that conviction, I venture to think impossible. I do so, not from the apparent force of the evidence adduced, (respecting which it is no part of my purpose to say anything,) but from your Lordship's speech in the House of Lords on the motion for the second reading of the Bill of Degradation. I there see that in express terms you admit and lament that 'impropriety of conduct,' that 'matters of great suspicion' had been established; but 'they did not amount to the fair conclusion of guilt, which alone could justify the verdict of guilty;' that in the outset your prejudices and feelings were unfavourable to the Queen; that you did think it possible that a case would be made out, which would compel you to vote for the bill; but as it then stood, the only vote you could reconcile to your honour and judgment was, with a profound sense of duty, to lay your hand upon your heart and say, not guilty."

Mr. Phillpotts then goes on to show what Lord Grey's conduct would have been if he had really believed that the Queen was innocent:—

"And while I form my conclusion from what you did say, I find it most materially strengthened by what you did not say. You did not say, my Lord, that you thought her innocent. And yet, if you had indeed thought so, your feelings as a man must have impelled you to give to her the full benefit of your favourable opinion. You could not, while you heard an opposite judgment strongly expressed by

many even of thofe who voted againft the bill, as well as by
the majority who fupported it—you could not have forborne
to declare yourfelf, in the broadeft and plaineft terms, in
favour of an unfortunate lady—that lady a Queen—that
Queen one whom, fourteen years before, when Minifter of
the Crown, you had felt it confiftent with your duty to
treat as, I am quite fure, your Lordfhip heartily wifhes fhe
never had been treated."

Having thus guarded his vote in the Houfe of
Lords in fuch a way as effectually to exclude him
from the number of thofe who believed in the Queen's
innocence, Lord Grey came before the meeting at
Durham, and liftened without remark to fpeakers
who affirmed that fhe was guiltlefs, joined in refolutions which were founded on this fuppofition, and afferted that " the witneffes againft the Queen had been
proved to be totally unworthy of credit," and that
" the evidence of the only witneffes brought forward
in fupport of the charge had been moft completely
overthrown by the teftimony of unimpeachable witneffes on the part of her Majefty."

Mr. Phillpotts thus fums up the cafe againft his
lordfhip :—

" My Lord, when I put thefe things together, and at the
fame time bear in mind the irrelevant matter fo unwarran-
tably introduced into your proceedings—the vehement condemnation of all the policy of his Majefty's Government,
both at home and abroad, and, laftly, the threat of a fpeedy
revolution if that policy is not changed—I have no difficulty
in ftating my reafons for confidering your Lordfhip as one of
thofe to whom the words of which you complain are juftly
applicable. In faying this, I add, with perfect fincerity, that

I believe you to have deceived yourfelf—to have been influenced by views and actuated by motives which you would be the firft to renounce, if you thought them inconfiftent with the welfare of your country."

A very injudicious fentence in Lord Grey's fpeech, which was evidently intended as a fop to the extreme Reformers of the day, gives Mr. Phillpotts an opportunity, which he was not likely to mifs, of defcending upon him with terrible force :—

"You fay that, 'if the adminiftration of affairs were offered to you to-morrow, you would not accept it, without being enabled to effect a complete change in the prefent fyftem of government.' This, my Lord, is fpeaking plainly. In truth, an ardent and impetuous politician, like your Lordfhip, who has been for nearly forty years engaged in vehement oppofition, can hardly fail to have difqualified himfelf for office. In the courfe of his long and unfparing hoftility to almoft every meafure of Minifters, it is fcarcely to be hoped that he fhould not have committed himfelf by pledges which he cannot, when in power, abandon without difhonour, nor redeem without ruin to his country. Your Lordfhip has once been tried, for a very fhort period, as a Minifter ;* and, whether juftly or otherwife, many of your old fupporters charged you then with incurring the former part of this alternative : if the trial be repeated, we may all have occafion to deplore that you now prefer the latter."

But Lord Grey, having "exhaufted," as Mr. Phillpotts fays, "the copious ftores of his own eloquence

* On the acceffion to office of the Fox and Grenville Miniftry, in 1806, Lord Grey was appointed Firft Lord of the Admiralty, with a feat in the Cabinet. On the death of Fox he fucceeded to the vacant poft of Secretary for Foreign Affairs; but the Miniftry was fhortly afterwards diffolved.

in railing at the clergy," has recourfe to a quotation from holy Scripture to juftify his arguments, and give point to his farcafm. He defcribes the clergy who figned the Addrefs in the words of David—" Their communing is not for peace, but they imagine deceitful words againft thofe that are quiet in the land." After a well-deferved rebuke for this trifling with facred words, Mr. Phillpotts exclaims:—

" Quiet in the land! Why, your Lordfhip and your friends are now the prime agitators in thefe northern parts. Be the fpirit of modern Whiggifm what it may—a fpirit of health, or one of a very different defcription—be its intents wicked or charitable—if it is in any degree an honeft fpirit, it will at leaft not afk us to call it a quiet one. A revolution muft have already begun, and have begun in the underftanding and reafon of Englifhmen, before we can bring ourfelves to acknowledge the peaceful politics of Mr. Lambton, or the dove-like demeanour of Earl Grey."

It has been faid already that this letter created a profound impreffion, and it deferved to do fo. Mr. Phillpotts had matched himfelf againft one of the acuteft intellects in the land, the impetuous eloquence of whofe oratory had earned for him the title of the Hotfpur of his party, and had fucceeded in fhowing that he could command powers of logic and fatire which it would not be well for an adverfary, however gifted, lightly to provoke. His pamphlet was ftrictly defenfive, and, although written under no ordinary provocation, was not remarkable for any needlefs afperity either of fentiment or of language. But ftill it is a queftion whether it would not have been wifer, as affuredly it would have been more praifeworthy, for a clergyman to withdraw himfelf altogether from the arena of party ftrife, and refrain from writing a letter which could fcarcely be viewed otherwife than as a political expedient. The temptation, no doubt, was ftrong. Party fpirit was running high. The fpeech of Lord Grey was fingularly irritating, and, if un-anfwered, was likely to do all the mifchief that his great and honoured name enabled it to do. The Durham dignitaries, too, had all along exhibited an unhappy propenfity to meddle with politics. Mr. Phillpotts, therefore, muft be judged with due regard to the circumftances of the times and the habits of thofe with whom he was affociated. The memory of his pamphlet did not foon pafs away; and if it fhielded the clergy from the unmerited attack of Lord Grey, it alfo expofed them to the hatred of adverfaries. This hoftility was not long in bearing fruit, for foon after its publication a confultation of eminent Whig lawyers was held, at the exprefs inftance of fome of the moft zealous affertors of the freedom of the prefs, for the purpofe of detecting fomething libellous in it, but the attempt was abandoned.

But matters did not reft here, for on Auguft the 18th, 1821, an article appeared in the *Durham Chronicle*, charging the clergy, and efpecially thofe of the cathe-dral, with " brutal enmity " to the Queen, becaufe they had not caufed the bells to be tolled at her death, and afferting that they clung to temporal power, and loft, in their officioufnefs in political matters, even the femblance of the character of minifters of religion. This led to an action for libel againft the publifher of the paper, John Ambrofe Williams, who was tried at Durham, Auguft the 6th, 1822, before Mr. Baron Wood and a fpecial jury. Mr. Brougham was retained for the defence, and made a fpeech the vehemence of which may well caufe one to marvel at the latitude accorded to popular orators in troublous times. Mr. Phillpotts himfelf thus defcribes* it:—

"Though delivered in fupport of a defence, it contains nothing at all apologetical, and not much that can be reprefented as even conciliatory. It is criminative, contemptuous, and defying. The tone throughout is that of proud fuperiority and command, and its general ftrain and character may be compendioufly defcribed by the fingle word terrible."

It was, however, without avail, for Williams was found guilty of a libel on the clergy of the cathedral at Durham. Dr. Phillpotts (for he had now taken his doctor's degree) evinced great intereft in the trial, and was prefent during the whole time it lafted. He was not, indeed, as was commonly fuppofed, one of the promoters of the fuit, for Mr. Scarlett, the counfel for the profecution, diftinctly afferted that the Bifhop of the diocefe was the profecutor. In truth the libelled clergy knew nothing of the profecution till they were informed of it through the public prints.

Though the defendant expreffed himfelf againft

---

* "Letter to Francis Jeffrey, Efq."

the clergy more coarsely than Lord Grey had done, yet the object of both was the same—to bring them into contempt. Thus, then, the verdict of a jury completed what the letter of Mr. Phillpotts had begun.

CHAPTER VII.

*Further Attacks upon the Clergy of Durham. Peculiarly ob-
noxious to the Enemies of the Church. Article in the* Edinburgh Review. *Dr. Phillpotts fingled out by Name. Defcription of the Article. Reafons for a Reply. Letter by
Dr. Phillpotts to Francis Jeffrey, Efq., the reputed Editor.
His Defence of the Doctrine of the Real Prefence. Expofure of the hiftorical Inaccuracy of the Reviewer. Improper
ufe by him of the Cafe of Williams. Reference to Williams
in a former Letter to Lord Grey denied by Dr. Phillpotts.
Extreme Forbearance which he had fhown towards him. Refutation of the Charge of not having caufed the Bells to be
tolled at the Queen's Death. The difingenuous Way in which
the Reviewer performed his Task. The Defendant's Libel
compared with the Defcription given of it by the Reviewer.
Remarks on the Way in which the* Edinburgh Review *was
conducted. Mr. Jeffrey's Reply. Nothing faid which affects
the Merits of the Cafe. A ftinging Reproof by Dr. Phillpotts. Offer of an Irifh Bifhopric by Lord Liverpool declined. His Promife to the Bifhop of Durham.*

BUT the troubles of the Durham clergy
were not deftined fo eafily to ceafe. The
iffue of the trial of Williams only ftimulated their enemies to further acts of aggreffion. Dr. Phillpotts defcribes himfelf and his
brethren* as "a body which feems to have earned in
a peculiar degree the hoftility of every enemy to our
Eftablifhment." And this was true enough. They
were decidedly unpopular. The *Edinburgh Review*

---

* "Letter to Francis Jeffrey, Efq."

in particular had marked them out for vengeance, and in November, 1822, an article appeared headed, " Durham Cafe—Clerical Abufes." Dr. Phillpotts was the only one of the clergy mentioned by name, and it is eafy enough to fee why this mark of diftinction fhould have been accorded to him. The article is defcribed by him as evidently written " by fome inferior hand, who, without the flighteft pretenfion to the ftrength of the ferpent, can only exhibit the flime and the venom." This is a fingularly happy defcription; applicable, unfortunately for the credit of journalifm, to other articles befides that in the *Edinburgh Review*. After this ftatement it is almoft a pity that he fhould have attempted any reply. There can be no pleafure in hunting down a loathfome reptile through maffes of filth. When you have caught it you can do nothing with it. It feemed, however, to Dr. Phillpotts that the extenfive circulation of the Review, and the inferences already drawn from the filence of the clergy, under charges moft unceafingly brought againft them, demanded that fome notice fhould be taken of the attack. If any notice was to be taken, moft people would agree that he was the man to take it. His anfwer affumed the form of a letter to the Editor of the *Edinburgh Review*, dated the 30th of December, 1822.*

* " A Letter to Francis Jeffrey, Efq., the reputed Editor of the *Edinburgh Review*, on an Article entitled, ' Durham Cafe—Clerical Abufes,' by the Rev. H. Phillpotts, D.D., Rector of Stanhope."

The reviewer had thought it needful to enter largely into what he took for theology. His blunders, however, are not to be regretted, as they afforded to Dr. Phillpotts an opportunity of expreſſing himſelf on the doctrine of the Real Preſence, which he declares to be "diſtinctly and unequivocally affirmed" in the Thirty-nine Articles. This is a valuable teſtimony, and none the leſs ſo from occurring in a place where one would ſo little expect to find it.

To ſhow that the hiſtorical knowledge of the reviewer was about on a level with his theological attainments, the following remarks of Dr. Phillpotts will ſuffice :—

> "Can a writer expect to be anſwered who will ſeriouſly quote Biſhop Burnet for a recommendation and authority to the Epiſcopal bench of our days to live 'abſtracted from courts, from cabals, and from parties ?'—ſcenes in which that good biſhop bore a buſier part than the moſt ſecular of our prelates for a century paſt, and where by his zealous ſupport of Whig principles he raiſed himſelf to that eminent ſtation, which, together with his numerous virtues, would enſure him, if now living, a full ſhare in the invectives of his preſent panegyriſt."

The miſerable equipment, however, of his aſſailant does not, in the Doctor's judgment, prohibit a reply ; and he proceeds to expoſe "the meaneſt artifice, and the moſt daring falſehoods," which "are reſorted to without ſcruple or reſtraint," in the courſe of the review. After dealing with the attack on modern biſhops, which had been made by the reviewer, with ſpecial reference to a recent ſpeech by the Biſhop of

G

London, on the fubject of the Queen's degradation,
Dr. Phillpotts goes on to ftate that the proceeding of
Williams, in publifhing an account of his trial for libel,
has afforded " to the congenial fpirit of this reviewer
an opportunity of reviling the clergy and the Church
of England, of which he has not failed to avail himfelf
to the utmoft."

" Decency," he adds, " and juftice might have feemed to
require that he fhould at leaft wait till the proceedings have
been completed ; but decency and juftice are antiquated
reftrictions, which a modern reformer has long fince learned
to defpife. Befides, if he did not fend forth his ftrictures
without delay, it might chance that the affertions, on which
they were to be built, might lofe even the faint femblance
of probability which it was convenient to throw around
them."

A ftatement in the letter of Dr. Phillpotts to Lord
Grey, in reference to " the miferable mercenary who
eats the bread of proftitution, and panders to the low
appetites of thofe who cannot, or who dare not, cater
for their own malignity,"* caufes the *Edinburgh
Review* to faften this fomewhat ungraceful defcription
on Williams, the defendant in the action for libel.
Dr. Phillpotts denies the allufion, and humoroufly
fays :—

" After this we may find no difficulty in believing that
the ingenious perfon who converted ' The Whole Duty of
Man' into a feries of libels, by labelling each vice with the
name of the fquire, the churchwarden, and fo forth, was no
other than an Edinburgh reviewer."

---

* See page 69.

The description evidently does not appear to have been as flattering to Williams as it was useful to the purposes of the reviewer, for in his affidavit before the King's Bench, in January 1822, he declared that he did not know who was intended by it.

" By what means," says Dr. Phillpotts, " he afterwards improved so wonderfully in the most important of all sciences —the knowledge of himself—or how he managed to ' screw his courage to the swearing point,' I shall not trouble myself to inquire."

And a little further on he adds :—

" In truth he was not idiot enough to fit the cap to his own head, till he fancied he could serve a desperate cause by wearing it."

So far from having assailed Williams, Dr. Phillpotts had carried forbearance to a point that must have been very trying to him. Week after week, and month after month, had Williams been dealing out the coarsest and foulest abuse of him in the columns of the *Durham Chronicle*, and it would not have been difficult to find passages that might have given rise to criminal proceedings. So far as it appears, Dr. Phillpotts did not retaliate, at all events in public, and with the exception of the single sentence in the letter to Lord Grey, which the reviewer claimed as describing Williams, nothing can be produced to show that he felt any irritation, or indeed was conscious of the attacks of the press.

Dr. Phillpotts next proceeds to that portion of the

review which relates to the conduct of the Durham clergy, in not caufing the bells to be tolled on the death of Queen Caroline. "To that body," he fays, "I did not belong: over the bells of any church in Durham I had no more control than the defendant or his reviewer." A little further on he declares that all the reviewer's clamour againft the Durham clergy, for taking a prominent and violent part on the queftion of the Queen's guilt, is as wholly devoid of truth as his other affertions concerning them.

"They actually forbore," he fays, "taking any part at all, till having been included in the defcription of a county meeting,* which threatened the Sovereign with a revolution, in confequence partly of the proceedings againft her Majefty, but chiefly of other alleged grievances, they exercifed that right which none but thofe 'who,' in the cant of the reviewer, 'efpoufe liberal principles,' would deny them, and difclaimed all fhare in the acts of that meeting. But even in doing this, fo little ground did they give for the charge of violence, in their language refpecting the Queen, that, as far as the proceedings of the county meeting related to her Majefty, they confidered it fufficient fimply to declare their diffent."

Speaking of the difingenuous way in which the reviewer had performed his duty, Dr. Phillpotts fays :—

"I will not purfue the difgufting tafk of tracing all the frauds and artifices of this perfon, whoever he be, who has thruft himfelf into the feat of juftice, and, in conjunction with his brother reviewers, profeffes to decide equally and impartially on all kinds of merit and demerit, literary, political, and moral."

------

* See page 66.

He then exhibits the defendant's libel, and the defcription of it as given in the review, fhowing that, to anfwer the reviewer's purpofes, it is ftripped of every fingle expreffion which marks its libellous character. Not one line of the libel occurs in a long article which occupies nine-and-twenty pages of clofely-printed matter. "What honeft motive," afks Dr. Phillpotts, "can be affigned for fuch a fuppreffion? Why is he thus anxious to hide from his readers the extent of the defendant's crime?"

The letter concludes with fome withering remarks on the manner in which the *Edinburgh Review* was conducted. Not even the character of Jeffrey could be proof againft fuch charges as Dr. Phillpotts heaps upon him. They deferve to be known, not indeed for the purpofe of reflecting upon the memory of one who is no longer able to anfwer for himfelf, and who for once forgot his high fenfe of honour in dealing thus with a clergyman of diftinguifhed pofition, but to fhow that whatever bitternefs may appear in portions of this letter, and in other places where this topic is referred to, was juftified (if ever there can be juftification for afperity of language) by a feries of affronts and invectives, unworthy alike of the *Edinburgh Review* and of the diftinguifhed critic who conducted it.

" If by inadvertence," fays Dr. Phillpotts, " anything falfe, unjuft, or culpably offenfive to the feelings of an individual, fhould for once have crept into his Journal, at leaft he would be anxious to prevent all recurrence of the injury. Has fuch been the conduct of the editor of this review? An

article was publifhed in his fixty-fourth number,* reflecting in
the coarfeft terms on my character. I anfwered that article
by proving the wilful falfehood of its main allegations, and at
the fame time called on the author to defend his own veracity.
Under that challenge he fat down in filence. He feized indeed (or fome one for him) on fome fubordinate particular,
and with much confidence of manner, and frefh fcurrility of
language, triumphed over my fuppofed mifapprehenfion of a
point of law. Here too he was defeated; his ignorance of
the law was expofed, as his lefs venial practices had been
detected before. Having done this, I addreffed the Editor of
the Review in terms of forbearance, perhaps I might fay of
courtefy, on the juft grounds of complaint which I might
urge againft himfelf. After an interval of three years, being
again affailed in the fame Journal, with equal groffnefs, and
as I have proved, with equal falfehood, I now tell the editor
before the world, that on him will light all the ignominy of
this fecond outrage; I tell him too that he would rather
have forgone half the profits of his unhallowed trade, than
have dared to launch againft any one of his brethren of the
Gown, the fmalleft part of that fcurrility, which he has felt
no fcruple in circulating againft Churchmen. To you, Sir, I
make no apology for addreffing you on this occafion. If
you are not, what the public voice proclaims you to be, the
Editor of the Review, you will thank me for thus giving
you an opportunity publicly to difclaim the degrading title.
If you are, it is henceforth to me a matter of indifference
what fuch a perfon may think or fay."

That Mr. Jeffrey fhould give utterance to fome
wails of pain under fuch a mercilefs caftigation as this

---

* This article appeared in the number for October, 1819,
and was entitled, "The Neceffity of Parliamentary Enquiry."
It related to the degradation of Queen Caroline.

was nothing more than might have been expected. Accordingly, in the next number of the *Edinburgh Review* (February, 1823) there appeared an editorial " note on Dr. Phillpotts," extending over upwards of four pages. Denying any *merit* to his pamphlet, the writer alleges its exceſs of violence and ſcurrility as its only claim to diſtinction.

As an example of the meekneſs with which he intends to ſchool Dr. Phillpotts into better behaviour for the future, he begins by ſtating that every one of the charges brought by him againſt the reviewer is *utterly unfounded,* and that his errors are to be aſcribed to *the violent paſſion* in which he evidently writes. After this conciliatory preface, he proceeds to examine certain ſtatements in the letter to Jeffrey in a tone which renders it impoſſible to follow him, and which plainly proves that the wounds inflicted by the laſh of Dr. Phillpotts were ſtill green and aching. Nothing, however, is ſaid which in the leaſt affects the merits of the caſe, and the concluding ſentences, in which all the previous charges againſt Dr. Phillpotts are reiterated and endorſed by the editor, can only have the effect of making every one regret that the manager of ſo diſtinguiſhed a Review ſhould have been wanting in the courteſy to confeſs that he was wrong, and refuſe to an injured clergyman the only reparation which it was in his power to give.

That Dr. Phillpotts ſhould have again adverted to the conduct of Mr. Jeffrey is not to be wondered at. The only marvel is that any ſkin, even if it were as

tough as the fevenfold fhield of Ajax, fhould be able
to endure a caftigation fo mercilefs.

The terrible denunciation which follows muft have
had its effect upon that motley brood of literary
vipers, one characteriftic of whom has ever been—

> " The tongue that licks the duft,
>   But, *when it fafely dares*, is prompt to fting ; "

and it is no wonder that Scotch theologians and critics
fhould henceforward have done their beft to keep themfelves out of reach of the Doctor's arm.

" The editor's own feelings on this occafion," he fays,
" may perhaps give him fome lafting touches of remorfe for
more than twenty long and guilty years of wanton or wilful
difregard of the feelings of others.   Let him, in his prefent
mood, look on the catalogue of honourable and diftinguifhed
names, which he and his confederates have laboured to
make the fport or the victims of their fpleen, their arrogance,
or their party fury.   Let him reflect on the meannefs, as
well as the injuftice, of abufing the power, which the extenfive circulation of his Journal gave him, to ' blazon thofe
names' in every quarter to which Englifh literature could
reach, ' in connection with epithets' fcarcely lefs painful
(except that they were, for the moft part, unmerited), than
thofe, under which he now writhes, with the bitter confcioufnefs that they are deferved.   Let him remember, that,
during fo long a period, he has by himfelf, or his minions,
pandered to all the envious and malignant feelings of his
readers—ufed every engine of literary torture that could
wound and lacerate ingenuous minds—left uneffayed no
fingle gradation of cruelty, from ruffian violence down to
the fubtler and fafer expedients of mock candour and contemptuous commendation—to eftablifh a defpotifm of the
pen, which, like other defpotifms, has ended in deftroying

itfelf. Let him read in the indignation, or the pity, of every impartial mind, his own large fhare in the common ignominy which has long been thickening round his band—and then, let him, if he will, affeft to hide his fhame under the babyifh plea, that he did not load the piece, he only primed it and drew the trigger—that he has, in fhort, only hired himfelf out to a bookfeller, for fome ftated hundreds of miferable pelf, to be the midwife and the nurfe to every un-fathered brood of calumnies which the malice of his faftion fhall engender. If he will, let him talk thus, and perfift to defend what he knows is indefenfible. But, rather, let him feek, in this, his day of deep humiliation, the real benefit which he ought to draw from it. Let him meditate on the painful contraft of what he is, with what he might have been —and what he yet may be. And then let him caft off at once the vile flough with which he is encumbered—again ftand forth in fome ingenuous form, and vindicate anew his title to that high refpeft, of which no man but himfelf could rob him. Let him do this, and he will yet have reafon to rejoice that in one, whom he had doomed for his viftim, he has found a monitor and a friend.''

This mafterly defcription of the effefts of perverted journalifm may be commended to the confideration of one, at leaft, of our modern Reviews, which, in its reftlefs eagernefs to provoke a laugh, miftakes invec-tive for wit, and is willing to purchafe a reputation for clevernefs at any price demanded by an infatiate public.

But, if Dr. Phillpotts had reafon to complain of the malignity of his enemies, he was alfo rapidly making friends for himfelf in high places. The vigour of his writings, the fubtlety of his wit, and the force and decifion of his charafter, pointed him out as a valu-

able ally to any Government.   It was about this
time, therefore, that overtures were made to him by
Lord Liverpool, who was defirous of raifing him to
the Irifh Epifcopal Bench.   The See of Clogher, then
vacant by the deprivation of the Hon. Percy Jocelyn,
with its princely income of 14,000*l.* a-year, would
have been a tempting offer to moft men ; but, with
greater fagacity, Dr. Phillpotts declined the honour,
rightly enough concluding that his talents and reputation would foon open the way to equal or greater
dignities in England.   That he himfelf expected that
this would be the not unnatural termination of his
labours, is evidenced by his having made a promife to
the Bifhop of Durham (Dr. Barrington), on his prefentation by him to the Rectory of Stanhope, that he
would not accept a bifhopric during his lordfhip's lifetime without his confent, nor after his death, unlefs
it fhould feem to him that, if that prelate were alive,
he would approve of his acceptance of it.

CHAPTER VIII.

Mr. Charles Butler's Book. The Answer of Dr. Phillpotts. Motives for undertaking it. Odium inevitable to it. No Desire to see the Restrictions of Roman Catholics strengthened. The Difficulty and Unpopularity of the Task. The Courage of Dr. Phillpotts. Value of his Letters to Mr. Butler. Devotion to the Virgin Mary and other Saints. Roman Catholic Explanations of the Way in which they receive the Prayers of Men. Their Futility. Doubtful Character of certain Roman Saints. An Example. Image-worship. S. Thomas Aquinas contrasted with the Second Council of Nice. Awkward Dilemma. Specious Attempts of Roman Catholic Writers to disguise the Doctrine of Image-worship shown (1) from the Theory of their Church, and (2) from its Practice. Examples. Summing-up of the Question. Dr. Lingard's Unfaithfulness in Quotation. Attempts of Roman Catholic Writers to soften down the Doctrine of Purgatory. Dr. Milner's Definition of it. A True Statement of it. Authority attributed by Bellarmine to Visions in support of Purgatory. Summarily disposed of by Dr. Phillpotts. S. Augustine improperly claimed in favour of Purgatory. Means of relieving those who are confined there. Effect of the Doctrine of Vicarious Satisfaction. Declarations of the Bible and the Church of Rome contrasted. Indulgences. The Ground on which the Doctrine rests. The Practice of the Roman Church. Confession and Absolution. A Clergyman compelled to give Evidence of a Confession in a Court of Justice. Impropriety of this shown by Dr. Phillpotts. S. Augustine and Pelagius. Dr. Phillpotts' Statement of Doctrine of Real Presence. Defective, as ignoring the Objective Presence. Archbishop Wake defended against Imputation of favouring Roman Doctrines. The Assertion that Bishop Hoadley had many Followers among the Clergy refuted. The Power of the Pope examined. Examples of its Exercise. The Treatment of Heretics. Illustration of the Doctrine that Oaths are

not to be kept with them. The Spirit of the Papacy un-
changed, as proved by the Recall of the Jesuits and the Revi-
val of the Inquisition. Character of Dr. Phillpotts' Letters
to Mr. Butler.

HE year 1825 was remarkable in the life
of Dr. Phillpotts for witnessing the pro-
duction of the most important literary
work upon which he had yet engaged.
Mr. Charles Butler, a Roman Catholic layman, and
member of Lincoln's Inn, distinguished no less for his
amiable qualities than his undoubted talent as a con-
troversial writer, had published a learned and laborious work, entitled, *The Book of the Roman Catholic
Church*. It was in answer to this, or rather to the
tenth Letter of it, entitled, *View of the Roman Catholic System*, that Dr. Phillpotts came forward to
correct what seemed to him to be a very erroneous
statement, in some respects, of the doctrines of his own
Church, but in a much greater degree of those of the
Church of Rome. It was a congenial task, and the
result of his labours was the production (April, 1825)
of fifteen Letters addressed to Mr. Butler,* and dedicated, together with an Appendix, to his old friend
and patron, Dr. Barrington, Bishop of Durham.

---

* "Letters to Charles Butler, Esq., on the Theological
Parts of his 'Book of the Roman Catholic Church,' with
Remarks on certain Works of Dr. Milner and Dr. Lingard,
and on some Parts of the Evidence of Dr. Doyle before the
two Committees of the Houses of Parliament, by the Rev.
Henry Phillpotts, D.D., Rector of Stanhope."

In undertaking the tafk Dr. Phillpotts does not feek to difguife the probability that he will be charged with reviving paft differences. But, whatever the effect of fuch a charge may be, with perfect manlinefs he avows:—

"It furely cannot be neceffary for a clergyman of the Church of England to apologife, at any time, for bringing forward the real grounds on which his Church found itfelf compelled to feparate from the Church of Rome."

Such a diffidence, in truth, would argue, not fo much tendernefs towards the principles of an adverfary, as a cowardly furrender of one's own. He is confcious, alfo, that the appearance of his work, at a time when men's minds were agitated as to the propriety of removing the remaining political reftrictions under which the Roman Catholics laboured, would be conftrued into the wifh of feeing thofe reftrictions ftrengthened and perpetuated.

"I think it proper to declare," he fays, "that fuch is very far from being the motive of my prefent undertaking. If the time of this publication may feem to argue the contrary, let me remind you that this time is not of my choofing, but of yours. At any period, and under any circumftances, I fhould have judged it right to expofe fo important a mif-ftatement as I confider yours to be: and I am not prevented from fo doing by an apprehenfion that I may be thought defirous of fupporting one fide of a great political queftion by the indirect influence of a theological argument."

Surely this frank and manly avowal fhould have fhielded Dr. Phillpotts from thofe cruel attacks which were afterwards made upon the purity of his motives

and the confiftency of his principles. He had taken
upon himfelf a difficult and a thanklefs tafk. The
great reputation of Mr. Butler, fupported by Dr.
Milner's *End of Controverfy*, could not fail to have
worked irreparable mifchief, if his ftatements had
remained uncontradicted. It was, indeed, an unpopular
undertaking to contradict them, for the utmoft fkill
and ingenuity of the advocates of Roman Catholic relief
had been exhaufted in endeavouring to make it appear
that the creeds of the Englifh and Roman Churches
were as fimilar as poffible. So great was the " liberalifm" of the day that points of difference were rapidly
vanifhing, and plain men began to wonder why there
had been fuch a turmoil about the Reformation.
But thanklefs as was the office of awakening the
nation from the eafy flumber of indifferentifm into
which it had fallen, lulled by the moft foothing tones
of its chofen orators, yet Dr. Phillpotts fhrank not
from it. God had given to him the learning and
ability to overthrow the fophiftry of adverfaries, and
right manfully did he do his work. This confideration alone fhould have fhielded him from railing
tongues.

Want of fpace will render it impoffible to go through
thefe mafterly letters in detail, more particularly as
portions of them will be touched upon in connection
with Dr. Phillpotts' letters to Mr. Canning. The
utmoft, therefore, that can be attempted will be to
direct attention to fome of the moft interefting fubjects
referred to in them. And this is done with the pro-

foundeſt reverence for the learning, ſkill, and temper diſplayed throughout the whole. As long as any controverſy ſhall exiſt between the Churches of England and Rome, ſo long, it may ſafely be affirmed, will theſe letters remain a ſtorehouſe of knowledge for every ſtudent of theology.

In the ſecond Letter, which is occupied with a conſideration of the " Devotion to the Virgin Mary and other Saints," Dr. Phillpotts takes occaſion to examine what is meant by the *veneratio* and *invocatio* which the Roman Church enjoins to be paid to them. After ſhowing that the Council of Trent aſſigns to them one of the diſtinguiſhing attributes of God—a knowledge of what paſſes in the hearts of men, inaſmuch as *mental prayer* is included in the devotion to be paid to them, and that another attribute aſcribed to them is preſence throughout the habitable globe at the ſame time, as a neceſſary conſequence of the duty of praying to them, he continues :—

" I am aware, indeed, that ſome ingenious expedients have been ſuggeſted [to avoid the conſequence ariſing from the above poſitions]. For inſtance, that God is pleaſed by immediate revelation to inform the Virgin, and the ſaints, of every ſupplication addreſſed to them ; and this ſeems to be the ſolution favoured by Dr. Milner. But, as you tell us that prayers are offered to the ſaints, only that they may offer prayers to God on our behalf, it follows, that God firſt reveals to them what we entreat them to pray to Him for us,—a proceſs which is not very ſatisfaĉtory to men of plain underſtanding. It is told of a great man who had the miſfortune of writing very illegibly, that he was in the habit of accompanying every letter written by his own hand with a tranſcript of it by his ſecretary, in order that he might at the ſame time teſtify his reſpect, and conſult for the convenience of his correſpondent. Now this, which is the very reverſe of the ſuppoſed mode of availing ourſelves of the aſſiſtance of the ſaints in our prayers, ſeems to be much the more rational courſe of the two.

" But another ſolution of the difficulty has been deviſed: —that the ſaints have their information, not from God, but from the angels. This, however, I fear, removes the difficulty but a ſingle ſtep. For whence have the angels a knowledge of our prayers ? What ſupports the tortoiſe ? Accordingly, a third plan has been thought of : — that the ſaints ſee *in the mirror of the Deity* all that it is His pleaſure they ſhould ſee, and, among other things, the prayers of their ſupplicants. A fourth mode of explaining the matter is, the ſuppoſition of an inconceivable celerity in the locomotion of angels and ſaints—a celerity which, if it be ſufficient for its purpoſe, is ſo near akin to ubiquity, that it leaves us where it found us."

A little further on Dr. Phillpotts ſuggeſts another and a ſerious difficulty relating to the amount of honour to be paid to the ſaints :—

" As you are in the habit of addreſſing a good many ſaints, the merits of very few of whom are mentioned in Scripture, a plain man might aſk, What aſſurance you have that they really are ſaints ? Is it not poſſible that very awkward miſtakes may occaſionally happen ? That you may, for inſtance, addreſs your petitions to perſons of very different characters, and occupying a very different place in the world of ſpirits, to that which you ſuppoſe ?"

The anſwer to this is the ſolemn canonization of deceaſed perſons under the eſpecial cognizance of the Pope ; and Dr. Phillpotts mentions the caſe of Pope

Alexander III, who had occasion to reprehend certain persons for worshipping, as a martyr to the cause of true religion, a man who was in truth only a martyr to the strength of his wine, having been killed in a state of drunkennefs.

In the third Letter Dr. Phillpotts expoſes the diſhonefty of Roman Catholic writers on the ſubject of " Image-worſhip." As a proof of this he ſets the authority of S. Thomas Aquinas againſt that of the Second Council of Nice. The former maintained that the image of Chriſt receives no reverence, as it is a piece of wood, or other ſubſtance, but is reverenced as repreſenting a rational being, and that therefore the reverence paid *to the image of Chriſt* muſt be *the ſame* as that which is paid to *Chriſt Himſelf.* The Second Council of Nice,* on the other hand, decreed that, like the image of the precious and life-giving Croſs, the venerable and holy images be ſet up, ſo that they who behold them may pay them " ſalutation and reſpectful honour ; not indeed that true worſhip which is according to our faith, which only befits the Divine Nature," &c. Dr. Phillpotts thus remarks upon the diſcrepancy :—

" S. Thomas's doctrine (though in accordance with that of S. Bonaventure, Cardinal Cajetan, and others) was in direct oppoſition to a much higher authority than any of them—I mean the Second Council of Nice ; the ſcandal whereof is ſo great that Bellarmine is driven to conjecture

---

* Aſſembled, in 787, by the Empreſs Irene, to reverſe the decrees of Conſtantinople, and eſtabliſh image-worſhip.

H

that S. Thomas had never feen the Acts of that Council—a fuppofition which is rather awkward, confidering that one of the characteriftics of a General Council is, that ' their found is gone out into all lands, and their word unto the ends of the world;' and yet the greateft of fchoolmen, it feems, five hundred years after the Council had fat, was an utter ftranger to its proceedings ! But awkward as this fuppofition is, it is neverthelefs abfolutely neceffary; other-wife a ftill more awkward alternative prefents itfelf. For either the Second Nicene Council, approved by Pope Hadrian, accepted by the whole Church, and declared to be a General Council by the infpired affembly at Trent, was no General Council, and fo the infallible Church hath erred ; or elfe S. Thomas, the angelic Doctor, in fpite of his fainthood, aye, and S. Bonaventure too, the feraphic Doctor, who is declared in the bull of his canonization· to have ' difcourfed on thefe matters as if the Holy Spirit fpoke by his mouth,' were no better than rank heretics."

The fpecious arguments with which Roman Catholic writers difguife the worfhip which is fhown to images are well expofed by Dr. Phillpotts. " Decent refpect" is all that Dr. Milner pretends to demand for them in his *End of Controverfy*; and he maintains that the object for which pious pictures and images are re-tained in churches is "the fame for which pictures and images are made and retained by mankind in general— to put us in mind of the perfons and things they repre-fent." The falfity of this is fhown by Dr. Phillpotts (1) from the *theory* of the Roman Church as contained in the decrees of the Second Nicene Council, on the perfect infallibility of which the infallibility of the Roman Church depends. Some curious cafes are re-corded of the teftimony rendered by bifhops and others

at this council in favour of the worfhipping of images.
There is one ftory (recited from the *Limonarium* of
Sophronius, Archbifhop of Jerufalem) attefting the
hatred which the devil bears to images, which is too
edifying to be omitted. A certain hermit was ha-
raffed by the demon of incontinence. One day the
devil prefented himfelf before him, and promifed that
he would tempt him no further, if he, on his part,
would fwear to obferve what he told him. The hermit
fwore. " Do not worfhip this image," faid the devil,
pointing to one of the Bleffed Virgin with the Child
Jefus in her arms, " and I will never attack you again."
The hermit felt that he had been incautious, and demanded time for deliberation; whereupon the devil went
away. Having confulted the Abbot Theodore, and
told him all that had paffed, he was difmiffed with the
following affurance, " You had better not leave a fingle
brothel in this city unvifited, than refufe to worfhip
our Lord Jefus with His mother in image." The
conduct of this hermit is compared by the Fathers of
the Council to S. Peter's denial of our Saviour with
an oath, and afterwards repenting !

" It is but juftice to the liberality of the council," fays
Dr. Phillpotts, " to ftate, that the quality of the perfonage
to whom the hermit had taken his oath is not permitted to
affect the argument. They are determined folely by the
matter of the hermit's oath, as it involved a renunciation
of the worfhip of images : fo that to my Proteftant readers
the judgment of thefe holy fathers may be more fimply ftated
thus ; *it is a greater fin to keep the fecond commandment than
to break the third and the feventh.*"

But the falſity of the ſtatements of Roman apolo-
giſts about image-worſhip is alſo ſhown (2) from the .
praſtice of their Church.   Dr. Phillpotts quotes paſſages from the Miſſal where " the miniſters of the altar,
and the reſt in ſucceſſion, *adore the croſs,*" and where
" the *adoration of the croſs being finiſhed,* the deacon re-
verently receives the croſs, and carries it back to the
altar."   He alſo quotes prayers from the *Pontificale Ro-
manum,* "*De benediſtione novæ Crucis,*" in the courſe of
which the pontiff kneels before the croſs, and "*devoutly
adores it.*"

Dr. Phillpotts then demands whether the Roman
doſtrine of image-worſhip is the harmleſs thing it is
repreſented to be.   If it implied nothing more than
" decent reſpeſt,"—

" Could it," he aſks, " have ſo often led its followers to
the praſtice of direſt idolatry ?   Or could the rulers of your
Church have heſitated one inſtant to forbid all images,
when the uſe of them was ſo little neceſſary, and the abuſe
ſo common and tremendous ?   If it were only this, could cardinals, and popes, and ſaints, have ſo groſſly miſconceived,
or ſo impiouſly perverted it ?   If it were only this, could the
aſſembled piety and wiſdom of the univerſal Church ; above
all, could that Holy Spirit, Whom the Lord of life and love ſent
into the world to bleſs, to comfort, and to ſupport His children, could He, guiding by His ſecret influence the deciſions of
a general council, condemn the impugners of ſuch a doſtrine
to eternal torments ?   Could He, for ſo ſlight an error, have
ſhut us out from all hopes of mercy, have denied us all ſhare
in our Redeemer's merits, made us outcaſts from His love
and aliens from His inheritance ?   Is it thus His bleſſed promiſe is fulfilled, that ' even the bruiſed reed He will not

break, and the fmoking flax He will not quench?' Has
that Holy Spirit told us that ' we fhall not make to ourfelves
any graven image, nor the likenefs of anything in heaven,
in earth, or under the earth ; that we fhall not bow down to
them, nor worfhip them ;' and does the fame Spirit cut us
off for ever, if yet we fcruple to refpeft and venerate them ?
Is the exact meafure of obfervance due to images, by the
will of God, fo very nice, fo very delicately poifed, and yet
is miftake on either fide big with danger to our foul's falvation ?

" Will you dare to anfwer thefe queftions in the affirma-
tive ? If you will not, you muft acknowledge that the reprefentation of your Church's doctrine, made by your modern apologifts, is, in this inftance, falfe and deceitful."

The fourth Letter, relating to Dr. Lingard, the Roman Catholic hiftorian, an old antagonift of Dr. Phillpotts,* and his unfaithfulnefs in quotation, is well
worthy of careful ftudy, as fhowing the petty artifices
which even the more refpectable among Roman Catholic
controverfialifts fhrink not from adopting to fupport
a tottering caufe. After fhowing the unfcrupulous way
in which he had garbled fome remarks of Anaftafius
Bibliothecarius, in his Preface to the Seventh Synod
(the Second Nicene), Dr. Phillpotts concludes,—

" Perhaps, however, you will by this time underftand
why I now attend not to what Dr. Lingard may fay, but to
what he may prove ; and that to a hiftory by that writer I do
not attend at all."

The attempt of Roman Catholic writers to foften
down the doctrine of " Purgatory" next engages the

---

* See page 12.

attention of Dr. Phillpotts in the fifth Letter. Dr. Milner had not feared to assert that there are only two points defined by the Roman Church, viz. that there is a middle state, called Purgatory, and that the souls detained in it are helped by the prayers of the faithful on earth. This, it must be confessed, is a comfortable, if not a satisfactory, way of getting out of the difficulties involved in this dogma. But Dr. Phillpotts is not so easily satisfied : he therefore proceeds to state what purgatory is according to authorized Roman writings. For brevity and accuracy it is probable that a better description does not exist.

" It is the doctrine of the Church of Rome, that, although in Baptism all sin previously committed is freely forgiven, and all punishment on account of it, temporal as well as eternal, is fully remitted, yet after Baptism, mortal sins are not dealt with so leniently; even when they have been remitted in the sacrament of penance, and so the guilt of them (*reatus culpæ*) and the eternal punishment in hell on account of them, have been removed. In short, there still remains due to Divine justice a temporary punishment; and those who have not satisfied for this temporary punishment by their works or their sufferings, in this life, must suffer for them in purgatory after death. And so necessary an article of faith is this held to be, that an anathema is expressly denounced by the Council of Trent against all who shall deny it."*

He then speaks of the authority attributed by Bellarmine to visions, as attesting the existence of purgatory. That author, the depth of whose learning

---

* Sess. vi. c. 30.

and the ftrength of whofe arguments muft ever give him a foremoft place amongft controverfial writers, diftinctly afferts that it has pleafed God fometimes to raife His fervants from the dead, and to fend them to announce to the living what they have really beheld. This affertion, and the two narratives which follow in fupport of it, are moft happily difpofed of by Dr. Phillpotts :—

" Here it is obvious to remark, how much more gracious God is reprefented to have been to your Church in this particular, than might have been expected from His declaration in the Gofpel, ' If they hear not Mofes and the Prophets, neither will they be perfuaded, though one rofe from the dead.' It may indeed be faid, and I am ready to admit the whole force of the fuggeftion, that neither ' Mofes and the Prophets,' nor Chrift and His Apoftles, have faid a fingle word about purgatory, and therefore an efpecial revelation in proof of it was by no means fuperfluous."

It is well known that S. Auguftine is claimed by the Roman Catholics as an authority in favour of their doctrine of purgatory ; but the flendernefs of the grounds on which this claim is founded is not fo generally underftood. Dr. Phillpotts goes into the queftion at confiderable length in his fixth Letter, and expofes the unfairnefs of Dr. Milner's quotations and deductions.

"The truth is," he fays, " that the real words of Auguftine, though a moft undeniable evidence in favour of facrifices of the altar, and of alms for the dead, are a ftrong teftimony *againft* the Roman doctrine of *Purgatory*."

That prayer for the dead was in ufe in the early

Church Dr. Phillpotts readily enough admits, but contends that it was a very different thing from the modern Roman practice, and proceeded on very different grounds. So much fo indeed—

"That, in Augustine, passages which prove the practice of prayer for the dead, are in general found in company with others which negative a belief in purgatory, never (as far as I have seen, or Dr. Milner has shown), with any which affirm it."

In the feventh Letter Dr. Phillpotts proceeds to confider the means of relieving those who are confined in purgatory. And here he has recourfe to the authorized documents of the Roman Church, which fet forth that "God has mercifully granted to the infirmity of the human race, that one man may be able to fatisfy for another;" that is, to fatisfy for the temporal punishment due to mortal fins, whose guilt and eternal punishment are already remitted. This certainly is a comfortable, if not an edifying, article of belief, for it is in the power of furviving friends to make that fatisfaction for the fins of the deceafed which he omitted to do before he died. On this arrangement of vicarious fatisfaction Dr. Phillpotts remarks with as much of pleasantry as force :—

"As these friends of the deceafed may chance to be unmindful of them, or may have enough to do on their own account, a prudent penitent, if he be alfo an opulent one, will take care, in contemplation of the pains of purgatory, to make his testamentary dispositions in fuch a manner as shall fecure the performance of an adequate number of maffes for his relief. The Council [of Trent], with laudable attention to the equity of thefe tranfactions, ftrictly enjoins that the money fhall not have been received, without a return of the money's worth : that ' whatever fhall be due for the faithful defunct, according to the foundations of teftators, or on any other fcore, fhall be difcharged, not perfunctorily, but by the priefts and minifters of the Church, and others whom it may concern, with diligence and accuracy.' "

After pointing out that the " faithful" in former days had not been flow or niggardly in this comfortable way of turning the mammon of unrighteoufnefs to a ferviceable account, he continues :—

" Let us hear, then, the conclufion of the whole matter. ' How hardly fhall he who trufts in riches enter into the kingdom of God,' fays the Gofpel of Chrift Jefus. ' How hardly fhall he, who trufts in riches, be kept out of the kingdom of God!' fays the gofpel of the Church of Rome. If it be one of the high diftinctions of the former, that to the poor the Gofpel is preached, it may be not lefs the appropriate boaft of the latter, that by it the cafe of the rich has been no lefs happily provided for. Charles II. had good reafon for faying that yours is the only religion for a gentleman."

The eighth Letter is occupied with the confideration of " Indulgences," the real nature of which it is the aim of Roman Catholic writers to difguife. After expofing fome of the expedients to which they fcruple not to refort, Dr. Phillpotts proceeds to give a clear and concife view of the ground on which the doctrine refts, the correctnefs of which it would be eafy to fuftain by authorities of the higheft credit in the Roman Church.

"It refts, (as I need not remind you, though you have made it neceffary that I fhould remind your readers,) on the alleged 'treafure of your Church,' a treafure which is abfolutely inexhauftible; for it confifts, firft, of all the merits of Chrift's fufferings beyond what was neceffary for the redemption of mankind; and as thofe merits were infinite, their value could not be diminifhed by that or any other application of them; they muft ftill, therefore, continue infinite. But over and above, and (what is fomewhat remarkable) in aid of this infinite treafure, you have in the fecond place, a fubfidiary hoard, namely, the merits of all the works, which all or any of the faints have ever performed beyond what was neceffary to fatisfy for themfelves; thefe you, of courfe, regard as a very large fum; the Virgin Mary's merits in particular muft have been enormous; for fhe had not even venial fin of her own (as we have already feen) to curtail their amount. Now, all thefe merits, I fay, are a facred treafure to be difpenfed at the difcretion of the Church, that is, with rare exceptions, of the Pope, to meet the exigencies of the faithful. Accordingly, Bellarmine has faid that an 'indulgence is nothing elfe, than an application of the fatisfactions, or penal works of Chrift and the Saints.'"

Having ftated the doctrine, he next proceeds (2) to the *practice* of the Roman Church in refpect of indulgences.

The earlieft inftances on record were thofe granted to the Crufaders, who, in confideration for their zeal in fighting for the recovery of the Holy Land, received from the Pope " remiffion of all their fins," or, in other words, entire exemption from the pains of purgatory.

" And this," fays Dr. Phillpotts, " it muft be allowed, was only putting the armies of the Crofs on an equal footing with thofe of the Crefcent. Mahomet had promifed to his followers, that all who fell in battle on his side fhould be admitted at once to the joys of Paradife ; and was it reafonable that the Pope fhould be backward in affording fimilar encouragement to Chriftian warriors?"

The cafes of Innocent III. and Honorius II. are then cited, both of whom levied armies, in which immunity from purgatory formed the chief part of the pay.

" But thefe are all military and fomewhat perilous works," fays Dr. Phillpotts. " There were other indulgences granted on more peaceful and ordinary occafions. Such was that of Pafchal II. in favour of all who devoutly vifited the churches of the Apoftles at Rome ; fuch, too, was that in favour of thofe who affift at the Pope's folemn benediction on Eafter Day. In procefs of time, indeed, indulgences, even plenary ones, were to be had on extremely reafonable terms. In the pontificate of Leo X. they were fome of the moft marketable commodities of the day, and feem to have been fold fufficiently cheap."*

---

* "Thus were men taught to put their truft in riches ; their wealth being thus invefted, became available to them beyond the grave ; and in whatever fins they indulged, provided they went through the proper forms, and obtained a difcharge, they might purchafe a free paffage through purgatory, or at leaft an abbreviation of the term, and a mitigation of its torments while they lafted. How fevere thefe torments were to be, might in fome degree be eftimated by the fcale appointed for thofe who were willing to commute, at a certain rate, while they were alive. The fet-off for a fingle year was fixed at the recitation of thirty pfalms, with an accompaniment of one hundred ftripes to each : the whole pfalter, with its accompaniment of fifteen thoufand, availing only to redeem five years."—SOUTHEY's *Book of the Church*, vol. i. chap. x.

The ninth Letter, on " Confeſſion and Abſolu-
tion," will be more appropriately conſidered further
on in this work, in reference to a letter by Dr.
Phillpotts to the Dean of Exeter on the ſame ſubjeсt.
It was reprinted in a ſeparate form, and obtained an
extenſive circulation among the clergy.

The tenth Letter, (a very ſhort one,) " on the ſuppoſed legal neceſſity of a miniſter of the Church of
England giving evidence in a Court of Juſtice, of
what has been confided to him in confeſſion," aroſe out
of the following circumſtances.   At the aſſizes for
Northumberland, a priſoner, who was on his trial for
murder, had confeſſed his guilt to a prieſt of the
Church of England.   That clergyman was required
to give evidence of the confeſſion, and an objeсtion
to it taken by the priſoner's counſel was over-ruled by
Mr. Juſtice Wilſon, before whom the caſe was tried.
The importance of this queſtion it would be hard to
over-eſtimate.   While Dr. Phillpotts inclines to the
belief that confeſſion to a prieſt would fall under the
application of the ordinary law of evidence, and ſo be
required to be divulged in a Court of Juſtice, he nevertheleſs maintains that there is ſpecial ground for
proteсtion in the caſe of prieſts of the *Engliſh* Church.
This ground is to be diſcovered in the Liturgy and
Rubrics, which, if not aсtually part of the law of the
land, are regarded by it " as pointing out, in all
particulars included in them, the real duty of Chriſtians."   He refers to the rubric in the Office for the
Viſitation of the Sick, which, " in certain circumſtances,

enjoins fecret confeffion to a prieft, as a part of Chriftian duty," and points out that the Liturgy, in the exhortation to Holy Communion, " fpecially invites " the penitent to fimilar confeffion.

" Does, then, the Law of England," he inquires, " fubjeet to civil mifchiefs of the graveft kind, thofe who comply with what it admits to be their duty as Chriftians, becaufe they comply with it? Is it thus that the great boaft of Englifhmen is realized, that Chriftianity is part of the common law of the land? But this is not all. If the clergyman is bound to reveal in evidence what has been communicated to him in confeffion, he is alfo bound to reveal it, in cafe of felony, without waiting to be fummoned as a witnefs at all. If he does not, he is guilty of mifprifion of felony. Will a principle, drawing this monftrous confequence after it, be maintained? Shall the clergyman be fubjeeted to fine and imprifonment for not difclofing to man what the law of God commands him to conceal? But to this extent the principle, if it be a found one, muft be confeffed to lead."

The thoroughly fenfible and praetical view taken by Dr. Phillpotts in the above extraet entitles him to the refpeetful thanks of every Englifh Churchman.

The eleventh Letter, on " Auguftine and Pelagius," requires no comment, as it merely fets forth that, in Dr. Phillpotts' judgment, Mr. Southey, in his *Book of the Church*, has not formed an accurate eftimate of the points in controverfy between them, inclining more to the fide of Pelagius than is confiftent with any very rigid notions of orthodoxy.

The twelfth Letter, on " Tranfubftantiation," affords to Dr. Phillpotts an opportunity of ftating what he conceives to be the doetrine of the Church of England

on the Real Prefence.   Reference has already been
made to places* where he treats the doctrine in general terms ; but here his ftatement is far more explicit:—

" She holds that after the confecration of the bread and
wine they are changed, not in their nature, but in their *ufe ;*
that, inftead of nourifhing our bodies only, they now are
inftruments by which, when worthily received, God gives
to our fouls the Body and Blood of Chrift to nourifh and
fuftain them ; that this is not a fictitious or imaginary exhibition of our crucified Redeemer to us, but a real though
fpiritual one ; more real, indeed, becaufe more effectual,
than the carnal exhibition and manducation of Him could
be, (for the flefh profiteth nothing.)   In the fame manner,
then, as our Lord Himfelf faid, ' I am the *true* bread that
came down from heaven,' (not meaning thereby that He
was a lump of baked dough, or manna, but the true means
of fuftaining the true life of man, which is fpiritual, not
corporeal,) fo, in the Sacrament, to the worthy receiver of
the confecrated elements, though in their nature mere bread
and wine, are yet given truly, really, and effectively, the
crucified Body and Blood of Chrift ; that Body and Blood
which were the inftruments of man's redemption, and upon
which our fpiritual life and ftrength folely depend.   It is in
this fenfe that the crucified Jefus is prefent in the Sacrament
of His Supper, not in, nor with, the bread and wine, nor
under their accidents, but in the fouls of communicants ; not
carnally, but effectually and faithfully, and therefore moft
really."

This extract is given, not as containing the true
doctrine of the Church of England on the fubject of
the Holy Eucharift, but for the purpofe of hereafter

---

* Pages 36 and 81.

comparing it with other ſtatements by Dr. Phillpotts.*
Meanwhile, it may ſuffice to ſay that this expoſition of
doctrine riſes not at all above the level of Zuinglian-
iſm, ſince it is founded throughout on the notion of a
mere *ſubjective* preſence, the *objective* being never taken
into account. In the laſt paragraph it ſeems to be
forgotten that the thing received in the Holy Euchariſt conſiſts of two parts, different indeed in character,
yet inſeparably united one to the other—the *ſacra-
mentum* and the *res ſacramenti ;* and that in receiving
the former we alſo receive the latter. Whether, however, we alſo receive the *virtus ſacramenti* is another
queſtion, and one which depends upon the diſpoſitions
with which we receive that holy ſacrament.

The commencement of the thirteenth Letter is occupied with a defence of Archbiſhop Wake againſt the
imputation of favouring Roman doctrines. The idea
having been firſt ſtarted by the Biſhop of Norwich in
his place in Parliament, it was eagerly adopted by Dr.
Milner, and turned againſt the clergy of the Church,
for the purpoſe of ſhowing their intolerant ſpirit. The
conduct of the Archbiſhop has already been referred
to ;† it will be needleſs, therefore, to ſay more than
that Dr. Phillpotts thoroughly expoſes the diſingenuous
uſe which Dr. Milner had attempted to make of his

---

* Particularly in reference to a reply to an Addreſs of the
Clergy of the Dioceſe of Exeter on the caſe of Archdeacon
Deniſon.

† See pages 34—37.

revered name. With equal force and ability does he difpofe of the charge that a large proportion of the Church of England were difciples of Hoadley, and, as fuch, denied the exiftence of Sacraments. After afferting that in the experience of his whole life, fpent under circumftances which gave him unufual opportunities for obferving the opinions of thofe with whom he had to deal, he had never met with a fingle minifter of the Church who held the notion imputed to them, Dr. Phillpotts continues :—

" The truth is, (and for teftimony to it I appeal to all men of all fects and parties who have any opportunity of obferving,) that, whatever faults may be afcribed to the prefent clergy of the Church of England, indifference to the tenets of that Church forms no part of their character. There is, on the contrary, an increafed and increafing fpirit of earneftnefs in inveftigating, and of zeal in preaching them ; nor could an adverfary at any period fince the Reformation, with lefs fhadow of juftice than at prefent, have arraigned the Eftablifhed Church for unfaithfulnefs to the Articles of their religion. Nay, even in Hoadley's own time, fo little were his notions countenanced by the clergy, that the Lower Houfe of Convocation paffed a ftrong vote againft him ; nor could anything have fhielded him from the further confequences of their indignation, had not the injuftice or the timidity of Government prevented that body from ever deliberating again."

Letter the fourteenth is on " the Power of the Pope," which Dr. Phillpotts characterizes rightly enough as a monftrous claim to a pre-eminence, not of rank merely, but of authority and jurifdiction over the greateft princes of the earth—a right to depofe them for herefy and favouring herefy, and a confequent right to abfolve fubjects from their allegiance. After quoting the Council of Florence, the Fourth Lateran Council, and the canons in fupport of this view of the Papal power, he proceeds to fhow that it was no mere empty honour, but was often exercifed in a way at once energetic and formidable. A Roman Catholic witnefs before the Committee of the Houfe of Commons having afferted that the Popes refted their title to temporal interference upon fome temporal right previoufly acquired by themfelves or their predeceffors, Dr. Phillpotts continues :—

"I may be permitted to afk, What temporal right had been acquired by Gregory III. over the Eaftern Empire, entitling him to forbid taxes to be paid to Leo the Iconoclaft, who had been excommunicated by him? Again, who had given Zachary, or any of his predeceffors, any temporal right over the kingdom of France, by virtue of which he actually depofed Childeric on account of his being indolent and ufelefs, and fubftituted Pepin in his place?"

He might alfo have inquired, with equal force, what right Alexander the VIth had to beftow America on Spain, and India on Portugal.

After an examination of Bellarmine's doctrine of the Pope's power in temporals, a fomewhat inftructive portion of which is that the Church does not always exercife the right, "*either becaufe it has not fufficient ftrength, or does not think it expedient,*" Dr. Phillpotts goes on to confider the treatment of heretics. Fully admitting the right of the Church to cut off its unworthy members,—

I

" Therefore," he fays, " if excommunication were all the penalty which the Church of Rome had claimed a right to inflict, there could be no fair ground of complaint againft her ; even though the civil power, acting on the judgment of the Church, fhould, of its own motion, inflict on thofe whom the Church had excommunicated any meafure of punifhment whatever."

But, fo far from this being the cafe, the Great Lateran Council * had decreed that heretics were to be delivered over to the fecular power, to be punifhed in the manner that is due.

" What that manner is," fays Dr. Phillpotts, " I need hardly remind my readers. It was death—death in its moft appalling form, death by burning. This accurfed fentence was the invention of the Church of Rome ; its canons recognize it, thofe canons to which councils refer."

As to the queftion whether oaths with heretics are binding, after quoting the well-known cafes of John Hus, and Jerome of Prague, Dr. Phillpotts mentions another, which, if lefs widely known, is equally to the point :—

" It is the cafe of Paul V, who is faid to have adopted a more ingenious, and hardly lefs fatisfactory courfe, than the Council of Conftance followed in Jerome's inftance. Father Fulgentio, the friend of the illuftrious Paul Sarpi, was prevailed with to come to Rome under a fafe-conduct granted by the Pope. When there, he was treated as a heretic, and on appealing to his fafe-conduct was anfwered, that *the conduct was fafe for his coming thither, but not for his going thence.* After this, who will deny the ftrict fidelity of the Church of Rome to all its engagements with heretics ?

---

* Convened by Innocent III. in 1215.

Among thefe engagements, it has always reckoned as the moft facred that of labouring for the fpiritual good of its rebellious children, 'the deferters from its camp,' as the Catechifm of Trent calls them, by a little gentle corporal correction."

In the fifteenth and laft Letter Dr. Phillpotts afferts that the fpirit of the Papacy is ever the fame, and that if it is now lefs imperious in its demands than formerly, it is from lack of power to enforce them.

" Not that there is any ground of hope," he fays, "that the fpirit of Rome is grown at all more tolerant, lefs ferocious, or lefs ambitious. It is declared by its own advocates to be unaltered and unalterable. The hiftory of ages attefts the momentous truth. Twelve hundred years have now paffed over the heads of men fince this fpiritual tyranny firft fhowed its portentous form ; during that period ftates and empires have difappeared from the face of the earth ; but Rome, Papal Rome, is ftill the fame—ftill adheres with undiminifhed zeal to that one fubtle, daring fyftem, which, through every variety of power and fortune, it has contrived to cherifh, and commonly to advance."

He then inftances the recall of the Jefuits by Pius VII, after they had been banifhed by Clement XIV, and the revival of the Inquifition, as evidence of the unyielding fpirit of Rome, and the pertinacity with which fhe returns to her original principles. Speaking of the Inquifition, he denounces it as—

" That accurfed inftrument of fpiritual tyranny, which no Englifh Proteftant, even in the fecurity of his own land, can think on without horror. The office of the Inquifition, which owed its rigour at leaft, if not its birth, to the fame Pontiff who convened the great Lateran Council, and there devifed thofe decrees againft heretics which nothing but fuch an inftitution could execute,—that Inquifition which Paul IV. afcribed to the fpecial infpiration of the Holy Ghoft, and with his dying breath commended to his cardinals as *effential to the very exiftence of the authority of the Church*,—that Inquifition is again in being, not in Spain only, but in Italy.   Need I fay more.   The monfter lives !''

The Letter concludes with fome well-turned compliments on the character and abilities of Mr. Butler, and an earneft deprecation on the part of Dr. Phillpotts of any afperity which inadvertently may have appeared.

But, fo far from any harfhnefs being traceable in thefe Letters, they are in truth models of courtefy. Never for one moment does Dr. Phillpotts forget what is due to his own character, and that of his opponent ; nor can a fingle inftance be cited in which he endeavours to ftrengthen his argument by any uncandid ftatement of facts.   An air of fairnefs breathes through every line.

Well might the writer fay to his adverfaries :—

> " There is no terror in your threats,
>   For I am armed fo ftrong in Honefty,
>   That they pafs by me as the idle wind,
>   Which I refpect not."

Would that all controverfialifts would follow in the fteps of Dr. Phillpotts and not regard the end, without jealoufly watching over the means !

If his language occafionally affumes the tone of indignant proteft, it is due to thofe fpiritual guides of Mr. Butler who mifled him on points where his own judgment would never have feduced him. Arduous as was the talk of hunting profeffed controverfialifts through every citation they made, yet all muft admire the forbearance of Dr. Phillpotts while expofing even the moft difingenuous and clumfy of their devices. His temper never fails him under circumftances the moft irritating. From beginning to end he mingles a quiet humour with his argument, which relieves the fubject of its tedioufnefs, and reveals the almoft boundlefs refources of his wit. That Mr. Butler himfelf was powerfully impreffed with the courtefy of his opponent may be gathered from the fact of his feeking an introduction to him, and cultivating his acquaintance.

CHAPTER IX.

*Supplemental Letter to Mr. Butler. Its Origin. Dr. Kelly's
Attempt to explain away Prayers addreſſed to the Virgin.
His Sophiſtry expoſed. Examples of Blaſphemous Prayers.
Image-worſhip evaded by Roman Catholic Writers. Mira-
culous Images. The Bambino and Winking Virgin of An-
cona. Profuſeneſs of theſe Wonders. Their authority ſup-
ported by Official Documents. Dr. Murray's View of
Indulgences. His Diſingenuous Dealing. An Example. The
Length of Time for which Indulgences are available. Diſ-
honeſty of Roman Catholic Writers. Confeſſion. Flagrant
Example of its Abuſe. Prohibition of the Free Uſe of the
Scriptures. Fearful Terms in which they are ſpoken of by
Roman Catholic Writers. The Power of the Pope. At-
tempt of Dr. Doyle to ſoften it down expoſed. Danger of
the Doctrine in a country like Ireland. The Interference of
Government in the Appointment of Iriſh Roman Catholic
Biſhops. Allowed by the Pope, but repudiated by the Roman
Catholic Biſhops themſelves. Prevarication of Dr. Doyle.
The Oath taken by Roman Catholic Biſhops to the Pope. Its
Origin. Canonization of Gregory VII. The Third Canon
of the Fourth Council of Lateran. Attempt of Roman
Catholics to repudiate it expoſed. The Caſe of John Hus
fully conſidered. The Doctrine of Excluſive Salvation as
taught by the Church of Rome. Its Danger. Diſinge-
nuous Uſe of the 18th Article of Religion by Roman Catholic
Writers. An Expoſition of it. Peril of admitting Roman
Catholics to a Share in the Legiſlature. Pretenſions of the
Roman Church as ſtated by Dr. Doyle. Poſition of Members
of the Eſtabliſhed Church according to the Roman Theory.
Examples of the Overbearing Spirit of the Roman Church.
Appeal to the more Moderate Members of that Communion.
Eſtimate of Dr. Doyle.*

ARLY in the following year, 1826, a fecond Letter to Mr. Butler* appeared, dedicated to the Bifhop of London (Dr. Howley). This was caufed mainly by the evidence taken before felect Committees of the two Houfes of Parliament, appointed in the feffions of 1824 and 1825 to inquire into the ftate of Ireland,— fome idea of the ponderous character of which may be gathered from the fact that a digeft of it occupies two moderately thick octavo volumes. In the courfe of their examination the Irifh Roman Catholic Bifhops had endeavoured to give fuch a view of the doctrines and practices of their Church as was both at variance with facts and calculated to excite an undue feeling of fympathy for the caufe of Roman Catholic relief. Much credit, therefore, belongs to Dr. Phillpotts for expofing the deception, and tearing away the flimfy veil of fophiftry with which they had fought to difguife the deformity of their modern inventions.

Dr. Kelly, the Roman Catholic Archbifhop of Tuam, and confequently no mean authority in his Church, had endeavoured to perfuade the Committee

---

* "A Supplemental Letter to Charles Butler, Efq., on fome Parts of the Evidence given by the Irifh Roman Catholic Bifhops, particularly by Dr. Doyle, before the Committees of the two Houfes of Parliament in the Seffion of 1825, and alfo on certain Paffages in Dr. Doyle's 'Effay on the Catholic Claims,' by the Rev. Henry Phillpotts, D.D., Rector of Stanhope."

of the Houfe of Commons that the nature and object of prayers addreffed to the Bleffed Virgin were commonly mifunderftood—that fhe cannot, as was reprefented, grant favours of herfelf, but that fhe may, through her powerful interceffion, obtain favours from God for us. The following prayer was then adduced: "Te deprecor ut mea inopia fublevetur, ut per te purgationem peccatorum obtineam;" upon which Dr. Kelly remarked, with more of ingenuity than honefty, that "the ufe of the word *per* conftitutes it a prayer of interceffion; that it is through her interceffion only that all thefe favours are fought to be obtained by this prayer." This was too fpecious an argument to be allowed to pafs, and therefore Dr. Phillpotts replies :—

"Now this, at leaft, is making the diftinction to be very finely drawn, and fufpends the whole weight of the honour due to God on a very flender thread. To any one who may chance to ufe this prayer, without underftanding this folitary prepofition in Dr. Kelly's fenfe, (which is by no means its only or its moft obvious fenfe,) it is then an act of the utmoft impiety; it is a transfer to a mere creature of the honour due, by the Word of God, to God only."

He then quotes extracts from books of devotion in common ufe among Roman Catholics, to fhow the extravagant nature of the prayers addreffed to the Virgin. Whether they harmonize as completely as could be wifhed with the explanation of Dr. Kelly may be judged from the following, where fhe is invoked as "*the great Mediatrix between God and* *man,* obtaining for finners all they can afk and demand of the Bleffed Trinity,"* (p. 293 ;) and again, " Hail, Mary, Lady and Miftrefs of the world, *to whom all power has been given both in heaven and earth,*" (p. 206.)

After quoting other blafphemous prayers to the Virgin Mary commonly ufed in England, Dr. Phillpotts continues, and every devout mind muft fhare his honeft indignation :—

" I will not wound the feelings of my Proteftant readers by producing any more of this difgufting, this polluting trafh. But I call on Dr. Kelly, or any other apologift of your Church ; above all, on Dr. Milner, by whofe authority thefe abominations profefs to be fet forth for the edification of the ' Faithful of the Midland Diftrict,' to produce, if he can, fome lurking prepofition, as in the former inftance—fome potent particle, which may refcue thofe who ufe them, and efpecially the Apoftolic Vicar, who has fanctioned the ufe of them, from the charge of direct and moft atrocious blafphemy."

Paffing from this fubject, he goes on to difcufs the honour paid to images. Dr. Kelly had wifhed to make it appear that Roman Catholics attached no importance to them beyond their ufe in reminding the faithful of circumftances connected with religious duties. But if the Committee of the Houfe of Commons was fatisfied with this explanation, the humour

---

* " Devotion to the Sacred Heart of the Bleffed Virgin Mary. By R. R. John Milner, Bifhop of Caftalaba, Vicar Apoftolic. Keating and Brown, 1821."

of Dr. Phillpotts is not fo indulgent towards the apolo-
getic prelate.   Accordingly, he brings forward the
cafe of *miraculous* images,—" images which, as having
at fome time been the inftruments, or media, of fuper-
natural effects, are expected to repeat their prodigies,
and are reforted to with much confidence and veneration accordingly."   Thefe wonder-working images are
by no means uncommon in Roman Catholic countries,
and an edifying volume might be compiled in attefta-
tion of the prodigies which they have effected.

The ftory of the Bambino of Ara Celi—which, having been taken away from its niche to perform the
office of Lucina to a lady of quality, arrived at the
door of the church in the middle of the night, figni-
fying its prefence by a tremendous knocking, and, on
being admitted, went ftraight to its accuftomed place,
throwing down an intrufive image—is too well known
to need repeating.   But, perhaps, even this marvellous and pugnacious image is furpaffed by the ftatue
of the *Winking Virgin* in the Cathedral of Ancona, in
honour of which a pious fraternity was inftituted by
the Pope, under the name of the " Sons and Daughters
of Mary."   Not that this was by any means a folitary
inftance of miraculous power ; for—

" It would be great injuftice to the other images of the
Virgin Mary in Italy," fays Dr. Phillpotts, " to fuppofe that
they continued idle, while their illuftrious fifter at Ancona
was thus delighting the good people of that city.   Far from
it : at Rome, at Civita Vecchia, at Macerata, at Afcoli, at
Frafcati, &c. &c., the Madonnas were everywhere on the
alert, and there was an abfolute rivalry and emulation in
winking among thefe holy images."

He then proceeds to quote the official memoirs of miraculous images, of which it is hard to fay whether they are moft ludicrous or profane. Dr. Phillpotts finds in thefe ftories a congenial field for the exercife of his wit, and if he indulges in pleafantry at the expenfe of weeping and perfpiring images, it certainly is no more than they deferve. The painful part of the whole is that thefe monftrous legends are no mere vulgar fuperftition, but are extracted from legal proceffes inftituted in Ecclefiaftical Courts, and duly certified as true. No wonder that Dr. Kelly was afhamed of them. We may pardon him for trying to get rid of them, even at the rifk of bringing down upon himfelf the avenging lafh of Dr. Phillpotts.

The fubject of Indulgences is next brought forward. The Roman Catholic prelates had endeavoured to fhow that they did not relate to a future ftate, but (in the words of Dr. Murray, Roman Catholic Archbifhop of Dublin) only to "a certain portion of the temporal punifhment due to fin." This was, in effect, finking all idea of purgatory, and reducing the doctrine to the leaft offenfive fhape.

"It would be interefting to know," fays Dr. Phillpotts, "what that 'certain portion' is; and it would be ftill more interefting to learn what courfe the Church of Rome would take with the Archbifhop, if, inftead of making this convenient infinuation before .an affembly of heretics, he fhould venture to deny categorically, before the world, the power of the Church to grant a full remiffion of all the temporal punifhment of fin in fuch cafes."

He then recounts the unworthy expedients to which

Dr. Murray, and his brother prelates, fcrupled not to refort, in order to foften down the harfhnefs of the doctrine of Indulgences, which, when ftated in its bare form, muft ever be repulfive to Englifh ears. Their examination before the Committee of the Lords is an example of evafion and difingenuous dealing, which may fpeak highly for the acutenefs of their intellects, but which will not be loft upon thofe whofe bufinefs lies with the Roman controverfy. Thefe gentlemen are very ecclefiaftical chameleons ; firft one colour, then another, and, occafionally, all colours at the fame time.

One of their many variations of hue muft fuffice. Dr. Murray had ftated, that " Indulgences can be ap-lied to fouls in purgatory only by way of fuffrage, that is, as a prayer ;" and had fpoken of this as " our belief," " our doctrine." The attempt to confound " fuffrage " with " prayer " is more ingenious, perhaps, than honeft ; but the expreffions, " our belief," " our doctrine," as applied to the ftatement above, involve, unhappily, fomething more than a mere exercife of ingenuity.

" If," fays Dr. Phillpotts, " they mean merely to exprefs, each in the fulnefs of epifcopal authority, that fuch is the belief or doctrine of himfelf individually, it is clear they are cajoling the Committee, whofe inquiry is folely directed to the belief and doctrine of their *Church.* If, on the other hand, they mean, as it would be reafonable to fuppofe, the belief and doctrine of their Church, they affirm what they cannot but know to be utterly unfounded. For they muft know perfectly well that the opinion, which they afcribe to their Church, would be held in abomination by the great majority of Divines who have treated on the subject, and is in direct contradiction to the Papal bulls by which Indulgences are granted."*

The length of time for which indulgences are available next comes under confideration. Upon this point the Roman Catholic bifhops appeared fufpicioufly ill-informed. The utmoft that could be extracted from them was, that no indulgence was recognized "for a period beyond that of feven years." Without ftopping to refrefh the failing memory of thefe worthy prelates, by a reference to the authoritative writings of their own Church, Dr. Phillpotts mentions a circumftance which, if it fails of conveying all the edification it is capable of, is yet very appofite to the matter in hand :—

" I have now before me an engraved portrait of the Virgin Mary's foot, taken from her true fhoe, recently publifhed in Italy, conferring, by authority of John XXII. and Clement VIII, an Indulgence of three hundred years on all who fhall kifs it three times, and recite thereupon three Ave Marias."

Any one in poffeffion of this precious relic might, with the aid of the winking image, feel tolerably eafy about purgatory, even though the Irifh prelates cannot grant him relief for more than feven years.

The next fubject on which Dr. Phillpotts remarks is Confeffion, as practifed in the Englifh and Roman

---

* For the real doctrine of Indulgences, as taught by the Roman Church, fee Dr. Phillpotts' firft Letter to Mr. Butler, page 106.

Churches; but, as this ſubject will be fully handled
hereafter,* for the purpoſe of ſhowing the maturer ſentiments of Dr. Phillpotts on this important doctrine,
it will not be neceſſary to enter upon it now, any further than to ſhow the evil uſe to which it is ſometimes turned by Roman prieſts.   In regard to the
much-vaunted ſecreſy of the confeſſional, it deſerves to
be known that their practice has not always kept pace
with their theory.   Dr. Phillpotts cites, on the authority of the hiſtorian Du Thou, a flagrant example
of this—no leſs a perſonage than Pope Sixtus V, who—

" After he had ſucceeded to the Papal chair, availed himſelf, in many caſes, of the ſecrets formerly confided to him in
the confeſſional, at a time when his great ſanctity had rendered him the moſt popular confeſſor in Rome.   He kept a
regiſter of theſe matters, and not only brought many perſons
to juſtice for crimes which had been ſo communicated to
himſelf, but he likewiſe ſent for the oldeſt confeſſors, and
required them to communicate to him whatever crimes had
been confeſſed to them.   Several complied, and Leti juſtifies the proceeding by the neceſſity of the times."

The prohibition of the free uſe of the Scriptures by
the Roman Catholics is next conſidered.   Dr. Doyle
had taken great credit to himſelf and his brethren that
ſeven editions of the Bible had been publiſhed in Ireland ſince the invention of printing.   It is eaſy enough
to print books, but if they are not allowed to be read
when they are printed, it comes to much the ſame as
if they had never been printed at all.   And this is how

---

* See firſt Letter to Mr. Butler, page 108.

the Bible fared in Ireland; for, by way of reply to this
felf-glorification of the Roman Catholic prelates, Dr.
Phillpotts quotes the fourth rule *De Libris prohibitis,*
" approved and confirmed by Pius IV," which provides that whofoever fhall prefume to read bibles (tranflated, be it obferved, by *Roman Catholic authors*)
without the poffeffion of a faculty in writing, fhall
not be capable of receiving abfolution of their fins,
unlefs they have firft given up their bibles to the
ordinary. If, then, the feven editions had been multiplied to feventy, it would not have made much difference, as long as the Pope remained in fuch a mind.
But this was the reftriction of a darker age, it may be
thought. We would thankfully admit the plea, had
not Pope Leo XII, no later than 1824, in an encyclical
letter, defcribed the Holy Scriptures, tranflated into the
vulgar tongue, as " *poifonous paftures,*" and declared
that " if the facred Scriptures be everywhere indifcriminately publifhed, more evil than advantage will arife
thence, on account of the rafhnefs of men." Terrible
as is this language, it is only the reproduction of the
blafphemies of bygone days. " Vain is the labour which
is fpent on Holy Scripture," is the language of Cardinal
Hofius, a papal legate at the Council of Trent; " it is
but a creature, and a beggarly element." Another member of the fame council declares that it " is only lifelefs
ink;" while a writer of eminence fhrinks not from calling it " a nofe of wax, which allows itfelf to be pulled
this way and that, and to be moulded into any form you
pleafe." But fearful as was the language of Leo, it was

endorfed by the Irifh prelates, as in duty bound, who
averred, " In this fentiment of our head and chief we
fully concur." Is it too much, after this, to fay, with
an eminent living divine,* " Scripture is to be treated
as its Divine Author was by the fervants of Caiaphas,
and the foldiers of Pilate—firft blindfolded, buffeted,
and fpit upon, and then put to death."

The power of the Pope is next confidered, as Dr.
Doyle had declared on oath that it was the doctrine
of his Church that " the Popes have no right whatever
to interfere with the temporal fovereignties or rights
of kings or princes." To any one but moderately
acquainted with hiftory this affertion muft be ftartling.
Great, indeed, muft have been Dr. Doyle's effrontery to
have ventured upon fuch a ftatement in the prefence
of educated Englifh gentlemen, and greater far muft
have been his credulity, if he could expect that it fhould
be believed. Rightly enough does Dr. Phillpotts fay :—

" There are fome pofitions which it is difficult to refute,
without appearing to depart from the refpect which an author
ought always to feel for the underftanding and information
of his readers : and if there ever was an inftance of this kind,
the prefent may pre-eminently claim to be fo regarded."

Without taking advantage, then, of the enlarged term
of nine centuries, during which, if Dr. Doyle was to
be believed, the Popes had never exercifed the power fo
ftrangely imputed to them, and fuppofing that fuch
perfonages as Innocent III, Gregory VII, and Boniface VIII, had never exifted, Dr. Phillpotts limits his

---

* Dr. Wordfworth : Letters to M. Gondon.

inquiry to three centuries, commencing with the Bull *in Cæna Domini*, put forth by Paul III. in 1536, and ending with the excommunication of Buonaparte by Pius VII. in 1809. The result of this investigation it is needless to dwell upon; neither is it pleasant to pause longer than is necessary to contemplate the woe-begone figure of Dr. Doyle, as he strives to shelter himself from the merciless pelting of his adversary's facts.

That the power of the Pope, as far as most European nations are concerned, is at the present time little more than a name, will be readily admitted; but it is no less true that this name, empty as it is, may produce the most terrible results in minds which are debased by crime or enervated by superstition. To such as these the Papacy of the present day is all that it was in the days of Hildebrand; and even though the Holy Father may be a prisoner in the hands of the " eldest son of the Church," he has but to speak the word, and the kings of the earth will come to do him homage. Little of this feeling may survive in Italy, but it burns with a brightness, which centuries of bloodshed have not been able to quench, in many an Irish cabin. Harmless, therefore, as the pretensions of the Pope may be in more enlightened countries, among the Roman Catholic population of Ireland they are full of peril.

" Its truth," says Dr. Phillpotts, " is written in characters of blood in the history of Ireland itself: and be it always remembered, that while the lights and intelligence of other nations have been incalculably progressive, the Irish (the Roman Catholic Irish multitude I mean), continue nearly

what they were in the middle of the seventeenth century, in
the days of Ormond and Rinuccini. That multitude could
again be ſtimulated by an ambitious prieſthood to defeat the
honeſt efforts of the nobles and the gentry of the land, whoſe
wiſhes and whoſe views muſt always ultimately be for peace—
and to re-plunge their country in all the horrors of civil war."

The next ſubject referred to is the interference
of Government in the appointment of Iriſh Roman
Catholic Biſhops. Although the Pope himſelf had,
in the year 1815, given his expreſs and formal aſſent
to a propoſal of this deſcription, yet Dr. Doyle had
the hardihood to affirm that it would be inconſiſtent
with the diſcipline of the Roman Catholic Church to
admit any interference, direct or indirect, of the Proteſtant Sovereign of this country in the appointment
of Roman Catholic Biſhops in Ireland. The prevarication of this prelate is an edifying ſtudy to thoſe
who may have the curioſity to ſee what latitude is
allowed to Roman Catholic controverſialiſts, when the
intereſt of their Church is at ſtake. The Committee
of both Houſes find it impoſſible to get a ſtraight-
forward anſwer from him. He unites all the ſlipperi-
neſs of the eel to the wilineſs of the ſerpent. It is
only when he falls into the hands of Dr. Phillpotts
that he finds there is no eſcape, and then the real
value of his aſſertions are ſeen. All his ſophiſtry
avails him not. His moſt ſpecious arguments crumble
into duſt at the touch of his remorſeleſs antagoniſt.
He ſtands forth convicted of a wilful attempt to diſguiſe, if not to pervert, the truth.

The oath taken by Iriſh Roman Catholic Biſhops to

the Pope next comes under confideration.* Dr. Phillpotts fhows that it is of a feudal chara&ter, and " had its
origin not merely in the feudal times, but in the pretenfions of the Pope to be the fupreme feudal chief, of
whom all temporal princes, even emperors and kings,
were feudatories and vaffals." It was originally of
much fmaller dimenfions than at prefent ; but if it has
developed, the theory of it is ftill the fame—to give
to the Pope that dominion over the nations of the
earth which has been fo arrogantly claimed and fo
mercilefsly ufed. Pius V, as is well known, was
canonized for the vigour which he difplayed in the
exercife of this power ; but Dr. Phillpotts cites—

" A name far more eminent than his, the noted Hildebrand—that Gregory VII. who claimed the univerfal dominion of the world as an appendage of his See—whofe life
was one unceafing effort to realize this claim—who was as
little turned afide from the profecution of his holy purpofe
by confiderations of his own fafety, as by a regard for the
peace and tranquillity of mankind—that Gregory of whom
Dr. Doyle himfelf fays, that the unhappy Rodolph (who
had been fet up by him to fill the Imperial throne, of which
he had deprived the lawful owner), when about to pay the
forfeit of his crime, ' confeffed that, induced thereto by the
Pope, he had rebelled againft his Sovereign '—that Gregory
of whom Dr. Doyle further tells us, on the authority of the
chronicler Sigebert, that ' when he found himfelf near his
end, he acknowledged that *he had, at the inftigation of the
devil, ftirred up enmities and ftrife amongft mankind,* and fent
to the Emperor to folicit his forgivenefs—that very Gregory
of whom the moft charitable judgment which can be paffed

---

* For the terms of this oath, fee Appendix B.

is that he was a crack-brained fanatic—was, in the 18th century, by Benedict XIII. placed among the faints!—a holy fervice was appointed to his honour—all good Catholics were called upon to bend the knee in adoration to him—and the worfhip of God Himfelf was profaned by thanking Him for giving this firebrand to the world, and by *praying* that *his example might ftill edify* and ftrengthen the Church."

Moft people will probably think that Dr. Phillpotts has done but fcanty juftice to the memory of one of the greateft of thofe whoever wore the triple crown.   That Hildebrand lived only to make the Roman Pontiff the fovereign of the world may be true enough ; but no one who has watched the inflexible determination with which he followed up his purpofe, and the fkill with which he difpofed of his refources, can fairly call him " a crack-brained fanatic." Here, then, a pardonable zeal for his caufe has carried Dr. Phillpotts too far.   The account alfo which he gives of Hildebrand fending to the Emperor to fue for his forgivenefs differs from the commonly-received verfion, which reprefents him as abfolving and bleffing his enemies, with the refolute exceptions of the Emperor and the Anti-Pope.

The next fubject confidered is the Third Canon of the Fourth Council of Lateran, which enforces on the faithful the duty of exterminating heretics.   It was natural enough that, in their prefent yielding temper, the Roman Catholic prelates fhould defire to difown the obligation of fuch a canon, particularly in a country where the probability of its ever being carried into effect happened to be very remote. But in their exceflive defire to pleafe they involved themfelves in a ferious difficulty. Not content with repudiating the doctrine laid down in the Canon, they threw difcredit upon the Canon itfelf, and aflerted roundly that it was not to be found in the Acts of the Council at all. This was taking the bull by the horns with a vengeance. They had calculated, doubtlefs, upon no one being at the pains to refer to the Acts of the Council, and expofe their audacity. In this cafe all would have been well. But Dr. Phillpotts had had too much experience of the amount of credit due to the ftatements of thefe complaifant prelates to truft them over much ; and fo, having examined every printed edition of the Council's Acts, he tells them plainly that the repudiated Canon appears *in every one of them*, and that there does not exift the flighteft intimation of any doubt as to its being genuine. This announcement muft have ftartled Dr. Doyle and his brethren, if they had hoped to efcape detection ; and, if anything was wanting to complete their difcomfiture, it was furnifhed by the mafterly way in which Dr. Phillpotts expofed their blunders and mif-ftatements, weaving together fuch a chain of condemnatory evidence as it would have been hopelefs to attempt to break.

The next matter referred to is the proceeding of the Council of Conftance againft John Hus, which Dr. Phillpotts rightly ftigmatizes as a " cruel and treacherous murder." And indeed it can be fairly called by

no lighter name.   The ftory is well known.   Having
been charged with holding the doctrines of Wicliffe,
Hus was cited, in 1414, to appear before the Council
of Conftance.   Having obtained from the Emperor a
fafe-conduct to and from that city, he prefented himfelf before the Council.

Vain was it for Dr. Murray to affure the Committee
of the Commons that the fafe-conduct given to Hus
by the Emperor was nothing more than *a travelling
paffport,* fuch as is commonly ufed on the Continent at
the prefent day.   The terms of the document forbid
any fuch conftruction as this ; and the diftrefs of the
Emperor Sigifmund when he heard of the condemnation of Hus,—a diftrefs which was only appeafed
by the affurance that the decree of the Council was
fuperior to his own authority,—can only be reconciled
on the fuppofition that he believed that his honour had
been forfeited.   The attempt alfo of Dr. Doyle to
fhow that the city of Conftance was wholly independent of the Emperor, and that, confequently, he was
not anfwerable for the act of its magiftrates in burning
Hus, is a miferable piece of fhuffling—too pitiful,
indeed, to find place anywhere but in a caufe that was
already defperate.   So far from the city being " free,"
in any fenfe, to exclude the authority of the Emperor,
Dr. Phillpotts fhows, on the authority of Nauclerus,
a chronicler dear to Dr. Doyle himfelf, that the
circumftance of Conftance being fixed upon as the feat
of the Council gave great delight to the Emperor,
" *becaufe it was a city fubject to him,*" while Pope John

XXIII. was correfpondingly depreffed at the felection ; as well he might be, if he had the power of predicting that the Council would decree that a General Council was fuperior to the fucceffor of S. Peter, while it depofed one of the rival Popes, compelled the other to refign, and elected a frefh Pope.

As a further example of the accuracy of Dr. Doyle's affertion it may be remarked that, in the courfe of a fermon preached before the Council by the Bifhop of Lodi, the Emperor was fpecially invoked to " deftroy all herefies and errors ; and, *above all, this obftinate heretic :* " (Hus.) That this might only have been a fpecimen of fomewhat fervid pulpit rhetoric it would be pleafing to believe, were it not for the fequel of the fermon, when we find Hus delivered by the Council to Sigifmund, while he in turn hands him over to Louis, Elector of Bavaria, who in due courfe caufes him to be burnt, much to the edification of the faithful, and the terror of all unbelievers. Whether Rome thinks it needful to keep faith with heretics it would be wafte of time to inquire, as long as the Acts of the Council of Conftance are acknowledged by that Church, otherwife a ftartling commentary on her practice might be collected from the writings of Hofius, Simanca, and Albert Pighius.

The fate of Hus leads Dr. Phillpotts on naturally to examine the doctrine of exclufive falvation in the Church of Rome. And here he fays truly enough : —

" Even the claims of its fpiritual head to a right of inter-ference, whether direct or indirect, in the temporal concerns of states (if they were universally acknowledged), would be of far less practical moment, than the doctrine which excludes from salvation all those who dare to separate themselves from the Roman Church."

That this was perceived by the Roman Catholic prelates themselves is plain from their endeavours to soften the obnoxious tenet. But here, at least, their sophistry served them not.

"It stands," says Dr. Phillpotts, "in the very front of their whole system; nay, it makes a part of every other dogma; for all are commended to the acceptance of the faithful under the awful sanction of an anathema if they be rejected."

Dr. Doyle having recriminated on the Church of England, and asserted that she taught the same exclusive doctrine in the 18th Article, an opportunity is afforded to Dr. Phillpotts of vindicating and explaining that Article. After quoting it,* he proceeds:—

"In other words, those are to be accursed who presume to say that the great work of redemption by Christ was not necessary for the salvation of man; but that men of any religious persuasion, if they live according to the law or sect which they profess, and to mere natural light, shall be saved *thereby;* whereas Holy Scripture tells us that all who shall be saved, of whatever sect or persuasion they may be, will

---

* "Article XVIII. *Of obtaining Salvation only by the Name of Christ.*—They also are to be had accursed that presume to say that every man shall be saved *by* the law or sect which he professeth, so that he be diligent to frame his life according to that law, and the light of nature. For Holy Scripture doth set out to us only the Name of Jesus Christ, whereby men must be saved."

be faved only by the Name of Jefus Chrift—only by reafon of Him and His merits. That this is, in one fenfe, a doctrine of exclufive falvation, I am quite ready to admit; but let us fee of what it is exclufive,—it is not of the fubjects of falvation, for it abfolutely excludes none; but only of means, or authors, of falvation. In fhort, it does no more nor lefs than *exclude all other Saviours than our Lord Jefus Chrift.* Here then the whole parallel between the Churches of Rome and England, in refpect to the dogma of exclufive falvation, as far as our Article is concerned, falls abfolutely to nothing."

Whether members of the Roman Church, while maintaining the doctrine of exclufive falvation, can be fafely entrufted with a fhare of legiflative power among a people the majority of whom fhe regards as out of the pale of falvation, is a queftion about which no fober man will doubt. The marvel is that the claim fhould ever have been ferioufly entertained. As if it were not enough that Rome fhould have pronounced the Englifh Church to be no true part of the Church of Chrift, but abandoned to the guidance of the devil in this world, and to eternal perdition in the next, fhe muft alfo claim as *a right* to legiflate for that Church which fhe denounces, and for that State of which, if her allegiance to the Pope be more than a name, fhe is a faithlefs member.

The pretenfions of the Roman Church are thus fet forth by Dr. Doyle himfelf:*—

" ' It *is the worft of herefy*, and a virtual apoftafy from the Chriftian religion *to affert that* the gates of hell have ever

---

* " Addrefs to Clergy of Carlow, Auguft the 28th, 1825."

prevailed againſt this Church—that is, that *the paſtors and, people who compoſe it, have ever, at any period, even for a ſingle hour, profeſſed error.*' A ſentence," ſays Dr. Phillpotts, " by which every national Church, every denomination of Chriſtians throughout the world, which differs from Rome in the minuteſt point of faith, is pronounced to be in a ſtate of the moſt damnable hereſy."

The members of the Engliſh Church, then, in the eyes of Rome, are in evil caſe ; nor are matters much improved when the ſpecious plea of " invincible ignorance " is ſet up on their behalf. For, although Baptiſm cleanſes original ſin, and all actual ſin committed before that holy Sacrament, yet every mortal ſin committed after Baptiſm can only be remitted (according to the Church of Rome) in the ſacrament of penance.

" Here then," ſays Dr. Phillpotts, " is the amount of the utmoſt conceſſion which can be made, even to thoſe whoſe involuntary error, and invincible ignorance keep them out of the pale of the Church of Rome. They will be ſaved— if they do not commit any actual ſin. But if they ſin, for *them* there is no remiſſion—the Blood of Chriſt has been ſhed in vain—the Goſpel of Chriſt has been preached in vain. If they ſin, they have no ſhare in the common bleſſing promiſed to Chriſtian ſinners. If they ſin, they have *not* ' an Advocate with the Father '—' Jeſus Chriſt the Righteous is *not* the Propitiation for *their* ſins.' They have fallen from grace given in Baptiſm, and to them no ' place of repentance ' is left, though they ſeek it with tears of anguiſh, and ' groans which cannot be uttered.' Their ' broken and contrite hearts '—the Church of Rome hath ſaid (and who ſhall dare to gainſay it ?)—' their broken and contrite hearts, O Lord, Thou *ſhalt* deſpiſe.' "

Dr. Phillpotts then proceeds to enumerate certain cafes in which Rome delights to difplay her overbearing fpirit, commencing with the admonition of the rubric to parents " not to truft their children to be in any wife fuckled or nurfed by heretic women," down to the refufal of Chriftian burial (in countries where it may fafely be done) to heretic corpfes.   But this is not all.

" The fame odious fpirit," fays Dr. Phillpotts, "which makes it a fubject of grave precaution that herefy be not fucked in with the nurfe's milk, and which violates the decencies of our common nature in refufing the protection even of a fecure grave to the bones of a deceafed Proteftant, has intruded itfelf into the deareft connections of domeftic life, and fought to make the marriage-bed a fcene of difcord and polemic altercation."

Then follows a refcript of the Pope, publifhed in 1825, " while the Committee of the Houfe of Commons was fondly catching the honeyed dew of peace and brotherly love, as it trickled from the guilelefs lips of Drs. Doyle, Murray, Kelly, and Magaurin ;" which, if obeyed, would have the effect of introducing diforder into every home where the hufband or wife chanced to be a Roman Catholic.

With fuch terrible examples of the intolerance of Rome before our eyes, it is hard to account for the infatuation which could plead for the admiffion of its children to a feat in the Legiflature.   Dr. Phillpotts brings the queftion to its legitimate iffue when he fays :—

" If thefe tenets be not effential, let the authority, be it what it may, which can declare what is or is not effential, renounce and difclaim them. If this be not done, no adequate fecurity can be given to any Proteftant ftate againft the arrogant pretenfions, the rancorous malignity, of their Church itfelf. If this be not done, let thofe among them (and there are many fuch) who cherifh the feelings of Chriftian charity, and refpect the rights of other Chriftians, either emancipate themfelves from the bonds of religious tyranny, or candidly acknowledge that it is not the Crown, it is not the Heir to the Crown, it is not the Houfe of Lords, it is not the people of England—it is the Pope, it is the Church of Rome itfelf, which bars the entrance of the Britifh Senate, and condemns them to a ftate of mortifying but neceffary exclufion."

Dr. Doyle next receives fevere chaftifement at the hands of Dr. Phillpotts for the fhamelefs way in which he contradicted himfelf in relation to Paftorini's prophecies, and the queftion of Roman Catholic Emancipation. That diftinguifhed prelate makes but a forry figure, it muft be confeffed, and it is hard to fay whether he moft moves our laughter or contempt. His fyftem of fcheming, fubterfuge, and evafion culminates in the ftatement, pronounced, it is to be hoped, with gravity fuited to its fincerity, that, if ever he took part in political difcuffions, *it was with great reluctance.* If anything could have awakened the confiding Committee of the Houfe of Commons to a fenfe of the character and motives of the man with whom they had to deal, it muft have been this perilous affertion. That I. K. L.* fhould defire to forget his

* The initials under which Dr. Doyle wrote—James Kildare and Leighlin.

fedition was reafonable enough; but that any one
fhould believe that this political firebrand had been
dragged an unwilling victim into conflicts which his
peaceful foul abhorred, was as unlikely as that they
fhould learn to venerate the lying wonders of his
Church.

" Yet this," fays Dr. Phillpotts, in conclufion, " is Dr.
Doyle ! This is, or lately was, (for thefe glories are not
often very long-lived,) the idol of the liberal party in our
Englifh Houfe of Commons ! one whom ftatefmen have
not fcrupled to laud in good fet fentences as a paragon of
talent, and the very mirror of honefty ! In exhibiting him
in his real colours, in holding him forth in his own recorded
words and fentiments, to the indignation of every man, to
whom truth and plain dealing are not empty names, I have
performed a duty painful and difgufting to my own feelings ;
a duty, by the difcharge of which I may perhaps draw down
upon myfelf the ribaldry of Scotch critics, the revilings of
Irifh orators, the fneers of Englifh liberals, and the half-
vented rebukes of the friends of conciliation. Be it fo !
From all thefe cenfors I appeal to the unbiaffed judgment
and honeft fympathy of the Britifh people ; and if my caufe
be as good, as my own confcience tells me it is, to that tri-
bunal I fhall not appeal in vain."

CHAPTER X.

*Bill for Roman Catholic Relief carried in the Houſe of Com-
mons. Thrown out in Houſe of Lords. Outrages and Famine
in Ireland. Mr. Canning's Bill for Conceſſion carried in the
Houſe of Commons, but rejeЕted by the Lords. Continuation
of Diſturbances in Ireland. Further Motions in Parliament.
The Roman Catholic Aſſociation in Ireland referred to in the
King's Speech. Mr. Goulburn's Bill for its Suppreſſion.
Mr. Brougham's Defence of it. The Motion carried, and
the Bill paſſed by both Houſes. Further Motions in Parliament. The Declaration of the Duke of York againſt the Roman
Catholics. Opinion of Lord Eldon. Strong Feeling in the
Country againſt further Conceſſion. Sir F. Burdett's Motion
in 1827.*

R. PHILLPOTTS had now fairly em-
barked in the Roman Catholic queſtion; and
it was in February of the next year, 1827,
that he publiſhed the firſt of his celebrated
Letters to Mr. Canning on the propoſed meaſure of
relief. But, before conſidering the part which he played
in a conteſt the moſt important of any that have agitated
the country ſince the Revolution, it will be well to take
a general ſurvey of the political condition of the Roman
Catholics, and examine the various efforts made on
their behalf, terminating in the Relief Bill of 1829.
If it be pleaded that ſuch a ſurvey forms no part of
the *Life* of Dr. Phillpotts, it muſt be remembered
that this work is alſo a hiſtory of his *Times*, and
that no ſuch work would be complete without giving
ſomething like a comprehenſive view of this momentous ſtruggle.* The various ſtages of the meaſure are
ſo little known to the majority of Engliſhmen, that,

---

* A ſimilar mode of treatment will be adopted further on,
in reference to the " Oxford Movement."

even at the rifk of a certain tedioufnefs infeparable from an examination of details, it is believed that a fervice will be rendered by fhowing how the queftion of Roman Catholic relief ftruggled on from fmall beginnings till it affumed the proportions of one of the moft gigantic evils which it was ever the lot of the country to confront.

And here it may be faid, generally, that in every reign, except that of James II, fome frefh feverity had been enacted againft the Roman Catholics. A thoughtful writer fupplies us with reafons for thefe acts of legiflation :—

" The ftatutes againft Popery in England and Ireland were the reftrictions, not of a religious faith, but of a political faction, enacted not againft diffidents from the Church of England, but againft rebellious partifans of the Houfe of Stuart. The queftion was one, not of the Liturgy, but of the fword. The Stuarts loft the day. They were exiled ; and the foldiers whom they left behind were difabled by the provifions of law from again ftirring up rebellion, and again fhedding the blood of freemen in the caufe of tyrants and flaves."*

So numerous were thefe ftatutes that no lefs than feventy pages are occupied in Burn's *Ecclefiaftical Law* with an enumeration of them.

Popifh priefts who fhould officiate in Romifh churches or chapels were declared guilty of felony, if foreigners, and of high treafon, if natives. Rewards were payable on the difcovery of popifh clergy—50*l.* for difcover-

---

* Croly : " Life of George IV," p. 476.

ing a bifhop, 20*l.* for a prieft, and 10*l.* for a popifh-ufher. No Proteftant was allowed to marry a Papift. No Papift could purchafe land, or take a leafe for more than thirty-one years; and if the profits of the land fo leafed amounted to more than a certain fum, the property was to pafs to the firft Proteftant difcoverer. No Papift could be in a line of entail, but the eftate was to pafs on to the next Proteftant relation. No Papift could hold any office, civil or military, or dwell in certain fpecified towns, or vote at elections. The wives of Papifts were to have an increafe of their jointure on converfion. Two juftices were empowered to compel any Papift, above eighteen years of age, to difcover every particular which had come to his knowledge refpecting popifh priefts, celebration of Mafs, or popifh fchools, under penalty of imprifonment for a year if he refufed. Nobody was allowed to hold property in truft for a Roman Catholic. In every cafe growing out of the penal ftatutes the juries were to be exclufively Proteftant. Papifts in towns were to provide Proteftant watchmen, and were incapacitated from voting at veftries. They were alfo incapable of being called to the bar, and barrifters or folicitors marrying Papifts were confidered Papifts, and were liable to all the confequent penalties. Perfons robbed by privateers during war with a popifh prince were indemnified by money levied upon Roman Catholics only. Any prieft found guilty of celebrating a marriage between a Proteftant and a Roman Catholic was to be hanged.

L

Such is an outline of the penal code to which a portion of our fellow-subjects was liable. But, neceſſary as theſe enactments may have been, they were certainly hardſhips and diſqualifications which nothing but the moſt imperious neceſſity could juſtify. They were deviſed to meet a preſſing evil; and, as that evil paſſed away, moderate men began to feel that they might be relaxed without danger to the State. It is true that many of theſe Acts had for a long time remained a dead letter; but they were ſtill to be found in the ſtatute book, and might be enforced, even at the riſk of ſowing the ſeeds of family diſcord, and looſening the very frame-work of ſociety itſelf.

Among the earlieſt Acts of legiſlative conceſſion may be ranked that of 1778, when a bill for relieving Roman Catholics from the operation of many ſevere ſtatutes was introduced, and paſſed with little oppoſition. But where a little is yielded, it is invariably made a ſtepping-ſtone for further demands. This was ſpecially the caſe with the Roman Catholics; and, in the year 1781, an eminent member of that body made no ſcruple to ſay* that "the boaſted excellencies of the Britiſh Conſtitution are nothing to me, who am deprived of the common rights of humanity; they only ſerve to make my condition more irkſome, and to *create a reſtleſs deſire of change and revolutions.*"

In May, 1789, the Engliſh Catholic *Diſſenters* (for

---

* In a pamphlet entitled, "The State and Behaviour of Engliſh Catholics from the Reformation to the Year 1781."

that was the fomewhat doubtful title under which they now figured) prefented a petition to the Houfe of Commons, praying to be relieved from the difabilities under which they laboured. The petition was drawn up with great care and ·ingenuity. They acknowledged no infallibility in the Pope, and affected to pay no great reverence to the decrees of councils. King George was their fole lord and mafter, and no Pope or council could depofe him. It was altogether fuch a document as would drive the Wifemans and MacHales of the prefent day to frenzy, and is not without its inftruction, as fhowing the elafticity of the Roman fyftem, in fpite of its vaunted unchangeablenefs, and how well that Church knows how to relax or tighten its pretenfions according to the temper of the times. This petition was received with confiderable favour; and, early in the feffion of 1791, Mr. Mitford (afterwards Lord Redefdale) moved for leave to bring in a bill "to relieve, upon condition, and under certain reftrictions, perfons called Protefting Catholic Diffenters from certain penalties and difabilities to which papifts, or perfons profeffing the popifh religion, are by law fubject." In the courfe of an able fpeech he commented with great feverity on the exifting laws againft Roman Catholics, and after enumerating the various oaths of fupremacy which had from time to time been devifed, he ftated that the relief which he fhould propofe for the protefting Roman Catholics would be a bill fimilar to that which had paffed in Ireland for the relief of the Roman Catholics fome years fince; and, as no ill confequences had been found to refult from it in a country where the Roman Catholics were fo much more numerous, he trufted that the Houfe would fee no impropriety in the propofition.   The motion *was fupported by Mr. Pitt*, who expreffed a hope that the Houfe would be unanimous in receiving the bill.   He was followed by Mr. Fox, who thought, however, that the meafure was too narrow in its views. He wifhed to go much further, and eftablifh complete toleration.   The bill was eventually carried through the Houfe of Commons without a divifion.   On the fecond reading in the Houfe of Lords a debate enfued upon the propriety of feveral claufes.   The Arch-bifhop of Canterbury, and the Bifhops of S. David's, Peterborough, and Salifbury, gave the bill their fup-port, and it was paffed on the 4th of June, a flight variation having been made in the form of the oath.

And now that the Roman Catholics were relieved from the feverity of penal ftatutes, it was determined that an effort fhould be made to free them from *poli-tical* difabilities as well.   The attempt originated in Ireland in the early part of 1795, where affemblies of the moft influential of the Roman Catholics were held, in which it was determined to addrefs the Throne for a remiffion of political difqualifications, and a full parti-cipation in the rights of their fellow-fubjects.   It was well known that the Prime Minifter, Mr. Pitt, was favourable to their demands, provided that fufficient fecurities could be given; but it was alfo known that the King was moft determinately hoftile, and it was not thought that in the face of the Irifh legiflature, compofed entirely of Proteftants, any material conceffions would be granted.* Ultimately, however, the exifting laws were fo far relaxed as to permit Roman Catholics to intermarry with Proteftants, to take apprentices, to keep fchools, and to plead at the bar, together with fome leffer privileges hitherto withheld from them.

But, important as thefe relaxations were, they were received with little favour. The Roman Catholics had tafted enough of the fweets of liberty to make them long for more. The ftudy of human nature proves the truth of the French proverb, *L'appetit vient en mangeant;* and nothing would now fatisfy them but a deliverance from difqualifications of *every kind.* It was at this junéture that Lord Fitz-William was appointed Lord-Lieutenant of Ireland. From his well-known inclination to moderate counfels, and the favourable difpofition of the government which had appointed him, large conceffions were not unreafonably expeéted. It was believed that he was fpecially charged to carry over to Ireland a final deliverance from difqualifications of all kinds on religious grounds. The Roman Catholics faw, therefore, that this was the time to prefs their advantage, and Mr. Grattan was

---

* The unconquerable nature of the King's fcruples is forcibly defcribed in his well-known fpeech :—"I can give up my crown, and retire from power ; I can quit my palace, and live in a cottage ; I can lay my head on a block, and lofe my life : but I can *not* break my oath."

put forward to advocate their claims. A Relief Bill was already in courſe of preparation, when the Government, finding that the King would never give his conſent to it, took alarm, and declared its hoſtility to the meaſure. Lord Fitz-William, who, it muſt be confeſſed, had ſhown but little tact in ſo eaſily allowing himſelf to become the tool of the Iriſh party, was recalled, and Lord Camden was appointed as his ſucceſſor. This led to the moſt ſerious manifeſtations of diſpleaſure both in the Iriſh Parliament and out of doors. One party was for impeaching Mr. Pitt, while the more excitable vented their indignation in tumultuous meetings, which were only diſperſed by the ſoldiery. Meanwhile, however, a conceſſion of another and more perilous kind was granted to the Iriſh Roman Catholics. Up to this time the ranks of the prieſthood had been recruited from foreign colleges; but the French Revolution had ſwept moſt of theſe ſeminaries away. The Roman Catholics were now in an evil caſe, and if Government had not ſpeedily come to their aſſiſtance, their Church in Ireland muſt have expired from inanition. This was, therefore, thought to be a favourable moment for founding an inſtitution in Ireland for the training of Roman Catholic youths for the prieſthood, and thus prevent their forming foreign connections, involving themſelves in foreign relations, and bringing home to their own country foreign affections. Eight thouſand pounds were, accordingly, granted from the public money, in the year 1795, and the college of Maynooth was founded—an eſtabliſhment which from that day to the prefent has furnifhed a ceafelefs ground of irritation and debate. The grant was made, beyond queftion, in a liberal and conciliatory fpirit; but experience has fhown that the college has proved an entire and hopelefs failure.

And now the projected union of Ireland with Great Britain fhared for a while the thoughts and occupied the energies of politicians of every grade, jointly with the meafure for Roman Catholic Relief. It was believed that, when the Act of Union paffed, in July, 1800, immediate fteps would be taken by Government to releafe the Roman Catholics from their remaining difabilities. As long as the two kingdoms had diftinct legiflatures, it was impoffible to open the avenues of Parliament and public offices to Roman Catholics in Ireland, fince they outnumbered the Proteftant population in the ratio of three to one. Such a meafure would have had the inevitable effect of eftablifhing a Roman Catholic Government and Church in Ireland. But when one common legiflature was eftablifhed for both countries, it was not thought that the admiffion of a very fmall and uninfluential minority of Roman Catholics into Parliament would exercife any improper influence on the councils of the nation. Many, therefore, of the leading Tory ftatefmen were favourable to their admiffion, Mr. Pitt among the number; but the determined oppofition of the King rendered any fuch ftep for the prefent impoffible. He was abfolutely inflexible, and was, moreover, fully perfuaded that any further relaxation

would involve a violation of his coronation oath. He
was fupported in his determination by the opinion of
the Chancellor Loughborough, who was, it is to be
feared, merely humouring the King's prejudices for
his own private ends; and the confequence was that
the King refufed to have the fubject mentioned in his
prefence any more.   This led to a coldnefs between
the King and Mr. Pitt; and it was not long before the
adminiftration of the latter, which had been carried on
with unparalleled benefit to the country for feventeen
years, came to an end.   To increafe the pain and per-
plexity which were felt on all fides at this eventful time,
the minifters were charged with having caufed that
calamitous affliction under which the King laboured.
So acutely did Mr. Pitt feel the imputation, little as
he deferved it, that, on the King's reftoration to health,
he promifed that he would not again bring forward the
Roman Catholic queftion during his Majefty's lifetime.

For the prefent, then, further conceffion was not to
be thought of.   But its advocates, though repulfed,
were not daunted, and, like fkilful generals, gathered
up their forces for a frefh attack.   Lord Grenville had
efpoufed the caufe of Roman Catholic relief with great
warmth, and on the 10th of May, 1805, moved the
order of the day in the Houfe of Lords to take into
confideration the petition of the Roman Catholics in
Ireland, prefented on the 25th of March, and, in a
fpeech of great power, advocated the removal of exifting difabilities. Special importance attaches to the de-

bate which followed, as it was the *firſt time* that the queſtion had been brought forward *ſince the Union.* The Lords debated, until four o'clock in the morning, whether or not the petition ſhould be referred to a committee, and then adjourned until Monday the 13th, when, after ſitting till ſix o'clock on the following morning, they rejeĉted the motion by 178 to 49. Mr. Fox's motion in the Commons, on the preſentation of a duplicate petition, met with a ſimilar fate on the following day, being rejeĉted by a majority of 336 to 124. The voice of the country was plainly againſt making any change in the Conſtitution at a time when the whole of Europe was convulſed, and many who were otherwiſe favourable to the meaſure gave their vote againſt it. The debate in the Commons was chiefly remarkable for giving occaſion to the *débût* of a new member, Henry Grattan, who had with difficulty been perſuaded to ſit in Parliament, and had, through Lord Fitz-William's intereſt, been returned as member for Malton. His ſpeech, which laſted for an hour and a-half, elicited marks of very warm approval even from Mr. Pitt, and placed him at once in the front rank of parliamentary debaters. From this moment to the end of his brilliant career he was the moſt zealous champion of Emancipation ; and, although not permitted to ſee his labours crowned with ſucceſs, it was to his untiring energy that the ultimate paſſing of the meaſure was chiefly due.

The year 1807 was marked by the grant of an additional ſum of 5000*l.* to the college of Maynooth.

Petitions continued to be prefented to both Houfes of Parliament; and, on the 13th of May, 1810, Mr. Grattan brought forward a motion in the Houfe of Commons for a committee to confider the Roman Catholic claims. Seldom had the walls of S. Stephen's echoed with fuch fervid eloquence. But though this memorable fpeech led captive the judgment of even fober men, and gave to the opponents of the meafure a temporary check; yet, the magnitude of the danger attending further conceffion fpeedily re-afferted its power, and, after an adjourned debate, the motion was loft by a majority of 104. On the 6th of June a motion to the fame effect was made in the Houfe of Peers by the Earl of Donoughmore, which was loft by a majority of eighty-fix, the Lord Chancellor Eldon having been its chief opponent.

Early in the following year (1811) the Roman Catholics again occupied a large fhare of the attention of Parliament—the firft of the Regency. Political agitators in Ireland had conceived the plan of a National Reprefentative Affembly, which was to hold its fittings in Dublin, and, under pretence of petitioning Parliament, levy money, and take into its hands the general protection and management of Roman Catholic interefts. The danger of fuch a proceeding was too great to allow of delay, and the Irifh Government promptly checked the project by fending a circular letter to the fheriffs and chief magiftrates of all the counties in Ireland, directing them to arreft, under the Convention Act, all perfons who might in any way be concerned in promoting fuch an affembly. The remedy was fharp, but decifive, and led to an animated debate in the Englifh Parliament, Mr. Wellefley Pole, Secretary to the Lord-Lieutenant of Ireland, appearing in his place in the Houfe of Commons to give an account of his conduct; but there were no refults, beyond a difplay of irritated feelings. It was of this benefit, however, to the Roman Catholics, that it kept their claims frefh before men's minds, and helped to increafe the growing conviction that further conceffions were inevitable. On the 31ft of May, in the fame year, Mr. Grattan repeated his motion in the Houfe of Commons on behalf of the Roman Catholics, and this time with fomewhat better fuccefs, for the majority againft the motion had now decreafed to fixty-three. On the 18th of June a fimilar motion was alfo made in the Houfe of Lords by the Earl of Donoughmore. The debate was chiefly remarkable for a fpeech by the Bifhop of Norwich, Dr. Bathurft, in favour of the Roman Catholic claims; the motion, however, was loft by a majority of fifty-nine, being twenty-feven lefs than upon the former occafion. In proportion as the majorities againft thefe annual motions decreafed, fo did the hopes of the Roman Catholics rife. They felt that the conteft might be prolonged, but that victory was fecure; and thus, while noify agitators were doing their work out of doors, Parliament was inundated with petitions from all quarters, not a few of them coming from Proteftant fources. On the 21ft of April, 1812, Lord Donoughmore renewed his motion, and, in the long debate which followed, every argument which had been previously used was again brought forward, decked out with the choicest ornaments of oratory. It was a subject the charm of which seemed to make speakers insensible to weariness. But the hopes of the Roman Catholics were not as yet to be realized, for the government at this time was essentially a "no-popery" administration, and the motion was lost by a majority of seventy-two. A similar motion was made by Mr. Grattan in the House of Commons on April the 23rd, and was lost by a majority of eighty-five. The *third* memorable defeat which the Roman Catholic claims, so pertinaciously urged, had suffered in Parliament. Undaunted by these failures, and confident that the fears of their opponents would one day grant what their better judgment withheld, the favourers of the measure rose, Antæus-like, from their overthrow, and next time with Mr. Canning and Lord Wellesley at their head.

On the 22nd of June, 1812, Mr. Canning moved a resolution, pledging the House to an early consideration, in the next session, of the Roman Catholic claims, with a view to their final and conciliatory adjustment. In the debate which followed, *the motion was carried* by the decisive majority of 235 to 106. In the House of Lords, the stronghold of the Anti-Catholic party, the majority against the motion was only *one*. Seldom has any division shown such an extraordinary balance of opinion in that House. The Ministers were not agreed among themselves, for it had been understood

for fome years that this fhould be left an open queftion. The Bench of Bifhops itfelf was divided; and
of the five Royal Dukes three voted on one fide and
two on the other.

And now the Roman Catholics had good reafon to
congratulate themfelves upon the improved afpect of
their fortunes, and to predict the hour of victory. But
feventeen years of reftlefs agitation were to intervene.

On February 25, 1813, Mr. Grattan, emboldened
by the fuccefs of the previous year, renewed his annual
motion for a committee on the claims of the Roman
Catholics. The *debate which followed continued
during four days*, fo exhauftlefs did the fubject promife to be ; and fome idea of its prolixity may be
formed from the fact that its printed report is the
fize of an ordinary volume. At its clofe there was
a majority of forty in favour of the motion ; a great
falling off as compared with the majority of the preceding year, and attributable to the reactionary alarm
which had fet in throughout the country at the magnitude of Roman Catholic pretenfions.

In order to occupy the ground which had already
been gained by Mr. Canning, Mr. Grattan, on March
the 9th, moved the order of the day for a committee
of the whole Houfe on the Roman Catholic queftion.
He then propofed a refolution that it is highly ad-
vifable to provide for the removal of the civil and
military difqualifications under which his Majefty's
Roman Catholic fubjects labour, with fuch exceptions,
and under fuch regulations, as fhould be found necef-

fary. On a divifion of the Houfe there was a majority of fixty-feven in favour of the motion.

On April the 30th Mr. Grattan introduced his bill, and moved that it fhould be read a firft time and printed, which was agreed to. On May the 13th the bill was read a fecond time, after a ftout oppofition. It was confidered in committee on May the 24th, and after a powerful fpeech againft the meafure by the Speaker, the Right Honourable Charles Abbott, it was rejected by a narrow majority of four. But the hopes of the Roman Catholics had now rifen fo high that even the meafure of conceffion which was propofed altogether failed to excite their gratitude, or indeed to meet their approval. This is clearly fhown from the following letter of the Roman Catholic Prelates, affembled in Dublin, to the Clergy and Laity of the Roman Catholic Churches in Ireland :—

" Reverend Brothers—Beloved Children—Peace be with you. Solicitude for the fpiritual intereft of our beloved flocks, obliges us once more to fufpend the exercife of our other paftoral duties, in order to deliberate, in common, upon the prefent pofture of our religious concerns.

" We haften to declare to you the lively feelings of gratitude excited in our breafts by the gracious condefcenfion of the Legiflature, in taking into its favourable confideration the difabilities which ftill affect the Catholic body. With thefe feelings deeply and indelibly impreffed upon our hearts, it is with the utmoft diftrefs of mind that we are compelled, by a fenfe of duty, to diffent (in fome points connected with our emancipation) from the opinions of thofe virtuous and enlightened ftatefmen, who have fo long and fo ably advocated the caufe of Catholic freedom.

" Probably from a want of fufficient information, but un-
queftionably from the moft upright motives, they have
propofed to the Legiflature the adoption of certain arrangements refpecting our Ecclefiaftical difcipline, and particularly
refpecting the exercife of epifcopal functions, to which it
would be impoffible for us to affent, without incurring the
guilt of fchifm, inafmuch as they might, if carried into effect,
invade the fpiritual jurifdiction of our Supreme Paftor, and
alter an important point of our difcipline, for which alteration his concurrence would, upon Catholic principles, be
indifpenfably neceffary.

" When the quarter is confidered from whence the claufes
have proceeded, it might perhaps be imagined, were we to
continue filent, that they had our unqualified approbation.
On this account we deem it a duty which we owe to you,
to our country, and to God, to declare, in the moft public
manner, ' that they have not, and that in their prefent fhape
they never can have, our concurrence.'   As, however, we
have, upon all occafions, inculcated the duty of loyalty to
our moft gracious Sovereign, (the fecuring whereof is the
profeffed object of the propofed ecclefiaftical arrangements,)
fo we would be always defirous to give you the moft convincing proofs that we are ready, in the moft exemplary
manner, to practife it ourfelves.   We have fworn to preferve inviolate the allegiance which every fubject owes to
his Sovereign—we are not accufed of having violated our
oaths.

" Should any other oath, not adverfe to our religious
principles, be yet devifed, which could remove even the
unfounded apprehenfions of any part of our countrymen,
we would willingly take it.   We owe it to our God to be free
from difloyalty.   We owe it to our countrymen to endeavour,
at leaft, to be free from fufpicion.

" Upon thefe grounds, Reverend Brothers, Beloved Children, we announce to you the following refolutions, which,
after invoking the light and affiftance of God, we have
unanimoufly adopted, viz :—

" 1. That having seriously examined a copy of the Bill, lately brought into Parliament, purporting to provide for the removal of the civil and military disqualifications under which his Majesty's Roman Catholic subjects labour, we feel ourselves bound to declare that certain ecclesiastical clauses or securities therein contained are utterly incompatible with the discipline of the Roman Church, and with the free exercise of our religion.

" 2. That we cannot, without incurring the heavy guilt of schism, accede to such regulations; nor can we dissemble our dismay and consternation at the consequences which such regulations, if enforced, must necessarily produce.

" 3. That we would, with the utmost willingness, swear, (should the Legislature require us to do so,) that we never will concur in the appointment or consecration of any Bishop, whom we do not conscientiously believe to be of unimpeachable loyalty and peaceable conduct; and further, ' that we have not, and that we will not have, any correspondence or communication with the Chief Pastor of our Church, or with any person authorized to act in his name for the purpose of overthrowing or disturbing the Protestant Government, or the Protestant Church of Great Britain and Ireland, or the Protestant Church of Scotland, as by law established.' Reverend Brothers, Beloved Children, the Grace of our Lord Jesus Christ, and the Communion of the Holy Ghost be with you all, Amen.

" *Dublin, May* 26, 1813."

(*Here follow the Signatures.*)

In spite, however, of the rejection of Mr. Grattan's motion, the session of this year did not pass away without a considerably increased measure of relief being granted to the Roman Catholics. A bill was brought forward in the Lords by the Duke of Norfolk, and subsequently passed into law, which provided that

Roman Catholics holding any civil or military office granted to them in Ireland under the Act 33, George III, c. 21, who fhould have taken the oaths prefcribed, fhould not be liable in England, in the navy, or in Jerfey and Guernfey, to any of the penalties of 25 Charles II, c. 2, or to any penalties for not taking tefts ; and that any Roman Catholic having taken thofe oaths, and having received in Ireland a commiffion in the army, fhould not, on receiving a higher commiffion in Great Britain, be liable to any of the faid penalties.

In the following year, 1814, the proceedings of the Roman Catholic board in Ireland were fo violent and menacing, that the Lord-Lieutenant, with the advice of the Privy Council, iffued a proclamation, declaring it contrary to law. This led to a monfter meeting of Roman Catholics in Dublin, under the prefidency of the Hon. Thomas Ffrench, at which Mr. O'Connell diftinguifhed himfelf by more than his ufual fluency of invective. For a time the violence difplayed by political agitators in Ireland occafioned ferious injury to the caufe of Roman Catholic relief, and promifed to retard for many years the fulfilment of hopes fo fondly cherifhed and fo warmly urged. Once more, therefore, it was determined to have re-courfe to more conftitutional meafures, and on May 11, 1815, a petition was prefented to the Houfe of Commons by Sir Henry Parnell, on behalf of the Roman Catholics of Ireland, praying it " to grant to them the redrefs of the oppreffive grievances of which they fo juftly complain ; and to reftore to them the

M

full and unreftricted enjoyment of the rank of free fubjects of the empire."

On the 30th of the fame month a long debate enfued, in which all the former ground was traverfed afrefh by the various fpeakers, and in which Mr. Grattan fhone with even more than his wonted brilliance. The motion, however, was loft by a majority of eighty-one; and a fimilar motion made by Lord Donoughmore in the Houfe of Lords, on June the 8th, was rejected by a majority of twenty-fix.

Meanwhile the agitation in Ireland continued unabated, and this, combined with a confederacy in crime which manifefted itfelf in a fyftematic oppofition to all laws and municipal inftitutions, fufficed to keep the country in a ftate of the greateft uneafinefs and alarm. The danger of further conceffions to the Roman Catholics is well fhown in a letter written about this period by Mr. (afterwards Sir Robert Harry) Inglis to Lord Sidmouth.

"Nothing," he fays, "that I have yet feen or heard in Ireland has weakened my conviction that it is neceffary to ftop fhort of any further conceffion of political power to the Roman Catholic body. If we could be morally certain that unconditional fubmiffion to their prefent demands would enfure to us the permanent peace and union of all claffes, we might, perhaps, admit the anomalies of the meafure; but every new conceffion has furnifhed only the difpofition and the means to extort more. 'Afk where's the North, at York it's on the Tweed;' and the North will thus recede from us 'till all be theirs beneath the Arctic fky.' Catholic emancipation will be followed by the abolition of the tithes, the erection of a Roman Catholic eftablifhment, or the

feparation of the two countries as fucceffive objects of popular excitement; and O'Connell and O'Gorman, who, we
are told, would completely lofe their confequence by the
fuccefs of their own prefent efforts, would quickly find in any
one or all of thefe, or fome other of the 'thirty thoufand
grievances,' fome moft animating fubftitute for the war-cry
which they now raife."

The Parliamentary tranfactions of 1816, in reference
to the Roman Catholic claims, were opened, on April
the 26th, by a petition being prefented to the Houfe
of Commons by Sir Henry Parnell, and the efforts were
continued to the clofe of the feffion. On the 15th and
21ft of May petitions were alfo prefented; and upon the
laft occafion Mr. Grattan moved that the Houfe fhould
take into its confideration the ftate of the laws affecting
Roman Catholics, with a view to a final and conciliatory adjuftment. It deferves to be recorded that upon
this occafion the motion was fupported by Lord
Caftlereagh, and oppofed by Mr. Peel, Secretary for
Ireland. It was loft by a majority of thirty-one. On
the 30th of May the queftion was revived by Sir Henry
Parnell, and again alfo on the 6th of June—fo determined were the Roman Catholics to force their claims
upon the nation. In the Houfe of Lords the fubject
of Roman Catholic relief was taken into confideration
on June the 21ft—the chief feature of the debate being
the fpeech of the "liberal" Bifhop of Norwich (Dr.
Bathurft) in favour of the motion. It was rejected,
however, by a majority of four. And here it may
not be out of place to notice the fact that this great
queftion, involving a change in the conftitution of the

country, was fcarcely ever brought forward till near
the clofe of the feffion, when, according to the very
advocates of relief, it was too late to take any fteps in
the matter. The queftion was again revived May
the 9th, 1817, by Mr. Grattan unfuccefsfully moving
the adoption of the refolution of 1813. It was rejected
by a majority of twenty-four; and on May the 16th
a fimilar motion was negatived in the Houfe of Lords
by a majority of fifty-two.

The year 1818 was fignalifed by a refpite from
Parliamentary debates on this interminable fubject; but
on May the 3rd, 1819, Mr. Grattan again preffed it
on the attention of the Houfe of Commons, and in a
very full Houfe there was a narrow majority of two
againft his motion. In the Houfe of Lords, on May
the 17th, a fimilar motion was rejected by a majority
of forty-one.

On the 25th of the fame month Earl Grey introduced a bill to relieve Roman Catholics from taking
the declaratory oaths againft Tranfubftantiation and
the Invocation of Saints.* The bill was read a firft
time, but on the fecond reading (June the 10th) there
was a majority againft it of fifty-nine.

But before the Roman Catholic caufe could again
be brought before Parliament, its chief fupport was no
more. Mr. Grattan had, indeed, come to London to
attend the feffion of Parliament; but his health was
broken, and he never again raifed his voice in public

---

* For an account of this, fee " Letter to Earl Grey,"
page 28.

in defence of that queſtion which had engroſſed the beſt of his time and talents. His laſt thoughts, however, were given to his darling ſcheme, and his dying words were thoſe of warning to the Roman Catholics, entreating them to abſtain from endeavouring to turn the diſſenſions of the times to their own profit, but quietly to wait for the victory which was ſure to come. His loſs in the Houſe of Commons was irreparable. The rival of Pitt, Fox, and Sheridan, with a force of eloquence and a power of illuſtration which were all his own, upon whom ſhould his mantle fall?

In the early part of the ſeſſion of 1821 the claims of the Roman Catholics were again brought before both Houſes of Parliament. On February the 28th, Mr. Plunkett moved in the Commons that a Committee of the whole Houſe ſhould conſider the exiſting laws as affecting the Roman Catholics, and inquire whether it would be expedient to alter or modify them. The oppoſition was led upon this occaſion by Mr. Peel, whoſe hoſtility to further conceſſion was moſt energetic; but the motion was carried by a majority of ſix, in a very full Houſe. Leave was then given to bring in a bill. This was done on the 7th of March, and the ſecond reading was fixed for the 16th of the ſame month. Among thoſe who ſpoke in favour of the meaſure were Mr. Wilberforce, Sir James Macintoſh, and Mr. Canning. Upon a diviſion there was a majority of eleven for the ſecond reading of the bill; and on the 2nd of April, on the queſtion being put for the third reading, it was carried by a majority of nineteen. Thus, then, the efforts of the Roman Catholics were crowned with partial fuccefs.

The bill was carried up to the Houfe of Lords on the 3rd of April, and was read a firft time without any debate. Meanwhile numerous petitions were prefented againft it; and it is worthy of remark, as evidencing the fpirit of aggreffion which had at this time taken poffeffion of the Roman Catholics, that they themfelves were among the number of thefe petitioners, expreffing very ftrong difapprobation at the propofed regulations which were intended as fecurities; fo quickly had the fpirit of the encyclical letter of the Irifh Bifhops, already quoted, leavened the entire community.

The fecond reading was fixed for the 16th of the fame month, when, after a long and wearifome debate, the motion was negatived by a majority of thirty-nine. Upon this occafion, as on all others, Lord Eldon fhowed himfelf an inflexible opponent of the meafure, and the Duke of York expreffed fentiments, which, as coming from the heir-prefumptive to the Crown, could not fail to exercife a depreffing influence upon the hopes of the Roman Catholic party. Lord Liverpool, alfo, continued his oppofition, declaring that there were not three lines in the bill to which he could agree.

The year 1822 was fignalifed by riotous proceedings of a more than ordinary atrocious character, and by a famine, in Ireland. This, however, did not at all prevent a renewal of the difcuffion of Roman Catholic claims, though they were not urged this year

under the comprehenfive form of Catholic Emancipation. Mr. Canning had now taken Mr. Grattan's
place as the advocate of entire conceffion ; but for the
prefent he contented himfelf with moving, on the 30th
of April, for leave to bring in a bill to relieve Roman
Catholic Peers from the difabilities impofed on them
by the Act of 30th Charles II, with regard to the
right of fitting and voting in the Houfe of Lords.
This was a fkilful way of introducing the thin end of
the wedge, and the hopes of the Roman Catholics not
a little revived when the motion was carried by a majority of five. The fecond reading of the bill took
place on the 10th of May, when Mr. Peel continued
his oppofition with unabated force and eloquence, but
without effect, for it was carried by a majority of
twelve, and no difcuffion or divifion took place on the
third reading. But, yielding as the Commons had
now become, the Peers were not infenfible of the impending danger ; the bill was thrown out in the Houfe
of Lords, on its fecond reading, by a majority of
forty-two.

Difturbances and outrages continued in Ireland
during the year 1823, and the ftate of that country
had now become a fource of ceafelefs difquiet to Englifh legiflators. It was the one problem which feemed
capable of no folution. So ferious was the afpect of
affairs, that many of the more moderate of the Roman
Catholics were for poftponing all further confideration
of their claims ; but the voices of the violent party
prevailed, as they moftly do prevail in troublous times,

and the subject was again brought before the Houfe of Commons on the 17th of April. It was upon this occafion that Sir Francis Burdett declared his intention of withdrawing from all further confideration of the queftion, ftigmatifing the annual motion as a farce. A violent difcuffion then took place, in confequence of the alleged defection of Mr. Canning from the caufe. That right honourable gentleman defended himfelf with great warmth, and the debate affumed all the appearance of a perfonal quarrel. Nothing refulted beyond this difplay of bitternefs, and the queftion was allowed to drop. Other motions were made during the feffion, varying the nature of the Roman Catholic claims, and calculated to bewilder their opponents from their very variety; but no meafure was paffed.

The ftate of Ireland had greatly improved as the fpring of 1824 advanced, and it was felt that the opportunity was favourable for renewing the confideration of Roman Catholic relief. Two bills were introduced into the Houfe of Peers by Lord Lanf-downe for abolifhing fome of the difabilities of the Englifh Roman Catholics. One bill conferred on them the elective franchife, and the other admitted them to act as magiftrates, and hold certain fubordinate offices, particularly in the revenue. Both bills, however, were rejected.

The Affociation in Ireland already referred to,* which levied money under colour of protecting Roman

---

* See page 154.

Catholic interefts, was now felt to be an infufferable evil, and to be totally oppofed to the fpirit of the Conftitution. The King's fpeech at the opening of Parliament, on the 3rd of February, 1825, referred to its illegal proceedings, and called upon the Houfes to confider the means of applying a remedy. On the 10th of the fame month Mr. Goulburn moved for leave to bring in a bill to amend the Acts relating to unlawful focieties in Ireland. The debate which followed was keen and fierce, and lafted over four nights. The motion was carried by a decifive majority of 155. Meanwhile, the Roman Catholics began to feel that they had gone too far, that the patience of the nation was well-nigh exhaufted, and that they ran the moft imminent rifk of feeing the hopes of years altogether extinguifhed. On the 17th of February, therefore, Mr. Brougham appeared in the Houfe of Commons as their advocate, and prefented a petition fetting forth their grievances in language the moft fpecious, and praying that the Houfe would adopt no meafure againft the Catholic Affociation, or againft any portion of the Catholic people of Ireland, without firft affording to the petitioners a full opportunity of vindicating their principles and conduct at the bar of the Houfe, and of being heard, if neceffary, as well by witneffes as by their counfel.

On the fame night Mr. Brougham moved that the Roman Catholic Affociation fhould be heard, by themfelves or their counfel, at the bar of the Houfe, and after a fharp debate, in the courfe of which Mr. Peel made a brilliant speech against the motion, it was re-jected by a majority of 133.

Mr. Goulburn's bill was read a second time on the 21st of February, and a third time on the 25th. It was then carried up to the House of Lords, where it was read a third time and passed on the 7th of March, and on the 9th received the Royal assent. The Act was to commence ten days after it passed, and was to continue two years in force. The Roman Catholic Association, seeing that resistance was hopeless, expired without a struggle; only, however, to revive again with increased power of vitality and mischief.

And now the thoughts of the Roman Catholic party were turned towards Mr. Canning. His popularity was unbounded, his feelings were known, and the most extravagant ideas were formed of what might be effected by his all-powerful support. On the 1st of March (so short was the repose given to the House of Commons) a petition to examine Roman Catholic claims was presented by Sir Francis Burdett, who seems to have reconsidered his determination to retire altogether * from a contest which was destined to afford a perpetual outlet for party feeling. Mr. Canning spoke in favour of it, as well as Mr. Plunkett and Mr. Brougham. The motion was stoutly opposed by Mr. Peel; but it was carried by a majority of thirteen. On the 23rd of March a bill was brought in and read the first time. A long and animated debate

---

* See page 168.

enfued, and it was ultimately read a third time and paffed on the 10th of May, by a majority of twenty-one.

Previoufly to the reading of this bill in the Houfe of Lords, a moft important event had occurred—the declaration by the Duke of York againft further conceffions to the Roman Catholics. It would be difficult to defcribe the effect of his fpeech, and the new courage it gave to the Anti-Catholic party. Thoufands of copies of it were printed and circulated throughout the country. It was the moft decifive check that the queftion had yet fuftained.

Whatever therefore the fate of the Bill might be in the Houfe of Lords, it was confidently believed that it never would receive the Royal affent. Truly enough did Lord Eldon fay, that " if the fame attention had been paid by the people to this concern between Popery and Proteftantifm, in any early ftage of the bufinefs, all had been well."

But fevere as was the check which the Roman Catholic party had now received, they determined to prefs the matter on without delay. The bill was, therefore, carried up to the Houfe of Lords on the 11th of May, and, after a very long and tedious debate, in which all previous arguments were repeated with as much relifh as if they were the moft brilliant novelties, it was thrown out by a majority of forty-eight. During the feffion of 1826 the queftion of Roman Catholic Emancipation was not formally preffed upon the notice of Parliament. The recent vote in the Houfe of Lords, coupled with the ftrong Proteftant reaction which had fet in throughout the country, muſt have been enough to convince its moſt enthuſiaſtic advocates of the utter hopeleſſneſs of obtaining any further conceſſions at preſent, either from the hopes or the fears of the nation.   Leſt Roman Catholic claims, however, ſhould be allowed altogether to fade away, they were aſſiduouſly kept before public notice by means of numerous petitions addreſſed to both Houſes of Parliament.   The Roman Catholic Aſſociation alſo ſtill held its meetings, the laws againſt it never having been put into force, and continued to pour forth an uninterrupted ſtream of ſlander and ſedition.

Early in the year 1827 the Roman Catholics were determined to improve their laſt victory in the Houſe of Commons, and, on the 5th of March, Sir Francis Burdett moved, " That this Houſe is deeply impreſſed with the neceſſity of taking into immediate conſideration the laws inflicting penalties on his Majeſty's Roman Catholic ſubjects, with the view of removing them."   After a moſt animated debate, in which all the leading ſtateſmen of the day took part, the motion was loſt by a majority of four, the numbers being, for the motion, 272 ; againſt it, 276.   Thus, then, the queſtion ſeemed as far from ſettlement as ever.

CHAPTER XI.

*Dr. Phillpotts' Firſt Letter to Mr. Canning. His Induce-
ment for entering upon the Roman Catholic Queſtion.
Securities a Part of every Roman Catholic Relief Bill.
Mr. Canning himſelf an Advocate for them. Gradual
Departure from Original Principles. The Menacing Atti-
tude of the Roman Catholics. An Anecdote in Illuſtration of
Mr. Canning's Retroceſſion. The Bill of 1825 conſidered.
Its Securities compared with thoſe of 1813. Its Inferiority
to Previous Bills. Exceſſive Deference ſhown to Roman
Catholics. Inſolence of the Iriſh Roman Catholic Aſſociation.
No Voice allowed to the Sovereign in the Appointment of
Roman Catholic Biſhops. A Board of Commiſſioners propoſed
to certify the King of the Loyalty of the Biſhops-eleſt. Com-
poſition of the Board ridiculed by Dr. Phillpotts. The
propoſed Way of dealing with Bulls and other Inſtruments
from Rome. Summary of the Bill. Mr. Canning's Conduſt
deſcribed.*

T was at this ſtage of the Roman Catholic
Queſtion, that Dr. Phillpotts publiſhed
his Letters to Mr. Canning, the firſt
being dated the 23rd of February,* and
the ſecond, the 7th of May, 1827. Among the
many remarkable publications which iſſued from the

---

* " A Letter to the Right Honourable George Canning on
the Bill of 1825, for removing the Diſqualifications of his
Majeſty's Roman Catholic Subjeſts, and on his Speech in
ſupport of the ſame, by the Reverend Henry Phillpotts,
D.D., Reſtor of Stanhope."

prefs, during this eventful controverfy, none received, or deferved, more attention than thefe brilliant letters. It will be neceffary, therefore, to examine them at fome length.

Dr. Phillpotts ftates, at the outfet, that his inducement for entering upon a difcuffion of the Roman Catholic claims was to vindicate certain doctrines of the Englifh Church from the grofs mifconception and mifreprefentations to which they had been fubjected by the unfcrupulous arts of Roman controverfialifts. The theological and political afpects of the queftion were by no means infeparable ; but the two had become fo clofely interwoven that it was hardly poffible to keep them apart. Mr. Canning, in dealing with the political fide of the cafe, had found himfelf irrefiftibly drawn into a difcuffion of the theological. This afforded to Dr. Phillpotts the opportunity of putting forth one of the moft fplendid treatifes on the bearings of the Roman Catholic queftion which ever iffued from the prefs.

He proceeds in the firft place to fhow that a fyftem of *fecurities* had formed part of every plan of Roman Catholic relief, from the time of Mr. Pitt in 1799, down to 1813, and that politicians of all fhades of opinion, including Mr. Canning himfelf, had united in thinking it undefirable to make conceffions to the Roman Catholics without afking from them in turn the obfervance of certain conditions which were deemed indifpenfable to the welfare of the State. This part of the fubject deferves efpecial attention, as it was

afterwards endeavoured to be shown that Dr. Phillpotts had, for the most unworthy motives, seen fit to
change his opinions on the question of securities. He
thus speaks upon the matter :—

"This, Sir, was the epoch of the most secure and
honoured state of our Protestant establishments since the
time when they were first assailed by the claims of the
Roman Catholics. No statesman, on either side of either
House of Parliament, ventured then to recommend the unqualified concession of those claims ; or the concession of
them at all, without requiring real, effectual, and adequate
securities. But from this our high and palmy state the
hopes of the Protestants were soon doomed rapidly to decline. The advocates of concession, though still loud and
ardent in their professions of a wish for mutual satisfaction
and security, began to adopt a looser phraseology ; instead of
precise pledges, we now had, from most of them, only vague
unmeaning generalities ; even the tone of just indignation
against the treachery or waywardness of the Irish Roman
Catholics themselves, began to give way before 'candid
allowances,' and we soon heard little else but lamentations
over 'the disappointment of a nation's hopes ;' with very
small consideration of the causes to which that disappointment was mainly to be ascribed. In short, they were but
too apparently preparing to slide into a totally different line
of sentiment and conduct."

Dr. Phillpotts next refers to Mr. Canning's aban-
donment of his earlier principles on the question of
Roman Catholic relief, and speaks of the peril of
making concessions at a time of popular excitement,
and under the pressure of intimidation. The attitude
of the Roman Catholics themselves is very happily
described as follows :—

".It fhould feem, that, in the judgment of fome of our ftatefmen, a very peculiar principle of political calculation applies to this fubject, by which the neceffity of precaution is found to be in an inverfe ratio to the magnitude of the danger. Not many years ago, a meek and imploring fuitor was not to be admitted into the outer court of the temple, without firft demanding from him ample fecurities for his good bearing; but, now, every barrier may be fafely broken down—nay, every obftruction and inconvenience muft be carefully fwept away, in order that the armed ruffian, with defiance on his front, and menace on his tongue, may find a free and unencumbered paffage to the very fanctuary of our laws and our religion."

Mr. Canning's retroceffion, in prefence of the menaces of the Irifh Roman Catholic party, headed by O'Connell, is humoroufly illuftrated by the following ftory:—A celebrated wit, the beft fcholar of his day both at Eton and Oxford—a firft-rate fpeaker, too, in Parliament, whofe only fault was a little over-anxiety, in feafon and out of feafon, to get the laughers on his fide—happened one day, in driving along a narrow road, to meet a heavy-loaded waggon. What was to be done? he wifhed to be accommodating, but for both to proceed was impoffible: afferting, therefore, the privilege of his ariftocratic vehicle, he peremptorily ordered the farmer to get off the road. " Off the road! not for thee nor any man in England; —and if thou doft not take that gimcrack of thine out of my way directly, I'll do—what I fhould be very forry to be obliged to do." Our hero, though by no means deficient in manhood, yet wifely confidering that no honour could be gained in fuch an encounter,

foon determined to take the difcreeter part. Therefore, fettling the matter of dignity as he could, with
the beft grace poffible, and with admirable management of his reins, he contrived to back out of the
difficulty, and at length lodged himfelf and his cur-
ricle on a piece of fmooth turf, at a confiderable diftance in the rear. " And now, my friend," faid he,
" fince I have done this purely for your accommodation, be fo good as to tell me what you meant by
faying that if I did not get out of your way, you'd do
what you would be very forry to be obliged to do ?"
" Why, pleafe your honour," fays the honeft York-
fhireman, pulling off his hat, and making his loweft
reverence, " if you had not backed, *I muft.*"

The bill of 1825, which Dr. Phillpotts defignates
as an infult to the common-fenfe of the country, next
comes under confideration ; and he compares the fecurities with which the conceffions were to be accompanied with thofe of the bill of 1813; for thefe, as
he truly fays, are the only fubjects worthy of inquiry,
the conceffions in both bills being nearly the fame.
Thefe fecurities were two-fold ; a new oath, and a
Royal Commiffion charged with certain duties touching,
firft, the appointment of Roman Catholic bifhops and
deans; and fecondly, the reception of bulls and other
inftruments from Rome.

The fummary way in which the firft of thefe is
difpofed of is moft thoroughly characteriftic of Dr.
Phillpotts, and fhows that his wit was as ready as his
perception was keen. He fays :—

N

"It contains nothing which has not been already prefcribed by the Irifh Act of the 13th and 14th of George III,
or by that of the 33rd of the fame king. So far, therefore,
we gain nothing. I beg pardon ; we gain the exchange of
and for *or* in two of its claufes. Firft, as the law now
ftands, the Irifh Roman Catholic ' renounces, rejects, and
abjures ' the opinion that ' princes excommunicated may be
depofed *and* murdered.' Your new fecurity-oath would have
made him renounce, etcetera the opinion, that princes excommunicated ' may be depofed *or* murdered ;' and for
the microfcopic vigilance which enabled you and your fellow-
labourers in this good caufe to fuggeft fuch an amendment
in the exifting law, I truft you will receive your due meed
of praife. The matter is really more important than the
Proteftant reader may at firft fufpect ; for the perfons whofe
loyalty requires to be fecured by thefe provifions are prodi-
gioufly nice and accurate in eftimating the exact quantum
of obligation which they undertake. ' Is it fo nominated in
the bond ?' is their conftant inquiry. ' If not,—

> " be't but fo much
> As makes it light or heavy in the fubftance,
> On the divifion of one-twentieth part
> Of one poor fcruple,"

they will have nothing to do with it.' "

He then proceeds to cite a marvellous inftance of
Roman Catholic cafuiftry which may, perhaps, provoke
a fmile, but which alfo fhows that he was not infenfible to the importance of the apparently trifling
change of *and* into *or*.

After pointing out the omiffions of the new fecurity-oath, and infifting that the prefent attempt at
legiflation was inferior, in many important particulars,

to preceding ones, Dr. Phillpotts inquires for the caufe of this retroceffion, and explains it on the affumption that the whole proceeding was regulated according to the views and wifhes of the Roman Catholics themfelves :—

"Of the very perfons againft whofe apprehended hoftility new checks and fafe-guards were to be devifed. Mr. O'Connell wrote to his Dublin friends that fuch was the liberal wifh for conciliation in England that he himfelf was employed to draw the Bill! And though the dignity of our fenators took fire at the intimation, the internal evidence proves, moft conclufively, either that Mr. O'Connell faid what was literally correct, or at leaft that he was allowed 'an effectual negative' on your deliberations. I fufpect that Dr. Doyle was alfo of the party; for the interefts of his order were too amply and warily provided for, to have been altogether the work of laymen however liberal. In fhort, nothing feems to have been infifted upon which the Roman Catholics could find any difficulty in yielding; if any objection on their part arofe, the point itfelf was abandoned; and this whole procefs of arranging the terms of the oath was no better than allowing you to march out with the honours of war, and fparing you the fhame of a furrender at difcretion."

That this ftatement is not overdrawn will be acknowledged by every one who has been at the pains to read the tranfactions of the Roman Catholic Affociation in Ireland; the boaftfulnefs of its language, and the arrogance of its claims might well juftify the fears of every well-wifher of the State. The marvel is that minifters fhould have toyed with a danger which called for an immediate exercife of repreffive

energy, and which, by being left unchecked, was deſtined, only two years later, to react upon the conſtitution with deſtructive power.   If no other merit belonged to this letter of Dr. Phillpotts, it would have
at leaſt this claim on the gratitude of Engliſhmen, that
it warned them of the danger towards which they
were drifting.

Having ſhown the inſufficiency of the oath, he
next goes on to examine the ſecond ſecurity.   The
bill proceeds to declare " that regulations touching
the appointment of Biſhops and Deans of the Roman
Catholic Church in Ireland are deemed neceſſary ;"
and truly enough he ſays, when the portentous powers
poſſeſſed, and exerciſed, by theſe functionaries, in the
preſent ſtate of that unhappy country, are borne in mind
—ſtill more when it is recollected who and of what character are ſome of the perſonages who now fill the ſtation
of biſhops there, that one of them, under the ſignature
of I. K. L.,* is by far the moſt daring and ſeditious
libeller of the day—that another ſcruples not (if the
public papers do not belie him) to addreſs an aſſembly
of thouſands of the moſt ignorant of his countrymen
in terms hardly ſhort of excitement to immediate in-
ſurrection, it will readily be conceded, that " regulations touching the appointment of them " are indeed
" *neceſſary.*"

The bill of 1813 gave the Sovereign the power of
ſignifying his approbation or diſapprobation of the

---

* James Kildare and Leighlin (Dr. Doyle).

appointment of Roman ecclesiastics in Ireland, but this important provision was omitted in the bill of 1825.

" Our Sovereign was not to be permitted to exercise any power whatever," says Dr. Phillpotts, " no, nor to possess the smallest influence, over this Irish hierarchy, though it is notorious that the schismatical Emperor of Russia, and the heretical King of Prussia, exercise in the appointment of the Roman Catholic bishops of their dominions a power far exceeding the utmost ever proposed to be given to His Majesty, and have each of them an accredited agent at Rome chiefly for the exercise of it."

It is worthy of remark that Pius VII, in 1816, had not thought it beneath the dignity of the Papacy to allow a veto to the British Sovereign, on the appointment of bishops in Ireland. That, however, which was granted in days of weakness may, on the Roman theory, be revoked in days of power ; and it was now proposed that a Board of Commissioners should be created, whose duty should be " to certify to His Majesty the appointment of any Bishop or Dean, to be hereafter appointed in the said Roman Catholic Church in Ireland." Dr. Phillpotts rightly says, " that, so far from this being a *security*, it was in reality a new and very important concession, being, in fact, nothing else than giving them what the law has seen fit to withhold—the public and formal recognition of their rank and character of bishops."

The structure of this Board of Commissioners next occupies the attention of Dr. Phillpotts. The description of it is conceived in his happiest vein :—

" But of whom was the Board to confift ? *Solely* of the Roman Catholic Bifhops themfelves. Such men as thofe to whofe proceedings I have juft now adverted are to vouch for the loyalty of their future colleagues ! Sir, I will not abufe the patience of my readers by commenting on fuch a provifion. I will only entreat you to follow up your own principle, and recommend to your brother Secretary of State, Mr. Peel, that in his amendment of the criminal law he give us the benefit of this new fecurity for our lives and properties, and provide that in future every perfon charged with felony fhall be tried by a jury taken out of Newgate."

Dr. Phillpotts next comments on the remaining fecurity—the power given to the board, confifting of Roman Catholic bifhops, of infpecting and reporting upon bulls and other inftruments from Rome ; and fhows that the real effect of this would be another great conceffion. Independently of the extreme improbability of any bull from Rome appearing to them to be in any way injurious to the fafety or tranquillity of the United Kingdom, or to the Proteftant Eftablifhment in Church or State, it would give to the bifhops of the Roman Catholic Church in Ireland a legalized right to communicate, as they pleafed, with the Pope, and to circulate, as they pleafed, whatever mandates he might think fit, or be induced to iffue. He then fums up the merits of the propofed meafure as follows :—

" And now, Sir, having toiled through the bill, permit me to recapitulate the fair and full amount of the new ' fecurities' therein devifed. Two of the three provifions which you are pleafed to dignify by that name are found, in truth, to be new and large conceffions to the Roman Catholics ;

the other, the fole remaining fruit of feven-and-twenty years of hard labour, given fucceffively by fome of the acuteft and moft powerful intellects which England and Ireland have ever produced, to the momentous problem of ' combining Catholic freedom with Proteftant fecurity,' is the amendment of two claufes of the Irifh oath of 1793, by changing therein the conjunction *and* into *or*.

" Really, Sir, if the dignity of your ftation and character did not forbid the fuppofition, I fhould imagine that you had no other purpofe in recommending fuch provifions than to laugh at the whole proceeding. But no : it comes from you in very fober earneft ; and the moft charitable way of view-ing the whole matter is, to believe that you have fo tied and hampered yourfelf with this unhappy queftion, that you muft fee it difpofed of at any hazard. You dare not fcrutinize the particular meafure devifed for the purpofe, whether by yourfelf or others. You are afraid of looking into its details, left they fhould be found too abfurd, or too mifchievous, for even the powers of your eloquence to make them decently producible to an affembly of educated Englifhmen. You, therefore, difpofe of the whole of them in a lump ; and the majority of the Houfe, equally tired of the queftion, and equally committed upon it, with yourfelf, cheers you while you fay that ' you will not now enter into the queftion of fecurities, further than obferving that *you do not think we can have any better than thofe propofed.*' "

CHAPTER XII.

Dr. Phillpotts' First Letter to Mr. Canning continued. The General Character of Mr. Canning's Speech in support of the Roman Catholic Relief Bill of 1825. The Oath against Transubstantiation assailed. The Arguments of those who desired its Repeal. Their Fallacy exposed. The True Statement of the Case. Answer of Dr. Phillpotts to Mr. Canning's Remarks on Transubstantiation. Advantage of selecting that Doctrine as a Test. Treatment to which Oaths of Allegiance to Temporal Sovereigns are obnoxious at the hands of Roman Catholics. The Oath of 3 James I. The Gunpowder Treason not the only Cause of it. Objections against the Athanasian Creed. Mr. Canning's Use of it admirably illustrated by Dr. Phillpotts. Object of the Creed explained. Doctrines of Roman Catholics render them unfit to legislate for Established Church. Fallacy of supposing that Roman Catholic Laymen, if admitted into Parliament, would not busy themselves with Ecclesiastical Questions. Doctrine of Absolution enforced. The Roman Catholic Doctrine of the Merit of Good Works. How used by Mr. Canning. Calvinists and Roman Catholics contrasted. The Pope's Supremacy not merely a Spiritual Question. Specious Arguments of Roman Catholics. Different Foundations of Papal Authority in different Countries. The Council of Florence. Doctrine of Papal Supremacy not likely to receive much Favour in England. Danger of its Reception in Ireland. The Bulls "Unam sanctam" and "Unigenitus." The Peril of admitting to a Share in the Legislature those who hold the Doctrine. The Pope determines the Point at which the Allegiance of Subjects to their Sovereign ceases. The Fourth Lateran Council on the Deposition of Kings. Dr. Phillpotts fully justified in his Remarks upon the Pope's Supremacy.

D R. PHILLPOTTS then proceeds to examine the chief points in Mr. Canning's speech in support of the Roman Catholic Relief Bill of 1825, the merits of which he had just submitted to so severe a scrutiny.

The general character of it is thus defcribed by him :—

"And here, Sir, I cannot but exprefs my aftonifhment that fuch a fpeech fhould ever have iffued from your lips. That there are in it, as there muft always be in every con-fiderable effort of yours, proofs of uncommon talent, fplendid imagery, felicitous expreffion, I need not fay. But the total abfence of everything like reafoning, the careful avoidance of all grappling with the real difficulties of your fubject, the fabrication of foolifh objections for the mere purpofe of knocking them down ; above all, the tone of exaggeration, of forced paffion, of idle menace, nay, of palpable contradic-tion which mainly diftinguifh it, form fuch a contraft to your happier, I fhould fay your ordinary, ftyle, as to give it the air of traveftie, rather than of a genuine production of your rare genius. I am not ignorant that it was character-ized by one of the ableft of your hearers as ' unanfwerable ;' but in fober truth I can hardly imagine a more amufing ex-hibition than an anfwer to it from yourfelf. How would the unhappy wight who had ventured in your hearing to utter fuch an harangue in oppofition to you have been made to wince, and writhe, and groan, under the fting of your far-caftic tongue ! You would have filenced him for the re-mainder of the feffion."

The chief efforts of the fupporters of the bill were directed againft the application of a religious teft as a qualification for the enjoyment of political privileges. The oath againft Tranfubftantiation, therefore, had to meet the firft affault. Why, it was argued, fhould religion be made a crime, and perjury a qualification for office ? The treatment of the Roman Catholics was contrary to the principles of all Government, fince no Government has a right to eftablifh an inquifition

into the thoughts of men, nor to puniſh any one purely
for religion. As to the qualifying oath, it was ſaid
that a Diſſenter of any kind, or even a Deiſt or Atheiſt,
might take it, while the Roman Catholics alone were
excepted. Why, then, ſhould the doctrine of Tranſubſtantiation be ſelected as a particular ſubject for
denunciation and abhorrence ? A man might believe
in Jupiter or Oſiris, in all the hoſt of heaven, and all
the creeping things in the earth, and yet enjoy the
honours and emoluments of thoſe offices from which
the Roman Catholic was excluded. Was this right—
was it reaſonable ? Should a man be puniſhed for
believing too much ? Should there be any other teſt
than to allow every man to follow his own form of
religion, without reſtriction and limitation, ſo long as
he continued to live a peaceable member of the ſtate ?

Such was a plauſible way of ſtating the caſe ; and,
tranſparent as is its fallacy, it found much favour,
even with people who ought to have been able to diſ-
tinguiſh ſophiſtry from reaſon. It was all very well
to aſk, Was the Roman Catholic likely to be a worſe
legiſlator than the Deiſt ?—and, if not, to what was
his diſqualification to be traced ? The anſwer was
eaſy. The Roman Catholic was not diſqualified *becauſe*
he held certain doctrines, but becauſe the Church which
taught theſe doctrines committed him to a political
combination inimical to the State, and which was liable
to make him at any moment the tool of a foreign and
hoſtile power. The Roman Catholic, then, was excluded from office, not becauſe his religion was con-

fidered as his crime, but becaufe it was looked upon
as evidence of his poffible, and not improbable, difloyalty. Lamentable, therefore, as it muft always be to
offer a religious teft, and, more particularly, one involving the deepeft myftery of religion, to candidates for
office under Government, fuch a teft had been thought
to be neceffary ; and, if neceffary, it would be hard to
find one more fearching in effect than the denial of
Tranfubftantiation,—a doctrine interwoven with the entire fyftem of the Roman Church. A fubftitution for
this oath, fuggefted by Dr. Phillpotts, and which puts
the queftion upon its proper bafis, occurs further on.
Meanwhile, the danger of thinking lightly of this oath,
as Mr. Canning and his adherents fought to do, or of
abolifhing it without receiving in return ample fecurities for the loyalty of Roman Catholics, is forcibly fet
forth by Dr. Phillpotts.

In the courfe of his fpeech, Mr. Canning remarked
that, while a man was excluded from Parliament for
his belief in Tranfubftantiation, one who believed in
Confubftantiation enjoyed every privilege of the Conftitution. Without afferting that there was no difference between the two opinions, he added, that " the
man who could make it a ground of exclufion from
political power muft have a minute perception of the
niceties of ratiocination, for which he might be envied
as a logician, but which was wholly ufelefs for the
purpofes of common life."

Dr. Phillpotts fhows the value of this ftatement by
putting a parallel cafe :—

"In order to protect the Bank of England from forgery, it is highly penal 'for any one to have in his poffeffion a frame for making paper with waved lines.' Imagine, then, fome fagacious country gentleman, frefh from Burn, to come down to the Houfe, and denounce, with becoming felf-complacency, the monftrous injuftice, that while ftraight-lined paper may be made with impunity, any honeft man who happens to have a curved-line frame in his houfe is liable to be fent to Botany Bay. 'I do not deny,' fays he, 'that there is a difference between ftraight and waved lines; but the man who thinks that difference fo great that the poffeffor of the waved-line frame is unfit to abide in the fame hemifphere with him of the ftraight, has an acutenefs of fenfibility to lineal rectitude which, however it may demand our admiration, is utterly unfit for ordinary life.'"

But there was one advantage in felecting Tranfubftantiation as a teft—it was a doctrine which might not be diffembled. While Roman Catholics, therefore, might find authorities to fupport them in practifing mental refervation with reference to any oath, even if it were that of allegiance or fupremacy to the King, the doctrine of Tranfubftantiation was one upon which it was not lawful to equivocate or diffemble. So far, then, the teft was adopted with great fagacity. Dr. Phillpotts gives one or two examples of the fort of management to which oaths of allegiance to temporal fovereigns (on Roman Catholic principles) are obnoxious:—

"In the firft place, any one who holds the fupreme power of the Pope, even in temporal matters, may fafely fwear that he has 'no temporal or civil power, direct or indirect, within this realm,' becaufe his power, though it operates in temporal matters, is not temporal, but fpiritual. Again, by any general, though negative declaration, againft any authority in general to be in the Pope, is only intended to deny his having an *ordinary* authority; it does not extend to his extraordinary, cafual, celeftial, divine authority, on great and unufual contingencies. Once more, there is a very important diftinction between the *fpecificative* and *re-duplicative* fenfe. This will be beft explained by an example. In Father Walfh's time, the Irifh clergy were willing to fubfcribe to this propofition:—'It is our doctrine, that we fubjects owe fo natural and juft obedience to our King, that no power, under any pretext foever, can ever difpenfe with or free us of the fame.' Here, the re-duplicative fenfe applies to '*we fubjects*,' that is, *while* we are fubjects—which we fhall not be when the Pope, by a judicial procefs, or bull, fhall denounce the King excommunicated and deprived of the crown. The re-duplicative fenfe applies alfo to 'our King,' that is, *while* he is our King, &c. Such were the principles of the congregation of Irifh clergy in 1666, according to this honeft Francifcan. Nor would they be moved from them by the precepts of the Apoftles commanding obedience to the civil powers, even under the reigns of the moft tyrannical emperors. 'They fay, with Bellarmine,' (thefe are Walfh's words) '*the Apoftles*, with the Fathers and other primitive Chriftians, *diffembled on this point, becaufe they had not ftrength enough of men and arms to oppofe.*' In what degree the living generation of Irifh priefts may have departed from thefe principles of their predeceffors, is more than I can prefume to fay. If charity teaches us to hope the beft, it does not forbid us to take all reafonable precaution againft the worft.''

Dr. Phillpotts next proceeds to confider the Oath for Roman Catholics prefcribed by 3 James I, c. 4. s. 15,* which had been defcribed by Mr. Canning as a "taunt" againft their religion. So far from this

---

* See Appendix C.

being the cafe, he fhows, moft conclufively, that its
object was not to affix a brand on any loyal fubject,
but to protect the State againft the machinations of
thofe who were agents of foreign powers. After ftating that the Gunpowder Treafon was the proximate
caufe of this oath being impofed, he alleges that, though
the proximate, it was very far from being the only,
caufe.

"That Treafon itfelf was, in truth, a natural fruit of the
doctrines then almoft univerfally taught in the Church of
Rome. In particular, as you need not to be informed,
feminaries were founded and endowed at Rheims, at Douay,
at Rome itfelf, for the education of Englifh Priefts; whofe
firft duty it was to poifon the minds of their people againft
the heretical government under which they lived. The
right of deftroying heretics was (I wifh I could fay that it
no longer is) a part of the Canon Law; that right had been
recently exercifed againft the facred perfons of fovereign
princes. The fame Canon Law (as we have already feen)
held, and ftill holds, it a venial offence to put to death an
excommunicated perfon, whatever be his ftation, provided
that *it be done from zeal for religion.*

"Thefe, and fuch as thefe, were the reafons for impofing
this oath, which you have thought fit to defcribe as an idle
taunt."

The next topic in Dr. Phillpotts' letter deferves fpecial
attention, if only for the mafterly way in which he
deals with objections which are raifed againft the Athanafian Creed on the fcore of its illiberality.* Generation after generation are thefe objections revived, and

---

* See "Letter to Lord Grey on the Teft Act," page 38.

succeffive attempts at legiflation (abortive up to the prefent time, through God's mercy) teftify to the reftleffnefs with which man's unchaftened fpirit fubmits to anything like dogmatic enunciation of truth. When fpeaking of the doctrine of exclufive falvation, as held by Roman Catholics, Mr. Canning had brought forward the Athanafian Creed, which expreffly declares "that they who differ from it cannot be faved,"* as an argument why Roman Catholics fhould not be "excluded from the enjoyment of their civil rights, on the ground of believing the doctrine of exclufion."

The attempted parallelifm affords to Dr. Phillpotts the opportunity of dealing upon his adverfary fome terrible blows.

"Sir, the laws of the old Athenian legiflator Draco were faid to be written in blood : for he annexed the penalty of death to every offence whatever. Suppofe, now, that a citizen of Megara had obferved to a friend at Athens, on the cruelty of this fanguinary code—'This is a dreadful fyftem of yours, to put a man to death for ftealing a few figs, or breaking into his neighbour's olive ground.' 'Why, my dear friend,' anfwers the Athenian, 'how can you talk fo abfurdly ? Did not you yourfelf hang a man laft week for murder ?' This, Sir, affords but a very faint illuftration of the wifdom of putting our ufe of the Athanafian Creed on a par with the tyrannical and intolerant principles of the Church of Rome. That Church, among a thoufand fimilar extravagancies, fentences a man to the lofs of all hope of Chriftian falvation who fays that it is contrary to the inftitution of Chrift *to mix water with wine* at the holy Communion : the Church of England, in the Athanafian Creed,

---

* Mr. Canning's Speech.

pronounces the same of one who impugns the fundamental truths of Christianity; and you are pleased to say, that this deprives us of all right to find fault with the exclusive spirit of Rome.

" As to the Athanasian Creed being ' a human *exposition* of the great mysteries of Christianity,' you must forgive my telling you that, if you had taken the trouble of acquainting yourself with the nature of that formulary, you would not have thought it a fit subject of sneer or banter. The Athanasian Creed is not an *exposition* of any mysteries ; it does not aim at anything so absurd. But it *states* the fundamental doctrines of the Gospel, and, in respect to the doctrine of the Trinity, accompanies the statement with certain distinctions, which were rendered necessary by the attempts of heretics to corrupt the doctrine itself by their own daring innovations. It also accompanies its statement with denouncing the awful sentence on unbelievers which our Lord Himself denounced, when He gave to His Apostles the solemn charge ' to go and preach the Gospel to every creature.' ' He that believeth not shall be damned.'

" You will perceive, therefore, that the main question respecting the Athanasian Creed is, first, whether its doctrines be true ; secondly, whether they be fundamental. The Church of England holds them to be both true and fundamental, and therefore scruples not to receive and use the Creed, notwithstanding the strong terms in which the danger of unbelief is there set forth."

The real complaint against the Church of Rome Dr. Phillpotts declares to be, not that it excludes from salvation those who impugn doctrines which it thinks fundamental, but that it teaches its members to regard every other Church but its own as necessarily leading to perdition. Now, as one of the objects of Parliament is " to consult for the safety and defence of the

Church of England,"* it is manifeftly inconfiftent with
the fpirit of the Conftitution that members of the
Roman communion fhould be entrufted with the legiflative powers of the State, when thofe powers muft
neceffarily be exercifed, if their own principles are carried out, to the detriment of the National Church.

"This, Sir," fays Dr. Phillpotts, "is the argument for ex-
cluding Roman Catholics from Parliament, which we found
on their doctrine of exclufive falvation; and you will, I am
fure, perceive that it remains completely untouched by your
pleafant commentary on the Athanafian Creed."

But while it was felt that the doctrines of the
Roman Church, if acted upon, would make it unfafe
that members of that communion fhould be entrufted
with a voice in the legiflature of the country, yet it was
argued that thofe Roman Catholic laymen who might
obtain a feat in Parliament would not be likely to
trouble themfelves with queftions relating to the National Church. Dr. Phillpotts forcibly enough remarks :—

"Sir, I certainly will not infult the members of a different
communion by fpeaking or thinking fo ill of them as to fuppofe that if they hold the doctrine of their Church in this
particular, it will be perfectly inoperative. On the contrary,
thofe who really hold it muft feel every inducement and
temptation to act upon it; their fpiritual inftructors will be
ready enough to apprife them of this duty, and their own
paffions will make them very willing to acquire the merit of
obeying it. In a Church which keeps fo accurate a ledger
of each individual's merits and demerits, and allows fo large

---

* Writ of Summons.

a premium on acts of obedience to itself, we may be quite fure that there will be no want of inclination to comply with fo eafy a demand. It may be faid, however, that there are many profeffed members of the Church of Rome, who do not hold this doctrine, whatever their Church may tell them. I really believe that there is much truth in this obfervation, and if you could afcertain correctly who thefe are, I for one fhould not be afraid of feeing fuch men in Parliament. But in the meanwhile it is quite idle to fpeculate on the poffible conduct of thefe mere *entes rationis*."

The doctrine of Abfolution next engages Dr. Phill-potts' attention. Mr. Canning, for the purpofe of foftening down the Roman practice and its confe-quences, had ftated that in the abftract the doctrine was " *abfurd*."

" I truft, Sir," fays Dr. Phillpotts, " that you meant to confine your cenfure to the extravagant doctrine of the Church of Rome ; not to extend it (as your words feem to imply) to abfolution generally : for if the latter were intended, I am bound to tell you, that, in the plenitude of your parliamentary privilege, you have prefumed to vifit with your ban one of the moft folemn acts and declarations of our bleffed Lord Himfelf. After His refurrection from the dead, when ' all power had been given to Him in heaven and in earth,' He conferred on His apoftles and, in them, on their fucceffors to the end of time, the power of abfolution, foberly and foundly underftood."

The next topic in the letter relates to the " over-weening value" which, as Mr. Canning affirmed, Ro-man Catholics attach to the merits of good works.

" I will boldly venture to affert," fays Dr. Phillpotts, " and to appeal to your own better recollection for the truth of the affertion, that you never yet met with man, woman, or child, quite fo filly as to advance this objection, which you are pleafed to honour with a moft grave, laboured, hiftorical, theological, and (need I add) triumphant reply. But how, it may be afked, can fo portentous an hallucination have come over you? I will here hazard a conjecture. It is not improbable that in the courfe of your morning's reading, preparatory to a debate which was to crown your other high diftinctions with the honours of a dilettanti degree in divinity, you happened to find that one of the charges fometimes brought againft the Church of Rome was the exceffive value afcribed by it to the works of man. This theological objection you haftily miftook for a political one. And how was it to be treated? A man of ordinary genius would have been content to fay, that however erroneous the tenet might be, its obvious tendency is to render thofe who hold it good and ufeful fubjects ; that it is the height of injuftice, therefore, to make it, in any degree, a plea for abridging their political privileges. But this was very far from fatisfying your afpirations. You aimed at higher glory than a dull matter-of-fact argument, however convincing, could beftow. You were pleafed, therefore, to contraft the alleged error of the Church of Rome with what you, I doubt not, ferioufly believe to be a notion of the modern Calvinifts. ' Would it not,' you fay, ' be more dangerous to a ftate to make *good works nothing* and faith everything? I prefer the man who infifts on the neceffity of good works as part of his religious creed, to the man *who confiders himfelf controlled in all his actions by an inexorable fate.'* "

Mr. Canning then contrafts the Calvinifts of Charles the Firft's time with the Roman Catholics of his own, demanding who were they who brought the monarch to the block? and who ftripped epifcopacy of all its fpiritual authority and temporal poffeffions? The anfwer to thefe queftions is, of courfe, not the Papifts —

who, in Mr. Canning's eſtimation, are a lamblike, un-
offending ſet of men,—but the Calviniſts, who were
moſt violently oppoſed to them.

Dr. Phillpotts retorts :—

" Your argument now ſtands thus ; becauſe great miſchief
was inflicted on our Church and nation by one ſet of mad-
men two hundred years ago, therefore it is unjuſt or fooliſh,
or both, to guard againſt the avowed hoſtility of another
claſs of enemies in our own days ; becauſe the Dutch fleet
burned Chatham in the ſeventeenth century, therefore none
of our dockyards ought to be protected againſt a French fleet
in the nineteenth.

" I am afraid, Sir, we gain but little by this improvement
of the argument. Leaving, therefore, this very favourite
piece of eloquence (for ſo the cheers which attended it
prove it to have been) to the ſatisfaction of yourſelf and
the admiration of your hearers ; I will remind you of a real
political objection againſt the Roman Catholics, founded on
the value they attach to good works, but then it is to the
good works of others, not their own—and conſequently it
has no tendency to improve either their loyalty or their
morals. On the merit of the ſupernumerary ſatisfactions of
departed ſaints, the doctrine of indulgences—remiſſion, that
is, of the pains of purgatory—has been built. Theſe indulgences have often been employed in Ireland as means to
ſtimulate and reward the diſloyalty of the people to their
heretical Sovereigns."

Dr. Phillpotts next proceeds to examine the doctrine
of the Pope's ſupremacy. And this muſt not be
thought to be merely a *ſpiritual* queſtion, ſurrounded
with entanglements which the ſubtleſt theologians have
hitherto been unable to unravel. It has its *political*
bearings alſo, and thoſe of ſuch magnitude and impor-

tance, that no ſtateſman can ſafely overlook them.
On behalf of the Roman Catholics it was urged that
they acknowledged all the principles of the Conſtitution, and lived as peaceful ſubjeƈts, in obedience to
the laws. How could they, then, attribute to the
Pope any abſolute power, or any temporal authority,
as interfering with the conſtitution and laws? The
only ſupremacy which they acknowledged in the Pope
was *purely ſpiritual.* The allegiance which they paid
to the Holy Father had not hindered them from ſhed-
ding their blood, at their country's call, upon every
battle-field of Europe; and were they ſtill to be
charged with diſaffeƈtion, and ſuſpeƈted of revolt?

Now, if all this had been ſtriƈtly true, the Roman
Catholic would have had much indeed to complain of.
But argue as ſtateſmen might, they could not gainſay
the faƈt that the authority claimed by the Pope, when
carried to its legitimate reſults, ended in *temporal*
dominion, none the leſs galling becauſe it happened
to be *eccleſiaſtical.* It is to this point that Dr. Phillpotts addreſſes himſelf with ſingular clearneſs and
vigour.

Mr. Canning had declared that he ſaw no valid
objeƈtion in the argument drawn from the belief in the
ſpiritual ſupremacy of the Pope. In his judgment
the queſtion was not whether this doƈtrine was aƈted
upon by Roman Catholics, but whether it was aƈted
upon in ſuch a way as to make them dangerous to the
State.

Dr. Phillpotts proceeds, in the firſt place, to ſhow

that different foundations of Papal authority exift in different countries. His obfervations on this point are very valuable.

"The French look to the Councils of Conftance, Pifa, and Bafil, not only as truly œcumenical, but as having fo fixed the fuperiority of Councils over the Pope, and in other refpects fo limited his power, that not even the decrees of fubfequent Councils, much lefs the conftitutions of Popes themfelves, can work any material change in the principles there eftablifhed. But befides this general fecurity they procured for themfelves what was called ' the pragmatic fanction,' which recognized on the part of Rome a very large meafure of independence in the Church of France, and though this pragmatic fanction was afterwards difplaced by a lefs favourable inftrument,—the concordat between Francis I. and Leo X,—ftill the refult has been the eftablifhment of fo ftrong a barrier againft the worft ufurpations of Rome, that the liberties of the Gallican Church have formed a proud exception to the general ftate of fpiritual bondage, in which other countries of that communion have been all, more or lefs, enthralled. For by the reft, the acts of the councils, which I have mentioned above (excepting the decrees of Conftance againft heretics) were all rejected ; and in their place the decrees of the Council of Florence (which was held by Eugenius IV. at the fame time with the Council of Bafil, and in exprefs oppofition to it) were univerfally received. Now, the Fathers of Florence afcribed fo large and fweeping an authority to the Pope, that the French have not only uniformly refufed to recognize this council as valid, but when at Trent there was an attempt to obtain the re-enactment of the Florentine Decree, the Cardinal of Lorraine, and the other French prelates, pofitively declared, that they would quit the council, and proteft againft its decrees, unlefs the meafure were abandoned."

Dr. Phillpotts then quotes the Decree of the Council
of Florence * as the recognized ftandard of orthodoxy
on the doctrine of the Pope's fupremacy.

"' We define, that the Holy Apoftolic See, and the Roman
Pontiff, have a primacy over the whole world, and that
the Roman Pontiff himfelf is the fucceffor of S. Peter,
the chief of the Apoftles, and true Vicar (or reprefentative,
τοποτηρήτης) of Chrift, and that he is head of the whole
Church, and the Father and Teacher of all Chriftians; and
that to him in S. Peter was delegated, by our Lord Jefus
Chrift, full power to *feed, rule, and govern* the univerfal
Church; as alfo is contained in the Acts of General Councils,
and in the holy canons.'"

Dr. Phillpotts then proceeds :—

" On the authority of this decree, it is not wonderful that
the moft inordinate extent of power has often been claimed
by the Popes, and too often conceded to them. It is admitted by thofe who are moft eager to foften the harfher
features of the papal fyftem, by Mr. C. Butler in particular,
that the ultramontane doctrine, as it is called, the affertion
of the Pope's right to fupreme power, whether direct or indirect, in all the temporal concerns of ftates, the power of
depofing fovereigns, of interfering with the rights and duties
of fubjects, may here find apparent fupport. That doctrine
is not contradicted by any ecclefiaftical authority, it is
favoured at Rome,—and, everywhere elfe, it is tolerated by
thofe who do not affent to it. We may be aftonifhed at this;
we may think it impoffible for any, who diffent from a
doctrine fo pregnant with crime and mifchief of the moft

* The Council of Florence was firft affembled at Ferrara
by Eugenius IV, who attempted to tranflate the Council of
Bafle thither in 1437. Two years later the Council of
Ferrara was tranflated to Florence.

gigantic kind, to efteem it worthy of toleration and endurance.   But fo it is; individuals may difclaim the doctrine
for themfelves ; but, as we have already feen, they are not
permitted to condemn it as contrary to religion.''

That the doctrine of the Papal fupremacy, when
carried to its extravagant refults, would not be likely to
gain much favour in England is admitted by Dr.
Phillpotts; but he maintains that the cafe is different in
reference to Ireland, where the moft audacious claims
of the Pope are acknowledged and refpected.   As a
proof of this he inftances the Bull *Unam fanctam*, included in the clafs-book at Maynooth, which teaches
that it is altogether a point neceffary to falvation for
every creature to be fubject to the Roman Pontiff.
One would imagine that the profanity of this affumption would caufe it at once to be rejected by all who
profefs refpect for the principles of religion ; but fo far
from this—

" It is the doctrine," fays Dr. Phillpotts, " now taught to
the ftudents who are training in the College at Maynooth for
the miniftry in Ireland, and thofe among them who fhall follow
their own common fenfe, (which, be it remembered, they
are in this particular freely permitted to do,) and fhall underftand the Bull of Boniface according to the plain meaning of
the words, and the confeffed intention of the writer, will
here find a complete and infallible authority for preaching
the fupreme power of the Church in temporals in its fulleft
extent."

The Bull *Unigenitus,* and the canonization of Pius V,
for depofing Queen Elizabeth are next referred to, for
the purpofe of fhowing that the Papal fupremacy is no
mere empty claim.

" Sir, I muſt think," ſays Dr. Phillpotts, "that a claim to ſupremacy ſuch as this, acknowledged and acted upon by all the eccleſiaſtics in communion with Rome—entering into, and directing, their devotions—hallowed by aſſociation with all that is moſt ſacred in their religion,—is not a matter to be treated with contempt."

He then proceeds to ſhow the danger likely to ariſe out of the doctrine of the Pope's ſupremacy, from a conſideration of the fact that the power of determining the preciſe point at which the allegiance of ſubjects towards their ſovereign terminates reſts with him alone.

" Now, Sir, can any Government be ſafe if its ſubjects are thus at liberty to apply to any authority, foreign or domeſtic, to aſcertain whether and when their duty of allegiance has ceaſed ? Certainly the danger is not leſſened, but greatly increaſed, by that authority being eccleſiaſtical, for a ſacredneſs is thus thrown about it, which makes its reſponſes infinitely more venerable and convincing than any merely human ſanctions could ever give. But the conſideration of greateſt moment in the account is this,—that there is a ſpecific quarter to which reſort may be had for the ſolution of the doubt. This muſt facilitate the application for the ſolution, and, ſtill more, muſt facilitate and encourage the growth of the doubt itſelf. Where the conſcience of the individual muſt decide, if he be indeed conſcientious, he will of courſe be ſo deeply impreſſed with the ſacredneſs of the obligation under which his oath has laid him, that he will be eager to keep down every naſcent ſurmiſe unfavourable to his ſworn allegiance ; nothing but the ſtrongeſt and the moſt palpable caſe of tyranny will overcome his honeſt ſcruples. But if there be an eccleſiaſtical ſuperior who can authoritatively pronounce on the validity of his ſurmiſe, he feels himſelf quite at liberty to give it a full and free vent ; to communicate

it to that ſuperior, and in communicating to ſet it forth in
the ſtrongeſt colours, and ſo to confirm and augment its
native force.   Beſides, if there were no external quarter to
which to have recourſe for ſolution of ſuch doubts, every
individual muſt be inclined to keep them to himſelf, until
the caſe be of ſo grave and overpowering a neceſſity as to
unite the whole maſs of the people in one common feeling.
On all theſe as well as other accounts the doctrine of the
ſupremacy of the Pope is one which muſt make every wiſe
legiſlature, particularly every Proteſtant legiſlature, cautious
how they increaſe the power of thoſe who hold it ; and can
this ſeem of little moment when Iriſh Roman Catholic
biſhops, who to the maſs of their people muſt appear to ſpeak
with authority ſcarcely leſs ſacred than that of the Pope himſelf, are deſcribing an intolerable tyranny as even now exerciſed by the government of their own land ?''

Such, then; being the claims put forward by the
Roman Church, it is evident that the queſtion of the
Pope's ſupremacy can never be a matter of indifference
to any ſtateſman who labours for the honour and independence of his country.   Nor muſt it be imagined
that Dr. Phillpotts has, for the ſake of indulging his
ſatire, at all overſtated Roman pretenſions.   The fourth,
or great Lateran Council, which was preſided over by
Pope Innocent III, declares—

" That the ſecular powers ſhall be admoniſhed, and, if
neceſſary, be compelled by eccleſiaſtical cenſures, to make
oath that they will, to the utmoſt of their power, ſtrive to
exterminate from their territory all heretics, declared to be
ſuch by the Church ; and further, that if any temporal lord
being required and admoniſhed by the Church, ſhall neglect
to purge his territory from all taint of hereſy, he ſhall be excommunicated by the metropolitans and other provincial

bifhops ; and if he contemptuoufly omit to give fatisfaction within a year, it fhall be fignified to the holy Pontiff, in order that he may thenceforth proclaim his vaffals abfolved from fealty to him, and may expofe to Catholics his territory to be occupied by them who, having exterminated the heretics, may poffefs the fame without contradiction.''

After this authoritative approval of wholefale murder and fpoliation, it would be vain to fhut one's eyes to the monftrous refults which might well follow from Roman claims. Nor will it be thought that Dr. Phillpotts has fpoken too ftrongly in pointing out the danger which would arife if the queftion of the Pope's fupremacy were treated as belonging merely to the region of fpirituals.

CHAPTER XIII.

The Letter to Mr. Canning continued. The Errors of the Roman Catholics charged upon "our Perfecution." The excited ftate of the Country caufed the wildeft Statements to be received. Extract from Speech of Mr. Grattan. The Cry of Perfecution deftitute of all Foundation. Shown by reference to the Laity's Directory. Extracts from that Work, fhowing the Gratitude of Roman Catholics for the Conceffions which had been made to them. The Rapid Strides made by that Body in England. An Account of their Hierarchy, Colleges, Monafteries, and Convents. Dr. Phillpotts expofes the Difhonefty of the Cry of Perfecution. Examples. The Power of the Priefthood in Ireland. Its Abufe. " The Prieft's Curfe." Conduct of the Roman Catholic Bifhops. A Teft fuggefted by Dr. Phillpotts in place of Denial of the Doctrine of Tranfubftantiation. Difficulty of coming to an Arrangement with the Roman Catholics defcribed by Lord Eldon. Dr. Phillpotts' later Opinion of his fuggefted Teft. His Regret that it had never been changed from a Speculative to a Practical Form. A more Elaborate Scheme of Legiflation on this Subject propofed by Dr. Phillpotts. A Defcription of it. Conclufion of Firft Letter to Mr. Canning. Its Effect upon that Statefman. Opinion of the Edinburgh Review. Conduct of Mr. Canning's Friends.

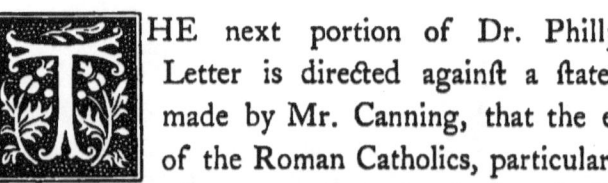

HE next portion of Dr. Phillpotts' Letter is directed againft a ftatement made by Mr. Canning, that the errors of the Roman Catholics, particularly in Ireland, were due to *" our perfecution."* A ftrange charge it may be thought; but in making it this gifted ftatefman was only echoing a popular cry.

Like men of lefs perception, he had fuffered his reafon
to be led captive by idle clamour. A fpell was on
the nation, and the loftieft intellects were proftrated
by its power. No falfehood was too improbable to
be believed. The wildeft ftories were related as if
they were the moft fober truths. Not merely had
the Irifh Roman Catholics been crufhed, fo it was
faid, but their Church had been depreffed, to make
room for that which they believed to be no Church,
the very exiftence of which was only fecured by difqualifying the people, and compelling them at the
fame time to pay for its fupport.

" A Church fuch as this," faid one of their warmeft advocates,* " could not be called Chriftianity. It would be
a Church of ambition, of avarice, of bigotry, and intolerance;
a Church baptized in the iniquities of mankind, and wickedly
apoftatifing from God; a Church bearing the vices and
policy of man in one hand, and the people and God in the
other."

If fuch was the language held by ftatefmen and
fenators, it is little wonder that it fhould find a ready
refponfe in the breafts of the ignorant and difaffected.
It was not the firft time in hiftory that political capital had been realized out of the cry of intolerance
and *perfecution.* But never, furely, was fuch a cry
raifed with fo little reafon. The notion of perfecution was merely an after-thought of the Roman Catholics to compafs their ends. Already had their

* Mr. Grattan.

gains been not a few, and now, that they could quietly count them over, they were greedy of more. Dr. Phillpotts fhowed the abfurdity of this clamour, and the evidence of Dr. Moylan, as cited by him, was an arrow fledged with their own feathers. But in addition to this, a Roman Catholic almanack, called " The Laity's Directory, publifhed by authority," contains fome curious and inftructive evidence as to the way in which the conceffions, which from time to time had been made in favour of the Roman Ca-tholics, were received among them. The teftimony is valuable as coming from a fource which they them-felves are bound to refpect.

" In 1778," according to the *Laity's Directory*, " the Roman Catholics of England were freed from a part of the galling penalties and reftraints which, through mifconcep-tion of their principles and conduct, had been accumulating upon them during the greater part of two centuries and a-half."

This Act is defcribed by Bifhop Walmfley, in a letter addreffed on the occafion to the Roman Ca-tholic clergy of the weftern diftrict, as " *an extraor-dinary favour*," fhowing " the great humanity of go-vernment towards them," and " fuggefting a propriety of behaviour on their part, in ufing *the prefent indul-gence* with caution, prudence, and moderation."

" In 1791," according to the fame Directory, " a partial enjoyment of the rights of free fubjects was extended to them [the Roman Catholics] by the legiflature, and in par-ticular they were indulged with the important privileges of

educating their children in their own religion, and of prac-
tiſing it in all its eſſential duties, except the Sacrament of
Matrimony."

Upon the paſſing of this Act, Biſhop Douglas addreſſed a paſtoral to the clergy and laity of the London diſtrict, ſaying that " the day was at length arrived, when he could congratulate them on the greateſt
of bleſſings—*the free exerciſe of their religion*"—ſince
" *a humane and generous legiſlature* had ſeen the op-
preſſion under which they laboured, and, by an act
worthy of its enlightened wiſdom, *had redreſſed the
grievances* of which they complained." He then goes
on to ſay that—

" As their EMANCIPATION from penal laws muſt awaken
every feeling of a grateful mind, they ſhould haſten to cor-
reſpond on their part with the benignity of government ; to
give to their gracious Sovereign the teſt of loyalty which the
legiſlature called for, and diſclaim every principle dangerous
to ſociety, and to civil liberty, which had been erroneouſly
imputed to them."

Biſhop Gibſon alſo ſpoke of "*the mildneſs* and
condeſcenſion of the legiſlature," and called upon the
Roman Catholics of the northern diſtrict " to expreſs
their obligations and gratitude for it." Biſhop Talbot
praiſed the king as " the beſt of ſovereigns," and " the
legiſlature" as "*indulgent, compaſſionate, enlightened
and wiſe.*" And " upon the Duke of Cumberland
viſiting Rome (*Laity's Directory*, 1793), the Pope
deſired him to convey to his Royal Father expreſſions
of thankfulneſs for the indulgences lately granted to
the Roman Catholics of England," expreſſing " his

wifh that every member of the legiflature fhould be
informed of the grateful fenfe in which that indulgence
was held."

In the year 1792 a great number of the French
clergy, who had been banifhed from their own country, fought refuge in England, where they were not
only received with great hofpitality, but a fubfcription
was fet on foot for their relief, and was enforced by a
royal letter.   To commemorate this act of national
benevolence, the Pope iffued a brief, dated Rome,
September 2, 1793, in which he defcribed it as " a
glorious defign," and went on to fay that " the King's
humanity and munificence *fhould ever be remembered
with the fincereft gratitude."*

In 1794 many religious communities, driven from
their homes by the French Revolution, fought refuge
in England.

"The Benedictine Dames of Bruffels," fays the Directory,
" landed at S. Katherine's ftairs, July the 6th, where they
met *with the utmoft humanity and refpect, even from the loweft
ranks of Englifhmen."*

Again :—

" The Benedictine Dames of Ghent received from the
Duke of York, during the late campaign, on every occafion,
the *kindeft protection ;* and from Britifh officers and foldiers
in general *fuch civility and refpect as ftill excites their aftonifhment and gratitude."*

" The Regular Canoneffes of the Holy Sepulchre of Liege
turned their eyes towards England for refuge, with hope and
confidence of finding, in their diftrefs, a fhare in *the unparalleled benevolence, charity, and generofity,* which have been exhibited to fo many of their fellow-fufferers."

" The Benedictine Dames of Paris arrived at Dover in 1795, where they were kindly welcomed. It will be their pleafing duty to pray for the welfare of their native country with redoubled earneftnefs, *after having experienced its liberality, and enjoyed the bleffings of its free conftitution,* fo widely different from the boafted liberty, but real tyranny, from which they have efcaped, and in particular for *the beft of Sovereigns,* that he may long reign over a happy and a united people, and may fucceed in his gracious endeavours to bring about univerfal peace and philanthropy."

So much for the cry of *perfecution.* But our fympathies, it may be alleged, were extended mainly to continental Roman Catholics, who happened at the time to be fpecial objects of commiferation. Not a word is faid about Ireland. While the yoke was being relaxed in other quarters, it was being tightened in that unhappy country. Let the *Laity's Directory* again be witnefs :—

" In 1796, the deftruction of the greateft part of the Irifh Colleges on the Continent, having alarmed the (Roman) Catholic Bifhops in Ireland, they prefented a memorial to Lord Weftmoreland, then Lord-Lieutenant, praying to obtain permiffion to educate the Irifh clergy at home. They at the fame time requefted a clergyman of their own communion, refident in London, to converfe with the Britifh Miniftry on the fubject, and after a few converfations Earl Fitz-William, who was fhortly to affume the government of Ireland, was inftructed to eftablifh and endow a college for the education of the (Roman) Catholics of that country. The plan not being completed during the fhort Viceroyalty of the laft-named nobleman, it was taken up by his fucceffor, Earl Camden, who, not fatisfied with obtaining from Parliament the neceffary grants, both for the fubfiftence and neceffary buildings of the college, *went in perfon, accompanied by the*

Lord Chancellor and the three chief Judges, befides the ufual
attendants of his high office, *to lay the firft ftone;* all the
neighbouring noblemen and gentlemen, and an immenfe concourfe of people, with the Prefident and ftudents, attending,
who teftified the moft unbounded joy and loyalty on the occafion.
After the conclufion of the ceremony, his Excellency com-
miffioned the Prefident of the College to conduct fuch of the
(Roman) Catholic Bifhops as attended, in his own carriages,
to dinner at the caftle, where a fplendid entertainment was
prepared, and, as a mark of further refpect to the ceremony,
he called upon the (Roman) Catholic Archbifhop of Armagh
to fay grace. Thefe laft circumftances cannot appear too
trivial for memory to record, when it is confidered that *this
was the firft time fince the Revolution that a (Roman) Catholic
Bifhop was permitted to dine or to fit in company with any Lord-
Lieutenant of Ireland.* The whole meafure was carried into
effect *with fo generous, fo liberal, and fo cordial a protection,* as
to endear him perfonally to the Catholics of Ireland, and to
imprefs them with fo grateful and fo affectionate a loyalty to
His Majefty's Government AS TIME CAN NEVER EFFACE."

Comment would be idle. If the Roman Catholics
could exprefs themfelves in language of fuch apparently
heartfelt gratitude, and within a few years could raife
a cry of oppreffion and perfecution againft their bene-
factors, it is only one more proof of the effentially
aggreffive fpirit of their Church, and of the need there
was to exact fecurities for their peaceable behaviour.

And here it may not be amifs to dwell for a moment
upon the refults of Roman Catholic agitation, as exhibited in the rapid ftride made by that body in England
during the laft thirty years. Few people are aware of
the extent of the Roman Catholic population in England and Scotland; and thofe who are aware of it can

only think with forrow and alarm of the conceffions wrung from a pliant Parliament by political agitators, ftimulated by prieftly craft. Freed from all reftrictions, and hampered by no unpalatable fecurities, the intrufive Roman Church raifes her head fo proudly as to make her a dangerous rival to the Eftablifhed Church. Having gained fo much, why may fhe not afk for more? Already fhe has in England 19 bifhops, including one cardinal archbifhop, 1196 priefts, 824 churches, chapels, and ftations, 50 communities of men, 153 convents, 10 colleges, and in Scotland 4 bifhops, 169 priefts, 195 churches, chapels, and ftations, and 2 colleges. Such is the machinery which the Roman Church has at its command for winning back the population of this ifland to " the true faith." That fuch a refult fhould ever arrive is probably more than even the moft ardent of the " faithful" looks for ; but with fuch an agency at work, with organization fo perfect, with a network of religious houfes fpread acrofs the land, and with a priefthood largely recruited from the ranks of our own clergy, it would be mere folly to clofe our eyes to the fatal legacy which our fathers bequeathed to us, when they yielded, in a haplefs moment, to the cry of " perfecution," and gave to the Roman Catholic all and more than he had dared to hope for.

After ftating the neceffity of defending the laws and Government from the reproaches fo inconfiderately caft upon them by Mr. Canning, Dr. Phillpotts proceeds to cite the teftimony of the very men who had been paraded as the miferable victims of oppreffion and perſecution.   He quotes a letter of Dr. Moylan, a Roman Catholic Biſhop, (16th of April, 1798,) in which he informs the faithful of his dioceſe that they "*poſſeſs the advantages of the Conſtitution,*" that "the penal laws under which our fathers groaned have been almoſt all done away," and that "*theſe are favours that ſhould excite and call out all our gratitude.*"   He then remarks upon theſe ſtatements :—

"You, Sir, will not be able to read language ſuch as this without deploring the lamentable degradation to which the exiſting penal code had thirty years ago reduced its victims ; they were, it ſeems, ſo far debaſed by it that they could even hug their chains and fancy themſelves happy, till Mr. O'Connell, and Mr. Cobbett, and Mr. Canning, (have we lived to witneſs the aſſociation ?) in the overflowing torrent of their benevolence, have kindly aſſured them that they are perfectly miſerable.   To call on Ireland to value the Conſtitution in her preſent ſtate, is, according to you, 'to ſuppoſe her either utterly incapable of appreciating the benefits of *emancipation*' (ſhade of William Pitt! does he who calls himſelf your diſciple dare ſo to abuſe that word ?) 'or altogether unworthy of it.'   And yet, Sir, ſo late as the 16th of March, 1821, you were yourſelf ſo inſenſible to the wrongs of that injured country that you could thus ſpeak of the condition in which the laws have placed her.   'From that time (1774) the ſyſtem was progreſſively mitigated, until the year 1793, which *crowned and conſummated the gift of civil liberty, and left only political conceſſion imperfect.*'"

In what follows, Dr. Phillpotts expoſes a moſt fruitful ſource of miſchief in Ireland—the unwarrantable power claimed by the prieſthood ; a power which, as he ſhows, their prelates refuſed to ſanction, however much they might find it convenient to wink at it.   This

power difplayed itfelf in denunciations from the altar;
and, after making allowance for all explanations, it
muft be confeffed that anathemas of this kind partook
of the charaĉter of aĉtual excommunication.

And here it muft not be thought that Dr. Phillpotts was fetting himfelf up as an antagonift of that
Ecclefiaftical difcipline which from the earlieft times
has been held neceffary for the well-governing of the
Church, which derives its authority from Holy Scripture, which has been enforced by an unbroken line of
writers, beginning with S. Clement, and which has
received the fanĉtion of a long feries of Councils and
Synods, including the famous one of Nice. No, he
was too true a Churchman for that. With his Prayer-
book in his hand, declaring (*Art. of Relig.* XXXIII.),
" That perfon which by open denunciation of the
Church is rightly cut off from the unity of the Church,
and excommunicated, ought to be taken of the whole
multitude of the faithful as an heathen and publican,
until he be openly reconciled by penance, and received
into the Church by a Judge that hath authority there-
unto"—he was not likely to fay anything to throw difcredit upon this falutary ordinance. But he held it as a
fcandal upon Religion that the priefthood fhould be
allowed, often for no higher motive than to infure the
return of a favourite candidate at an eleĉtion, to fow
curfes broad-caft over the land. The educated might
think as lightly of them as they deferved, but the unlet-
tered would recognize the Voice of God. To chronicle
the outrages and murders committed in Ireland under

the ſacred name of Religion would be to tranſcribe the darkeſt page in the hiſtory of that unhappy country.

Boldly does Dr. Phillpotts attack this abuſe of ſacerdotal power, and ſhow the expedients to which even prelates would condeſcend, in order to ſhift the reſponſibility from their own ſhoulders :—

" Sir, I muſt not wholly omit to notice the power of excommunication, as one of the moſt efficacious cauſes and inſtruments of the tyranny of the Iriſh Prieſthood. Ex-communication, I need not ſay, is a ſentence of abſolute excluſion from all the rites and ſacraments of the Church—and that, in the eſtimation of every ſincere member of the Church of Rome, it is therefore an abſolute excluſion from the means of Grace, and from the hopes of Heaven.

" This ſentence cannot, according to the principles of that Church, be pronounced by any but the Biſhop, or delegate of the Biſhop. Yet in Ireland the Pariſh Prieſts are continually in the habit of exerciſing a power ſhort of formal excommunication, but which has almoſt equal effect on the terrified minds of the people ; and what is not leſs worthy of remark, the Biſhops are in the habit of contem-plating the exerciſe of this power in perfect ſilence. It is called ' The Prieſt's Curſe.' "

Dr. Phillpotts then cites inſtances of the exerciſe of this dreadful power, and continues :—

" Yet, notwithſtanding the notoriety of theſe and other ſimilar proceedings, we have not heard of a ſingle inſtance in which any one of theſe Clergy was called to account by his eccleſiaſtical ſuperiors, for what Dr. Doyle has deſignated as ' a thing ſo wrong in its own nature, that it muſt ſtrike every Chriſtian,' namely, ' that a Prieſt, appointed to mi-niſter between the people and God, ſhould convert his miniſtry into a curſe.' And while the Biſhops have thus looked on in filence, the laity, even in England, have given their fanction to this exercife of fpiritual authority in temporal matters, by returning folemn thanks to them for their exemplary zeal and fervices."

The next point in Dr. Phillpotts' letter relates to a Teft which he propofes in place of the denial of the doctrine of Tranfubftantiation. Some fuch a teft as that fuggefted by him would at once have filenced thofe noify agitators who were clamouring for "religious liberty," and who maintained that, in difqualifying men for office on account of any particular creed, Parliament was arrogating to itfelf the power of the Almighty. But it fhould be remembered that, with the Roman Catholics, the queftion did not lie between the denial of Tranfubftantiation and any other teft, but between that and *none.* They were now fuing for admiffion into the legiflature on equal terms with Proteftants, and were not prepared to give fecurities for their good behaviour. The day might come when thefe fecurities would be inconvenient. It was wifer then to be unfettered. The nation juft now was in a pliant mood. It required but a little gentle preffure to gain that which, a few years before, the wildeft agitator had not dreamt of.

Speaking of the attitude of the Roman Catholics, and the difficulty of making any fatisfactory arrangement with them, Lord Eldon fays, in a letter to Dr. Phillpotts, September the 28th, 1828 :—

" I prefume that arrangement has not become more eafy, when the Irifh Roman Catholics fay that they *muft* be put upon an *equality*, at least, with the Protestants; that they *must* have a Reform in Parliament, and the right of suffrage continued to the freeholder under the influence of the Roman Catholic priesthood, or still more largely established; and when they tell you that they not only will not be contented with this, if they receive it of your gift, but *that they will have it, and can have it, whether you choose to give it them or not*. I cannot imagine to myself what it is you can concede to them with safety to the Established Church, if you are to negotiate about concessions to them, in possession, *in fact*, of the Government of Ireland, and professing to treat *with the Government of the United Kingdom*, on the part of 'the people of Ireland,' as a body, in fact, though not in law, no part of *the people of the United Kingdom*, separated at least from that kingdom *de facto*, as they allege. If their *power can wrest from you now what they ask*, will your granting what they now ask disable them, by the exercise of that same power, to wrest from you whatever they may further please to demand ?"

The new Test suggested by Dr. Phillpotts runs as follows:—

"I, A. B., do declare, in the presence of Almighty God, that I do not hold, nor believe that it is necessary, in order to their eternal salvation, that his Majesty King George, or any of his liege people being Protestants, be or shall become in any way subject to the Pope, or to any authority of the See of Rome; and I do declare, that I do not hold, nor believe, that the Protestant Church of England and Ireland, as by law established, is in such wise heretical, that any of the members thereof are, on that account, excluded from the promises of the Gospel, or cut off from Christian salvation; and I do faithfully promise and swear, that I will not use any power, right, or privilege, which does or shall to me belong, for the purpose of destroying, or in any way weakening, the Protestant Church and the establishment thereof, as it is now by law maintained. So help me God."

He then goes on to fay :—

" Sir, I bear no man's proxy, and am not fure that fuch a teft would fatisfy any other individual of any party.

"That it would not fatisfy the Irifh leaders I am well aware, and, in plain truth, I fhould have no fort of confidence in any that would. That it would be offenfive to the Church of Rome, and to all the bigoted members of that Church, I have as little doubt, and for that very reafon I fhould have more reliance on its efficacy. The great defideratum has always been to feparate between the bigots and the moderate members of that Church; to bear with as light a hand as poffible on the latter, and to control the hoftility of the former with the moft effectual reftraints that the wifdom of the Legiflature can devife. I fhould hope that, among the nobles and the educated laity of that communion, both in England and Ireland, many would be found who would fpurn the mandates of their Church, if fhe fhould refufe to let them give to their Proteftant countrymen fuch a fecurity for the fafe and honeft exercife of their functions as legiflators."

Speaking of this fuggeftion for a new Teft, Dr. Phillpotts fays, feveral years later :*—

" In looking back at this paffage, I frankly own that I do not think it was marked by ' abfolute wifdom,' though I do not the lefs claim it as a teftimony of my fincerity."

A little further on Dr. Phillpotts expreffes his regret—and it is one in which every thoughtful man muft join—that the experiment of changing the teft from a *fpeculative* to a *practical* one had never been tried.

---

* " Letter to Sir Robert Inglis."

" One great advantage would neceffarily follow," he fays ; " there would be no longer occafion left for declamatory harangues on the hardfhip of punifhing men for fpeculative errors ; there would be no more prattle heard about nice diftinctions between Tranfubftantiation and Confubftantiation; and you, Sir, and men like you, would be fpared the feeling of felf-reproach, which the confcioufnefs of having recourfe to fuch wilful fophiftry can hardy fail to inflict.   In fhort, thofe who would be excluded by fuch a teft could not be held up as martyrs.   It could not be any longer faid that they are ftigmatized as idolaters,—that they are punifhed for following the dictates of their confcience.   But the real truth would be made manifeft, that they are the perfecutors in fpirit—that if there be any ftigma it is ftamped by themfelves—that they are kept out of Parliament becaufe their confcience itfelf would compel them to abufe the power of legiflation into an engine of fpiritual tyranny, and of aggreffion on the confcience of others."

And here it will not be out of place to notice a more elaborate fcheme of legiflation on this fubject fuggefted by Dr. Phillpotts in 1828.   It occurs in a letter to Lord Eldon, and is worthy of all attention, as fhowing the profound knowledge and ability which he brought to bear upon a fubject that was diftracting ftatefmen, and caufing the wildeft apprehenfion throughout the country.   In this fcheme, it is to be obferved, as elfewhere, he infifted that the time of *exclufion* was gone by, and that nothing remained but to grant a meafure of *conceffion*, accompanied, however, with fecurities of the moft ftringent kind.   What thefe fecurities were to be he himfelf fets forth ; and if exception be taken to certain portions of his plan, it muft be remembered that he has only failed where the greateſt intellects had failed before him, and it muſt be allowed that upon the whole the ſcheme is juſt, reaſonable, and ſalutary.

The following obſervations give an admirable view of the poſition :—

" Permit me, in the outſet, to ſay, that the longer I have conſidered the ſubject, and the more cloſely I have been able to watch the progreſs of events, the more firmly am I convinced of two things, apparently at variance with each other;—firſt, that the true principles of the Britiſh Conſtitution require that conceſſions ſhould *not* be made ; and, ſecondly, that the wretched degeneracy of our preſent race of Parliamentary orators, their ignorance of thoſe principles, and, ſtill more, their heedleſſneſs of them—the want of energy in moſt of our public men, the want of authority in Government on this queſtion (on which, ſixteen years ago, Government moſt—what ſhall I ſay ? moſt unhappily—abdicated all authority)—above all, the lamentable abſence of almoſt everything that was wont to characterize an Engliſh Houſe of Commons, combine to make it certain that, ere it is very long, conceſſions *will* be made."

He then goes on to ſay that if this is a correct view of the ſtate of things, the preſent is the time when conceſſions may be made with the leaſt hazard.

As a preliminary, however, to any act of legiſlation, he holds that the honour of Government ſhould be vindicated by the immediate ſuppreſſion of the Iriſh Aſſociation. He then ſuggeſts that the queſtion of conceſſion, coupled with full and complete ſecurities, ſhould be brought before Parliament in a ſpeech from the Throne. What thoſe ſecurities ſhould be he next proceeds to conſider.

" And now for the plan of fecurities to be propofed.

" I will fet out, with obferving, that it would appear to me utterly intolerable, in framing thefe fecurities, to have recourfe to any Roman Catholics, leaft of all to the Pope. I fhould hope that Parliament would adopt, in their fulleft fenfe, the words of the Duke of Wellington—' We muft legiflate for ourfelves, and we muft legiflate firmly and fear-leffly.' I will next fay, that it would appear to me of main importance, in framing fuch fecurities to *avoid all mention of Roman Catholics*, and to make laws in general terms, which, while they operate on all, fhall yet be fo devifed as to provide againft the particular dangers to be apprehended from that fe&t.

" I. Let there be an Act for limiting the right of voting for Members of Parliament for Counties in *Ireland*, to perfons having eftates in fee or in tail, or on leafe for lives renew-able for ever, if the value of the land is 40*s*. per annum, and lefs than 20*l*. per annum, leaving the right as at prefent to all perfons having any freehold eftate in land above that value, the value of the land to be in all cafes eftimated according to the *rent* which it would obtain if let. The obvious benefit of this firft fecurity would be to reclaim the power of choofing Members of Parliament for Irifh counties from pauperifm to property, and thereby to fecure the elections, for a long time, almoft entirely to Proteftants. In the in-ftances in which Roman Catholics would be chofen, they would at leaft be men of property, and probably men of education; in either cafe not likely to be the flaves of the priefthood.

" It is faid by all perfons acquainted with Ireland as it is now, and as it was thirty years ago, (before the eftablifhment of Maynooth College,) that there is *now* one marked change. The priefts are of a lower grade in fociety, they are not, as they formerly were, guefts of the Popifh gentry; on the contrary they are kept at a diftance, and have little or no influence over them.

" A Proteftant gentleman of large fortune refident in the county of Clàre, who has been with me lately, fays that the Roman Catholic gentry are more annoyed, if poffible, than the Proteftants, at the prefent domination of the priefthood and the demagogues.

" II. An Act, requiring all members of either Houfe of Parliament before they fit or vote, to take an oath, or make a folemn declaration, founded either on the writ of fummons to Parliament, or on the declaration recently fubftituted in lieu of the facramental teft, *for the fecurity of the Church of England and Ireland;* the preamble of this Act recognizing this Church as *a fundamental and effential part of the Conftitution.*

" The benefit to be obtained from fuch a ftatute might be found greater than at firft appears, for it would give to the Church the pledge, not only of Roman Catholics, but of *all other Members of Parliament,* none of whom are at prefent under any engagement to it. If individuals would difregard, or explain away fuch a pledge, it might be at leaft hoped that the great body of either Houfe of Parliament would feel and refpect its binding nature. At any rate it would ftrengthen the claims of the Church, and could not fail to affect powerfully the opinion of the people againft any open attempt to injure it.

" This meafure would be ftoutly oppofed. Lord Holland protefted againft it by anticipation, during the debates on the repeal of the Teft Act. So did fome one in the Houfe of Commons. But if no meafure is to be adopted which will be oppofed, the Conftitution may as well be given up at once. After all, fince men of all parties are weary of the Popifh queftion, and eager to get rid of it, any meafure, ftrenuoufly infifted on as a neceffary adjunct to the fettlement, might be carried, perhaps with lefs of refiftance than under other circumftances could be hoped. The propofed *recognition of the Proteftant Epifcopal Church of England and Ireland as an effential part of the Conftitution* was made *in the preamble of the bill of* 1813, as amended in the Committees of the Houfe of Commons of that year; and it is enacted in the Act of Union that the prefervation of the faid United Church fhall be deemed an effential and fundamental part of the faid Union.

" III. An Act *declaring* it to be unlawful and prohibiting all perfons from calling themfelves or others *in any printed book or paper*, under any qualification, Bifhops of any See, Deans of any Chapter, or Rectors of any Parifh, of which there are according to law Bifhops, Deans, or Rectors of the Eftablifhed Church of England and Ireland. The penalty for the firft offence, a fine of   ; for the fecond, the party to be required to withdraw himfelf from the realm, and if he return without licence under the Great Seal, tranf-portation.

" The neceffity of fome fuch ftatute is becoming every day more imperative. The Popifh Bifhops call themfelves, and are called Bifhops of the Irifh Sees without fcruple, and often without qualification. If it be urged (as it was urged by Mr. Pitt) that in an *Epifcopal Church there muft be Bifhops*, at leaft let the Popifh Bifhops be compelled to imitate the modefty of the Proteftant Bifhops of the Epifcopal Church of Scotland, who abftain not only from all titles of *Lordfhip*, but even from calling themfelves publicly Bifhops *of Sees*, though there are no other perfons entitled by law to thofe Sees. Within the laft two months this abufe and ufurpation in Ireland has extended beyond Bifhops, and even beyond Deans. The Parifh Priefts are now called by the Affocia-tion, *Catholic Rectors*, and fometimes fimply *Rectors* of fuch and fuch parifhes. But for this invafion of the rights of the Eftablifhed Church there is abfolutely no femblance of ex-cufe: it is fheer, unmixed, unmitigated hoftility; it is an avowal of a determination to ufurp the character of the National Church, in defiance and in derogation of the law-ful rights of the Proteftant Epifcopal United Church of England and Ireland.

" IV. A Statute, prohibiting all perſons in Holy Orders, or pretended Holy Orders, or pretending to Holy Orders, and all Miniſters or Teachers of Diſſenting Congregations in Ireland, from in anywiſe interfering in any conteſted election of members of Parliament in Ireland, whether by aſking votes, or otherwiſe, making any candidate ineligible, and conſequently all votes given to him thrown away, who ſhall, by himſelf, or by his agents, uſe, or knowingly permit the aid or interference of ſuch perſons, ſaving, however, the right of ſuch perſons to vote themſelves, and to ſolicit the votes of perſons who are tenants under them of any land or tenement, and are qualified to vote.

" This, it will be ſeen, is here confined to *Ireland*, but if in order with the better grace to exclude the influence of the Popiſh Prieſt, it be thought fit to extend the operation of the propoſed meaſure to England alſo, it is a reſtraint which I think would not do us any harm ; nor would it, I believe, excite any feelings of annoyance or diſſatisfaction in the minds of the Proteſtant Clergy of this country. Perhaps even our fair influence would not be leſſened by it.

" V. A general oath of allegiance and ſupremacy to be taken by all perſons in *Ireland* as a qualification for office, or on any other occaſion when either the common oaths of allegiance and ſupremacy are required at preſent, or the oaths preſcribed in the Acts of 21 and 22 Geo. III. and 33 Geo. III, to be taken by Roman Catholics (in lieu of the oaths now required by law) :—

" I, A. B., do take Almighty God and His only Son, Jeſus Chriſt, my Redeemer, to witneſs, that I will be faithful and bear true allegiance to our moſt gracious Sovereign Lord King George the Fourth, and him will defend to the utmoſt of my power againſt all conſpiracies and attempts whatſoever that ſhall be made againſt his perſon, crown and dignity, and I will do my utmoſt endeavour to diſcloſe and make known to his Majeſty and his heirs, all treaſons and traitorous conſpiracies which may be formed againſt him or them; and I do faithfully promife to maintain, fupport and defend to the utmoft of my power the fucceffion of the Crown in the heirs of the body of the Princefs Sophia, Electrefs and Duchefs Dowager of Hanover, being Proteftants, againft any perfon or perfons whatfoever; and I do declare that I do not believe that the Pope of Rome or any other foreign Prince, prelate, ftate or potentate hath, or ought to have any temporal or civil jurifdiction, directly or indirectly, within this realm. (I do further declare that our Sovereign Lord King George is over all perfons and in all caufes ecclefiaftical and civil, to the laws of this kingdom in any wife appertaining, within his dominions fupreme.) And I do fwear that I will defend to the uttermoft of my power the fettlement and arrangement of property in this country as eftablifhed by the laws now in being. I do hereby difclaim, difavow, and folemnly abjure any intention to fubvert the prefent Church Eftablifhment; and I do folemnly fwear that I will not exercife any privilege to which I am, or may become, entitled to difturb or weaken the Proteftant *Church of England and Ireland, as by law eftablifhed, or the Proteftant Government* in this kingdom.

"So help me God.

" The whole of this form of oath is taken from thofe already prefcribed to be taken by the Irifh Roman Catholics, by 21 and 22 Geo. III. c.—and 33 Geo. III. c. 21 (Irifh), except the words defcribing the fucceffion of the Crown and the fhort claufe within brackets, and except the alteration of the laft claufe into words more diftinctly expreffing the intention of the legiflature, and lefs obnoxious to unfair interpretation than thofe in the exifting ftatute. The claufe fo altered refembles one *propofed by Mr. Canning in 1813, and making part of the Bill as amended in the Committee of the Houfe of Commons of that year.*

" In *England* it would not feem neceffary to make any change in the oath of allegiance, or oath of abjuration. The Oath of Supremacy (to be taken by all perfons whenever the prefent Oath of Supremacy is required), might be as follows, taken from the 37th Article of the Church :—

" I, A. B., do declare that the King's Majefty hath the chief power in this realm, unto whom the chief government of all eftates of this realm, whether they be ecclefiaftical or civil, in all caufes, doth appertain, and is not, nor ought to be, fubject to any foreign jurifdiction.

" So help me God.

" *Provifo*—That the prefent oaths be continued to be taken by all perfons holding any office, benefice, place, or dignity in the united Church of England and Ireland and the Church of Scotland, by all Judges in every Ecclefiaftical Court, by perfons holding office in all Univerfities, or taking degrees in Englifh or Scotch Univerfities or Colleges, or fchools of Royal or State foundation.

" *Provifo*—That all Archbifhops, Bifhops, Priefts and Deacons of the united Church of England and Ireland, all Chancellors or Vicars-General of Diocefes, all Judges in any Ecclefiaftical Court or Court of Appeal, fhall take the oaths now required by law.

" The ftiffer Papifts may object to the concluding words, becaufe they hold that all baptized perfons are fubject, in fpirituals at leaft, to the jurifdiction of the Church and of the Pope.   But let thofe that will, object to fuch a form, their objection would only prove more ftrongly the neceffity of requiring it.

" The reafon for propofing different forms of oaths for the two countries is the different ftate of the law at prefent in the two.   The oath now taken by the Irifh Roman Catholics contains a claufe fo much more diftinctly engaging them to abftain from injuring the Proteftant Church, than any in the oath of the Englifh Roman Catholics, that it muft not be furrendered.   And it is not likely that it would be objected to by the Irifh Proteftants, if enjoined to be taken generally by all perfons in Ireland.   But if propofed as the oath to be taken by all perfons in England it would,

Q

without doubt, be ftrongly oppofed, nor would it be defirable to difturb the adjuftment made by the ftatute which repealed the Teft and Corporation Acts in the laft feffion.

"VI. An Act prohibiting any perfon from advifing the King in the difpofal of ecclefiaftical benefices who is not a member of the Church of England and Ireland; and enacting that if any ecclefiaftical benefices be in the patronage of any office under his Majefty, the perfon appointed to fuch office fhall at the time of taking the other oaths, required to be taken by him on entering thereupon, make and fubfcribe the following declaration :—

" I, A. B., do folemnly declare that I am a member of the united Church of England and Ireland.

" So help me God.

" In default whereof the exercife and enjoyment of the faid patronage fhall belong (during the continuance in office of fuch perfon), to any Privy Councillor whom his Majefty fhall appoint, fuch Privy Councillor firft making and fubfcribing the faid declaration.

" It may feem to be neceffary, confiftently with this meafure, to retain the exifting reftraints on Roman Catholics who are poffeffed of advowfons. And, in my opinion, there are obvioufly found reafons of juftice and policy againft permitting any perfons who are not members of the Eftablifhed Church to prefent to any of the benefices of that Church. But as other diffenters are permitted to enjoy this patronage it would perhaps be hardly neceffary or expedient to retain this one badge of fufpicion againft Papifts *alone.* If retained there might be a permiffion to the Catholics to fell advowfons, if entailed, purchafing lands with the money received for the fame, and making the lands fo purchafed liable to the fame limitations as the entailed advowfons.

" VII. An Act, charging all affeffments for the repair of churches and other church-rates in *Ireland,* on the landlord, and not on the occupier of lands, and tenements,—requiring the occupier to pay them to the collectors, but authorizing and empowering him to deduct the ſums ſo paid from the rent due to the landlord. Perhaps an appeal to the quarter ſeſſions might be given on the expediency or amount of any particular rate.

" I apprehend that, at preſent, in every caſe of fair letting of lands or houſes, the landlord does, in fact, pay the rates, inaſmuch as their amount is calculated as an outgoing, when the bargain is made; but in the exiſting ſtate of Ireland, where very little calculation often takes place, previouſly to the tenant taking his ſmall tenement, and exceſſive rents are blindly ſubmitted to, theſe rates do really fall upon the tenant, and from their very nature and object, being impoſed for the ſupport of a Church to which he is adverſe, they muſt be peculiarly galling. This is, perhaps, the moſt ſpecious of all the alleged grievances. But the neceſſity of requiring theſe rates to be paid by *all*, whether members of the Eſtabliſhed Church or not, reſts on a principle which muſt on no account be relinquiſhed, how vehemently ſoever it be aſſailed.

" VIII. A continuance at leaſt for ſome years of the prohibition againſt Roman Catholics in Ireland (not poſſeſſing certain qualifications in land or money) having arms in their poſſeſſion.

" It would be obviouſly prudent to effect this by ſilently retaining the preſent diſability. If it be oppoſed there is unanſwerable ground for inſiſting upon it, in the turbulent and perilous ſtate of that country.

" If this, or any other reſtraint, be retained (as ſome others muſt be—particularly in reſpect to advowſons, and alſo in reſpect to voting at pariſh veſtries, the founding of monaſtic eſtabliſhments, the prohibition of proceſſions, etc.) —it will be much better to follow the precedent of the Engliſh Act of 1791, which diſtinctly enumerates the laws to be repealed, than the Iriſh Act of 1793, which commences with a general repeal of all diſabilities, and then proceeds to ſpecial exceptions.

" IX. A proviſo ſimilar to that in 1813 for Act of Uniformity, etc.

" X. Proceſſions, etc.

" I have thus ventured to detail my opinions as to the
meaſures which ought to accompany conceſſion, if conceſſion
be made. For doing this at ſo great a length I offer no
apologies, for your Lordſhip has been pleaſed to require it of
me. It would be the higheſt reward I could receive, if your
Lordſhip ſhould be hereby induced to give your own mind
to a conſideration of this important ſubject. From you
would proceed a ſcheme of real ſecurities if any are attain-
able."

It has been thought adviſable to inſert this ſcheme
of ſecurities at full length, in conſequence of its important bearing on Dr. Phillpotts' alleged change of
ſentiment on this ſubject, which will come under conſideration further on.

The ſuggeſtion for a new teſt brings us to the concluſion of Dr. Phillpotts' firſt Letter to Mr. Canning.
And well may it be doubted whether his wit ever
ſhowed a keener edge or brighter poliſh than when
laying bare the ſophiſtry with which that great ſtateſman ſought to diſguiſe arguments which not even his
matchleſs eloquence could reſcue from ſo mercileſs a
diſſection. Writing to Sir John Copley, Mr. Canning ſpoke of this letter as " Dr. Phillpotts' *ſtinging
pamphlet.*" He might with equal truth have called it
withering, for it penetrated to the very heart's core of
the ſyſtem of expediency put forward in a ſpeech which
was vaunted as a maſter-piece of ſtate-craft. That
ſpeech was publicly characterized as " unanſwerable,"
and ſo perhaps it ſeemed, until a thinker as acute as
Mr. Canning, and one whoſe wit was both more ſubtle

and piercing, ftepped down into the arena to give him battle. Then it was that the vaunted armour of proof turned out to be no better than pafteboard.

The truth is, that, brilliant as were Mr. Canning's talents, he was overmatched by Dr. Phillpotts. It was one thing to encounter amateur theologians on the floor of the Houfe of Commons, it was another to meafure fwords with a man to whom theology was both a bufinefs and a paftime, and who, in this fenfe, had been a man of war from his youth. It is not, of courfe, to be expected that an eminent ftatefman fhould of neceffity be an eminent divine ; and therefore to fee a man like Mr. Canning ftepping out of the region of his own ftudies and refearch, and difcourfing glibly of doctrines and creeds, reminds one of Achilles in petticoats playing the amiable to the daughters of Lycomedes. An occafional awkwardnefs in gait is excufable, but fuch perpetual blundering and ftumbling reveals the deception. That the merits of this letter were too great to be fafely difguifed is confeffed by Dr. Phillpotts' old enemy, the *Edinburgh Review.* In March 1827, an article appeared entitled, " Late Vote of the Houfe of Commons," in the courfe of which the writer admits that " *he* certainly has been *quite confiftent* ;" and goes on to fay that " he has always ftoutly delivered his fentiments on one fide ;" that " he has juftly acquired the credit of being about the ableft of thofe who efpoufe that fide ;" and that " he now perfeveres in the fame courfe, at a time when the expediency of fuch conduct, for the interefts of him who holds it, becomes daily more queſtionable." This is high praiſe, but it is no more than he deſerved.

But while Mr. Canning was ſmarting from his wounds, his friends were doing their beſt to cover his retreat. And this they thought would moſt effectually be ſecured by diſcharging a volley of mud at the head of his aſſailant. He was called " a foul-mouthed parſon," " a libeller," and ſo forth. But all this time he was quietly occupying the field of battle and collecting his energies for another attack.

CHAPTER XIV.

Rapid Sale of Firſt Letter to Mr. Canning. The ſudden Change in that Stateſman's Views. Dr. Phillpotts' Second Letter to him. An Unguarded Expreſſion. The Attitude of the King in reference to the Roman Catholic Queſtion. Mr. Canning's Accommodation of himſelf to the new Order of Things. Dr. Phillpotts' Remarks upon it. Reflections on the Rapidity of the Change. Mr. Canning's careleſs Treatment of the Coronation Oath. The Real Obligation of that Oath deſcribed. The Reaſon why Lord Kenyon gave Dr. Phillpotts the Letters of George III. Dr. Phillpotts not averſe to Conceſſion to the Roman Catholics with adequate Securities. The Idea of Securities ridiculed by Mr. Canning. Inconſiſtent with the Tone of his earlier Policy. A Compariſon. Effect of Dr. Phillpotts' Two Letters to Mr. Canning. Their Tone. The Author vilified by Anonymous Writers.

HE firſt Letter to Mr. Canning rapidly paſſed through ſeveral editions ; and it is ſaid that Lord Lyndhurſt, while Maſter of the Rolls, made very liberal uſe of it in one of the moſt brilliant ſpeeches which he ever delivered in the Houſe of Commons. The ſecond and ſhorter Letter,* dated May 7, 1827, was called for by the neceſſity of examining ſome of the leading points in the ſpeeches delivered by Mr. Canning in Parliament ſince the publication of the former letter.

---

* "A Short Letter to the Right Hon. George Canning, on the Preſent Poſition of the Roman Catholic Queſtion. By Rev. Henry Phillpotts, D.D., Rector of Stanhope."

In the courfe of a very few weeks that diftinguifhed ftatefman had learnt the advantage of difcretion, and the danger there would be in forcing the confciences of fo many enlightened and religious Englifhmen to accede to a meafure from which they revolted. With thefe feelings in his mind, and with the defire of poft-poning the Roman Catholic queftion for the prefent, he fomewhat incautioufly fpoke of a better day which would hereafter dawn, and exprefled a hope that the prefent darknefs would be fucceeded by a light which would illuminate the profpect.

The opportunity afforded by this unguarded ftate-ment was not to be loft, and Dr. Phillpotts avails him-felf of it thus :—

" Sir, I need not fay that I am one of thofe who are in-volved in this darknefs which you venture to predict will be fo fpeedily difpelled. Our number is at prefent very large, and it is our pride, our boaft, the theme of our grateful, heartfelt acknowledgment, that our Sovereign himfelf has been pleafed exprefsly and folemnly to place himfelf at our head. With a firmnefs and determination worthy of the illuftrious ftock from which he is defcended, with the frank-nefs and manly candour becoming the King of a free people, with due veneration for that pure faith of which he is the hereditary and fworn defender, he has been pleafed to allay every uncomfortable furmife, which the felection of you, as his chief minifter, muft otherwife have caufed. He has voluntarily announced to the moft exalted members of our hierarchy, for the information of their brethren, and through them of the people at large, that he is unalterably attached to the religion of his fathers—that he fees and will repel the danger which muft follow the removal of thofe fafeguards with which the wifdom of our anceftors (a phrafe of which

I am not yet afhamed) has fenced and protected our Proteftant Church—*and that the oath which he took at his coronation* has bound him for ever to reject every fpecious pretence of political expediency which may be urged to divert him from his purpofe. I repeat that this affurance, fo folemnly given, far more than counterbalances any apprehenfion which the apparent triumph of the caufe of liberalifm in feveral recent appointments would otherwife excite."

The letter then goes on to congratulate Mr. Canning on the happy way in which he has been able to accommodate himfelf to the new order of things, and more particularly for his determination " not prematurely " to ftir up the feelings of the people of England, fince the object for which he had been fo earneftly ftriving was, after all, merely " a *theoretic*, though effential good."

" That this defcription contains fome very found and important meaning," fays Dr. Phillpotts, " I have not the fmalleft doubt ; but it is probably a confequence of that thick darknefs in which I am involved that I am unable to perceive how a merely ' theoretic' good can, at the fame time, be ' effential.' I am ftill more unable to comprehend how that which we have often heard defcribed by you as the greateft *practical* evil which can afflict the land, that which was ' perfecution' two years ago, and 'oppreffion' two months ago, is now only a *theoretic* evil, which may well wait on your convenience for its cure."

Then follows a brief review of Mr. Canning's language and conduct on this queftion, for the purpofe of fhowing the importance he attached to its fpeedy fettlement. The retrofpect does not reflect much credit on that ftatefman's confiftency.

Dr. Phillpotts next proceeds to comment on the abrupt and fufpicious change which had taken place in Mr. Canning's fentiments relative to preffing the Roman Catholic claims upon the feelings of Englifh-men.   It would be difficult to cite a paffage more thoroughly characteriftic of the writer's peculiar vein than the following :—

" Now all this, 'though I moft powerfully and potently believe it,' and though I cannot but think it infinitely wifer and more becoming an Englifh ftatefman, than the violent, and (pardon me when I fay it), almoft inflammatory language and fentiment in which you indulged on the two immediately preceding difcuffions.   Yet, I own, it excites my admiration.   I admire, not that your uncommon vigour of intellect fhould improve every paffing event, and turn it to the beft account—not that you fhould grow wifer, as you grow older ; but that you fhould grow fo very much wifer in fo very fhort a fpace of time ;—above all, that you fhould, apparently without any effort, attain at once to that higheft point of human wifdom, the power of knowing and acknowledging that you have been in error ; the capacity, in fhort, of eating up, at a fingle mouthful, every unwife or mifchievous fentiment you may have expreffed on a great queftion of national policy during half of your political life, and, after the moft grievous and the wildeft aberrations, fhould return to the very point of fober difcretion from which you ftarted fifteen years ago.   This it is which chiefly excites my admiration, and which, in my humble opinion, places you quite alone among ftatefmen—far above all comparifon with any of the vulgar herd of politicians of whom I have ever read or heard."

After fome obfervations on the rejection by the Roman Catholic prelates of the fecurities provided by the Bill of 1813, which has already been referred to, Dr. Phillpotts takes Mr. Canning to talk for the light and carelefs way in which he had fpoken of the Coronation Oath, faying that its day was gone by, and taunting a member of the Houfe of Commons with feeling an old-fafhioned reverence for it. " I hope," he continued, " at leaft one bugbear is difpofed of, and we fhall hear no more of the Coronation Oath." Such language, proceeding from fuch a quarter, is fhocking, and, if unrebuked, would have been productive of moft ferious mifchief. The dignified reply of Dr. Phillpotts merits the gratitude of every religious mind. He fhows wherein the obligatory nature of the Coronation Oath really confifts ; and it is hard to fay whether the vigour of his language, or its intrepid honefty has the largeft claim upon our admiration.

" *The Oath taken by the King is a purely perfonal act ; it is an act between himfelf and God.* To apply to it our little, convenient, political, or legal fictions—to talk of ' the omnipotence of Parliament,' as enabling it to annul, or difpenfe with, the oath of the Sovereign—to fpeak gravely of ' a keeper of the King's confcience '—to fay that, as ' the King can do no wrong,' as all his queftionable acts muft be regarded as the acts of his Minifters, therefore they muft direct him in fuch a cafe as this—would be more foolifh even than it would be prefumptuous. He might, and probably he would, communicate with thofe perfons—whether his political Minifters, or *others*—on whofe counfel he places moft reliance, in an affair of fo great fpiritual and confcientious moment to him ; but it would be the groffeft infult to the Monarch, it would be degrading him from the rank of a moral being, to fuppofe that he would regard the advice of

fuch counfellors, be they who they may, as acquitting him
of the awful refponfibility of acting in fuch a cafe on the
deliberate determination of his own confcience. Every
Sovereign, duly impreffed with the folemn nature of the
obligation of his oath, (as, thank God, our own gracious
Sovereign has eminently proved himfelf to be,) would feel
that that oath bound him, as he values the favour of God,
and the promife of that ' crown immortal,' before which his
earthly diadem fades into a worthlefs toy, to decide for himfelf whether the bill offered to his acceptance do indeed contain provifions at variance with one of the great and expreffed
objects of his oath, with ' the maintenance, *to the utmoft of
his power*, of the laws of God, the true profeffion of the
Gofpel, and the Proteftant reformed religion eftablifhed by
law.' The Minifter who fhould dare to tell his Sovereign
that he is exempt from this duty, that he may act on the
confcience of his Parliament, or of his Privy Council, inftead of his own, in fuch a cafe—I will go no further, and
will fay, that the Minifter who fhould dare to treat the Coronation Oath, in the prefence of his Sovereign, with half the
levity with which you have not thought it unbecoming to
treat it in your place in Parliament, would bring on himfelf
a refponfibility which no honeft man would incur for all that
kings or parliament can give or take away."

It was in confequence of reading this very ftriking
paffage that Lord Kenyon confided to Dr. Phillpotts
the letters of King George III, which will be referred
to in their proper place. A little further on Dr.
Phillpotts calls attention to the Treaty of Union
with Scotland, which provides, that every King or
Queen, at their coronation, fhall take an oath to maintain and preferve inviolably the fettlement of the
Church of England as by law eftablifhed, within the

kingdom of England and Ireland. He then continues :—

"Sir, when I read the terms in which this oath is conceived, it is to me a matter of high gratification, moft certainly, but of no furprife, that a prince, alive to the moft folemn of all obligations, fhould refolve, as our gracious Sovereign has refolved, never to concur in granting to his Roman Catholic fubjects fuch conceffions as they and their advocates in Parliament are accuftomed to demand. If, indeed, fuch meafures were propofed as the confcience of the Sovereign could regard as a real, fair, ample fecurity, of the great objects to the maintenance and prefervation of which he is bound by oath, the cafe would be different ; and you would then have the affurance afforded by every act of his illuftrious reign, that he would rejoice in extending an equal fhare of civil and political rights to all his fubjects. But who is prepared to offer fuch fecurities? You, Sir, have been pleafed to proclaim yourfelf ' no fecurity-grinder.' You have faid, in a tone of fneer and banter, which few of your hearers, and ftill fewer of your readers, have thought particularly appropriate to the occafion, ' the tafk of finding fecurities to fatisfy thefe over-fcrupulous gentlemen is fomething *like the tafk impofed on the prophet in the Bible, who was not only to find out the interpretation, but to guefs at the dream.'* We all remember a perfon, fome years ago, charged with intending to bring the Scriptures into contempt by his profane application of their language ; and he procured an acquittal from the jury by adducing inftances of fimilar irreverence (among others) from fome of your juvenile productions. Are you defirous that a future Hone fhall be able to cite in his defence the graver authority of your addreffes to Parliament, at your prefent mature age, and in the character of Minifter of the Crown ?"

Dr. Phillpotts then fhows how inconfiftent was Mr. Canning's fneer about fecurities—that thofe who felt

the danger fhould find them—with the tone of his
earlier and wifer policy :—

" Sir, I need not tell you that this point was not mooted
for the firft time on the 7th of March laft. Several years
ago a fpeaker in your own Houfe, of whom, in common with
a large portion of my countrymen, I was then a warm ad-
mirer, made upon it the following very judicious remark :—
' Is it not a little extraordinary that Proteftants fhould be
expe&ed to be of one mind as to granting everything to the
(Roman) Catholics, when fuch a difcordance of opinion reigns
among the (Roman) Catholics themfelves as to the terms on
which fuch grant would be acceptable to them? *It has been
argued rather whimfically, that the granting party fhould be
prepared to offer terms to the petitioning party; but furely it is
for thofe who feek a conceffion in their own favour to propofe
thofe means of fecurity, and thofe terms of arrangement, without
which, it is admitted on all hands, that conceffion could not be
rationally made.'* The fpeaker, of whofe words I have here
availed myfelf, is one with whom, if I may venture to judge
from your moft recent effufions, you are very far indeed
from being on fo good terms as your beft friends could wifh.
It was the Right Hon. George Canning, of May 25, 1810,
a gentleman from whofe fpeeches, about that period, it would
be eafy to adduce arguments in dire& contradi&ion to almoft
everything you have faid on this fubje& during the laft ten
years, up to the epoch of your return to founder views on
the night of Tuefday laft."

That thefe letters fhould have had the effe& of
creating a profound impreffion throughout the country
of the danger of further conceffion to the Roman
Catholics, without adequate fecurities, there can be
little marvel. They were eagerly bought and read;
they were the theme of univerfal converfation, and
they promifed to beftow on their author a more than

tranfient fame. The marvellous ability with which he had maftered the intricacies of a meafure that had exercifed the moft powerful intellects, and the concentration of analytical force which he was able to bring to bear upon the minuteft queftions that arofe from it, furprifed his friends and confounded his enemies. He was charged with having treated Mr. Canning with " fcurrility ;" but it may fafely be affirmed that even in the moft vehement paffages of his letters he never held any language towards that lamented ftatefman which might not fafely be ufed towards a public man on public affairs. It was eafy enough for anonymous writers to vilify him, but it was not fo eafy to anfwer him. Proudly confcious, therefore, alike of the nobility of his caufe, and the purity of his motives, he could feel that

> " we muft not ftint
> Our neceffary actions, in the fear
> To cope malicious cenfurers ; which ever,
> As ravenous fifhes, do a veffel follow,
> That is new trimm'd."

And plenty of this fmall fry were in his wake from this day forward. Few men have been more expofed to detraction than Dr. Phillpotts, and no part of his public career has been more relentlefsly affailed than his conduct on the queftion of Roman Catholic relief. Whether he remained confiftent to his principles, or whether, like Mr. Canning, whofe apoftacy he denounced, he firft wavered and then fell, will be feen in its proper place.

CHAPTER XV.

THE second Letter to Mr. Canning was followed almost immediately by another publication which bore the name of Dr. Phillpotts. This time, however, his labours were only editorial. Some important papers had passed between the late King, George III, and Lord Kenyon and Mr. Pitt, relative to the question of Roman Catholic relief. Lord Kenyon, who had formed a very high opinion of Dr. Phillpotts' talents as a controverfial writer, placed them in his hands, with authority to publifh them in any way he thought proper. Conceiving that the perufal of thefe remarkable documents could only have the effect of increafing the veneration felt by the country for the fingle-minded, uncompromifing, and confcientious regard of the obligation of his oath which the King had difplayed, under circumftances of no ordinary difficulty, they were given to the world. The opinion of the late King on the queftion of Roman Catholic Emancipation was well known; but his fubjects, as a general rule, were not aware of the pains which he had taken, and the confcientious anxiety which he had felt, to come to a right conclufion. Whether he was fucceffful or not in the attainment of that object is not the queftion; but one refult of the publication of his letters is to prove, if fuch proof were wanting, that the King was what has been juftly called " the nobleft work of God"—an honeft man.

Another motive for the publication of thefe letters is to be found in the fact that they reflected the greateft credit on the inflexible integrity of Mr. Pitt, who preferred to facrifice office, and peril the friendfhip of his Sovereign, rather than tarnifh his honour or defert his principles.

Thefe letters appeared on the 25th of May, 1827.*

---

* " Letters from His late Majefty to the late Lord Kenyon, on the Coronation Oath, with his Lordfhip's Anfwers; and Letters of the Right Hon. William Pitt to His late Majefty, with His Majefty's Anfwers, previous to the Diffolution of the Miniftry in 1801."

They are eleven in number, dating ˙from March 7, 1795, to Feb. 13, 1801. It forms no part of the defign of this work to enter into an examination of them, and they are only referred to on account of their having been put forth under the fanction of Dr. Phill-potts' name.

Whether he had acted with his ufual fagacity in publifhing thefe letters was a matter which was warmly debated. The advocates of Roman Catholic relief hailed their appearance as a triumph, affecting to fee in them a vindication of the principles for which they were ftruggling, while even the adherents of Dr. Phillpotts were doubtful whether a grave error in judgment had not been committed. Many of his oldeft friends began to regard him with disfavour, while fome fcrupled not to fhow their refentment by breaking off all intercourfe with him. It feemed neceffary, therefore, that fome explanation of the grounds of publication fhould be offered. Dr. Phill-potts was not the man to refufe the call, more particu-larly when he felt that his difcretion was not at fault, and his explanation affumed the form of *A Letter to an Englifh Layman,** which was publifhed early in the year 1828.

After a graceful tribute to the memory of Mr. Canning, he vindicates the pofition that the Church of

---

* "A Letter to an Englifh Layman on the Coronation Oath, and His late Majefty's Correfpondence with Lord Kenyon and Mr. Pitt, &c. By Rev. Henry Phillpotts, D.D., Rector of Stanhope."

England is an effential part of the Britifh Conftitution. This leads him to compare the various forms of Coronation Oaths which have been in ufe; and after fhowing at confiderable length that fecurity againft Popery and the perpetual maintenance of the Church of England was an efpecial objeét of the alteration made in that Oath at the Revolution, he expreffes himfelf as completely fatisfied that no monarch, as fenfible of the obligations of his oath as George III. was, could have done otherwife than rejeét every pro-pofition for repealing the Teft Laws.

The *Edinburgh Review* (June, 1827) had affeéted great delight at the publication of the Letters of George III. by Dr. Phillpotts, and had taken the opportunity of indulging in a moft cruel attack upon the under-ftanding of the late King. As the inftrument by which thofe letters had been given to the world, Dr. Phillpotts naturally felt it to be his duty to vindicate the memory of one of the beft of fovereigns from the malignant afperfions which had been caft upon it. This brought him once more face to face with his old antagonift Mr. Jeffrey. After referring to the claim of that gentleman to be confidered as verfed in the principles of the Britifh Conftitution, upon which he was fo careful to impart inftruétion to his readers, he continues, in reference to his refponfibility as editor of the Review,—

" He will prefent himfelf to his admiring hearers, as one, who, calling himfelf a Briton, could yet find a gratification in infulting the memory of the Father of his people—as one,

who could lift the hoof of brutal inſolence againſt the dead
lion of the Houſe of Brunſwick—as one, who could avail
himſelf (as he hoped) of a miſerable diſguiſe to outrage the
feelings of this whole nation towards a King, beloved,
honoured, and lamented, like George the Third.   This ſhall
be his high diſtinction ; and, if in the ſcorn of every truly
Engliſh mind he can find nothing to abaſh or diſconcert him,
his ſenſibilities ſhall yet be excited, for I will make him feel
that the publication which he has dared to put forth, is as
unfounded in principle, and as contemptible in argument, as
it is loathſome and deteſtable in ſpirit.''

Let any one read the next twenty pages of Dr.
Phillpotts' Letter, and ſay whether he did not redeem
his pledge.   To give extracts would only ſpoil the
harmony of the whole.

He next goes on to ſhow that the office of the King
is not merely *executive*, as the advocates of Roman
Catholic relief wiſhed to make out, but that he has
real power as a *legiſlator*, and that, as ſuch, he has an
independent right to pronounce upon the fitneſs of any
meaſure ſubmitted for his acceptance by the Houſes of
Parliament.   This appears from the very form of
making ſtatutes ; every new law being *enacted by the
King*, by and with the advice and conſent of his great
council, the Parliament.   " He enacts," ſays Dr.
Phillpotts, " by *willing* that their advice take effect ;
he refuſes his conſent, by announcing his purpoſe of
conſidering the matter with himſelf."

The next point is that the King, as legiſlator, is
bound by his Coronation Oath.   The courſe adopted
to prove this, although it diſplays Dr. Phillpotts' great
hiſtorical reſearch, can ſcarcely be made attractive to

the general reader. Suffice it to fay that he fhows, both by reafon and by authority, the utter futility of the notion that " the Coronation Oath applies to the conduct of the King, in his *executive* capacity only, not as a branch of the legiflature."

But it was alleged by the advocates of Roman Catholic relief that the Coronation Oath never prevented our princes from making fuch alterations in the laws affecting the Church, as on the whole they thought fit, and the cafe of Charles I. was cited, who gave his confent to a bill, which ferioufly curtailed the legitimate power of bifhops, for the purpofe of preventing the Church from finking into abfolute Prefbyterianifm. This was perfectly true. But it is equally true that nothing but the moft extreme neceffity could ever juftify fuch an act.

" Whenever fuch a neceffity fhall again occur," fays Dr. Phillpotts, " it will be for the King of England firft to fatisfy himfelf of its exiftence, and, if he be convinced that it really exifts, to follow the dictates of the higheft fpecies of prudence, that mafter virtue which balances conflicting duties, and decides which, in the collifion, is to be preferred ; decides, however, not according to the fhifting appearance of temporal expediency, but according to the eternal rules of truth and juftice."

But, in order ftill further to evacuate the obligation of the Coronation Oath, a happy expedient was hit upon by Mr. Charles Butler, the old antagonift of Dr. Phillpotts, who maintained that it was " made *to the people*, as reprefented by Parliament." The fallacy of this is admirably fhown by Dr. Phillpotts, who points out that, in order to make Mr. Butler's argument worth anything, the Oath fhould be made to the people *only*. The circumftances, however, under which it is taken—before God's Altar, and under the fanction of Chrift's Body and Blood—proclaim fuch an affumption to be wilful and criminal forgetfulnefs of Him by Whom Kings reign. " Where is the mortal legiflature," indignantly demands Dr. Phillpotts, " that fhall dare to abrogate this folemn vow ? "

" But neither is this all," he proceeds—and this confideration deferves to be noted—" the Oath is, in part, taken not only in favour of, but alfo *to* another human party, befides the people at large—the Bifhops and Clergy of the Church of England. Thefe have an intereft in the laft claufe of the Oath, which, whatever be the *power* of Parliament, it is certainly not within its moral competence to furrender."

As to the notion of the Coronation Oath being made to the people, *as reprefented in Parliament*, Dr. Phillpotts fhows its utter futility. Parliament, he truly enough fays, has nothing to do with the King's coronation : neither is there any reafon why that ceremony fhould take place during the fitting, or even the exiftence, of Parliament. The peers affift at it, not as lords of Parliament, but as peers of the realm, while the Houfe of Commons does not bear part in it at all. This was notably the cafe at the coronation of William III, when, according to Ralph, " the Commons, who had given his Majefty the crown, were not permitted to affift in putting it on." While the reprefentatives of the people, however, are excluded from

the ceremony, the bishops have always borne a con-
spicuous part in it, a portion of the oath being taken
to them. "It appears, therefore," says Dr. Phillpotts,
"not only that it is not to the people, *as reprefented
by Parliament,* that the oath is taken, but that a part
of it is not taken to the people at all."

The fact of the clergy being parties to this oath did
not efcape the notice of the advocates of Roman Catholic relief; but, while fome found it convenient to
diffemble their knowledge of its exiftence, others, with
more of ingenuity than honefty, tried to make it appear that the queftion of further conceffion depended
mainly, if not entirely, on the confent of the bishops
and clergy. It was a fkilful change of tactics, and,
under cover of this falfe attack, the Roman Catholics
hoped to gain poffeffion of the citadel. That they
did ultimately gain poffeffion of it was due in no
fmall degree to the odium which they had fo fuccefsfully ftimulated againft the clergy.

A little further on in the Letter, Dr. Phillpotts
anticipates Lord Macaulay as the panegyrift of William III. It is doubtful whether that diftinguifhed
writer, in his zeal to re-animate the decaying corpfe
of Whiggifm, ever indulged in more fulfome adulation
than Dr. Phillpotts himfelf, when he defcribes William
III. as "*one of the moft confcientious Sovereigns* that ever
fat on the Englifh throne!" It is painful to find that,
in his laudable vehemence againft Papal aggreffion,
Dr. Phillpotts fhould have allowed himfelf for a moment to forget incidents in the life of that monarch,

which may be palliated by a " liberal " hiſtorian, but which can ſcarcely be aſſociated, among upright men, with delicacy of conſcience, or refinement of moral ſenſe.

Reference has already been made, in an earlier part of this work, to a commonly-received belief that liberal conceſſions would be made to the Roman Catholics at the Union between Great Britain and Ireland. There were not wanting thoſe who ſcrupled not to affirm that pledges of conceſſion had been given. Mr. Butler, in particular, found it convenient to dilate in glowing terms upon the expeꝃations which had thus been held out to his co-religioniſts. It may ſerve to ſhow the remarkable eaſe with which hopes are excited in ſome minds, when it is ſaid that not a ſingle line occurs in any of Mr. Pitt's ſpeeches which Roman ſophiſtry can avail itſelf of as containing even the germ of ſuch a pledge. That no conceſſions were promiſed is ſhown by Dr. Phillpotts, by a reference to the ſpeeches of Mr. Fox, Mr. Pitt, and Lord Caſtlereagh, as well as the declaration of George III.

He then paſſes on to conſider thoſe portions of Mr. Pitt's letter to the King, dated January the 31ſt, 1801, which were claimed by the Roman Catholics as being favourable to their pretenſions. It does not fall within the ſcope of this work to examine Mr. Pitt's conduꝃ. If it did, it would be ſeen how little cauſe the Roman Catholics had to congratulate themſelves upon their champion. The ſumming-up of the matter by Dr. Phillpotts, deſcribing the vacillating policy purſued

towards Ireland, difplays as much accuracy in thought
as brilliance in compofition :—

"Whether the practical difficulties attending the fettlement of fuch a point would have been found too great even
for Mr. Pitt to overcome, is a queftion into which it is not
neceffary now to enter. That thefe difficulties, great in
themfelves, have fince his time become incalculably greater,
is unhappily too manifeft ; nor does there appear the fmalleft
reafon to believe, had he been fpared to his country to the
prefent day, that, according to the principles uniformly proclaimed by him, he would now be found among the advocates
for conceffion. It is true that he never would have endured
that the mifchief fhould have reached its prefent hideous
magnitude without any attempt to keep it down ; he never
would have endured that the known laws of the land fhould
be outraged with impunity—that they whofe duty it was to
execute and enforce thofe laws, fhould not only witnefs their
violation with calm complacency, but fhould, even in their
place in Parliament, themfelves pronounce the moft plaufible
excufe for paft delinquency, and adminifter the ftrongeft
provocative to future exceffes. Above all, he never would
have endured that the majefty of Britifh legiflation fhould
be made the fcorn and laughing-ftock of Irifh demagogues
—that an illegal affociation,* put down by an exprefs ftatute
in one month, fhould, in the next, rear its brazen front
without even the decent hypocrify of a change of name—
fhould beard Parliament with its infolent defiance, fhould
raife a revenue for the purpofes of feditious faction, fhould
even make the fhamelefs, but not the imprudent avowal (for
confidence in fuch a cafe is ftrength), that the collection of
this revenue is not merely a contribution for paft or prefent
charges, but a bond of union, and a pledge of future co-

---

* "The Irifh Affociation," often referred to in the courfe
of this work.

operation—in the revolutionary jargon of the day, it is a means of organizing and affiliating the people. All this, I repeat, would not have been endured had Mr. Pitt ftill guided the helm of government—aye, or any one truly Britifh ftatefman, who felt himfelf refponfible in his own individual fame for the refults of the policy which has been purfued. It was only when we were given over to divided councils and conflicting principles—worft of all, when the wretched fyftem was adopted of compromifing all difference of opinions by acting upon none—of banifhing even the name of Ireland from the deliberations of our rulers—of putting off to 'a convenient feafon' the moft perilous and urgent concerns of that diftracted country—*ftultâ diffimula-tione, remedia potius malorum, quam mala, differentes*—it was only then that we reached the full maturity of our prefent evils—evils fo great, that we can neither bear their preffure, nor endure their cure ; but we go on from day to day, from year to year, feeking, by any wretched noftrum the quackery of the age can furnifh, to palliate a corroding plague, which is faft eating to our very vitals.''

The conduct of Mr. Burke in reference to the queftion of Roman Catholic relief next paffes in review, and Dr. Phillpotts maintains that, if that eminent ftatefman were then alive, he would be adverfe to the Roman Catholic claims. The evidence which he ad-duces is moft conclufive, and a debt of gratitude is due to him for refcuing this honoured name from an affociation which he would have been the firft to difown.

The portion of the letter in which Dr. Phillpotts applies his preceding argument to the queftion of fur-ther conceffions to the Roman Catholics is mainly valuable as fhowing that he was not averfe to granting *all* conceffions, but that he thought that conceffions, if granted, fhould be accompanied with the *moft ample fecurities.* His language is clear and explicit, and fhows that he was as thoroughly alive to the aggreffive fpirit of the Roman Church as he ever had been. It was afterwards faid that the germs of his fubfequent alleged change of opinion were to be difcovered in this letter. But no affertion could be more groundlefs. It is true enough that, in common with moft other thoughtful men, Dr. Phillpotts faw that the temporifing policy of Parliament had made further conceffions inevitable; but this was a very different thing from defiring that thofe conceffions fhould be made without fecurity or reftriction. This was what the Roman Catholics had been aiming at throughout, and no one was more zealous in denouncing their machinations, and expofing the infolence of their pretenfions than Dr. Phillpotts. This prefent letter, if more tedious than his earlier writings, is a proof of the ftedfaftnefs of his principles, and of the clearnefs with which he forefaw the impending danger.

The language of the Irifh Roman Catholic clergy draws from Dr. Phillpotts a ftatement of their fentiments towards the Eftablifhed Church, which entitles him to the thanks of every one who would fhrink from feeing his country fall a victim to a tyranny too fearful to contemplate. Rightly enough does he defcribe their far-fighted policy, when he fays,—

" With a vigilance that never fleeps, with an elafticity of hope, which no degree of preffure can ever wholly keep

down, with a paſſionate and anxious longing for the reſto-
ration of the power of their Church and of their order—
they never omit a ſingle occaſion of ſerving that holy cauſe,
and of preparing for what they confidently expeẟ muſt one
day happen, its ſignal and enduring triumph."

Other topics are handled in this letter; but while
they are always treated with ability, it muſt be confeſſed that they are ſomewhat foreign to the purpoſe.
The letter is too diffuſe. Written, however, as it was,
one year before the fatal meaſure which gave to Roman
Catholics the unreſtriẟed enjoyment of civil privileges, it was natural enough that reference ſhould be
made to topics which might help to awaken the nation
to the greatneſs of the peril. It would have been
wiſe, however, if the dimenſions of the letter had
been curtailed. A volume of 100 pages would have
anſwered all the purpoſes of one of 330. But if the
letter is ſometimes tedious, it is always candid and
temperate. Faẟs are never perverted or overſtated.
The writing is clear, forcible, and manly, and every
one muſt riſe from the peruſal of this volume with the
conviẟion that the Author is as deeply verſed in the
conſtitutional law of the country as his other pamphlets have ſhown him to be in controverſial theology.

CHAPTER XVI.

The Death of Lord Liverpool, and its Effect upon the Roman Catholic Question. Ministerial Difficulties. Mr. Canning appointed Premier. His Death. Lord Goderich's Administration. The Duke of Wellington forms a Cabinet. Repeal of the Test and Corporation Acts. Immediately followed by a Motion to remove Roman Catholic Disabilities. Alarming State of Ireland. Hostility of the Roman Catholics to the Administration of the Duke of Wellington. The Irish Association. Rumours of intended Concession to the Roman Catholics. Subject referred to in the King's Speech. Alarm and Indignation of the Country. Ministers denounced. The Plans of the Duke of Wellington too well laid to be successfully opposed. Conduct of the King. Effect of the Measure on his Title to the Throne. Views of the Supporters of it. Remarks of Mr. Brougham. Difficulty of the Position acknowledged by the Duke of Wellington. Mr. Peel's Motion for removing Roman Catholic Disabilities. Anxiety of the Public to hear the Debate. Passing of the Bill. Symptoms of Disaffection in the Cabinet. Dismissal of Sir Charles Wetherall. The Bill carried up to the Lords and passed. Scene in the House. The Royal Assent given. Conduct of the King. Termination of this Memorable Contest. Lord Eldon's Prophetic Words. Remarks upon the Passing of the Bill.

UT while the Letters of Dr. Phillpotts were penetrating to the moſt diſtant parts of England, the hopes of the Roman Catholic party were ſtimulated by the illneſs and death of Lord Liverpool,* who for nearly

---

* He moved an addreſs to the King on the death of the

fifteen years had been prime minifter, and had ever
fhown the moft uncompromifing oppofition to their
claims.   A ferious difficulty immediately arofe.   The
Anti-Catholic part of the miniftry would ferve under
no head who would not pledge himfelf to refift further
conceffion, while the more " liberal " portion of the
Cabinet, reprefented by Mr. Canning, infifted upon
the nomination of a premier who was known to be
favourable to the Roman Catholic claims.   After much
negotiation and delay, Mr. Canning was appointed
prime minifter, and the Duke of Wellington, Lord
Eldon, Mr. Peel, and Lords Bathurft, Melville, and
Weftmoreland retired from the Cabinet.   Others were
introduced into their places who were moftly known
to be favourable to Roman Catholic relief; and although
they were not formally pledged to fupport any meafure of conceffion, yet it was commonly felt that the
Roman Catholic afpirations were never fo likely to be
gratified as now.   It is probable enough that Mr. Canning would have devifed fome fcheme of conceffion—
although it may well be doubted whether he would
have ventured to reproduce that bill which brought
down upon it fuch withering farcafm from Dr. Phillpotts—but his earthly labours were foon to ceafe.   He
was already ftricken with the hand of death, and four
months after his acceffion to office he expired at Chif-

Duke of York, February 12, 1827, and a few days afterwards was feized with paralyfis, which, although not fatal
at the time, entirely prevented him from again attending to
public bufinefs.

wick. Thus the " liberal party" was deprived of its leader, and the Roman Catholic cauſe of its champion. During the ſhort tenure of office by Lord Goderich, who ſucceeded Mr. Canning, nothing was done. The changes were too rapid to admit of thought being given to any meaſure of importance, much leſs to one of ſuch gigantic proportions as the Roman Catholic queſtion had now become.

At the commencement of the year 1828 it became evident that Lord Goderich's miniſtry was expiring, and that it could not be galvanised into vitality enough even for it to meet Parliament, which was appointed to aſſemble on the 29th of January. The conſtruction of a new miniſtry was therefore entruſted to the Duke of Wellington, and it was felt that the hopes of the Roman Catholic party were ex-tinguiſhed.

One of the earlieſt Acts of this ſeſſion was the repeal of the Teſt and Corporation Acts which ex-cluded Diſſenters from offices of truſt and power, and rendered them incapable of becoming members of any corporation, unleſs they conſented to receive Holy Communion according to the ritual of the Church of England. The meaſure was introduced by Lord John Ruſſell on the 26th of February, and became of great importance, as paving the way for the demand of further conceſſions by the Roman Catholics. This meaſure had ever been oppoſed by the greateſt ſtateſ-men as revolutionary and deſtructive of the Engliſh Church eſtabliſhed by law, nor will it be thought that the danger was over-rated when a Diffenting minifter of eminence had not fcrupled to declare, in reference to the projected conceffion, that he had laid a train of gunpowder under the Church which would blow it up ; and another Diffenting minifter had bleffed God that he could depart in peace, as the revolution in France would lead to the deftruction of all union between Church and State in England.

It was confidered an ominous fign that the archbifhops and moft of the bifhops declared themfelves in favour of the bill, and the Roman Catholics took courage.   Accordingly, the repeal of the Teft and Corporation Acts was immediately followed by a motion to remove the remaining Roman Catholic Difabilities, and after a debate it was agreed, on the 16th of May, that a conference fhould be held with the Houfe of Lords on the fubject.   This was held on the 19th ; and on the 9th of June the queftion was taken into confideration by the Houfe of Peers.   The debate lafted two days, and the motion was loft by a majority of forty-four.

Meanwhile the ftate of Ireland was fuch as to threaten the utter difruption of fociety in that country. In defiance of all law, Mr. O'Connell was returned as member for the county of Clare, and the Irifh Affociation declared openly that it would do everything in its power to prevent the election of every candidate who would not oppofe the adminiftration of the Duke of Wellington.   Nor were the operations of the Affociation confined to any particular locality.   Monfter meetings were held in the provinces, and county and parochial clubs were organized.

Nor was this all. Arms were provided, and the rabble were drilled to military duties. Riots quickly enfued, and it was hard to fay what would now fatisfy Roman Catholic rapacity, or where the mifchief would end.

It was under fuch circumftances as thefe that it began to be whifpered at the clubs that the Cabinet had determined on conceffion; and on the 5th of February, 1829, when Parliament was opened, the Royal fpeech contained a paragraph recommending it " to review the laws which impofe civil difabilities on His Majefty's Roman Catholic fubjects." This was, indeed, preceded by a paragraph which directed attention to the mifdeeds of the Irish Affociation, and called upon Parliament to affift his Majefty in enforcing the laws; but the Roman Catholics could well afford to put up with this affront upon their favourite inftitution, when, as Sir Jofeph Yorke truly enough remarked, " the affociation had now nothing to do but to fhut up its door; to put one of Bramah's beft patent locks upon it, and to put the key fomewhere where it would never be heard of again." This humorous fuggeftion was acceded to, and the Irish Affociation, after nine-and-twenty years of feditious agitation, clofed its meetings not many days afterwards, with an harangue from O'Connell.

The King's fpeech fell on the country like a thunderbolt, for there had hitherto been nothing either in the ſtate of the queſtion itſelf or the attitude of the miniſters to juſtify ſuch a ſudden change of policy. People began to believe that there was ſome truth in the French ſaying, " *le vrai n'eſt pas toujours le vrai-ſemblable.*" Thus, then, while the country was brac-ing its energies to offer a more reſolute reſiſtance to Roman Catholic aggreſſion, than any which had yet been ſeen, the miniſters were ſecretly betraying the cauſe which they had ſo long eſpouſed, and to which they were ſo deeply pledged. No whiſper of their treachery, however, was permitted to reach the public ear until the very eve of the aſſembling of Parliament, and their plans were by this time ſo ſkilfully arranged that ſucceſs could not for a moment be doubtful. The Duke of Wellington was not the man to do a thing by halves.

The indignation of the country was extreme. It felt that it was betrayed by the very perſons who had hitherto been the ſtouteſt opponents of any change. The victory was ſecure before the battle had begun, and although meetings were held in all parts of the country, and the Houſes of Parliament were deluged with petitions againſt further conceſſion, it was felt that no amount of energy could counteract the miſ-chief which was already done. The condition of the Anti-Catholic party at this time is well deſcribed by Lord Sidmouth.* "For the firſt time in my life I am diſheartened. We ſeem to be in a ſhattered boat,

---

* Pellew's " Life of Lord Sidmouth," vol. iii. p. 427.

and in a ftrange and agitated fea, without pilot, chart, or compafs." The King too—although, to do him juftice, he exhibited marked repugnance to the meafure—was placed in a moft painful and anomalous pofition, fince the projeƈt of Emancipation was founded on aſſumptions which, if juft, would have the effeƈt of rendering much which was done in 1688, and the Aƈt of Settlement on the Princeſs Sophia, and the heirs of her body *being Proteftants*—the forfeiture of the Crown by converfion or marriage—altogether unjuft; and, as Lord Eldon truly faid, the minifters of the Crown, in advifing him to confent to Emancipation, as it was afked, were in reality advifing him to give his aſſent to a libel on his title to the throne.

It is only fair, however, to the promoters of the meafure to fay that they looked upon it as a political neceſſity. The maintenance of a Cabinet on the principle of continued refiftance to Roman Catholic claims was, in their eftimation, impoſſible. And nowhere was this better underftood than on the oppofition benches.

" I contend," faid Mr. Brougham, " that there are no materials in exiftence for fuch a Cabinet. Suppofing the right hon. gentleman oppofite (Mr. Peel), unfortunately for his country, unfortunately for his own reputation, had continued to adhere to his opinion that the claims of the Catholics ought never to be liftened to, he alone muft have formed, of all the perfons here—he alone, with the exception of one or two other individuals on the bench above him, and with the exception of one or two noble perfons, members of a Houfe to which it would be diforderly further to allude—he alone muft have formed the Cabinet by which continual refiftance could have been made to the fettlement of the Catholic queftion."

To fhow the feelings of the Cabinet on this momentous meafure, it will be fufficient to quote the words of the Duke of Wellington. " This is a bad bufinefs," he faid to Lord Sidmouth, the day before Parliament met, " *but we are aground.*" It is true enough that the Duke fhortly afterwards difcovered and admitted that he had been miftaken; but ftill, for the moment, there appeared to him to be no door of efcape.

And now the queftion of Roman Catholic relief was once more to be debated within the walls of Parliament, and this time with fuch fuccefs as its earlieft advocates could never have dared to predict. On the 5th of March, Mr. Peel, who had been rejected at Oxford, but returned for Weftbury, moved " that the Houfe refolve itfelf into a Committee of the whole Houfe, to confider the laws impofing civil difabilities on His Majefty's Roman Catholic fubjects."

So great was the anxiety of the public to hear the debate on this all-abforbing meafure that every avenue leading to the Houfe of Commons was crowded before noon; and, although the call of the Houfe, moved for by Lord Chandos, prevented ftrangers being admitted into the gallery before fix o'clock, yet, fo far from the excitement having diminifhed, the number in attendance had gone on fteadily increafing with every hour. Some ladies of high rank were among the firft to rufh in as foon as the doors were opened, and there they patiently remained all the night, although feated immediately over the principal chandelier, and condemned, by their own felf-devotion, to fwallow all the poifonous vapour which arofe from the body of the houfe. Much time was occupied in the prefentation of petitions; but the anxiety. which filled every breaft to learn "the grand fecret" could be endured no longer, and the call for Mr. Peel became loud and general. On his rifing the deepeft filence prevailed, and, during the four hours and a quarter for which he fpoke, the attention of his hearers never feemed to flag. In an eloquent and elaborate fpeech he reviewed the whole queftion, and taxed his ingenuity to the utmoft to fhow that the meafure, which he had been fteadily oppofing for twenty years, was in reality for the benefit of the nation. On a divifion the motion was carried by a decifive majority of 188. And here it will be inftructive to notice that this bill required *no fecurities ;* but Roman Catholics might henceforward be admitted to the higheft offices in the State, with the exception of the Lord-Lieutenancy of Ireland, and the Chancellorfhip of England, and might hereafter become the King's advifers.

After paffing through its various ftages, each of which was fucceffively marked by long and ftormy debates, the bill was read a third time on the 30th of March, and carried by a majority of 178. The fcene in the Houfe towards the clofe of the debate was exciting in the extreme. The cheering of the fupporters of the bill was deafening, while upwards of fifty members from different fides of the Houfe thronged round Mr. Peel, and fhook hands with him in a cordial and enthufiaftic manner.

The rapidity with which this meaſure was hurried through the Houſe of Commons may well excite aſtoniſhment, eſpecially when it is remembered that it effected a greater change in the Conſtitution than anything which had taken place ſince the Revolution ; but the Duke of Wellington, having once decided on conceſſion, was too ſkilful a tactician to allow the country needleſs time for reflection.   This was the more neceſſary from ſymptoms of lukewarmneſs, if not of actual diſaffection, which had appeared in his own Cabinet ; and it is not unworthy of remark that the paſſing of the bill was ſignaliſed by the diſmiſſal of the Attorney-general (Sir Charles Wetherall) for having, in no meaſured terms of indignation, expoſed the fatal policy of the Miniſters, and denounced their apoſtacy.

On the 31ſt of March the bill was read a firſt time in the Houſe of Lords.   The debate on the ſecond reading commenced on the 2nd of April, and, having laſted during that and the two following nights, was carried by a majority of 105.   When the importance of the ſubject is remembered—being nothing leſs than a change in the Conſtitution of the country —the ability with which the arguments on either ſide were enforced, and the eſtimation in which the ſpeakers were held by their reſpective parties, this debate may fairly be conſidered one of the moſt memorable in the annals of the nation.   The third reading of the bill was moved by the Duke of Wellington on the 10th of April, when it was carried by a majority of ninety-

four, *in the fame Houfe which, in the preceding year,
had rejeɛted a fimilar bill by a majority of forty-five.*
The Houfe of Lords had never been fo full fince the
Queen's trial. The fpace about the throne and below
the bar was completely crowded, and the body of the
Houfe was filled with peers. All the Royal dukes
were prefent, as was alfo Dr. Doyle, the Roman Catholic bifhop, who had played fo confpicuous a part
in the agitation, and whofe unfcrupulous tactics had
been fo well expofed by Dr. Phillpotts in his Letters
to Mr. Butler and Mr. Canning. Mr. Peel, alfo, was
prefent, and remained in the Houfe during the greater
part of the debate. The Duke of Wellington, who
was the idol of the hour, Lord Grey, and feveral other
peers, were loudly cheered by the populace in Palace
Yard.

The bill received the Royal affent on April the 13th.
But this was given with no good grace. Oppofition
to fuch a meafure had now become the traditionary
policy of the Houfe of Brunfwick, founded, no doubt,
quite as much on political as religious confiderations.
If the proteftations of George IV. are to be believed,
he felt all the repugnance to conceffion which his
father and his brother (the late Duke of York) had
fhown, and, in a converfation with Lord Eldon, after
the paffing of the meafure,* " he declared that he had
been moft harfhly and cruelly treated—that he had
been treated as a man whofe confent had been afked

---

* Twifs's " Life of Lord Eldon," vol. iii. p. 84.

with a piftol pointed to his breaft, or as obliged, if he did not give it, to leap down a five-pair-of-ftairs window—what could he do ?   What had he to fall back upon ?"   He then went on to fay,*—"I am miferable, wretched ; my fituation is dreadful—nobody about me to advife with.   If I do give my affent, I'll go to the baths abroad, and from thence to Hanover. I'll return no more to England—I'll make no Roman Catholic peers—I will not do what this bill will enable me to do—I'll return no more—let them get a Catholic king in Clarence.   The people will fee that I did not wifh this."   But, in fpite of all this, and more, the affent was given ; not, indeed, by the King in perfon, but by a Commiffion, compofed of Lords Lyndhurft, Bathurft, and Ellenborough.   Very little intereft was felt in the ceremony.   There were fcarcely enough members of the Houfe of Commons prefent to attend the Speaker to the Upper Houfe, and amongft them were no perfons of diftinction or confequence, except Sir G. Murray.   On the Speaker's return there were about twenty members on each fide of the Houfe ; and, when he announced that the members had been in the Houfe of Peers to hear the Royal affent given to the Roman Catholic Relief Bill, there was fome cheering, in the midft of which a perfon in the fide-gallery exclaimed, in an audible voice, " Alas ! they know not what they do."   The meafure, therefore, had now paffed into law, and the only way in which

* Page 86.

the King could foothe his wounded feelings was by fhowing marked incivility at the following *levée* to all who had voted for it.

Thus ended the memorable conteft which had fo long agitated the country from one end to the other, and the magnitude of which it would be difficult to exaggerate. It was the confcioufnefs of the fatal conceffion which was being made that wrung from Lord Eldon the indignant declaration, that if he had a voice that would found to the remoteft corner of the Empire, he would re-echo the principle which he moft firmly believed—that if ever a Roman Catholic was permitted to form part of the legiflature of this country, or to hold any of the great executive offices of the Government, from that moment the fun of Great Britain would be fet. In defiance of all remonftrance, however, and as if in derifion of all prophetic forebodings, the meafure was carried with a high hand; not, indeed, by its original promoters, but by thofe who had hitherto fhown it the moft uncompromifing oppofition. Thus, then, the Roman Catholic hopes were crowned with fuccefs. The greatnefs of their victory was the prefage of ftill more unbounded triumphs. Time was when after the firft conceffions they were called ungrateful, becaufe they afked for frefh ones. Scarcely a voice was then raifed in their favour, and they themfelves had hardly learnt to feel any confidence in their ftrength. By degrees, however, they became confcious of latent power; that power was foftered and matured by external fympathy; firft of all they were pitied, then they were liftened to ; they quickly fhowed themfelves no contemptible opponents ; they made themfelves feared, and now behold them in their hour of victory ! Thus it was, then, that—" Roman Catholics were made members of that legiflature, which, by their religious tenets, they pronounce to be impious and heretical ; governors of that people which they pronounce to be incapable of falvation ; arbiters of that civil and religious freedom which it is the firft principle of Popery to extinguifh in all kingdoms, and counfellors of that King whom Rome denounces as a revolter from its fealty and religion."*

The courfe of events has been fomewhat anticipated, in order to bring the Roman Catholic queftion to a conclufion ; and now it will be neceffary to return to Dr. Phillpotts.

---

* Croly's " Life of George IV," p. 492.

CHAPTER XVII.

Dr. Phillpotts appointed Dean of Chester. Suit in the Ecclesi-
aftical Court against one of the Prebendaries. Ability dif-
played by Dr. Phillpotts. Accused of having changed his
Opinion on the Roman Catholic Question. Odium excited by
the Charge. Article in the Edinburgh Review. *The Falsity*
of its Allegations shown. Dr. Phillpotts not a Clerical Agi-
tator. His Vote for Mr. Peel at the Oxford Election of 1829.
Petition from the Dean and Chapter of Chester against Roman
Catholic Relief Bill. Letter to Dr. Ellerton. Remarks of
the Times. *Motives which guided Dr. Phillpotts in voting*
for Mr. Peel. His Opinion on the Roman Catholic Question
unchanged. Mr. Peel's Change of Sentiment. Hard to esti-
mate it aright at the Time. Fury of the Clergy. Combi-
nation of High and Low Church against Mr. Peel. The
Vote of Dr. Phillpotts given with pain. Estrangement from
Old Friends. Mr. Peel's Rejection. Satire and Rude Cari-
catures. Specimen of Verses. The Conduct of Dr. Phillpotts
in reference to the Roman Catholic Question in 1812. *Not*
an Advocate for Entire Exclusion. Meeting of the Clergy and
Resolution. His Amendment. His Views continued un-
changed. Reason of the Malice of his Adversaries.

ND now the labours of Dr. Phillpotts in
refisting the claims of the Roman Catholics
were about to receive a fubstantial and
appropriate recognition. The Deanery
of Chester having become vacant by the promotion of
Dr. Copleftone to the See of Llandaff, that office was
conferred upon him, and he was inftituted to it on the
13th of May, 1828. He continued to hold it until
his elevation to the Epifcopal Bench in 1831. It was

remarked at the time of his inftallation that both in perfon and voice he very clofely refembled a former dean, the Rev. Dr. Hodgfon—afterwards Dean of Carlifle.

No incidents of local intereft occurred while Dr. Phillpotts held the Deanery of Chefter, except the conduct of a difficult and complicated fuit carried on in the Ecclefiaftical and Civil Courts againft one of the prebendaries, who had leafed away part of the land attached to his prebendal houfe for building purpofes. This fuit was commenced by Dr. Copleftone while Dean of Chefter, and tranfmitted by him to his fucceffor. The extreme acutenefs and readinefs of reply which were manifefted by Dean Phillpotts, on fome occafions on which he was fuddenly called upon to give an immediate anfwer to difficult queftions of law or logic at the chapter meetings, were long re-membered. The fuit, however, poffeffes no intereft to the public.

It was while Dr. Phillpotts was Dean of Chefter that the meafure for the relief of Roman Catholics was carried ; * and it was now that he was accufed of having facrificed the convictions of a life for the fake of a mitre, which was to be the price of his perfidy. The odium created by this charge has lafted till the prefent day ; common juftice, therefore, demands that its truth or falfity fhould be eftablifhed.

Among the many periodicals which from time to

---

* See page 262.

time have lent themfelves to the propagation of this hideous charge, the *Edinburgh Review* may perhaps be ranked as the firft, both from its extenfive circulation and the credit of its writers. The opinions of this Journal, therefore, may well be allowed to do duty for the reft. In an article for 1852, the favage vindictivenefs of which does as little credit to the heart of the writer, as its gigantic diftortions do to his love of truth, the following occurs :—

" The Government which carried Catholic Emancipation was a Tory Government ; and Tory ftatefmen naturally defired to avert the lofs of that clerical fupport on which their power had fo mainly depended ; they knew the prejudices of the clergy, and felt how much they would be fhocked by the paffing of the meafure ; and they reafonably wifhed to fecure the fupport of that one of its moft prominent ecclefiaftical opponents, who had *oppofed it efpecially on religious grounds, and had moft fuccefsfully enlifted clerical paffions againft it.* His converfion and his arguments, it was hoped, might convince, or at leaft filence many who hitherto had hung fo fondly on his words. *Accordingly, the converfion of Dr. Phillpotts was effected at this critical juncture. He wrote in favour of the Bill, and he voted for the author of the Bill,* at the memorable Oxford election of 1829."

Now, if thefe charges were true, Dr. Phillpotts would, indeed, have been all and more than his anonymous defamer had wifhed to make him out to be. But the writer allowed his fpleen to carry him altogether out of the limits of truth, and having once fairly ftarted in the congenial region of romance, a powerful fancy, ftimulated by an atrabilious difpofition and impetuous temper, hurried him to lengths of invective which are happily unknown to lefs afpiring critics.

But falfe and cruel as thefe charges were, they claim a notice—more, however, for the fake of that diftinguifhed Magazine which permitted its pages to be fullied by the calumny, than for his who could proftitute mental powers of no mean order for the fake of indulging a paltry fpite.

It happens, then, that Dr. Phillpotts had *not* oppofed the Roman Catholic Relief Bill, " efpecially on religious grounds," in the fenfe imputed to him by the reviewer, nor had he " fuccefsfully enlifted clerical paffions againft it."

The fact was that Mr. Canning and others had fo blended the theological and political afpects of the queftion together that it was not eafy to deal with one without the other.   Nor was this confined to Parliament.   Every tavern orator who dafhed into the queftion imagined himfelf an Aquinas or a Luther as the Catholic or Proteftant fcale preponderated.   Like the figure of Fortune, then, the queftion had two faces, the religious and civil, and fo dexteroufly was the image turned about that you could not always tell which face it was that was looking at you.   Both, moreover, had become fo battered and dirty by ill-ufage that the delufion was helped in this way.   Meanwhile, as the figure revolved, the perpetual cry of its attendant priefts was for " toleration ;" a happily chofen word, as ambiguous as the refponfes of the oracle of old, and which might well do duty either for religion or politics, as need fhould arife.

Dr. Phillpotts was one of the firſt to ſee through this miſerable trickery. But what could he do? There was the queſtion in a hopeleſs tangle. Alexander himſelf might have found a difficulty in cutting the knot. If a hoſt of ſpeakers and writers perſiſted in thruſting forward *theological arguments* in favour of *political meaſures,* was Dr. Phillpotts to be blamed if he ſhowed that their theology was about as profound as their pretenſion to political knowledge? The taſk was not one of his own ſeeking, neither was it an agreeable one. It was forced upon him; and to the laſt he viewed it as a hard neceſſity. Of all men living, however, he was probably the beſt qualified to perform it. With a quickneſs of perception and a ſteadineſs of purpoſe which were abſolutely marvellous, he threaded his way through the mazes of this dreary controverſy. If his opponents, as in the caſe of Mr. C. Butler and Dr. Doyle, inſiſted upon throwing down the gauntlet of religious argument, he could not do leſs than ſtoop to take it up. But it was only to diſarm a miſchievous adverſary, and not to conſtitute himſelf the leader of a clerical faction. If, then, the clergy learnt to reſpect his talents, Mr. Butler and the reſt were to be thanked for having called forth their diſplay. And there the matter ended; for he was not qualified to become the leader of his brethren. Largely as he could ſympathize with them in their efforts againſt Roman Catholic aggreſſion, yet widely did he differ from them as to the way in which that aggreſſion was to be met. And this will preſently be ſeen.

But if the charge of being a clerical agitator brought Dr. Phillpotts into difcredit, the vote which he gave in favour of Mr. Peel at the memorable Oxford election of 1829, tended ftill more to inflame the prejudice which was already excited againft him. Early in that year it began to be rumoured that he had feen reafon to change his opinions on the queftion of Roman Catholic relief. The *Times* of February 3, gave publicity to this rumour, and fpoke of the " fpiteful dean who fo maligned the illuftrious Canning upon this very queftion," having " wheeled to the right about, as if by military command." He was alfo accufed of being the author of the forthcoming bill. And yet at this very time a petition to Parliament was being prepared by the Dean and Chapter of Chefter, bearing upon it evidence of Dr. Phillpotts' mafterly pen, in which, in his character as dean, he protefts againft " the extravagant demands of the Roman Catholics of Ireland," and declares that " no fcheme of fecurities has yet been brought forward which feems in any tolerable degree adequate to its profeffed object." Surely this was not the language of a man who had changed his principles, and was now ready to admit the Roman Catholics to civil privileges without any fecurities at all. The intimation of his intentions in reference to the forthcoming election is contained in the following letter to Dr. Ellerton, Tutor of Magdalene College, Oxford, dated the 20th of February, 1829 :—

" Dear Sir, I have received the favour of your letter, containing the recorded judgment of many moft refpectable

members of the Univerfity of Oxford, that Mr. Peel is unfit
to be 're-elected at the prefent crifis,' and inviting me to
vote for Sir Robert Inglis.

" On every perfonal and public ground I rejoice at the
felection of fuch a candidate by the opponents of Mr. Peel.
Sir Robert Inglis is one of my beft and moft valued friends ;
a man of the higheft character, and honourably diftinguifhed
by his zeal and ability in defence of our Proteftant Conftitution.

" But I am fure you will perceive that my vote, on this
occafion, muft be decided by one fpecial confideration.
Thofe with whom you act have, in a direct and manly manner, brought the matter to this iffue,—' Is Mr. Peel unfit to
be re-elected at the prefent crifis ?' I do not think that he
is. I will not, therefore, affift in cafhiering him.

" And now let me trouble you with a few words refpecting myfelf.

" You fay, ' reports are circulated here (Oxford) in refpect to a change of your opinions on a fubject on which you
have written fo ably and fo much. We are unwilling to give
credit to fuch rumours.'

" I thank you, and whoever elfe joins you in this fentiment, for your unwillingnefs to give credit to anything which
you may think difcreditable to me. In the prefent inftance,
the rumours you refer to, as far as they have reached me,
are either fo vague as to be unintelligible to me, or, if they
affume the fhape of an allegation of facts, are abfolutely falfe.

" As to my opinions, they remain unchanged ; they accord
with the fpirit of my Letter to Mr. Canning, pages 158—164,
and more efpecially with ' Application of the Argument,' in
my Letter on the Coronation Oath, pages 176—180. If
any of thofe who have done me the honour of reading thefe
works have happened to attend to fuch parts only of them
as fell in with their own preconceived opinions, it is rather
hard that I fhould be made anfwerable for their inadvertence.
Be this as it may, I have the gratification of knowing that

T

the moſt diſtinguiſhed of the names in the printed papers you have ſent to me are not in this error. They have ſtated (as I doubt not you have heard), in voluntary vindication of an abſent and ſlandered friend, that my writings had prepared them to expeƈt that I ſhould be favourable to the adjuſtment of the Roman Catholic queſtion, on terms compatible with the ſecurity of the Proteſtant Conſtitution.

" Whether the bill about to be brought into Parliament be of this charaƈter I do not know. If I ſhall deem it ſuch (and I heartily wiſh I may ſee reaſon to do ſo), I ſhall not be deterred by clamour, in any quarter, from avowing my opinion ; if otherwiſe, I ſhall not be backward in joining in any fit mode of expreſſing diſſatisfaƈtion.

" For the preſent, I content myſelf with citing to you, and to every one who may feel an intereſt in what concerns me, a ſingle ſentence (pages 179, 180), in my Letter, publiſhed laſt year on the Coronation Oath,—a ſentence which Mr. Wilmot Horton has with very good reaſon publicly treated as an invitation (he himſelf calls it a challenge), to conſider the matter of Securities on both ſides :—

" ' In one word, then, ſee whether you (the Roman Catholics) can offer us any real and adequate Security for our Church, if the boon you aſk be granted ; or try to find *the Securities which we, on our part, may deviſe,* ſuch as you can conſcientiouſly accede to.'

" Whether the writer of this ſentence can be juſtly charged with inconſiſtency, for now teſtifying, or aƈting upon, a wiſh, that adequate Securities may be propoſed, is a queſtion which I will not inſult your underſtanding by aſking you.

" You are at perfeƈt liberty to conſider this as a public Letter.

" I am, dear Sir,

" Your faithful Servant,

" Henry Phillpotts."

That this letter fhould have been regarded as evidence of defeĉtion from a caufe which he had ferved fo long and fo well, may reafonably excite aftonifhment in an unprejudiced mind. The *Times* of February 24, 1829, truly enough fays :—

" For the future it can only be wilful and obftinate perverfenefs that would charge him with having been hoftile to conceffion upon any terms ; but unprejudiced men could never have fallen into that error, on reading the Letter to which we have alluded,* if it had been conceived and written in a milder temper, and had treated the illuftrious ftatefman (as he deferved) with refpeĉt. However, people may now abufe Dr. Phillpotts as they pleafe for fupporting Mr. Peel, if that be matter of reproach ; but ' till they can rail the feal from off the bond,'—till they can obliterate what he has previoufly written—it *muft be impudently and glaringly falfe in them to tax him with ' change of opinions.'* "

The motives which guided him in recording his vote in favour of Mr. Peel are fupplied by Dr. Phillpotts himfelf in a letter to Sir Robert Inglis, written many years later :—

" It had been, and ftill is, the honourable diftinĉtion of the Univerfity of Oxford, when once it has eleĉted a Reprefentative in Parliament, to continue to him the undifturbed poffeffion of his feat, unlefs he fhould forfeit the confidence of his conftituents by fome flagrant departure from the principles which ought to aĉtuate public men. Upon this occafion, the queftion, which was to decide the votes of the eleĉtors, was not whether they approved the bill which had been paffed, but whether Sir Robert Peel had, by introducing it, deferved to forfeit the confidence of his con-

---

* The Firft Letter to Mr. Canning.

ftituents. It was my undoubting judgment that he had not, and I felt myfelf bound to vote for him accordingly, in oppofition to the wifhes and judgment of many whom I moft valued. I knew (or believed on grounds as fatisfactory as knowledge) that Sir Robert Peel had been brought to a conviction of the impoffibility of any longer effectually refifting the demand for conceffion to the Roman Catholics. I knew that he had ftated this his conviction to King George IV, and, having ftated it, had entreated permiffion to refign his office—thinking it better for his Majefty's fervice that the meafure fhould be carried by ftatefmen who had always fupported it, than by thofe who had hitherto refifted it. I knew that the King had refufed the permiffion which was afked, and had required that thofe minifters who had advifed the neceffity of conceffion, fhould themfelves give him their fervices in effecting it. Sir Robert Peel, in yielding to his Sovereign's very reafonable demand, thought it right to give to his conftituents an opportunity of declaring whether he had thereby forfeited their confidence. As one of thefe conftituents, honouring the integrity with which I knew he had acted, I deemed it my very plain duty to teftify that feeling by continuing to vote for him."

There is a manly tone about this ftatement which muft commend itfelf to every unprejudiced mind. Voting for Mr. Peel did not neceffarily entail any fupport of Roman Catholic claims. The opinion of Dr. Phillpotts on the great queftion of conferring upon Roman Catholics a fhare of the legiflature, without exacting from them ample fecurities, remained unchanged, and the vote which he felt bound to record in favour of Mr. Peel did not affect it. That a change of fentiment had unhappily found favour with that diftinguifhed ftatefman is known to every one, and after a lapfe of more than thirty years the motives which influenced his conduct can be accurately weighed and appreciated. But when men's paffions were inflamed to a degree almoft beyond precedent—when O'Connell was declaiming in the Rotunda at Dublin, and Moore was finging his patriotic fongs in the drawing-rooms of the Weft End—when, in a word, a Roman Catholic fever of unprecedented virulence feemed to have feized upon the country, and was rapidly approaching its crifis, it was not eafy—it was not poffible—to do juftice to this gifted man. Hence, many of the clergy, frefh from remote country parifhes, were furious, and haftened up to Oxford to record their indignant votes againft him. Never before, perhaps, was there fo extraordinary an exhibition of the violent temper of partifans, as in the fcene which then took place. High and Low Church forgot the differences of a lifetime in a coalition againft the " Ifcariot of the age," for fo Mr. Peel was fomewhat profanely called. Living out of the world, as many of the clergy did, and juftly meriting the reproach of Dr. Arnold,* that they were wanting in acquired knowledge and impartiality, they were as yet unconfcious of the tide of popular feeling which had fet in fo ftrongly. Dr. Phillpotts, however, and others like him, while they fhrank from the idea of conceffion without fecurities, could yet honour the ftatefman,

---

* " The Chriftian Duty of granting the Claims of the Roman Catholics," &c.

who, unable to refift his convictions, had laid his office
at the feet of his Sovereign.   For eighteen years he
had offered an uncompromifing, but a temperate, fair,
and conftitutional refiftance to making any further
conceffions to the Roman Catholics; it could have
been no light motive, therefore, which impelled him
to abandon principles of which he had for fo long
been the acknowledged and honoured champion.   But
what wonder is it that Mr. Peel fhould have fuccumbed
to what he regarded as a ftern neceffity, when fuch a
man as Lord Eldon, the hope and buttrefs of the old
Tory party, could fay on the eve of the meafure being
carried, " We fhall fight refpectably and honourably,
but we fhall be in a wretched minority ; but what is
moft calamitous of all is, that the *Archbifhops and
feveral of the Bifhops are againft us.*"

It is only due to Dr. Phillpotts to fay that the
vote which he recorded upon this occafion gave him
much pain, and caufed an eftrangement from old and
valued friends,—a circumftance which may well recall
the memory of more recent Oxford elections, when a
ftatefman as diftinguifhed as Mr. Peel, and once the
cherifhed reprefentative of the moft Confervative body
in England, faw his former fupporters ftand aloof, if
not foremoft in the oppofing ranks.   Ill muft it be
for him if he read not in the paft the tokens of his
future difmiffal !

If anything could have added to the pain with
which Dr. Phillpotts gave his vote, it was the fact
that he found himfelf in oppofition to his revered

friend Dr. Routh, Prefident of Magdalene College, who nominated Sir Robert Inglis. But this was not all. He voted on the lofing fide, Mr. Peel having been rejected by a majority of 146, after a conteft of three days, during which 1364 votes were polled. This pofition, agreeable at no time, was rendered doubly trying when rude fatire and coarfe invective were liberally employed to hold the haplefs voter up to ridicule.

Thus, while Mr. Peel was figuring in a caricature which reprefented Canning emerging from a tomb, and purfuing him with the words, " I am avenged !" the bookfellers' fhops were crowded with prints of " the great rat," as Dr. Phillpotts was called, with more of Fefcennine humour than truth. Squibs alfo, more or lefs highly feafoned to fuit the public tafte, were handed about from one common room to the other. The following fpecimen will fuffice :—

> " I faw a Bifhop in a confternation
> Refpecting a fcrap of erroneous Latin,
> Thinking about ' a new tranflation,'
> And afking what was the Greek for ' ratting.'
> I faw a man with a fhovel-hat,
> One who knows full well what's what ;
> ' Sir,' he faid, ' among my fancies
> I've been poring o'er S. Francis,
> And much light—much light—I've had ;
> Really 'tis not half fo bad.
> Truly, Sir, I can't but feel
> (My refpects to Mr. Peel),
> Oftentimes, dear Sir, and long
> I have done the Papifts wrong ;

And I'll haften to repair it,
For I know not how to bear it."

But there is another charge againft Dr. Phillpotts; that of having " moft fuccefsfully enlifted clerical paf-fions " againft the bill for Roman Catholic relief. This has already been referred to.* And here, again, he had much to complain of. So far from having affumed the character of a *clerical* agitator, for motives of worldly gain, as was pretty broadly hinted, he in reality *refufed to take any part* in the petitions againft the meafure which were fent up to Parliament from his own Diocefe. The great body of the clergy, in the excefs of their fears, believed that the only fecurity againft the aggreffions of the Roman Catholics was *entire exclufion* from civil privileges. Meetings in the feveral Archdeaconries and Rural Deaneries were haftily convened, and refolutions paffed which often exhibited more zeal than difcretion. But Dr. Phillpotts faw that the day for exclufion was paft, and that all that remained was to exact fuch fecurities from the Roman Catholics as might enfure their loyal and peaceable behaviour. So long ago as the year 1812, when the Bifhop of Durham (Dr. Barrington) had expreffed a defire that a Petition fhould be prefented to Parliament from the Clergy of his Diocefe againft the bill which Mr. Canning was about to introduce, Dr. Phillpotts told him, in the moft ftraightforward manner, that his own opinion was in favour of conceffion *if accompanied by adequate fecurities.* A meeting was convened by

---

* See pages 270, 271.

the Archdeacon, and the petition having been moved and ſeconded, an amendment was propoſed by Dr. Phillpotts, expreſſing confidence in Parliament that no ſuch bill would receive its ſupport, *unleſs due ſecurities were provided for the Church*, and its permanent connection with the State.   The amendment was carried.

That theſe views continued to actuate him' will be ſeen from an examination of his letters to Earl Grey, and Mr. Butler, as alſo his more recent letter on the Coronation Oath.   In each of theſe conceſſion is treated as poſſible—with the ſafeguard of ſufficient ſecurities.

And yet, in the face of this explicit declaration of his ſentiments, his motives were traduced and his character for honeſty was impugned.   The truth is, his aſſailants had adopted ſo much of his writings as they ſaw fit, and eagerly thruſt them forward as favouring their doctrine of entire excluſion.   But when Dr. Phillpotts declared that ſuch were not his views, and that he was not averſe to an adjuſtment of the Roman Catholic queſtion, provided that ſufficient ſecurities could be offered, their indignation knew no bounds, and they pretended to ſay that they had been betrayed. No charge could be more unfounded.   Few men acted with confiſtency equal to that of Dr. Phillpotts, throughout the whole of this trying controverſy, and no one had to make greater ſacrifices to the ſincerity of his convictions.

It will be neceſſary to return to this ſubject further on in this volume.

CHAPTER XVIII.

Dr. Phillpotts appointed Bishop of Exeter. His Election by the Chapter. Petition of the Inhabitants of Stanhope against that Living being held in commendam *with the Bishopric. Great Excitement in the Country. The Petition considered. Stanhope had previously been held* in commendam *by three Prelates. Spoliation of the See of Exeter at the Reformation. Examples of Bishops of Exeter who had held Livings* in commendam. *If a Living were to be held with Bishopric, special reasons why it should be Stanhope. Dr. Phillpotts refused to accept the See of Exeter unless he were permitted to hold Stanhope. Sir James Graham's Notice of Motion. Change of Government. New Ministry refuse to allow Dr. Phillpotts to hold Stanhope. The Hardship confessed. Promise of Further Preferment. Manner in which the Arrangement was carried out. Petition of Clergy of Exeter against the Appointment of Dr. Phillpotts to that See. His alleged Change of Sentiment on the Roman Catholic Question. Exculpatory Statement by Sir H. Hardinge. The Charge revived by Lord Radnor. Appeal of the Bishop to the Duke of Wellington. His Grace's Reply, fully exculpating him from the Charge.*

T the close of the following year, (1830,) Dr. Christopher Bethell, having been translated from Exeter to Bangor, the former See was offered to Dr. Phillpotts by the Duke of Wellington, and accepted by him. On the 11th of November the King was pleased to order a *congé d'élire* to pass the Great Seal, empowering the Dean and Chapter of Exeter to choose a bishop;

and on the 22nd of the fame month Dr. Phillpotts was elected, the confirmation taking place on the 9th of December following.

But no fooner was it known that he was to be elevated to the Epifcopal Bench than fome of the inhabitants of Stanhope prefented a petition to the King, praying that that important living might not be held *in commendam* with the diftant See of Exeter. The movement was fet on foot by a Mr. Rippon, who headed a fmall party of the moft violent Anti-Church fection of the parifhioners that could be collected. Thofe were the days when it was eafy enough to excite clamour againft a clergyman, more particularly one fo diftinguifhed as Dr. Phillpotts. Hence it was that this otherwife infignificant memorial created great excitement in the country; and as Dr. Phillpotts' conduct was very feverely canvaffed, it will be well to take a difpaffionate furvey of the circumftances of the cafe.

The chief points in the petition of the inhabitants of Stanhope were—1st, That "the population of which the rector has the fpiritual care confifts of 12,000 inhabitants." 2nd, That " he delegates the fpiritual care of thefe 12,000 fouls to a hireling." 3rd, That " the parifh pays him a tithe of 4000*l.* a-year, and therefore may claim the advantages of a refident rector."

Suppofing thefe allegations to have been true, it muft be confeffed that the people of Stanhope had good caufe to complain. But, unfortunately for the credit of their petition, the memorialifts had allowed their antipathy to Dr. Phillpotts to carry them into the region of romance. Thus, the population was ſtated as 12,000, while the cenſus preceding Dr. Phillpotts' appointment gave the number as 4600 leſs, and of the remainder nearly 5000 were not under the ſpiritual care of the Rector of Stanhope at all, but belonged to an ancient chapelry, which had its own miniſter, and its own endowment, and was in all reſpects an independent benefice. A ſecond incumbency had recently been erected within the limits of that chapelry ; and although the Rector of Stanhope had the right of preſentation to theſe cures, yet they were wholly independent of him. This left Dr. Phillpotts with the charge of about 3000 ſouls, being 9000 leſs than ſtated in the memorial. After this mis-ſtatement it might be thought to be ſcarcely worth while to inveſtigate the other allegations, were it not to ſhow the ſpirit in which the petition was conceived, and the amount of attention which was due to it.

The ſecond point of the petition was that the rector " delegates the ſpiritual care of 12,000 inhabitants to a hireling." The object of this was to inſinuate that Dr. Phillpotts was never reſident on his benefice ; than which nothing could be more untrue. Inſtead, however, of the charge being delegated " to a hireling," *two* reſident curates were employed, both of them men of education and high character. When his own ſervices are added, it muſt be confeſſed that the ſpiritual wants of the people of Stanhope were not inadequately provided for.

The third point was that " the pariſh pays to the

rector a tithe of 4000*l.* per annum, and therefore has a right to the advantages of a refident rector." This allegation was as unfounded as the others, for, although the income of Stanhope was large, yet the fum paid by the parifhioners to the rector did not exceed 600*l.* per annum !

The pecuniary calculations of the memorialifts were, therefore, as much at fault as their ftatiftics. The truth was that the bulk of the emoluments of the living arofe from an ancient donation of the See of Durham, which conferred on the Rector of Stanhope a portion of the ore raifed in the lead mines of the See fituate within the parifh. At the time of Dr. Phillpotts' appointment this amounted to about 3000*l.* per annum. The chief part of the income of Stanhope, therefore, was taken from *the revenues of the See of Durham,* and not from the tithe paid by the parifhioners ; and fince Stanhope was occafionally held *in commendam,* that See was made to contribute fomething from its princely revenue to a poorer bifhopric. Whether this might not have been arranged in a way lefs likely to caufe fcandal is, of courfe, a ferious queftion : but the fact remains. It was the *Bifhop of Durham* who mainly contributed to the endowment of Stanhope, and not the *parifhioners,* as was alleged.

Neither was it an unufual circumftance that Stanhope fhould be held *in commendam* with a bifhopric. That living had been held in this way by three prelates who were the immediate predeceffors of Dr. Phillpotts. Bifhop Butler (the author of the *Ana-*

logy), who held it with the See of Briftol, Bifhop
Keene with the See of Chefter, and Bifhop Thurlow
with the See of Lincoln.   Now it is well known that
the See of Exeter was fpoiled of much of its revenue
in the reigns of Edward VI. and Elizabeth, and although many people might be inclined to think that
2700*l*. a-year, with an epifcopal palace, and a feat in
the Houfe of Lords, is a fufficient worldly provifion
for a follower of Him who had not where to lay His
head ; yet this idea does not feem to have found much
favour with the Bifhops of Exeter, for during this
century three of them have held important livings in
addition to their See.   Bifhop Courtenay was rector
of S. George's Hanover Square, containing 43,936
inhabitants, as fcandalous a cafe as any on record.
Bifhop Pelham held a parifh in Suffex of 1907 inhabitants, while Dr. Bethell, the immediate predeceffor
of Dr. Phillpotts, held a living in the ftill more remote
county of Yorkfhire, containing 841 inhabitants.   It
was plain, then, that Dr. Phillpotts, in feeking to increafe his epifcopal income, was only following the example of his predeceffors, and the people of Stanhope
were no worfe off than they had often been before.
No doubt it is much to the difadvantage of any parifh
to be deprived of the fuperintendence of its rector,
and it is a happy thing for the Church that the abufes
of paft generations are no longer poffible.   The complaints embodied in the petition of the people of Stanhope, however, were not borne out by fact.   It would,
indeed, have been a noble act, and one which in days

when it was the fashion to scoff at holy things, would
have tended much to elevate his order in the eyes of
the people, if the newly-elected Bishop of Exeter had
declared his intention of claiming nothing but the revenues of his See. It would have been a proof, such
as the multitude could understand, that when a man
gave up a living of 4000*l.* a-year, besides a deanery,
for a bishopric whose value was under 3000*l.*, there
was something more intended by the Episcopal office
than that it should open the door to opulence. On
the other hand, it must be remembered that Dr. Phillpotts had at this time a large family growing up, and
it would be a serious question with every prudent
parent as to whether he were justified in accepting a
dignity which at the same time deprived him of half
his income. But if a living *was* to be held *in commendam* with the Bishopric of Exeter, there were special
reasons why that living should be Stanhope. When
Dr. Phillpotts was presented to that benefice he was
required by the Bishop of Durham, who was the
patron, to build a parsonage-house. The cost of this,
together with a residence for the curates which was
also built, amounted to 12,000*l.*, and this sum was
not charged upon the living, but was defrayed by Dr.
Phillpotts himself. It may, perhaps, be thought an
excessive sum for the erection of a glebe house; but
then the very largeness of the amount is a proof of
the liberality with which Dr. Phillpotts dispensed his
income. He might have died as soon as the house
was completed, and then his successor would have been

provided with a noble reſidence without the living being burdened to the extent of a ſingle penny. The fact, then, that he had ſunk property in Stanhope, to the extent of about 600*l.* per annum, was a reaſonable ground for requiring that if any living were to be held with his biſhopric, that living ſhould be Stanhope.

Nor muſt it be ſuppoſed that the deſire to hold Stanhope *in commendam* with the See of Exeter was an afterthought on the part of Dr. Phillpotts. As ſoon as ever it was notified to him that it was the King's intention to raiſe him to the Epiſcopal Bench he ſtated, with the utmoſt openneſs, that he ſhould be unable to accept the dignity, if he was not allowed to retain his living. His propoſal was aſſented to, and he was informed that orders would be given to prepare the proper inſtruments to enable him to retain Stanhope, upon which he immediately accepted the offer of promotion. But before this arrangement could be carried out a change of government had occurred.

Meanwhile, the matter was brought before Parliament, and, on November the 10th, Sir R. Peel ſtated, in reply to a queſtion from Mr. Beaumont, that it was the intention of government to allow the Biſhop of Exeter to hold Stanhope *in commendam*. Upon this Sir James Graham gave notice that he ſhould move an addreſs to the King on the ſubject. The next night Lord Belgrave, on behalf of Dr. Phillpotts, requeſted the Houſe to ſuſpend their judgments on the matter until a future night, when a ſtatement would be made. Meanwhile, he hoped that theſe *ex parte* allegations which had appeared in the newſpapers, and elſewhere, and to which it was evident that Dr. Phillpotts could not reply, might not be allowed to bias the judgments of thoſe whoſe duty it would be to pronounce upon the caſe. On November the 22nd the promiſed ſtatement was made in the Houſe by Mr. Phillpotts, Member for Glouceſter, the biſhop's eldeſt brother, relative to Stanhope; and on December the 9th, in reply to a queſtion by Mr. C. Wynne, Lord Althorp replied, on behalf of the new Government, that his Majeſty's Miniſters, upon finding a great ob- jection prevailing throughout the country on the ſub- ject of the living of Stanhope being held *in com- mendam* with the See of Exeter, had felt it their duty to adviſe his Majeſty to abſtain from iſſuing the in- ſtruments required for that purpoſe. The truth was that Sir James Graham—who had a notice on the order-book of the Houſe of a motion for an Addreſs to the Crown praying that leave might not be granted to hold Stanhope *in commendam*—had now become a member of the new Cabinet; and this circumſtance made it impoſſible to grant Dr. Phillpotts permiſſion to hold the biſhopric and the living together. On the other hand, it was repreſented by Dr. Phillpotts to Earl Grey, that, if permiſſion to retain the living were withheld, the income of the See of Exeter would be totally inadequate to his wants.

The ſubject was referred to again on December the 15th, when Lord Althorp ſtated that, in the deciſion to

U

which the Government had come they were not actuated by any perfonal confiderations towards Dr. Phillpotts, but that it was on public grounds alone that they had advifed his Majefty not to allow the living of Stanhope to be held *in commendam*. They confidered it a grofs abufe to permit a living of fuch importance, and requiring the conftant attention of the incumbent, to be held by a perfon who muft neceffarily refide at a diftance. At the fame time he was aware that a great hardfhip was inflicted on Dr. Phillpotts; for he had accepted the See of Exeter on the diftinct underftanding that he was to hold the living of Stanhope *in commendam*. Under thefe circumftances the Government had determined to add to the See of Exeter the firft Church preferment in the gift of the Crown which fell vacant, and did not involve the cure of fouls.

The arrangement coft Earl Grey fome trouble. The queftion, however, was ultimately referred to the Bifhop of Durham (Dr. Van Mildert), who offered the Rectory of Stanhope to the Rev. W. N. Darnell, a canon of the cathedral, and he, on his acceptance of it, refigned his ftall in favour of Dr. Phillpotts. This preferment he has continued to hold, together with his bifhopric, up to the prefent time, and his increafing years and infirmities do not prevent him from taking his regular turn of refidence, and difcharging the duties of his office with exemplary punctuality. The living of Shobrook, near Crediton, is alfo held by the bifhop, it having been annexed to the See of Exeter on the death

of Dean Carey in 1680. The bifhop never refides
there, and the duties are performed by a curate.

But while the inhabitants of Stanhope were petitioning the King, and the newfpapers were loud in their
invectives againft the bifhop defignate, a memorial was
forwarded to Government, by fome of the clergy of
the diocefe of Exeter, praying that the choice of Dr.
Phillpotts might not be confirmed. Nothing but the
moft extreme cafe could be held to juftify a ftep fo
unufual. Whether the Exeter clergy could plead this
juftification will be feen from the ground-work of
their petition, which alleged a change of fentiment, on
the part of Dr. Phillpotts, upon the queftion of Roman
Catholic Emancipation, as the reafon for their approaching the Throne. But it would have been wifer
—and affuredly it would have faved an ever-recurring
fource of bitternefs in days to come—if the petitioners
had taken the trouble to fatisfy themfelves that Dr.
Phillpotts really *had* changed his fentiments for the fake
of a mitre. An examination of his writings would
have convinced them that his fentiments were unaltered.
It is true that he had voted for Mr. Peel; but was
exclufion from the Epifcopal Bench an appropriate
punifhment for fuch an offence? There were other
confiderations alfo which might have helped them to a
right conclufion, for when the queftion of Stanhope
was under difcuffion in the Commons, Sir H. Hardinge
ftated that he felt it his duty to mention circumftances
attendant upon the promotion of Dr. Phillpotts. He

then proceeded to fay that the Duke of Wellington, by whofe authority he fpoke, had communicated with Dr. Phillpotts on the fubject of the Roman Catholic Relief Bill, and that Dr. Phillpotts, inftead of being, as was generally fuppofed, an approver of that meafure, had been in fact an opponent of it, up to the time when it paffed. He alfo ftated further, on the authority of the Archbifhop of Canterbury, that it had been the intention of Lord Liverpool to raife Dr. Phillpotts to the Epifcopal Bench. He alfo faid that the Duke of Wellington made the ufual communications to the Archbifhop of Canterbury, and the Bifhop of London, and that the noble duke received the affent of thofe prelates to the propriety of the appointment of Dr. Phillpotts to the See of Exeter. They had, indeed, faid that the appointment might be unpopular in the Church; but as the duke knew that the grounds on which Dr. Phillpotts was unpopular were altogether miftaken and unfounded, he felt that this could be no fufficient objection to the appointment.

It might be thought that this would have been fufficient to have fecured Dr. Phillpotts againft a repetition of thofe unmanly attacks to which he had been expofed. But once ftart a flander—no matter how improbable—and when it has gained poffeffion of the public ear, no proteftation of innocence on the part of its victim will ever be able to eradicate the mifchief. Lucky for him if he does not carry the ftigma to his grave! This was pre-eminently the cafe with Dr. Phillpotts. He was deftined to fare no better than many a man as wife and great as he.

Although it is fomewhat anticipating the courfe of events, it may not be out of place to refer to circumftances which led to a ftill more emphatic and complete vindication of his chara&er. After he had taken his feat in Parliament, and fome of the reforming lords had tafted his cauftic eloquence, and found it little to their liking, it was thought convenient to rake up this charge of having changed his opinions. " Turncoat " is a name from which all men fhrink, more particularly when that coat has been turned for gain ; and if this epithet could only be faftened on the bifhop, it would effe& more againft him than they could hope to do by a whole feffion of fpeeches. But it was not a pleafant fight to fee a noble lord calmly reiterating, before his brother peers, a charge which had been publicly refuted months before on the authority of the Duke of Wellington himfelf. And yet on March the 22nd, 1831, the Earl of Radnor thought it not beneath him to revive the old flander. Fortunately, the Duke of Wellington happened to be prefent, and taking advantage of this, the Bifhop of Exeter rofe and faid :—

" I do not mean to trefpafs long on the indulgence of your Lordfhips ; and I muft firft return my thanks to the noble Earl who has made the infinuation or charge, as it affords me an opportunity, by the ftatement of a few fa&s, of giving it a plain, but, as I hope, fatisfa&ory anfwer. What I am now about to fay is known to one of your Lordfhips, and one who, if I err in my ftatement, can immediately contradi&,

me. I refer to the noble Duke (Wellington) lately at the head of his Majefty's Government, and I entreat that noble Duke, if I fhould in the leaft err in my ftatement, to contradiƈt me. I fuppofe the noble Earl who made this charge concluded that I had pledged myfelf with the late adminiftration to give my unqualified fupport to the Catholic queftion. On that queftion I have always held decided opinions, and I have always thought that conceffion fhould not be granted without being accompanied with ftrong fecurities. My opinions on that fubjeƈt were well known. The noble Duke, when in office, had done me the honour to communicate with me on the fubjeƈt, and, having ftated his intention to propofe a meafure for the relief of the Catholics, had condefcended to afk my opinion. I told the noble Duke the fecurities I thought neceffary; and having afcertained, through the fame channel, the determination of the Cabinet, I told the noble Duke that I entirely difapproved of the propofed meafure, and in all my communications with the noble Duke I took the liberty of telling him that the propofed fecurities were inadequate. Having made this fhort ftatement, I again put it to the noble Duke, who alone knew of the communications, to contradiƈt me, if what I have ftated is incorreƈt.''

The Duke of Wellington felt bound in juftice to fay that not one word had been uttered by the bifhop which was not perfeƈtly correƈt. He had been often furprifed at the imputations which had been thrown out, and the injuftice which had been done to the Right Rev. Prelate refpeƈting circumftances which could not have been known to the public, nor indeed to any other perfon but themfelves. For his own part, he could fay that ever fince the correfpondence took place he had never mentioned it to any one, and he believed the Right Rev. Prelate had obferved a fimilar referve.

After a ſtatement ſo open and explicit, it would be idle to ſay more in refutation of the calumny. Truth muſt at laſt prevail, and until diſcredit is thrown upon the honoured name of the Duke of Wellington, Dr. Phillpotts has the proud conſcioufneſs of feeling that he was elevated to the Epiſcopal Bench by a ſtateſman whoſe views upon a great queſtion of national policy he had the courage to oppoſe.

CHAPTER XIX.

Dr. Phillpotts confecrated Bifhop of Exeter. Does Homage to the King. Arrival in Exeter. His Reception by the Mayor and Chamber. The Bifhop's Reply to their Congratulations. His Inftallation. Firft Sermon at the Cathedral. The Living of Tregony. Collated to a Stall at Durham. Meeting of Parliament. The Bifhop takes his Seat. His Firft Speech in the Houfe of Lords. The Parifh of Woodbury. The firft Piece of Preferment at the difpofal of the Bifhop. Tour in Cornwall. Parliamentary Seffion. Arrives at Ilfracombe. Vifits the Scilly Iflands, and confirms there. Anniverfary Meeting at Exeter of the Society for the Propagation of the Gofpel in Foreign Parts. The Bifhop's Speech. Increafed Circulation of the Bible. Tranquil State of the Diocefe. Lending Libraries. Condition of the Scilly Iflands. King's Letter for the Society for the Propagation of the Gofpel. Rumour of Reduction of Annual Grant to that Society.

HE confecration of Dr. Phillpotts to the See of Exeter took place at the Archiepifcopal Chapel, Lambeth, on Sunday, the 2nd of January, 1831, the confecrating prelates being the Archbifhop of Canterbury (Dr. Howley), the Bifhop of London (Dr. Blomfield), and the Bifhop of Llandaff (Dr. Copleftone). The fermon was preached by the Rev. J. Bartholomew, who afterwards became examining chaplain to the bifhop. It was printed at the command of the archbifhop.

Having done homage to the King at the Pavilion

at Brighton, the bishop very shortly afterwards set out
for his distant diocese, arriving in Exeter on Monday
the 10th of January. News of his coming had spread
through the town and neighbourhood, and, in consequence of the circumstances attending his appointment,
great anxiety was manifested to see him. His wel-
come, if not enthusiastic, was respectful. The children
of the Episcopal Charity Schools were drawn up in
line on the Heavitree road, and on the bishop's car-
riage making its appearance the senior boy came
forward and delivered an appropriate address. The
bishop was evidently much pleased ; and after ex-
changing compliments with the citizens, who mustered
in a strong body, he was escorted to the East-gate,
where the mayor and chamber and many of the clergy
were waiting to receive him at the house of the Rev.
Dr. Collyns, Head Master of the Grammar School.
The mayor (Paul Measor, Esq.) then addressed the
bishop, congratulating him on his advancement to the
See, and expressing a hope that the good understand-
ing which had so long subsisted between the Bishops
of Exeter and the civil authorities of the city might
continue unimpaired. The bishop, in an elegant and
characteristic speech, thanked the mayor and the other
members of the chamber for the reception they had
given him. He had expected, he said, to meet with
a kind congratulation from the chief magistrate on
his arrival, but had not been prepared for so impressive
an address as the mayor had just delivered. He was
fully sensible of the importance of the dignity to which

he was now called. It was well known that among all the cities of England none was more juftly renowned for its loyalty than Exeter ; and the kind expreffions of congratulation which he had juft heard led him to form the higheft hopes for the future. The bifhop again expreffed his thanks for the kind manner in which he had been received, and was then introduced by the mayor to the other members of the chamber. A proceffion was then formed, which proceeded down High Street and through Broad-gate into the Clofe, where the bifhop was met by the dignitaries of the cathedral, each of whom offered congratulations. The bifhop did not enter the cathedral upon this occafion, in confequence of the official mandate not having arrived from London, but proceeded to the palace. He was inftalled on the following Friday. On the next Sunday (January the 16th) his lordfhip preached for the firft time in the cathedral, from Matt. xiv. 1, 2 : "At that time Herod the tetrarch heard of the fame of Jefus, and faid unto his fervants, This is John the Baptift; he is rifen from the dead; and therefore mighty works do fhow forth themfelves in him." The text, which was taken from the fecond leffon for the day, was thought by many to be a fingular one for the occafion, and the fermon contained no allufion to his recent appointment.

The firft living to which the bifhop inftituted a clergyman (the Rev. J. L. Lugger), was Tregony, Cornwall, on the 19th of January, 1831. It is fomewhat remarkable that the right of prefenting to this living is now the fubject of protracted litigation between the bifhop and the patron, the nominee of the latter having been refufed inftitution by his lordfhip. Tregony, then, as is not unlikely, will be affociated with the earlieft and lateft days of his epifcopate.

On the following Sunday (January the 23rd) the bifhop preached again in the cathedral, from Matt. xxi. 19, 20, the fecond leffon for the day ; and it was generally thought that this fermon did more than the firft to vindicate the high reputation which he had brought with him into the diocefe.

It was in this month that the bifhop was collated to a ftall in Durham Cathedral, on the refignation of the Rev. W. N. Darnell.*

Parliament having met on the 3rd of February, the bifhop left Exeter on the 5th for Grofvenor Place, London, to affift in the bufinefs of the feffion. On the 7th he took the oaths and his feat in the Houfe of Lords. He was introduced by the Bifhop of Lin-coln (Dr. John Kaye) and the Bifhop of Llandaff (Dr. Edward Copleftone), and, after figning the De-claration, he took his feat on the bifhops' bench, where he received the congratulations of the Lord Chancellor. After this it became his duty to read prayers in the Houfe as junior bifhop.

The firft occafion of the bifhop fpeaking in Parlia-ment was on the 29th of March in this year (1831), upon a matter connected with his diocefe. Lord King

---

* See page 290.

prefented a petition from the parifh of Woodbury, in Devonfhire, complaining that, while 600*l.* a-year was levied in that parifh, and appropriated to the Choral Fund of the Cathedral of Exeter, only 50*l.* was paid to the curate, who performed all the ecclefiaftical duties in that parifh. The bifhop then briefly ftated that he had no jurifdiction in the matter, as it was one of thofe cafes in which the tithes were all in the hands of lay impropriators.

The hiftory of the cafe is as follows. In 1205, Henry Marfhal, Bifhop of Exeter, having acquired from Abbot Jordan and the Convent of S. Michael in Normandy, the Church of S. Swithin in Woodbury, with all its appurtenances, he made it over to the choral vicars of the cathedral, in confideration of the fatigue which they had to undergo in performing the Divine Office by day and night, and of the fmallnefs of their ftipends—20*s.* per annum; 40*s.* per annum being referved for the parochial incumbent, and 10*s.* for his clerk. This grant was confirmed by Bifhop Brewer on the 28th of May, 1227, who was alfo a liberal benefactor to their body. Shortly after this, Reginald de Albemarra, knight, from the motive of charity, granted them the right of pafture for a certain number of beafts and cattle, throughout the whole of his land of Woodbury, except in the wood and garden, with fome other perquifites and privileges.

The vicars choral are rectors of the parifh, and ufed to exercife all jurifdiction. This ceafed about fourteen years fince. The refident clergyman was

accuſtomed to act under their mandate, and uſually
without epiſcopal licence. In 1832 the incumbent's
income was raiſed from 50 *l.* to 82 *l.* per annum.*
It was ſubſequently augmented to 145 *l.* per annum.
Towards a parſonage-houſe the vicars choral gave
a ſite, as well as ſome money. The reſt was ſupplied by the indefatigable labour of the preſent excellent incumbent, the Rev. J. L. Fulford, who ſunk
a conſiderable ſum of his private property in its
erection, the total coſt being 1700 *l.* It is only due
to the vicars choral of Exeter to ſay that they are
unable to do what they could wiſh for the pariſh of
Woodbury, on account of the inſufficiency of their
ſalaries. The fault does not lie with them, but with
the Dean and Chapter.

The biſhop does not appear to have taken any ſhare
in the parliamentary debates of this ſeſſion.

On the 9th of May he conferred a ſtall in the cathedral on his chaplain, the Rev. John Bartholomew,†
vacant by the death of the Rev. John Bradford Copleſtone, the father of the Biſhop of Llandaff. This was
the firſt piece of preferment which fell to his diſpoſal.
On the 14th of the ſame month he arrived in Exeter
from London, and preached on the following day
(Sunday) to a very full congregation in the cathedral.
His ſtay upon this occaſion was of very ſhort duration,

---

* This is referred to again in Chap. XXII.

† This gentleman, in addition to his canonry, is now
Archdeacon of Barnſtaple, and Rector of Morchard Biſhop.

for on the Monday morning he left for Cornwall, on a vifit to Archdeacon Sheepfhanks, near Penryn. He remained in Cornwall for three weeks, infpecting many parifhes and churches, and returning to Exeter on June the 9th. The next morning he left for London to attend to his duties in Parliament, which met on the 21ft of June, after the diffolution. He did not fpeak at all during the feffion, and, on July the 2nd, he arrived with his family, by fteam-packet from Clifton, at Ilfracombe, a romantic watering-place in the north of Devon, where he remained fome weeks enjoying the fea-breezes, and making the acquaintance of the neighbouring clergy and gentry. During his fojourn he preached in the parifh church, much to the delight of the good people of the diftrict.

While ftaying at Ilfracombe, the bifhop conferred the living of Rockbeare, near Exeter, on the Rev. Henry Nicholls (22nd of July), an old and much-refpected clergyman of the diocefe, who for many years had been Head Mafter of the Grammar School at Barnftaple. This appointment gave great fatisfaction.

At the clofe of the following month (Auguft 30), he paid an epifcopal vifit to the extreme boundary of his extenfive diocefe, arriving at Scilly, in H. M. S. Hermes, accompanied by his chaplain and the Archdeacons of Cornwall and Totnes. Immediately on landing he proceeded to the houfe of John Johns, Efq., agent to the Duke of Leeds, where apartments had been prepared for himfelf and his fuite. After a fhort reft he proceeded to make a tour of the Iflands,

viſiting in turn S. Martin's, Treſco, and Bryer, in-
ſpecting the churches and ſchools in each place, and
making very minute inquiries into the ſtate of the
Pariſhes. In the evening his lordſhip dined with a
large party, including all the clergy, at the houſe of his
liberal hoſt, where taſte and munificence were alike
conſpicuous. On the following day the biſhop attended
Divine Service at S. Mary's Church, and preached a
moſt able and impreſſive ſermon on Confirmation, on
which occaſion the church was crowded in every part,
to a greater degree than was ever before witneſſed.
The appearance and ſolemn demeanour of the congregation, compoſed of perſons from all the Iſlands, was
pleaſing in the extreme, and could not fail to afford
ſatisfaction to their dioceſan. About 250 perſons received the ſacred rite of Confirmation ; ſhortly after
which the biſhop and ſuite proceeded to S. Agnes to
inſpect the ſchool there, and in the evening he left
Scilly for Plymouth, accompanied by the reſpectful
attachment of all who had had acceſs to him, and who
looked forward to the probability of a future, though
perhaps diſtant, viſit, with feelings of unmingled ſatiſ-
faction.

On his return from Scilly the biſhop proceeded to
Exeter for the purpoſe of attending the anniverſary
of the Societies for the Propagation of the Goſpel in
Foreign Parts, and for Promoting Chriſtian Knowledge, which was held September the 15th. There
was a ſpecial ſervice in the cathedral, attended by the
mayor and chamber ; the ſermon being preached by the

Rev. J. Barker, of Silverton, after which a collection was made amounting to 75*l*. The civic authorities then returned to the Guildhall, where the cuſtomary meeting took place, the biſhop in the chair. After the Secretary's and Treaſurer's Reports had been read, the biſhop addreſſed the meeting; and as his ſpeech embraces many topics of intereſt it will be well to give it entire.

" Gentlemen, it is my duty to ſay a few words upon the Reports which I have juſt had the honour of reading to you, —and they will be very few words, for when I recollect the illuſtrious individuals who have preceded me in this chair, in ſupport of theſe ſocieties, I feel that it would be a moſt unjuſt intruſion upon your time, and a tax upon your patience, were I to detain you long. Still, however, I will ſay a few words. In the firſt place, then, in reference to the Report of the Committee of the Society for the Promotion of Chriſtian Knowledge. Allow me to congratulate you upon the increaſed diſtribution of its tracts, and, above all, the enlarged circulation of its larger and moſt important works, I mean the Bible, the Teſtament, and Prayer-book, of which a larger portion than ordinary has been diſtributed during the paſt year—a year upon the ſucceſs of which I moſt heartily congratulate you. Gentlemen, I am ſorry to ſay that there has increaſed, in the courſe of laſt year, a ſpirit of inſubordination and diſaffection, which I am compelled to admit has been far too ſucceſsful in many parts of England, to entice our people to fly not only from their duty to their earthly rulers, but almoſt to riſe up in defiance of their God. I am pleaſed to be able to ſay that nothing of this kind has appeared in this Dioceſe—at leaſt nothing has ariſen which could at all approximate to that deſperate ſtate of things which we have had the melancholy taſk of witneſſing in other parts. It is, Gentlemen, with proud ſatisfaction that

I heartily congratulate you upon it. May it pleafe God that thefe two truly Britifh counties may ever preferve the true Britifh character, and be prevented from falling into that difgrace which has almoft made our countrymen in other parts of England forget that they are fo. Gentlemen, we muft recollect, however, that whatever caufe we have for congratulation in this particular, we can have little ground to hope that this occafion of congratulation will be continued to us if we do not ufe the proper and judicious means of forwarding thefe fentiments with the people; and I rejoice to find that this Committee have not confined their bufinefs merely to the circulation of religious tracts—that it has not confined its care merely to religious knowledge, but that it has promoted the general knowledge of the people alfo. I rejoice to find that *lending libraries* have been eftab-lifhed in no lefs than feventy places in this county. I re-joice that while they have been largely fupplied with religious works they have, by means of this Society, alfo been able to obtain a due portion of temporal knowledge. I venture to exprefs the importance of extending thefe libraries to dif-tricts into which they have not yet been introduced. Gen-tlemen, there is one other remark which I will ftill take the liberty of making with reference to the Report of the ' Society for the Promotion of Chriftian Knowledge,'—it tells us that it extends itfelf not merely through every part of England and Wales, but throughout every portion of Great Britain. Gentlemen, it has been my delight very recently to witnefs its operation in one of the remote parts of this diocefe—a part which I mean to fay is hardly recognized as belonging to England—and it is only in this way that I can reconcile it, that a clufter of iflands in fight of the Britifh fhore, but which is alfo the immediate property of the Britifh Go-vernment, as every inch of land is held from it, yet thefe iflands have been left almoft entirely to this Society, for the fupport of Chriftianity among their people. I am bound to ftate that, with one exception, I mean the ifland of S. Mary, the largeſt and moſt populous—this is the caſe. In that iſland there is a miniſter—paid by his Grace the Duke of Leeds, who is leſſee of the property under the crown. But he is the only one. In the five others, containing more ſouls but leſs means, not the ſmalleſt means of religious inſtruction is afforded by Government—but they have been freely afforded by this Society, which has been powerfully inſtrumental in the ſpread of true religion. Gentlemen, before I conclude upon this ſubject, I ſhould deprive myſelf of a very pleaſant duty if I did not bear the moſt faithful teſtimony to the readineſs of the noble Earl at the head of his Majeſty's Government to remedy this evil. As principal of this dioceſe, I took the liberty of informing him of the ſtate of the Scilly Iſlands; and he moſt readily and promptly returned me an anſwer of his willingneſs and deſire to know what was beſt to be done in order to remedy this evil. Having thus treſpaſſed on your patience with reference to this Society, I would refrain from ſaying anything with reference to the other Society (for Propagating the Goſpel in Foreign Parts), did not ſome circumſtances imperatively call for a few remarks. Gentlemen, it has pleaſed his Majeſty's Government in aid of that Society to iſſue a King's Letter empowering contributions to be made in every pariſh in the United Kingdom, and its cauſe to be advocated by every clergyman. I am quite ſure, from what I know of my clergy, that they will in all caſes exert themſelves to the utmoſt; and I venture to hope that the zeal which they have invariably ſhown will have its due effect upon their flocks. Gentlemen, it will be obvious to you that this letter is of the utmoſt importance, and has become abſolutely neceſſary, after what you have heard of the wants of this Society, which has ſtripped itſelf bare of its funded property, in order that there ſhall be no diminution of its uſefulneſs. Gentlemen, will you ſuffer its ſtreams to be dried up and its ſource to be exhauſted?—it is impoſſible. Let but the loſs be known, and Britain, I am ſure, will make it up.

Gentlemen, on this fubject I am bound to fay fomething more about the Government of the country. It is true that this Government has fhown its zeal by iffuing this letter to the clergy; and I wifh that this was all I had to allude to in refpect to Government; but I lament to fay that, while with one hand his Majefty has been advifed to iffue this letter,—on the other hand, if rumour does not deceive me, a rumour which I affure you I would not lightly allude to— but a rumour has reached me from authority, too facred to doubt, that it is the intention of Government for the Houfe of Commons to move for a very confiderable reduction of the annual grant which, up to this year, it has been in the habit of giving this Society. It may not be known to you, but this is the fact, that religious inftruction in Canada is chiefly given in this way:—when a diftrict is clear and a church is built, the Society is ready to give 200*l.* a-year for a clergyman to fettle there, and Government, as I conceive with only a juft fenfe of what is due, has been hitherto in the habit of granting the fum, I think, of 15,000*l.* a-year in aid of this great object. I grieve to fay that in thefe days of economy, the Government of this country—with a revenue of between fifty and fixty millions a-year—can think it too much to contribute that unimportant fum to the religious inftruction of one of the moft important colonies of the em- pire. Gentlemen, I do not ftand here fimply to ftate the fact; when I could uphold Government, I did it with confcientioufnefs and fincerity. What can be the right terms to apply to this conduct of Government, I will not fay. But let us fay with refpect to Government, that it is by no means blind to its important duties. No! but it is fo urged on every fide to the neceffity of economy that it is continually looking out for every means of reduction. Gen- tlemen, I cannot doubt but that Government would, in this particular, be glad if there were an expreffion of public feeling to keep the pruning knife from it. I think we fhould hear no more of this contemplated reduction, if a

confiderable number of petitions were to be poured into the
Houfe, fo that Government might have their hands ftrengthened upon this fubject.   Gentlemen, there is one more
point :—the main exertions of this Society, large and moft
fuccefsful as they have been, bring with them a neceffity for
increafed funds, and call for the increafed exertions of thofe
Englifhmen who are not indifferent to the wants of their
countrymen, whom neceffity has deprived of a home and
driven to feek for a place lefs facred to their feelings than
that which they have left.   Surely, Gentlemen, it is right,
for the fake of our own expatriated countrymen, and for
thofe millions of our fellow fubjects elfewhere, that we fhould
be eager to procure them thofe bleffings which the Gofpel
only can yield."

CHAPTER XX.

The Bishop goes to London. Lord King's Motion on the Pre-
scription Bill (Tithes). His Attack upon the Bench of
Bishops. Followed by the Lord Chancellor. Excited State
of the Country on the Subject of Reform. Menacing Language
towards the House of Lords. The Reform Bill thrown out
by the Lords. Outrages in the Provinces. Brutal Attack
on the Marquis of Londonderry. Inflammatory Articles in
the Public Prints. The Bishops the special Objects of Attack.
Extract from the Times. *Dauntless Conduct of the Bishop*
of Exeter. His Reply to Lord King's Attack. Earl Grey's
insulting Rejoinder. The Bishop's Reply. Conclusion of the
Discussion. The Bishop of Durham burnt in Effigy. The
Bishop of London threatened. The Parish of Clerkenwell.
Excited State of Exeter. Popular Agitators. Anticipated
Riot. The Yeomanry Cavalry called out. Address of the
Exeter Clerical Club presented to the Bishop.

HORTLY after this meeting the Bishop
proceeded to London, where he appeared
prominently for the first time in a Parliamentary Debate. On the occasion of
two petitions being presented by Lord King (October
the 11th), on the subject of the Prescription Bill
(Tithes), the noble lord made some very severe and
unjustifiable remarks in reference to the conduct of the
clergy, charging them with being "arch-disturbers
when their own interests were concerned, although
under other circumstances they were adverse to all

change." Lord Suffield thought it not beneath him to adopt the fame line, and roundly afferted that the bench of bifhops were ready to fupport the Government of the country fo long as it was arbitrary and oppreffive, but that as foon as a liberal Government produced a meafure for the benefit of the people at large, and for the extenfion and fecurity of the liberties of the country, the bench deferted that adminiftration, and threw all its power into the fcale againft it. Deplorable as this language is, it is ftill more painful to find the Lord Chancellor fo far forgetting what was due to his high office, and the auguft affembly he was addreffing, as to taunt thofe bifhops who had recently voted againft the Reform Bill, with the defire of " tripping the Government up." It may be difficult at the prefent day to eftimate correctly the effect of fuch language, coming from fuch a quarter : but in thofe days it was no light matter. It muft be borne in mind that Reform was the all-abforbing topic of the day. The bill, having paffed the Commons on the 21ft of September, was carried up, next day, to the Lords, by Lord John Ruffell, attended by about a hundred of its ftaunch fupporters in the Lower Houfe. It was read a firft time, on the motion of Earl Grey, without any remark being made, and was directed to be read a fecond time on the 3rd of October. Meanwhile, meafures were vigoroufly employed to intimidate the Peers into fubmiffion. Political unions, the prefs, and public agitators, rivalled one another in the loudnefs of their menaces.

" Let the Lords," ſaid Colonel Torrens, " refuſe this bill, *if they dare.* And if they do, dearly will they rue their obſtinacy hereafter. You all remember the Sibyl's ſtory. She preſented her oracles to Tarquin and his court, and her oracles were rejected. She burned a portion, and again offered them; but they were again rejected. After dimin-iſhing their number ſtill further, ſhe once more returned; and the remaining volumes were gladly purchaſed at the price which ſhe had originally demanded for the entire. We, however, mean to reverſe the moral; for ſhould the preſent bill be defeated, we ſhall bring their Lordſhips another bill, demanding a little more, and then, *ſhould they ſtill dare to reſiſt the might and inſult the majeſty of the people of England,* which Heaven forefend! united as one man will we come forward with a Bill of Reform, in which their Lordſhips will find themſelves inſerted in Schedule A."

And theſe ſentiments were received with favour! They were only too faithful an echo of the public voice. It was amid excitement, then, which can ſcarcely find a parallel in modern days, that Earl Grey, on Monday the 3rd of October, moved the ſecond read-ing of the bill. The debate continued for five nights, and at a quarter paſt ſix on the morning of the 8th of October the bill was thrown out by a majority of forty-one.

And now the ſupporters of the meaſure were excited almoſt to frenzy, and it ſeemed likely that they would carry their worſt denunciations into effect. In more than one inſtance the mob endeavoured to wreak their vengeance on perſons whoſe ſentiments were oppoſed to reform. At Derby the front of the mayor's houſe was demoliſhed, ſeveral other houſes were attacked by the mob, and the town-clerk received such severe injuries that it was for some time doubtful whether he would survive them. The town gaol was broken open, and all the prisoners liberated. The county prison was also attacked, and a severe conflict ensued between the constabulary and the mob. The soldiers were ultimately called out, and the riot was not suppressed until several lives had been lost. At Nottingham, among other lamentable excesses, the castle of the Duke of Newcastle was entirely destroyed by fire; while at Hastings placards of " Death or Liberty !" covered the walls.

As an evidence of the difficulties with which public men, who were obnoxious to the mob, were surrounded in the discharge of their duty, it may be enough to mention that the Marquis of Londonderry was assailed on the 10th of October (the day preceding the presentation of Lord King's petition) by a furious mob as he was going down to and returning from the House. They seized his cabriolet, endeavoured to drag him out of it, and one powerful ruffian struck him a violent blow with a stick. If the mob had succeeded in pulling him out of his cabriolet, there can be little doubt but that they would have murdered him. Fortunately, however, the horse sprang forward violently, and he escaped from the crowd. Such was the treatment which public men might expect who did not pander to the mob ; and well for them if it was no worse.

But fierce as was the rabble, the press was fiercer; and it would be hard to find language to characterize

the inflammatory articles which appeared even in prints
which laid fome claim to moderation. The bifhops
were the favourite objects of attack. Two only of
their number had voted in favour of the Reform Bill,
viz. the Bifhops of Chichefter and Norwich, while of
the reft twelve, including the Bifhop of Exeter, were
in their places, and gave their vote as " not-content,"
and nine voted againft the meafure by proxy. Nothing
was fpared to bring them and their office into contempt.
All that falfehood, barbed by party fpite, could do
againft them was done with an unfparing hand. The
flood-gates of licentioufnefs were opened, and for a
time it was doubtful whether the moft venerable
inftitutions of religion would not be fwept away.

The following extract from the *Times* may ferve to
illuftrate the language of intimidation which was fo
largely reforted to at this period :—

"Should the Bench of Bifhops," it fays, " be unhappily
found averfe to the reform of our political inftitutions ; and,
in the exercife of that hoftility, fhould they blight the hopes
of their countrymen, by adding to the votes againft the bill
juft fo many as may be fufficient to fecure the defeat of it,
while, had the meafure been left to take its chance among
the peers who are laymen, it would have paffed into a law ;
fhould, we fay, fo terrible a difafter happen, what will be the
pofition of the Church and of the prelacy ?—what the feelings of the whole Britifh Empire towards them ? Oh ! let
the bifhops be wife in time, and not realize, againft our
venerable Church, the only poffible anfwer to that inaufpi-
cious queftion. The Socinian, the Papift, the Jew, are all
in port, all exulting in their own increafed fecurity ; but the
Reformed Church of England will, by the unfkilfulnefs or

obſtinacy of her proper pilots, have been driven from her moorings in the hearts of the people, and expoſed to a hurricane the like of which was never blown. ' It is the biſhops,' will an exaſperated nation cry—' *it is the biſhops who have cruſhed our liberties, and deſtroyed us.* But for *them* we ſhould have had a free Parliament, a reſponſible Government, and the downfall of an oppreſſive oligarchy. Our character is loſt, and it is to the *anti-national ſpirit of the Church* we owe this grievous diſappointment. How SHALL WE FORGIVE THE CLERGY?'"

Such was the menacing language held even before the Reform Bill was thrown out by the Lords; and it may well be ſuppoſed that the poſition of the biſhops was not mended afterwards. But there were ſpirits among them which neither the lawleſſneſs of the mob, the ribaldry of the preſs, nor the coarſe invective of their brother peers could quell, and foremoſt among them ſtood the newly-created Biſhop of Exeter. When the Biſhops of London and Llandaff had indignantly hurled back the ſlanderous accuſations which had been brought againſt them, the Biſhop of Exeter roſe, and delivered a few ſhort but impreſſive ſentences.

"He was wholly aſtoniſhed," he ſaid, "at the remarks which had been made on the motives of the reverend Bench from the higheſt quarters. Noble lords aſſumed the right to cenſure the body of biſhops for the vote they had recently given. This cenſure came from thoſe too, who, from their office and ſtation, were bound to ſuſtain the inſtitutions of the country. He defied any noble lord to ſtate a ſingle inſtance in the hiſtory of the country when any members of that Houſe had been ſo vilified and inſulted as the biſhops had been within the laſt week, by a perſon of the higheſt ſtation in the realm. They had been accuſed of voting against the Reform Bill becaufe it was the meafure of a Liberal Adminiftration. Was this charge an inftance of liberality? and did the members of his Majefty's Government by thefe remarks intend to incite and encourage violence? He did not apologize for his warmth; for he fhould be afhamed of himfelf if he could be cool upon fuch a fubject. Had the attack upon the Bench of Bifhops been made at a moment of excitement, to that excitement he would have fubmitted; but, upon the mere prefentation of a petition, and that a petition of no confequence, one noble lord had abufed the Church as the great arch-difturber of all order; and another noble lord had charged the bifhops with being bound together in a confpiracy againft the liberties of the country, and againft all that could conftitute the welfare and happinefs of the people. Thefe were the notions that were propagated everywhere againft the Bench of Bifhops; and noble lords had, moreover, fpoken againft them in that Houfe in a tone of farcafm, if not of direct and pofitive cenfure, as a body actuated by felf-intereft at variance with the public good. Under thefe circumftances he had thought it his duty to addrefs their lordfhips."

The bifhop's manly eloquence had done its work; and Earl Grey, who immediately rofe, could fo ill difguife his feelings of irritation as to charge him with having "uttered the moft intemperate and unfounded infinuation that he had ever heard from any member of that Houfe." It may be hard to juftify fuch language as this; but the occafion demanded that fo zealous a champion of the Epifcopal Bench as the Bifhop of Exeter promifed to be fhould be crufhed at once; and fo, throwing all the indignation he could into his language—and that was not a little—the noble earl protefted that the bifhop was not merely contented with *want of truth* in what he had faid, " but had uttered it with all the appearance of a fpirit that but little became the garment he wore. It was the groffeft injuftice he had ever heard." The noble lord con-cluded a fpeech, which does his temper little credit, by calling on the bifhop to produce the proofs of what he had afferted.

The Bifhop of Exeter being thus appealed to, rofe and faid, that—

" He was not unwilling to admit, that, although he had charged the excitement which exifted againft the Bench of Bifhops throughout the country to the language which had been held in that Houfe, he had not meant to bring any charge againft the noble earl. He would now, however, proceed to prove the truth of what he had afferted. Irregular as it might be to refer to the debate that had recently taken place, yet, under the peculiar circumftances of his cafe, he hoped for the indulgence of their lordfhips in being allowed to refer to the proceedings in queftion. It muft be within the recollection of every noble lord who heard him that in the firft night of the debate upon the bill, the noble earl in ftating the cafe to the Houfe without any one thing to excite him from the Bench of Bifhops had thought himfelf juftified in calling upon the Bench ferioufly to take to mind what would be their condition in the country if there were to be found a narrow majority of lay lords againft the bill, and if it were to be difcovered that the bifhops had voted with that narrow majority. The noble earl had put this in a way to fhow that he expected that the Bench would be induced by the fear of odium to vote with minifters. To call upon any one fet of men—to call upon one of the great ftates of the realm as they were termed by the fages of the law, and by the law itfelf—to call upon them by way of a menace of popular in-dignation had the tendency—a tendency which the noble earl perhaps little fufpected—of exciting the odium of the people. Had not that odium been excited, and was not the Bench of Bifhops expofed to its effects? The noble earl had affumed the character of a prophet, and had told the bifhops 'to fet their houfes in order.' It was true that the noble earl did not conclude the fentence. He left that for themfelves to do, but it was impoffible not to know that he referred to where the prophet had threatened deftruction. The noble earl in the fame fpeech had taken fpecial care to remind the Bench of Bifhops that certain important queftions were in agitation which might take the turn that would prove favourable or unfavourable, according to the conduct of the Bench on that night. What were thefe queftions? Where were they in agitation, but in the councils of which the noble lord was at the head—he hoped fo at leaft, for he hoped the noble earl did not delegate his fuperiority to inferior minds. If the noble lord meant that fchemes of confifcation were contemplated—if the noble earl meant that the bold among the multitude would be encouraged, and that the multitude would be goaded on to more immediate execution—then he (the Bifhop of Exeter) could indeed conceive that the conduct of the bifhops that night might have the effect of driving the multitude to fuch purpofes. Had he faid anything but what the proofs he had adduced fully fubftantiated? The language of the noble earl had a tendency to implicate the prelates with the people, and to make them be regarded by the people throughout all the country as their foes. The people already pretty well echoed the noble Earl's fuggeftions, for they read the debates, and the fame language was repeated by the journals. The bifhops were threatened to be driven from their ftations becaufe they did not vote for minifters—becaufe for once they had thus voted upon the greateft queftion agitated fince the Revolution when the bifhops had acted in defiance of the Crown. Where would their Lordfhips have been but for the bifhops at the Revolution? The prefent was the firft occafion upon which the

Bench of Bishops had opposed the present ministers, and yet for opposing them this once they were charged with deserving all the mischief with which they had been threatened."

Earl Grey then asked the bishop why he had not made the serious charges he now brought forward, when the words he imputed to him were fresh in the recollection of the House, and when he could have made those charges in a regular manner. For his part he thought that the bishop's proofs corresponded very little with his assertions. He had charged his Majesty's ministers with having purposely done all in their power to encourage tumult and excite the mob to acts of popular violence.

Upon this the Bishop of Exeter said:—

" Most solemnly do I declare that I do not think I have used any such words.   Upon my honour and conscience I did not use those words.   I am quite sure that I never accused his Majesty's Government of exciting the people to out- rage."

After some further remarks by Earl Grey, and a vindication of the conduct of the Bench of Bishops by the Duke of Wellington, the subject dropped.

It may well be supposed that when peers of the realm could be found ready to ascribe the most sordid and unworthy motives to the rulers of the Church, the multitude would not be slow to imitate their example. Henceforward bishops were to contend, as best they might, against peers, public, and press, an unholy Triad!

The fruits of this alliance were soon matured. The Bishop of Durham was burnt in effigy before his own palace; and the Biſhop of London, who was advertiſed to preach at S. Anne's, Weſtminſter, was warned by the pariſhioners that the whole congregation would quit the church at the moment of his aſcending the pulpit. The *Times* truly enough ſaid of this,—

"Such a proof of public antipathy towards the entire 'order,' whoſe conduct in the Houſe of Lords was ſo conſpicuous on the ſecond reading of the Reform Bill is *without an example in modern hiſtory*, and is worth a whole library of comments."

In the important pariſh of Clerkenwell alſo the following requiſition was tranſmitted to the churchwardens :—

"*Wells without water.* We, the underſigned, inhabitants of the pariſh of Clerkenwell, moſt reſpectfully requeſt the churchwardens, that, in conſequence of the irreligious conduct of the biſhops in reſpect to the Reform Bill, they (the biſhops) ſhall not be again ſolicited to preach in the churches of this pariſh."

Ridiculous as this memorial ſounds at the preſent day, it was copied into provincial journals and received with great applauſe.

But nowhere did the noxious fruit come to maturity earlier than in the Dioceſe of Exeter. The plant had ſtruck its roots in a congenial ſoil. The people of the Weſt, among whom Cromwell, William of Orange, and Weſley had found their ſtouteſt adherents, were eaſily brought to believe that biſhops were enemies of progreſs, and the champions of a narrow faction, which deſired to repreſs their energies and curtail their liberty. Never, ſo their agitators told them, would the country breathe freely till every mitred head had been brought low, and the fooner churches were pulled down, and the parfons fet to mend the roads with the ftones, the fooner would England be great and free. More of the fame fort was faid, and much of it was unhappily believed. And fo, before the Bifhop of Exeter returned to his cathedral city, a ftrong party had been formed againft him, and at a large reform meeting three groans were called for and given with every indication of bitternefs at the mention of his lordfhip's name. And what made things worfe was that people whofe pofition and education fhould have taught them better were not afhamed to mingle their voices with the fhouts of the rabble. It was thought that the bifhop would have been burnt in effigy. No fuch fcandal, however, took place for the prefent; but as the annual Saturnalia of the 5th of November came round, it was feared that the mob would indulge in more than its wonted exceffes, and that a riot would take place. So active were the leaders, and fo ferious was the danger confidered, that the mayor proceeded to fwear in a large number of fpecial conftables, and Lord Ebrington attended as the Vice-Lieutenant, to command the yeomanry cavalry, who were haftily called out, and who were kept under arms the greater part of the night. This force, however, was with commendable prudence kept in referve, but the knowledge that it was clofe at hand exercifed a moft falutary effect, for no ferious demonftration was attempted.

But while "the great liberal party," as it was ftyled, were thus difporting themfelves at the expenfe of their bifhop, whofe only offence was that he had dared to give an independent vote, and had affifted the Houfe of Peers in maintaining its rights as an independent part of the conftitution, the clergy were not flow to recognize his fervices. At the monthly meeting of the Exeter Clerical Club, October 25th, it was unanimoufly refolved that a vote of thanks fhould be offered to the bifhop of the diocefe for the eloquent and manly part which he had taken in the debate in the Houfe of Lords on the 11th of October. *Laudatur ab his, culpatur ab illis;* and no doubt the bifhop knew whofe approval was worth the moft.

CHAPTER XXI.

The Return of the Bishop to Exeter. Anniversary of the Devon and Exeter Central Schools. Service at the Cathedral, and Sermon by the Bishop. Meeting at the Guildhall. The Bishop's Speech. His First Ordination. Neglect of Ember Seasons. Attention to the Affairs of his Diocese. Presentation of his Eldest Son to a Living. Dispute with the Parishioners of Stoke Damerel, Devonport, about a Burial-ground. Dr. Lushington consulted. A Vestry Meeting of the Parishioners. Libellous Resolutions passed. The Bishop applies to Court of King's Bench. A Rule obtained to show Cause why a Criminal Information should not be filed against the Chairman. Arguments of Counsel against the Rule. It is made absolute.

WEEK before the prorogation of Parliament, which took place on the 20th of October, the bishop returned to Exeter, and on the following Thursday was present at the Anniversary of the Devon and Exeter Central Schools. The children educated at these schools, headed by the mayor and civic authorities, and accompanied by many of the clergy, walked in procession to the cathedral, where Divine Service was performed and a most eloquent and impressive sermon preached by the bishop, his text being taken from 1 Pet. iv. 10, " As every man hath received the gift,

even fo minifter the fame one to another, as good ftewards of the manifold grace of God." At the conclufion of the fervice a collection was made at the door, amounting to 61*l.* 18*s.* 8*d.*, a larger amount than had been collected for many years before, but a pitiful fum enough as compared with what the fame clafs of people will fpend on a more congenial concert, or archery meeting. It furnifhed ground for congratulation, however, and as everybody was pleafed it would be out of place to do more than record the fact. In the courfe of the day a meeting was held in the Guildhall, the bifhop in the chair. After the report had been read and the ufual refolutions propofed and agreed to, Sir T. D. Acland rofe, and propofed a vote of thanks to the bifhop for the excellent difcourfe with which he had favoured them that morning, conveying, in the moft complimentary terms, a defire that his lordfhip would ftep beyond the direct terms of the motion, and caufe it to be printed.

Dr. MacGowan feconded the motion, which, having been put by the mayor, was carried with three hearty rounds of applaufe. The bifhop then rofe, and, as foon as he could obtain a hearing, faid :—

" Mr. Mayor, I affure you I fhould moft confult my own inclination if I were fimply to return thanks to you, and this moft refpectable meeting, for the high honour you have done me. But I feel it would be moft widely departing from the fingular example of kindnefs which has been fhown me this day if I were to do fo. I may be permitted to fay, without affectation, that my efforts are unworthy of the acknowledgement you have made—utterly unworthy, when compared with the silent, unpretending, and useful exertions which are made every day by those who have discharged the duties of sustaining these schools by the good effects of their control and supervision. Gentlemen, it is an easy matter for a man to sit down in his study, and put on paper those sentiments which every one must feel in the performance of a great Christian duty: to one whose disposition through life has been to be employed in such matters, it requires little effort to write upon such a subject as this. But I will go further. I will say that it is conferring upon him the highest pleasure to be called upon to advocate the cause of an institution like this. But, Gentlemen, I had my share of satisfaction in knowing that, whilst I was advocating the cause, I had a far more powerful advocate in the hearts of those who heard me. I know that in this place every hand will always be open to sustain so good a cause. Little ground, therefore, have I to claim thanks for the small services which I have rendered; but you, Gentlemen, have largely to claim my gratitude, for the very honourable mode in which you have been pleased to express yourselves of my services."

In seconding the vote of thanks proposed by Archdeacon Moore to the mayor and chamber for the use of the Guildhall, and their patronage of the Society, the Bishop said :—

" I have great pleasure in seconding the motion. I must be permitted to say, that no one feels more strongly than I do the important benefit of the co-operation of that distinguished body. And I really believe—I say it not in flattery —that in no city or town in England can it be said with more truth—I wish it could be said with as much truth in all—that the civic authorities are anxious on all occasions to record their testimony, and give their authority to the support of the Gospel, which they are well aware is their own best support."

After a vote of thanks to his lordfhip for his excellent conduct in the chair, the meeting feparated, much delighted at the courtefy of the bifhop, and the fuccefs of the day's proceedings.

On the following Sunday (October the 23rd) the bifhop held his firft Ordination in the Cathedral Church of S. Peter at Exeter. Upon this occafion there were fifteen deacons and fixteen priefts ordained, among the latter the bifhop's eldeft fon. It is to be regretted that the primary Ordination of fo eminent a prelate fhould be affociated with an irregularity—the neglect of the Ember Seafon. But, whatever may have been his earlier practice, no bifhop is now more careful to obferve the feafons appointed by the Church for the folemn purpofe of choofing and fending labourers into the Lord's vineyard.

During the whole of the next month, November, the bifhop devoted himfelf with great affiduity to the duties of his diocefe, receiving vifits from his clergy, and preaching in the churches of the city and neighbourhood. On the 4th of this month he prefented his eldeft fon, the Rev. William John Phillpotts,* to the vicarage of Lelant Uny with Towednack, Cornwall, twelve days after his ordination.

About this time the bifhop became involved in a difpute with the parifhioners of Stoke Damerel, the

---

* This gentleman is now Chancellor of the Diocefe of Exeter, Archdeacon of Cornwall, Prebendary of the Cathedral, and Vicar of S. Gluvias with Budock, Cornwall. The date of his appointments will be given as they occur.

mother church of Devonport.   It appears that, in the
year 1811, the churchyard of the parish being found
too small to meet the mortality of the place, Sir John
St. Aubyn, the lord of the manor, consented to give
a piece of ground for the purpose of adding to the
churchyard, in furtherance of which he conveyed the
ground in question to the parishioners for 5,000 years.
Thus matters stood till the autumn of the year 1831,
when it was found necessary still further to enlarge the
burial-ground; and application was made to the lord
of the manor, who again consented to meet the wishes
of the parishioners.   But, on inquiry, the deed of
1811, which conveyed the ground to the parishioners,
could not be found.   It was either lost or destroyed,
and, after deliberation, it was thought to be the safer
course to obtain a renewal of the old deed.   It was
necessary that the diocesan should be a party to the
conveyance, under an Act of Parliament of 43rd
George III, and application was made to him for his
consent.   The bishop replied that he had no interest
in the matter, and would act in it as he might be
advised to act by Dr. Lushington, upon a case to be
submitted to that learned civilian.   A case was accordingly laid before Dr. Lushington, without whose advice the bishop would not depart from the ordinary
rule.   That learned gentleman was of opinion that
the transaction would not be legal, unless the ground
were conveyed to the *incumbent*, and his successors, instead of the *parishioners*.   A second case, however, was
laid before Dr. Lushington, in which the bishop, after

fetting out facts, ftated that he did not inquire whether
he had the power to give or withhold his fanction from
the proceedings, but that he wifhed to afk whether,
under all the circumftances, Dr. Lufhington would
advife him to interfere one way or the other. The
anfwer was fuch that the bifhop deemed it right to
decline any interference. On this being made known
to the parifhioners, a cafe was directed by them to be
laid before Dr. Lufhington, who, on perufal of it,
gave his opinion that, though in ftrict law the conveyance ought to be to the *incumbent*, yet, as the original
deed, which had received the fanction of a former
bifhop, had conveyed the ground to the *parifhioners*,
and as, on the faith of that deed, burials had taken
place there for a number of years, the equity of the
cafe required that the new deed fhould be drawn up
in conformity with the purport of that which was loft.
The gentleman who acted on behalf of the parifhioners
prefented this opinion for the Bifhop's perufal; but he
declined to pay any attention to it. "I will not look,"
he very properly faid, "at an opinion given on a ftatement of facts not previoufly fubmitted to me for confideration." He added that, if the parifhioners had
any new facts to lay before him, he would confider
them, and act accordingly. He alfo declared his entire
willingnefs to abide by the advice of Dr. Lufhington.
Upon this the inhabitants of Stoke Damerel held a
meeting in veftry, when refolutions were paffed highly
derogatory to the bifhop, and fuch as made him feel
that he was called upon to apply to the Court of

King's Bench to vindicate his character. The veftry meeting took place on the 19th of October, and the following refolutions were agreed to, Mr. Clouter being in the chair :—

"Refolved,—That the meeting cannot but regret, from the ftatement made by Mr. Rodd, that the Bifhop of Exeter fhould fo far have forgotten himfelf as to deny to the parifhioners that juftice which they have a right to demand at his hands—viz. his fanction to the deed of conveyance. The parifhioners cannot reprobate fuch conduct in language too ftrong.

"Refolved,—That the utmoft cenfure be conveyed to the Bifhop for fuch his difhonourable and degrading conduct."

Thefe refolutions were figned by the Churchwarden, as chairman of the meeting; and it was ordered that they fhould be entered on the parifh books, and be printed and publifhed in the *Devonport Telegraph,* and in a Plymouth journal.

Application on behalf of the bifhop was made to the Court of King's Bench, at fittings in Banco, on Friday, Nov. 25, by the Attorney-general, when a rule to fhow caufe why a criminal information fhould not be filed againft John Clouter was granted.

On Monday, January 30, in the following year, Mr. Campbell appeared to fhow caufe againft the rule. He contended that the defendant could not be held liable, as from the nature of the fituation in which he was placed he was prevented from interfering in the bufinefs of the meeting. On the contrary, he was oppofed to the refolutions, and had refufed to fign them. The learned gentleman then went at great length into the circumſtances which had led to the meeting, at which the reſolutions had been adopted, with a view to ſhow that great excitement prevailed in the diſtrict from the refuſal of the biſhop to conſecrate the burial-ground. The Attorney-general and Sir James Scarlett ſupported the rule, and ſtated that the biſhop had refuſed to conſecrate the ground under the opinion of Dr. Luſhington. The Court were unani-mouſly of opinion that nothing could juſtify the lan-guage complained of by the biſhop, and directed the rule to be made abſolute.

The proceedings of the biſhop in this caſe created much ill-feeling againſt him throughout the dioceſe. Conſidering the unpopularity of his appointment, it would no doubt have been wiſer to have taken no notice of Mr. Clouter or his reſolutions; but the biſhop may have thought it more prudent at once to cruſh the riſing evil, and awe his adverſaries into ſilence, if not into approval of his conduct, by the ſtrong arm of the law.

CHAPTER XXII.

The Reform Bill. Impatience of the Country. Second Reading of the Bill in the Commons. The Bishop remains at Exeter. Freedom of the City presented to him. End of the first Year of his Episcopate. Opening of the Year 1832. The Reform Question. Bill carried in the Commons. The Ministerial Plan of Education for Ireland. Dissatisfaction of the Roman Catholics. The Kildare Street Society. Agitation in Ireland. Seditious Address of one of the Leaders. Infatuation of English Statesmen. Real Object of the Agitators to exclude Religious Instruction from Schools. The Rhemish and Douay Versions of the Scriptures. Feeling of the Authorities in Rome in reference to the Educational System in Ireland. Circular Letter from the Pope. Effect of it upon the People of Ireland. Neglect and Ignorance of the Scriptures in that Country. Infamous Treatment of them. Indignation of the Episcopal Bench at the Conduct of Government. Conduct of the Bishop of Exeter. His Forebodings of the Mischievous Consequences of the Bill. His Speech in the House of Lords. Effect of it. Lord Radnor's Remarks upon the Bishop. Lord King refers again to the Parish of Woodbury. The Bishop's Explanations.

ND now it will be neceſſary to return once more to the ſubject of Reform. The Parliament, which had been prorogued on the 20th of October, 1831, aſſembled again on the 6th of December. This was a ſhort receſs. No longer interval, however, could be granted, for the clamour of political unions and the impatience of the lower orders made it plain to the miniſters that an impelling force had been ſet in motion which it

would be vain for them to hope to control or refift. If they were to retain their office they muft be content, for the prefent at leaft, to be thruft forward by the rabble. Accordingly, a new Reform Bill was introduced into the Commons immediately on the meeting of Parliament. A vigorous debate followed, which ended in the fecond reading being carried, and then Parliament adjourned for the Chriftmas holidays.

The bifhop did not go up to London to attend this fhort feffion, but continued in the active fuperintendence of his diocefe, the great adminiftrative ability which he exhibited eliciting marks of warm admiration from all who had not made up their minds to be difpleafed with everything that he did. On the 15th of December the freedom of the city was conferred upon his lordfhip by a unanimous refolution of the corporation ; and on the 22nd of this month he prefented the Rev. Nicholas Lightfoot to the Rectory of Stockleigh Pomeroy, Devon, being the fourth piece of preferment which had fallen to his difpofal. Thus ended the firft year of his Epifcopate, without the occurrence of any further fubject of note, unlefs it deferve to be recorded that no churches or chapels were confecrated during this period.

The following year was deftined to be a very remarkable one. Parliament affembled on the 17th of January, after the recefs, and the reform queftion was proceeded with at once. Long and weary were the debates which followed. It was an oft-told tale. All that could be faid had been faid over and over again, and yet the speakers were never weary. On the 9th of March the Committee had gone through the bill, having entered upon the examination of it on the 20th of January. The report was considered on the 14th of March, and on the 19th the motion for the third reading of the bill was met by an amendment, moved by Lord Mahon, that it should be read a third time that day six months. The amendment was seconded by Sir John Malcolm, and was followed by a sharp debate, which was continued on the 20th and 22nd. On a division there was a majority of 116 for the third reading. This was decisive, and on the 23rd of March the bill was passed. But while this measure was occupying the attention of the Commons, another question, of scarcely less importance, was being debated in the House of Lords—the ministerial plan of education for Ireland, which was brought forward on March the 22nd.

An opinion had for some time been gaining ground that the existing system of Scriptural education was ill adapted to the peculiarities of that country, and that the Parliamentary grant made in the year 1816, and continued from that time, had not produced the desired effect. It does not appear, however, that any complaints were made until the year 1825, from which time, until 1831, the clamour rapidly increased, and the Government determined to abolish the Kildare Street Society (the object of which institution was to encourage local exertions in the establishment of schools), and supersede the existing system. In coming to this conclufion, there can be little doubt but that they were yielding to the preffure of demagogues who defired a change from *fome* religion to *none*. Reform was the order of the day, and education muft be content to come in for its fhare of it, even though in the procefs it fhould chance to be ftripped of everything that made it Chriftian. A plaufible pretext was ready at hand, and its favourers were not flow to make the moft of it.

The Roman Catholics confidered the unreftricted reading of Holy Scripture to be repugnant to their form of religion; and the confequence was that they refufed to allow their children to go to thofe fchools where inftruction in the Scriptures formed the bafis of education. To meet this difficulty it was fuggefted that two different fyftems fhould be introduced, one for the children of Proteftants, and the other for the children of Roman Catholics. This was objected to by the Roman Catholic prelates themfelves, who thought that the feparation of children was injudicious, and calculated to deftroy fome of the beft principles of human nature.

Thus the dragon's teeth were fown, nor was there long to wait for the crop. The Irifh people were taught by popular fpeech-mongers, whofe ftock-in-trade confifted of bitter hatred to England feafoned with blafphemy and ribaldry, that they had a grievance, and this "grievance" was oftentatioufly paraded before the world till it was fo thread-bare that it ceafed to be anything but a fcarecrow. Seffion after feffion, however, it continued to furnifh an unceafing political capital to a fet of noify demagogues, whofe frothy orations paffed for eloquence in Ireland, but moved all reafonable Englifhmen to laughter. One of the leaders of this faction, for fuch it really was, upon being advifed to follow moderate meafures, had the effrontery to tell his advifer that it was by violence alone that the Roman Catholics of Ireland had advanced their caufe to its prefent profperous ftate ; and this was true enough.

" Remember," he faid, " the conditions which were once required of us even by our prefent friends, and contraft with them the terms which we can now command. Was it our peaceable demeanour, our decorous language, which placed us on this vantage ground ? No ! it was the boldnefs with which we afferted our claims, the unflinching, uncompromifing tone of all our meafures, that has enabled us thus to look back with triumph, and forward with confidence. If, indeed, anything could have been gained by following the courfe which you gentle counfellors recommend, we might have been ready to play the pliant part, and liften to the men to *whom we now dictate.*"

This is plain fpeaking—plain enough, it might have been thought, to have opened the eyes of Englifh ftatefmen to what was going on in Ireland. But they feem to have been ftricken with a blindnefs fo obftinate that it feemed judicial. And fo political agitators and Romifh priefts were allowed to play into one another's hands, and to unfettle the country on the queftion of education, happy enough if in the general confufion they themfelves could fecure fome fubftantial fpoils.

What a fection of the agitators *did* want to do—but

they had not courage to avow it plainly—was to exclude religious inſtruction altogether from ſchools.
There was to be what was called " moral and literary
inſtruction," (an unfledged Mancheſter and Salford
ſcheme,) but nothing to teach the riſing generation of
Ireland a word about the hopes and promiſes of a
future ſtate, at all events according to the doctrine of
the united Church of England and Ireland.

If there was to be a bible at all, it muſt not be the
grand old tranſlation ſanctioned by law, and approved
by the confentient voice of a long line of ſcholars—a
tranſlation which has extorted even from infidels an
unwilling teſtimony to its ſublimity and beauty ; but
the Rhemiſh and Douay verſions —*per*verſions in ſome
places they might better be called—which, apart from
doctrinal differences, are as unlike the authorized verſion of the Holy Scriptures as they well can be, while
ſetting up any claim to be the ſame book.

And here it will be inſtructive to conſider the feelings which actuated the higheſt authorities in Rome in
reference to the educational ſyſtem in Ireland. They
will be beſt explained by the following circular letter
from the Pope to the Iriſh prelates on the ſubject of
bible ſchools.

" Rome, Court of the Sacred Congregation for the Propagation of the Faith. Sept. 18, 1819.

" My Lord,—The prediction of our Lord Jeſus Chriſt, in
the Parable of the Sower, that ' ſowed good ſeed in his field ;
but while people ſlept, his enemy came, and ſowed tares upon
the wheat,' (Matt. xvi. 24,) is, to the very great injury
indeed of the Catholic Faith, ſeen verified in theſe our days,

particularly in Ireland. For information has reached the ears of the Sacred Congregation that bible fchools, fupported by the funds of Catholics, have been eftablifhed in almoft every part of Ireland, in which, under the pretence of charity, the inexperienced of both fexes, but particularly peafants and paupers, are allured by the blandifhments, and even gifts of the mafters, and infected with the fatal poifon of depraved doctrines.

" It is further ftated that the directors of thefe fchools are, generally fpeaking, methodifts, who introduce bibles, tranflated into Englifh by ' the Bible Society,' and abounding in errors ; with the fole view of feducing the youth ; and entirely eradicating from their minds the truths of the ortho-dox Faith.

" Under thefe circumftances, your Lordfhip already per-ceives with what folicitude and attention paftors are bound to watch, and carefully protect their flock from the ' fnares of wolves, who come in the clothing of fheep.' If the paftors fleep, the enemy will quickly creep in by ftealth, and fow the tares ; foon will the tares be feen growing among the wheat, and choke it.

" Every poffible exertion muft, therefore, be made to keep the youth away from thefe deftructive fchools ; to warn parents againft fuffering their children, on any account what-ever, to be led into error. But for the purpofe of efcaping the ' fnares ' of the adverfaries, no plan feems more appro-priate than that of eftablifhing fchools, wherein falutary in-ftruction may be imparted to paupers, and illiterate country perfons.

" In the name, then, of the bowels of the mercy of our Lord Jefus Chrift, we exhort and befeech your Lordfhip to guard your flock with diligence, and all due difcretion, from thofe who are in the habit of thrufting themfelves infidioufly into the fold of Chrift, in order thereby to lead the unwary fheep aftray : and, mindful of the forewarning of Peter the Apoftle, given in thefe words, ' There fhall be alfo lying

masters among you, who shall bring in sects of perdition'
(2 Pet. ii. 8), do you labour, with all your might, to keep
the orthodox youth from being corrupted by them—an object
which will, I hope, be easily effected by the establishment of
Catholic schools throughout your diocese. And, confidently
trusting that, in a matter of such vast importance, your
Lordship will, with unbounded zeal, endeavour to prevent
the wheat from being choked by the tares, I pray the all-good
and Omnipotent God to guard and preserve you safe many
years.

> " Your Lordship's
> " Most obedient humble Servant,
> " F. CARDINAL FONTANA, Prefect.
> " C. M. PEDICINI, Secretary."

This document is pretty forcible, it must be admitted, even for a papal rescript, and its effect upon
the people of Ireland may easily be imagined. Trained
to regard the voice of the Pope as an infallible oracle,
it was not likely that the authorized version of the
Holy Scriptures would henceforward be received by
them with much veneration or favour.

" That the Scriptures should be neglected," says Dr.
Phillpotts, in his Letter to Mr. Canning, " and, in many
instances, utterly unknown, is only a matter of course. Mr.
Donelan, *a Roman Catholic gentleman, nephew of Lord Fingal,*
one of the inspectors of the Kildare Place Schools, states in
his evidence (p. 488) before the Commissioners of Education, 'that the peasantry could scarcely distinguish between a
Testament and any other book of the same size on a religious
subject ; that, in Connaught, *the peasant does not know what
a Bible or Testament is.* I think,' he adds, ' we may say, *in
general,* they do not understand that the Bible contains the
Word of God, the history of our Saviour, the history of the
creation, and the redemption of the world.' Another wit

nefs (Captain George Pringle, p. 686) informs the Commiffioners, that he 'had met with a great many who never faw
or heard of the Scriptures ; fome did not know what he was
fpeaking about, when fpeaking of the Bible. At laft they
cried, "Oh, yes, you are fpeaking about the *Black Book.*"
Some of them think that *Luther was the author of it.*' 'In
an inveftigation, which occupied nearly three whole days,'
fays Mr. Gordon, p. 716, 'during which I entered as many
cabins as that time would admit, only one copy of the Scriptures was found, a Proteftant Teftament, that belonged to a
child in attendance on a Proteftant fchool. The *perfons in
the cabin were afraid to touch it ; they handed it down on a
board*, becaufe they thought it *an heretical book.*'

"That this ignorance is encouraged by the Church of
Rome," continues Dr. Phillpotts, "as highly ferviceable to
its interefts, is manifeft not merely from the encyclical letter
of the Pope (quoted above), but alfo from the conduct of the
priefts, as narrated in the evidence before the Commiffioners. 'One lad of nineteen told me,' fays Captain
Pringle, '"If we read that Black Book, the prieft tells me
we fhall be vifited with thunder and lightning."' 'The
Roman Catholic clergy,' fays another witnefs (H. M.
Mafon, Efq., p. 746), 'have denounced the Irifh Scriptures from the altar in Kerry and Meath, and have
called our New Teftament, becaufe it is in fome inftances
bound in black, the *Black Book*, and have produced it as
fuch in its black coat, connecting it with *the powers of
darknefs.*'"

More of the fame kind might eafily be added, but
the picture is too unfightly already to require the introduction of frefh objects of horror. But, hideous as
it is, it is drawn from life ; for fuch was the ftate of
things revealed by a Commiffion appointed by Government, and for this deplorable ignorance it was only

too plain that the Romifh hierarchy were anfwerable. And now the queftion arofe, fhould Englifhmen, by a deliberate vote in Parliament, help to make this darknefs darker?   And, what is more to the purpofe, were the bifhops to ftand idly by?   Was no voice to be raifed in defence of God's holy Word?   Was it to be facrificed by ftatefmen at the call of a political faction? Was that which makes men wife unto falvation henceforward to be banifhed from every Irifh fchool?   No. Indignant voices were raifed from the Epifcopal Bench, and none more righteoufly indignant than that of the Bifhop of Exeter.   His was the noble part of expofing the infidious attempts of the Roman priefthood to fecularize the fcheme of education, in order to remain fole mafters of the field.   Moft forcibly did he fhow the real bearings of a bill fraught with fuch mifchievous confequences, that it might well be doubted if its promoters knew to what lengths they were committing themfelves.   It is probable that they did *not* know. But the penetrating glance of the bifhop could fee the evil which was coming, and, in a fpeech which would give him a lafting claim on the gratitude of pofterity, even if no other memorial of his public life remained, he denounced, with more than his ufual energy, and with a vehemence which muft have reminded his hearers of one of thofe heaven-infpired meffengers of old, the fin which would attach to the nation if fuch a bill fhould ever become the law of the land.

Early in the debate the bifhop fpoke as follows :—

" My Lords, I can affure the noble marquifs who has

just sat down that I will adhere to the advice which he has been pleased to give to your Lordships, and will confine myself strictly to the question before the House. I have in truth no temptation to wander from it; for the question itself is far more than sufficient for me to hope to do justice to it, and it is besides far more interesting in itself than any collateral matter could help to make it. My Lords, it is, I can assure your Lordships, felt to be so by thousands out of this House and by not a few I trust within it. It is a question which, as it will be my duty to endeavour to satisfy your Lordships before I conclude, has not only excited, but has also justified the greatest anxiety and alarm both in Ireland and throughout the empire at large.

" Before I proceed, my Lords, to enter upon the discussion of this most important subject, I will venture to make one remark in reference to an observation of the right reverend Prelate behind me (the Bishop of Chester), for whom I may be permitted to say I entertain the most sincere respect. That right reverend Prelate has said that he could not consent on this occasion to raise his voice in condemnation of His Majesty's Ministers, although he disapproved of the plan proposed by them. My Lords, I too wish to be understood in the observations which I am about to address to you, as meaning to say nothing unnecessarily disrespectful to His Majesty's Ministers. My remarks will be made against the measure and not against the men. And yet, my Lords, I shall not be restrained by any apprehension of incurring the censure of a noble Lord who has recently addressed you, of being called factious or belonging to a faction —an accusation pretty liberally bestowed of late on those who have considered it their duty, on public grounds, to oppose a public measure—I say, my Lords, I shall not be restrained by any apprehension of being charged as a member of a faction from speaking as becomes a member of your Lordships' House, and if I shall find it necessary to offer any very strong observations against the measure, I shall not scruple to do so, trufting that the noble earl at the head of His Majefty's Government and his colleagues will underftand that I wifh my obfervations to apply as little as poffible to them, but as much as poffible to the meafure itfelf. I fay this the more readily, becaufe I do not think that there are many among thofe noble lords, although officially refponfible for the meafure, who know what that meafure really is. My Lords, I do not make this charge on flight grounds, for when I hear noble lords who have fpoken in defence of the new plan, particularly the noble and learned Lord (Lord Plunket), declare that the principle of it has been fanctioned by all the commiffions and committees that have hitherto devoted their labours to the confideration of this fubject, it is plain to every underftanding, that they know not what this new plan really is. My Lords, inftead of being the fame in principle as that which has been recommended by the reports of previous commiffions and committees, I affirm that the prefent meafure not only has not the fanction of thofe reports, but is in direct oppofition to them all. If therefore, my Lords, I eftablifh this point to the fatisfaction of your Lordfhips, I think I fhall ftand excufed for faying that I very much doubt, or rather I do much more than doubt, whether the noble lords know what this meafure really is.

" My Lords, I will now beg leave to refer to the letter ad-dreffed to the noble duke at the head of the new board of education, whom I am moft happy to fee in his place, from the right honourable the Secretary for Ireland. And I will beg leave from that letter, which is the formal and official expofition of the new plan of national education in Ireland, to fhow what that plan is. It may be confidered as dividing itfelf into three diftinct particulars,—as refpects, firft, the moral and literary inftruction which it is propofed to afford to Proteftants and to Roman Catholics in common; fecondly, the feparate religious inftruction of Proteftants ; thirdly, the feparate religious inftruction of the Roman Catholics. From an examination of theſe ſeveral parts, I will undertake to ſhow that the real principle of this national plan of education is to exclude Scripture altogether from ſome of the ſchools ſupported by the State, and to lay the leaſt poſſible ſtreſs on Scripture as a part of that education in all. In truth, my Lords, ſtrange as it may ſeem, this official expoſition of the plan, I mean Mr. Stanley's letter, from the point at which it commences, the development of his plan is ſo conſtructed, as to avoid the very mention of Scripture at all.

" Firſt, as reſpects the common inſtruction of Proteſtants and Catholics, this is the proviſion :—' They will require that the ſchools be kept open for a certain number of hours on four or five days of the week at the diſcretion of the commiſſioners, for moral and literary education only. They will exerciſe the moſt entire control over all books to be uſed in the ſchools, none to be employed in the combined moral and literary inſtruction except under the ſanction of the board.' Now your Lordſhips will ſee here is no mention of any book of Scripture to be introduced ; no, not even of a book containing extracts of Scripture. I know it has been a ground of complaint againſt the plan that extracts are propoſed to be given from the Scriptures and not the Scriptures themſelves. This is matter of complaint which has been frequently adverted to in petitions to this Houſe, and ſome of your Lordſhips alſo have made the ſame complaint. My Lords, my complaint is of a contrary kind. I complain not that books of extracts of Scripture are to be uſed in theſe ſchools of moral inſtruction, but that they are not to be there uſed. My Lords, if volumes of well-choſen extracts from the Bible were to be uſed in the ſchools at the time of common inſtruction, I ſhould not think it reaſonable to complain, that the whole Bible is to be reſerved for the times of ſeparate religious inſtruction. I ſhould think this no more than a fair conceſſion to the peculiar circumſtances of the caſe ; but, my Lords, there is abſolutely no ſecurity whatever, that all books containing extracts from the Scriptures are not to be excluded—rather, there is actual proof that all such books will be excluded, as far as regards the moral inftruction of both Proteftants and Roman Catholics.

"I will take upon myfelf to fhow this prefently, but in the meanwhile, let me go on to ftate what the provifions of this plan are for the religious inftruction of Proteftants. 'They,' the Commiffioners, 'will exercife the moft entire control over all books to be ufed in the fchools; in the feparate religious inftruction none are to be employed, but with the approbation of thofe members of the Board who are of the fame religious perfuafion with the children for whofe ufe they are intended.' Why, then, my Lords, it is clear that there is no other fecurity for the ufe of the Bible, even in the religious in-ftruction of Proteftants, than that derived from the character of the individuals compofing that commiffion, and upon that point I fhall fpeak prefently.

"I obferve, that fome noble lords are difpofed to think that I am inclined to cavil upon this point, but I think when I come to enter further into the queftion, I fhall prove to them that I have too good ground for the opinion which I have expreffed.

"With regard to the feparate religious inftruction of Roman Catholics, the provifions are the fame as for the feparate religious inftruction of the Proteftants; neither the Old, nor the New Teftament is required—all is to be left to the Commiffioners of the two feveral perfuafions.

"Such is a general view of this new plan of national education. I proceed to a more particular inquiry into its three feveral parts.

"In refpect to the firft part, I think I fhall make it plain that the principle of this meafure, fo far as regards the joint moral and literary inftruction of Proteftants and Roman Catholics, is completely to exclude the ufe of the Bible, whether entire, or in extracts. In doing this, I fear that I muft pray the indulgence of your Lordfhips for fome tref-pafs on your time, becaufe I feel it neceffary to have recourfe to documentary evidence; and yet, however tedious that may be—and still more tedious the observations which I may consider it necessary to make on those documents—I venture to be confident that your Lordships will patiently bear with me, not only because I have not trespassed on your atten .on before, and am not likely often to do so again—but much more in consideration of the great importance of the question now before you.

" My Lords, I have said that the Holy Scriptures, whether in the entire volume, or in the form of extracts, are, in fact, excluded from the proposed plan of general education; and I think that this will appear in the clearest possible light, if I show that the exclusion or non-exclusion of them must depend on the good pleasure of the Board, and that there is one person placed upon this Board who is not only likely, but whose duty it is, to exclude them.

" My Lords, it must be borne in mind that this letter of the right hon. secretary refers to the acts of a preceding commission which took place some years ago. I mean the commission of 1824-27, at which latter period their labours were concluded. My Lords, the reports of that commission furnished ample details of the opinions of the Roman Catholics with whom they communicated. The Commissioners felt the great importance of the principle, that a literary and moral education should be based on the Scriptures. In their formal communication with Dr. Murray, on the subject of common instruction, a minute of which was made at the time, they thus express themselves :—' The Commissioners then stated that they could not consider any system of education as deserving the name, which should not seek to lay the foundation of all moral obligation in religious instruction —(so little notion had these wise and good men of any system of common instruction which should be moral and literary only). They, therefore, inquired of Dr. Murray, whether it would be objected to, on the part of the Roman Catholic clergy, that the more advanced of the Protestant and Roman

Catholic children ſhould, at certain times during ſchool hours, read portions of the Holy Scriptures together, out of their reſpective verſions, ſubject to proper regulations, and in the preſence of their reſpective Proteſtant and Roman Catholic teachers?' Dr. Murray anſwered, 'that ſerious difficulties would exiſt in the way of ſuch an arrangement; but he ſuggeſted an expedient—that of introducing collections from the Scripture and books of extracts.' Dr. Murray ſaid, 'No objection would be made to a harmony of the goſpels being uſed in the general education, which the children could receive in common, nor to a volume containing extracts from the Pſalms, Proverbs, and Book of Eccleſiaſticus, nor to a volume containing the hiſtory of the creation, of the deluge, of the patriarchs, of Joſeph, and of the deliverance of the Iſraelites, extracted from the Old Teſtament, and that he was ſatisfied no difficulties in arranging the details of ſuch works would ariſe on the part of the Roman Catholic clergy.' Thus it appears that the expedient of having books of extracts and collections from Scripture was firſt ſuggeſted by Dr. Murray; and that he then contemplated giving theſe extracts from the authorized Proteſtant verſion, is plain from what occurred at a ſubſequent meeting.

"My Lords, on the occaſion to which I have already referred, Dr. Murray came alone, and made this ſtatement before the Commiſſioners; but, in a few days afterwards, he returned, bringing with him the three other titular Roman Catholic archbiſhops of Ireland, and he ſaid,—'It appears to be the wiſh of theſe gentlemen,'—not at all implying that it was ſo much a matter of wiſh to himſelf, and certainly implying that it was not a matter of conſcience or principle to any of them,—'it appears to be the wiſh of theſe gentlemen, that anything given in the ſhape of Scripture ſhould be in the Douay verſion for the Catholic children.' Thus the matter ſtood on the 8th of January, 1825; yet, on the 16th of December, of the ſame year, it will be found that he poſitively objected, as of conſcience and neceſſity, to anything being read, as Scripture, in the prefence of the Roman Catholic children, unlefs it was in the Douay verfion; he retracted, in fhort, all he had faid, and objected to the ufe of any books that fhould give any part of our Lord's own words, unlefs it was in that verfion. But he went further, and faid that it was contrary to the difcipline of the Catholic Church that any books whatever fhould be placed in the hands of the Roman Catholic children in which there was even a quotation from the Bible of the Eftablifhed Church, where that Bible differed from the Douay verfion. Thus, it became apparent that no books of extracts from Scripture, *as Scripture*—no moral inftruction bafed on the Word of God, *as fuch*—could be admitted into the fchools of common inftruction, unlefs the bifhops of the Proteftant Church would confent altogether to forego the ufe of their own ver-fion—the only verfion, I muft be permitted to remind your Lordfhips, which the law of the land acknowledges as the Word of God. Not a text, or even a reference to it, would be tolerated by the Roman Catholics, if the reference to it were made as to the Scriptures—fo decidedly were they oppofed, within the fhort period of ten months, to their former ftatement in refpect of the facilities which they were willing to afford to one common principle of inftruction, and in order to promote the objects which the Commif-fioners had in view.

"And yet, my Lords, I muft be permitted to remark that, whenever it may feem neceffary, or poffibly expedient, for Dr. Murray and his friends to act on a fomewhat different principle from that which they have here announced, they find no difficulty in doing fo. No doubt, your Lordfhips will all remember that it was made a matter of great tri-umph, and adduced by the noble and learned lord, the Lord Chancellor of Ireland, as a convincing proof of the liberal and Chriftian fpirit of Dr. Murray, that a paper containing the firft leffon fet forth to be ufed under the new fyftem was moved for adoption by Dr. Murray; which leffon is to be

fufpended in every fchool, and enforced upon the mind of
every fcholar—a leffon, moft certainly, of a highly laudable
nature—a leffon of Chriftian benevolence towards thofe with
whom we differ in religious belief. Now, that very leffon
contains citations from the Holy Scriptures in the verfion of
the Church of England, even in texts where that verfion
differs from the Rhemifh (I fay Rhemifh, becaufe that word,
in ftri&nefs, refers to the tranflation of the New Teftament,
as the Douay verfion does to the Old), and, as I have faid,
is to be ftuck upon the walls of every fchool. This, I repeat, was propofed by Dr. Murray, although he had joined
before in faying, or, by his filence, had acquiefced in the
faying of his brother prelates, to the Commiffioners of 1825,
that it was contrary to the difcipline of the Roman Catholic
Church that the Roman Catholic children fhould have any
book or extra& with fuch a reference placed in their hands.
I ftate this to fhow how little confidence can be placed in
the fincerity of the Roman Catholic prelates, in any tranfactions in which the intereft of their Church are concerned.

"My Lords, it will be recolle&ed that the Commiffion of
1824 abandoned the experiment which they had endeavoured to carry into effe&, becaufe they found it impoffible
to get extra&s from the Scriptures to be read in the fchools.
The confent of the Roman Catholics could not be obtained
to the ufe of our verfion of the Holy Scriptures, even though
they were compelled to admit that their own verfion was
not, ftri&ly fpeaking, an authorized verfion; for it never
had received any fan&ion from Rome, and it had been repeatedly altered fince its firft publication. Our bifhops, on
the other hand, could not confent that the Proteftant Bible
—the only Bible acknowledged by the law of the land—
fhould be abandoned at the demand, or to conciliate the co-
operation, of the Roman Catholics. The confequence was,
as we very well know, that the Commiffioners of 1824
decided that the experiment could not go on ; for, as
a volume, or volumes, of extra&s from Scripture were

essential, in their judgments, to the proper teaching of morality to Christian children, and as no such volume could be agreed upon, nothing remained for them to do but to relinquish an attempt which was thus proved to be hopeless. Now, on this occasion Dr. Murray said, in a letter addressed to the Commissioners — ' I will avail myself of this opportunity to express an opinion, which you will not, I am sure, consider at variance with that respect which I sincerely entertain for the Board of Education inquiry : it is that the Board has created for itself a very needless difficulty by requiring, as a matter of necessity, any scriptural compilation to be used in schools for the purpose of general instruction.'

" It is quite manifest, therefore, that Dr. Murray thinks any such scriptural volumes unnecessary ; and, as he has also declared that any scriptural compilation from the Bible of the Established Church ought not to be used, he will not, and cannot, assent to its introduction into the schools of general instruction.   In short, my Lords, he must and will, if he have the power, exclude the Scripture from such schools altogether.

" But, my Lords, that he will have the power, I proceed to show to your Lordships—and this not merely from considering the deference which would necessarily be paid to his opinion resting on alleged grounds of religious scruples, but also from a very peculiar circumstance, which will be found to deserve the closest attention of your Lordships.   It certainly is most remarkable that Dr. Murray, or some one in the interest of Dr. Murray, has assumed for him a power which was not intended to be given by Mr. Stanley's letter : no less, in short, than a veto on all books proposed to be used for general instruction ; and this object has been effected by foisting in an important word into the regulations of the original.

" I am very happy to see in his place this day the noble Duke (the Duke of Leinster), who is at the head of the Board of Irish Education, because I shall be set right in respect

of what I call a moſt unwarrantable and unauthorized alteration of the inſtructions contained in that letter if I am in-
correct.

"My Lords, it will be obſerved that Mr. Stanley's letter
ſays : —' It is not deſigned to exclude from the liſt of books
for the combined inſtruction, ſuch portion of ſacred hiſtory,
or of religious and moral teaching, as may be approved of by
the Board.'

"Now under this regulation, certainly if the Board at
large ſhould think fit that a portion of the Scriptures ſhould
be uſed, any objection on the part of Dr. Murray would be
uſeleſs. [The Duke of Leinſter.—' Hear ! hear !'] I am
happy to find that the noble duke acquieſces in this, and calls
the attention of your Lordſhips to it ; for I am quite ſure that,
after I ſhall have ſhown what has been done, you will find
your attention has not been ill beſtowed. Your Lordſhips
will obſerve that a public notice has been given by the Board
of Education in Ireland, that they are ready to receive appli-
cations for aid, on the part of thoſe who may be diſpoſed to
eſtabliſh ſchools under the direction of the Board.

"My Lords, I hold in my hands the public advertiſement
of the Board to that effect. A noble lord near me ſays, in
a tone ſomething like that of taunt, that I am quoting from
a newſpaper. It is very true ; but it is the very ſame document as was cited for a different purpoſe, without objection
from any of your Lordſhips, ſome nights ago, by the noble
and learned Lord (Lord Plunket) ; and I muſt take leave to
ſay, that an advertiſement from a newſpaper is as regular a
document, and as fit to be cited here, as any other paper
which has not been formally laid on your Lordſhips' table.
I repeat, therefore, that my newſpaper is as authorized a
document as the noble and learned lord's ſheet, though this
latter be of handſomer form, and better type. Now, my
Lords, in this advertiſement, purporting to be the formal announcement of the Board's new plan of National Education,
and ſubſcribed by the Secretary to the Board, the reſt of the

regulation respecting the control of the Board over the books of general instruction is given *verbatim*, according to the terms of Mr. Stanley's letter; but, before the word ' Board ' is inserted, the word ' entire ' and the effect of the alteration, your Lordships will perceive, is to require the consent of all and every member of the Board, to the use of every particular book; thus giving, as I said, a veto to ˙Dr. Murray, and enabling him, even if he stand alone, to exclude all books of extracts of Scripture, or anything else which might displease him, from the list. [Earl Grey—' Where is the word? I do not find it here, and this is the paper issued by the Board.']

" Why, then, my Lords, if the Board has not in its own formal act inserted the word, it is quite plain that there is some power which can effect whatever alteration shall be deemed expedient in the acts of the Board, in spite of the intentions of the Board itself. This advertisement announces to the world the plan of education, and by it the conduct of the public in forming schools will be regulated, [Earl Grey intimated that he had found the word in his paper.]

" Oh, then, my Lords, it is in both papers—in the handsome official document, and in the more homely one in my hand, the word is equally to be found; and I cannot be sorry for the doubt which at first existed in the noble earl's mind on this point, as it must have increased your Lordships' attention to the circumstance, and, at the same time, perhaps, has testified the noble earl's sense of its importance. I repeat, this word ' entire' is something superadded to the instructions of Mr. Stanley—something not in any degree˙justified by those instructions; and I must take the liberty of saying, further, that it would be satisfactory, if the noble duke at the head of the Board could inform us how this unauthorized and most improper interpolation was made; I am perfectly satisfied that he was no party to it. I have heard much of the noble duke's high and honourable character—I am persuaded not too much,—and therefore, I feel myself warranted in affirming, that he never contemplated so important a change in the inſtructions and powers which the Board received, as is involved in the interpolation of the word 'entire.'

" My Lords, while I am ſure it is not the noble duke's act, I am not ſure whoſe act it was. But this I will ſay, it is not of Engliſh, it is not of Proteſtant origin—the taint of Jeſuit is ſtrong upon it.

" ' The offence is rank ; it ſmells to Heaven.'

" Such, my Lords, has been the mode by which power has been given to every ſingle member of the Board ; to Dr. Murray, therefore, in particular, who has declared himſelf bound in conſcience to uſe that power—to exclude all extracts from Scripture, if thoſe extracts be in the verſion which all Proteſtants conſider, and which alone the law of this land conſiders, as Scripture, from the ſchools of common inſtruction of Proteſtant and Roman Catholic children.

" My Lords, I proceed to the ſecond part of this plan of National Education—the ſeparate religious inſtruction of Proteſtant children. Here, too, I muſt remind your Lorſhips that we have heard this new plan repeatedly and ſtrongly defended, eſpecially by the noble and learned lord, the Lord Chancellor of Ireland, becauſe the ſeveral reports of the various Commiſſioners and Committees of the Houſe of Commons, aſſert principles in perfect accordance with thoſe upon which the Government plan of education has been founded. Now, I will take the liberty of aſſerting—and I fearleſſly refer your Lordſhips to the documents themſelves, to prove the correctneſs of my aſſertion—that, ſo far from this plan being ſanctioned by the previous reports, it is in direct oppoſition to all of them—in every part of it ; and not leaſt in the part to which I am about to invite the attention of your Lordſhips.

" My Lords, the whole control of the religious inſtruction of the Proteſtant children of Ireland will be placed, by this plan, in the hands of three Commiſſioners nominated by the Crown. I need ſcarcely tell your Lordſhips that I entertain for the Protestant portion of the Board the very highest respect; I have already spoken, and shall continue to speak, of the noble duke at the head of the Board with the most sincere respect; but sure I am your Lordships will agree with me, and I am also sure the noble duke himself will be perfectly ready to admit, that there is no great probability of his troubling himself much with minutely criticising the religious publications submitted to the Board. The duty of examining them must, then, of necessity devolve upon the other two Commissioners, namely, the Archbishop of Dublin and Dr. Sadleir. I know both those learned persons, and of both of them I think most highly. Of the Archbishop of Dublin, I will say, that I never knew a man of greater powers, or of a more richly cultivated mind. I never knew a man more strenuous in the pursuit of truth, more fearless in following whithersoever the pursuit may lead him. In short if ever I knew one man more than another who could be called a strict lover of truth, that man is the Archbishop of Dublin; and, to say of any man that he is a strict lover of truth, amounts to saying that he is one of the best of men. But, having said this, I trust it will not be imagined that I speak invidiously, when I say, that this very ardent love of truth in one, who happens to have erred in the pursuit of it, only makes him the more unsafe as a guide, much more as the absolute arbiter of the opinions of others. In short, my Lords, I must not be afraid of saying, that the known opinions of the Archbishop of Dublin upon an important theological question, are opinions which, in a great degree, disqualify him for the situation to which he has been called. That he is disqualified for that situation not merely because he must be thoroughly ignorant of the state of Ireland; not because he is, therefore, in imminent danger of being duped by the Jesuitism to which I have already adverted; but also because, as I have said, of those opinions.

"The opinions of this most reverend Prelate are no secret —they are known, I presume, to most of the noble lords

I have the honour to addreſs. His opinion denying the ſacredneſs of the Sabbath has been put forth to the world, and he is anſwerable for it to the world. Now, what I ſay is this, that any man holding ſuch an opinion, and not only holding it, but promulgating it to the world, is not qualified to have a veto on the books that ſhould be uſed in the education of Proteſtant children. Suppoſe a traɛt is put into his hand, the theme of which is, 'Remember that thou keep holy the Sabbath-day,'—I put it to any man, is he or is he not a perſon who ought to be intruſted with the power of deciding [as to the admiſſibility of ſuch a traɛt? My Lords, I perceive, from the demeanour of ſome noble lords near me, that they think this language invidious. My Lords, I diſclaim any ſuch intention, I mean nothing invidious. I, in common with the great body of the clergy of the Church of England, and with all, I believe, of my right reverend brethren near me, hold that this opinion is erroneous. I impute error, but nothing more than error : and I lament to think, in theſe days, that a man muſt either be ſuppoſed to be inſincere himſelf, or to aſcribe inſincerity to another, if he gives him credit for conſcientiouſly avowing and maintaining an error.

" But, my Lords, the caſe ſtops not here. Much worſe conſequences may flow from the principle on which this commiſſion is founded. The preſent Miniſters would not, I dare ſay, advance a man to the Epiſcopal Bench in Ireland who holds Socinian or Arian opinions. They would not knowingly do ſo. But there have been inſtances of ſuch appointments; even in our own times there was an Iriſh biſhop defamed as a Socinian. I will ſuppoſe ſuch a man appointéd to the Archiepiſcopal See of Dublin, and to a ſeat at this board, and then I find a Socinian veſted with full power to control the religious ſentiments of the riſing generation of Ireland.

" But, my Lords, the whole of this part of the meaſure is a flagrant violation of the ſpirit, and, I believe, even of the letter of the law of the land; it is, too, a gross usurpation upon the rights of the clergy of Ireland.

" By the statute law, it is the duty of the Protestant clergy of that country to make provision for the education of the people. The earliest Act to which I think it necessary to refer your lordships is an Irish Act of Parliament of the 28th of Henry VIII. This Act, after stating ' the importance of a good instruction in the most blessed laws of Almighty God;' and after further stating ' his Majesty's disposition and zeal, that a certain direction and order be had, that all of his (Irish) subjects should the better know God, and do that thing which might in time be, and redound to our wealth, quiet, and commodity,' proceeds, after other matters, to require an oath to be administered to every clergyman at ordination, and another at institution, that he will keep, or cause to be kept, a school for to learn English, &c. And this is re-enacted by the 7th William III, c. 4, (Irish). These provisions, as I presume I need not inform your lordships, impose no obligation upon the beneficed clergy to maintain those schools at their own expense; they merely convey to them a power, and impose on them an obligation, of seeing that these schools be established, and that no higher rate of payment be charged than the customary rate. In truth this Act does little more than add a pecuniary penalty to the sacred obligation which, without any such statute, would have been imposed upon the clergy of attending to the instruction of the young. It is their duty upon much higher grounds than those which any Act of Parliament can impose ; for at their ordination they receive a power, and at institution they receive the assignment of a particular place in which to execute that power, of preaching the Word of God ; and, by preaching, as I scarcely need tell your lordships, is not meant merely the delivery of sermons, but the whole spiritual care of their flocks. But the letter of the Chief Secretary for Ireland not only interferes with the obligation involved in the ministerial office,

ſo far as concerns this moſt important particular of the cure
of ſouls—the religious inſtruction of the children of the
poor—but it alſo puts an end, or profeſſes to put an end, to the
obligations which poſitive ſtatutes have created ;—for it, in
effect, takes out of the hands of the parochial clergy that
right and duty of ſuperintendence with which ſeveral ſtatutes
have inveſted them. This, I preſume, will be conſidered by
moſt noble lords as the aſſumption of ſomething very like
a diſpenſing power. Be this as it may, three Commiſſioners
are nominated by the Crown, who are to poſſeſs the abſolute
power of dictating what ſhall be the religious inſtruction
given to the children of Ireland ; thus taking from the parochial clergy in Ireland that which the laws of God and man
had intruſted to their fidelity and diſcretion. Now, my
Lords, we are told that this plan is perfectly identical with
that which was over and over again recommended by different Committees and Commiſſions. But ſo far is this
from being correct that the Commiſſion of 1824 left this
matter wholly and expreſſly in the hands of the clergy. The
firſt report of that Commiſſion, at great length, aſſerts and
eſtabliſhes the right of the clergy, by ſtatute, to the ſuperintendence of the inſtruction of the children of Ireland ; and
the Report of the Committee of the Houſe of Commons in
1828 left the ſelection of books for the religious inſtruction
of the Proteſtant children to the biſhops of the Church in
general, who might be conſidered as the fit repreſentatives
of the clergy. But this new plan abſolutely flies in the face
of all that went before ; and yet noble lords, and noble and
learned lords, defend this plan on the ground of its being
founded on the very ſame principles.

 " But I am come to the third part of this new ſcheme of
national education ; and I aſk, How does it provide for the
religious inſtruction of the Roman Catholic children ?

 " My Lords, I am not prepared to ſay that it is the duty of
the State to inſiſt on all perſons learning in the Bible ; but
this I ſay, that it is the duty of the State not to aid in any

form of education which excludes the Bible ; this I fay, that all perfons fhould have free accefs to the Bible, whether they will avail themfelves of it or not. We fhould recollect that the prefervation of a free accefs to the Scriptures is a duty impofed upon us by the law of God, and efpecially that every Proteftant legiflature, as fuch, is bound to take care that the people committed to its charge enjoy that privilege in its fulleft extent ; is bound to fee that, neither directly nor indirectly, it makes itfelf a party to any meafure adverfe to this prime and fundamental Proteftant principle.

"In making thefe ftatements, however, I am perfectly willing to admit that, in the prefent peculiar ftate of Ireland, it would be at once unwife and cruel not to give more than the Proteftant verfion of the Scriptures. All that I contend for is the duty of a Proteftant legiflature and a Proteftant government to fee that a verfion of the Scriptures, of fome kind or other, be acceffible to all ; and that it be actually ufed in the inftruction of all for whofe education the State fhall undertake to provide. Yet this the Roman Catholic hierarchy will not now permit. In truth, it cannot have efcaped the attention of your lordfhips that the prefent demands of that hierarchy are of a much more lofty character than thofe which they urged at a former period ; though, to do them juftice, their declared principles were then the fame as now. In proof of this I will refer to a petition of the Roman Catholic bifhops of Ireland to the Houfe of Commons, prefented in 1824, and publifhed in the firft Report of the Commiffioners of 1824, page 1. The words are thefe :—

" ' That the religious inftruction of youth in Catholic fchools is always conveyed by means of catechetical inftruction, daily prayers, and the reading of religious books, wherein the gofpel morality is explained and inculcated ; that Roman Catholics have ever confidered the reading of the facred Scriptures by children as an inadequate means of imparting to them religious inftruction, as an ufage whereby the Word

of God is made liable to irreverence, youth expofed to mifunderftand its meaning, and thereby not unfrequently to
receive, in early life, impreffions which may afterwards
prove injurious to their own beft interefts, as well as to thofe
of the fociety which they are deftined to form.'

" Such were the fentiments of the Roman Catholic bifhops at
the period to which I refer, deliberately laid before the other
Houfe of Parliament. I fhall now requeft your lordfhips'
attention to another document which I think not lefs interefting than important, for the purpofe of illuftrating and fuftaining the pofitions which it is my objeƈ to enforce. I allude
to an encyclical letter from Pope Leo XII. againft the ufe of
the Scriptures in the vulgar tongue, dated the 3rd of May,
1824, and publifhed in Ireland with ' Paftoral Inftruƈions
to all the Faithful' by the Roman Catholic archbifhops and
bifhops of Ireland, and is to the following effeƈ :—

" ' We alfo, venerable brethren, in conformity with our
apoftolic duty, exhort you to turn away your flock, by all
means, from thefe poifonous paftures (the Scriptures in the
vulgar tongue); reprove, befeech, be inftant in feafon and
out of feafon, in all patience and doƈrine, that the faithful
intrufted to you (adhering ftriƈly to the rules of our Congregation of the Index) be perfuaded that if the facred Scriptures be everywhere indifcriminately publifhed, more evil
than advantage will arife thence, on account of the rafhnefs
of men.'

" To this paffage the Irifh prelates, in their Paftoral Inftruƈions, refer in the following terms :—

" ' Our holy father recommends to the obfervance of the
faithful a rule of the Congregation of the Index, which pro-
hibits the perufal of the facred Scriptures in the vulgar
tongue, without the fanƈion of the competent authorities.
His holinefs wifely remarks that more evil than good is found
to refult from the indifcriminate perufal of them, &c. In
this fentiment of our head and chief we fully concur.'

"My Lords, you have here before you the folemn judgment

of the head of the Roman Catholic Church. You have likewife before you the folemn judgment of the whole Irifh
Roman Catholic hierarchy. I will·next ftate what an individual of that body—the moft influential among them, Dr.
Doyle—has faid of his own feparate fentiments—feparate
only in the fenfe that he fpeaks in his individual capacity, but
in no refpect different from the general fentiments of the
body. He fays,—

" ' The Scriptures alone have never faved any one ; they
are incapable of giving falvation ; it is not their object ; it is
not the end for which they were written.'

" Thefe are his fentiments, though S. Paul tells us that
the Scriptures ' are able to make us wife unto falvation.'
Dr. Doyle goes on to fay,—

" ' They hold a dignified place amongft the means of the
inftitution which Chrift formed for the purpofe of faving His
elect ; but if they never had been written this end would be
obtained, and all who were pre-ordained to eternal life would
have been gathered to the Church, and fed with the bread
of life.'

" Such are the notions of Dr. Doyle refpecting Scripture,
and not of Dr. Doyle only, but of all the Roman Catholic
prelates of Ireland. They will act in conformity to thefe
notions, and, armed with the authority of this commiffion,
they will expel the Scriptures from the religious inftruction
of all their fchools, even of thofe which are maintained at
the expenfe of this Proteftant State.

" But, my Lords does this accord with the recommendation of the Commiffioners of Irifh education of 1824 ? So
far from it, that they laid it down as a fundamental, an indifpenfable principle, that the Teftament fhould be put in
the hands of all children, Roman Catholics as well as Proteftants. This was a matter which they would not permit
to be brought even into queftion ; they infifted upon it as
effential (their own word, my Lords), and they required the
Roman Catholic prelates to furnifh them with a verfion of

the New Teſtament for the purpoſe. They permitted, indeed, that notes ſhould be ſubjoined, requiring only that theſe notes ſhould not contain matter of reaſonable offence to Proteſtants. My Lords, I have pleaſure in bearing teſtimony to the fairneſs and fidelity with which this has been accompliſhed. I have pleaſure in ſaying that I have read thoſe notes, and have found in them nothing whatever which can afford fair ground of offence to any reaſonable Proteſtant.

"My Lords, the Commiſſioners of 1824 inſiſted, I repeat, on this Teſtament being uſed in the religious inſtruction of the Roman Catholics, and on the children reading in it, not only the Epiſtles and Goſpels of the Sundays, but the Epiſtles and Goſpels of the whole week, including a large portion of the New Teſtament.

"My Lords, the Committee of the Houſe of Commons of 1828 followed in the ſame line. They, too, required that this New Teſtament ſhould be printed and ſupplied to the national ſchools for the religious inſtruction of the Roman Catholic children :—

"'Reſolved, that it is the opinion of the Committee that copies of the New Teſtament, &c. ſhould be provided for the uſe of the children, to be read in ſchool, &c. the eſtabliſhed verſion for the uſe of the Proteſtant ſcholars, and the verſion publiſhed with the approval of the Roman Catholic biſhops for the children of that communion.'

"Such was the reſolution of the Committee of 1828 ; but the new plan abandons the Teſtament altogether. It does ſo, even though it profeſſes to carry into effect the report of that Committee—it does ſo, even though ſome ſpecial management (I wiſh not to uſe the word in an invidious ſenſe, but ſimply to ſtate the fact, that ſome management) was neceſſary to effect the purpoſe. My Lords, on looking to No. 6 of the regulations of page 5 of the report of the Committee, and comparing it with No. 5 of the regulations in Mr. Stanley's letter, your lordſhips will perceive what I mean. In the latter, all mention of ſupplying ' books of

religious inſtruction' (which included Teſtaments) is ſtudi-
ouſly omitted, even where that letter is copying the very
part of the report which requires ſuch a ſupply.   Why, my
Lords, is this ?   Why is it that, in the plan of the preſent
Board of Education, which profeſſes to carry into execution
the recommendation of that Committee, there is no proviſion made for the ſupply of Teſtaments to any ſchool in
Ireland ?   Becauſe, my Lords, the power which dictates to
Government, in all that concerns the intereſts or the wiſhes
of the Roman Catholic Church, has choſen to demand the
ſacrifice—has choſen to demand that the Bible ſhould be
altogether excluded from their ſchools.   To this power our
Proteſtant government has conſented to ſurrender that which
never before was permitted even to be aſked.

    " My Lords, I have now gone through the various parts of
this new ſcheme of national education, and I think its merits
may be fairly ſummed up in this brief abſtract.   It has
divorced morality from the Word of God.   It has controlled the Proteſtant prieſthood in the exerciſe of one of
their moſt eſſential rights, and in the diſcharge of one of
their moſt important duties—ſubjecting them to a tyranny
which the laws neither of God nor of man have authorized.
It has conſpired with the Roman Catholic hierarchy to arreſt
the progreſs of the book of life—to exclude that bleſſed book
for ever (as vain man fondly deems) from every cabin of
every peaſant in Ireland—and to conſign the unhappy peaſant himſelf to a deeper, deadlier ſtate of darkneſs and of
bondage.

    " My Lords, I have done.   I have ſaid what I had to ſay,
and I thank your lordſhips for the patience with which you
have heard me.   Be aſſured that I will not often treſpaſs on
that patience.   My Lords, in the part which I have now
taken, I have only endeavoured to diſcharge ſome portion of
the duty which I owe to the high office in which I am
placed.

    " Why are men of our ſpiritual function called to mingle

in the councils of you, the mighty ones of this world, and to bear our part in legiſlating for the land? Why is this ſtrict union of Church and State?—an union which, for many more centuries than I can number, has been the glory and ſecurity of England. Why, I aſk, is this? Is it to make the Church political? No, my Lords; in the language of the moſt venerable man among you—one of whom, as he is now abſent, I can more freely expreſs my gratitude and admiration—I mean the noble and learned earl who for ſo many years ſat on that woolſack—it is not to make the Church political, but to make the State religious. Therefore, my Lords, it is that we ſit here. We ſit among you mainly and chiefly (not, indeed, ſolely, but mainly and chiefly) that we be at all times ready, when occaſion ſhall demand, to inſtil into your counſels the holy leſſons of Goſpel truth —to watch over the beſt and higheſt intereſts of thoſe for whom you legiſlate—to raiſe our warning voice againſt every attempt, from whatever quarter it may proceed, to ſever policy from religion, or to ſacrifice the ſmalleſt particle of that pure faith for which your forefathers, my Lords, drove a bigot from his throne, and our predeceſſors were content to be led by his beadles to a gaol! My Lords, I ſtand before you a biſhop of the united Church of England and of Ireland; the united Church, I ſay—for never may we forget that it is united—never! never! never!—leaſt of all, in this dark hour of ſuffering to the Iriſh branch, of common trial, of common peril (it may be both), to both. I ſtand here, and implore your lordſhips to give your moſt ſerious attention to the high-religious intereſts, aye, and I muſt be permitted to add, the high religious duties, which are involved in this night's queſtion. I ſtand here, and conjure you to caſt off, for one brief hour, all inferior thoughts, and to remember only that you are Chriſtian legiſlators.

" My Lords, four-and-twenty hours have ſcarcely paſſed ſince we humbled ourſelves in the houſe of God, deploring the ſins of a guilty people, and beſeeching Him to avert the

fearful fcourges which thofe fins have merited.   We all
then ' humbly acknowledged that, through our negle&t of
God's ordinances, through our mifufe of God's bounties,
offences have multiplied in the land.'   My Lords, of all thofe
ordinances, the moft facred is the due and free ufe of His
holy Word; of all thofe bounties, the moft precious is the
gift of that holy Word.   And will you then, my Lords, on
this, the firft night of your affembling together after that
folemn fervice—will you join in dereli&tion of your firft duty
—in deferting the caufe of God's own Word ?   My Lords,
I have no right to fpeak to you of my own feelings : if I
had, I would entreat, I would befeech you—I would not,
indeed, imitate the eloquent a&tion of the moft eloquent of
living men—I would not bend my knee in prayer to you,
for I pray not to mortal man—but if reverence did not forbid me to mingle the attitude and the words of prayer with
the excitement of this debate, I would humbly pray to Him
Whofe poor and worthlefs creatures we all are—aye, my
Lords, the higheft and the proudeft, no lefs than the lowlieft
and the meekeft—I would pray to Him that He would bow
the hearts of all here as of one man, ' to put away the accurfed thing from among you '—to difclaim all part in this
moft unhallowed work, even though the name and the feal
of our gracious Sovereign be upon it.

   " My Lords, that name and that feal, affixed to fuch a
commiffion—in execution of fuch purpofes—by fuch inftruments—fill the mind with ftrange mufings ; awaken affe&ting
recolle&tions ; invite, perhaps, to fome comparifons.   But
I forbear; I will not be further ftirred by them than to
warn the counfellors of a gracious prince—all whofe thoughts
and wifhes and intentions are, we know, for the good and
happinefs of his people—to warn them, ere it be too late—
while thrones are tottering, and crowns are falling around
us—while they themfelves are reminding us, moft properly
and moft wifely—I thank them for it—while they are reminding us that even now God's judgments are in the earth

—to warn them, I ſay, that He, by Whom kings reign, may be provoked to ſay again, what He once ſaid to a monarch whom He had himſelf placed over His own choſen people, ' Becauſe thou haſt rejected the Word of the Lord, He hath alſo rejected thee from being king over Iſrael.' ''

This ſpeech—the firſt conſiderable effort of the biſhop in the Houſe of Lords—placed him at once in the front rank of Parliamentary debaters, and inſpired even his enemies with the higheſt opinion of his ability and eloquence.

It was upon the occaſion of this debate that Lord Radnor, ever ready to caſt obloquy upon the Church or the clergy, made that diſgraceful attack upon the character of the biſhop which has already been referred to.

On the 27th of this ſame month (March), the Houſe having reſolved itſelf into a Committee on the Pluralities Bill, Lord King took occaſion to refer once more to the pariſh of Woodbury* in the dioceſe of Exeter, from whence, as alleged, the vicars choral of Exeter Cathedral drew an income of 600*l*. or 700 *l*. per annum, while they allowed the officiating clergyman only 50*l*. or 60*l*. a-year. The Biſhop of Exeter then expreſſed his gratification that Lord King had referred to this matter, as it gave him an opportunity of ſtating the real facts of the caſe. Inſtead of receiving 600*l*. per annum, as alleged, the vicars choral received only one third of that ſum, and the income of the clergy-

* See page 300.

man inſtead of being 50*l.* was 100*l.* per annum. It was true that he received only 50*l.* or 60*l.* from the choral fund, but the pariſh made up his ſalary to 100*l.*, and the vicars choral had ſince raiſed it to 150*l.* per annum.

CHAPTER XXIII.

*Anxiety as to the Fate of the Reform Bill in the House of Lords.
Rumoured Intention of creating new Peers. Defection of
Lords Harrowby and Wharncliffe. The "Waverers."
The Bill carried. The Royal Assent. The Bishop of Exeter
a Strenuous Opponent of it. His Intrepid Conduct. Aban-
donment of the Cause by some of the Bishops. Description of
the Bishop of Exeter's Speech. Anxiety to hear the Debate.
Excitement throughout the Country. The Bishop's Speech
against the Bill. Importance of Publication of Parlia-
mentary Debates. Conduct of the Editors of Newspapers.
The Bishop's Speech attacked by the* Times. *Charged with
Change of Sentiment on the Roman Catholic Question. Lord
Durham uses Violent Language towards the Bishop. He is
called to Order. He repeats his Charge. The Bishop's
Reply. The Duke of Buckingham declares that Extracts
from a Letter of his to the King had appeared in the* Times,
*as stated by the Bishop. Indignant Speech of Earl Grey.
Attack upon the Bishop. Exultation of the Radical Portion
of the Press. No Real Explanation given of the Appearance
of the Letter. Injudicious Conduct of Ministers. The Bishop
signs the Duke of Wellington's Protest against the Reform
Bill. Great Unpopularity in his Diocese. He returns to
Exeter. His Preaching. Sets out on a Confirmation Tour
through South Devon. Holds an Ordination at Exeter.
Leaves for London to attend Session of Parliament.*

THE successful progress of the Reform Bill
through the House of Commons has been
already noticed.* So far all had gone
smoothly enough; but its warmest supporters could not think of its probable fate in the

* See page 310.

Houſe of Lords without concern. It was rumoured that, if need ſhould ariſe, a ſufficient number of new peers would be created to enſure its ſucceſs. This would have had the practical effect of altogether depriving the Houſe of Lords of a voice in the council of the nation. They might paſs the meaſure indeed, but it would be by the preconcerted vote of a packed aſſembly. If the deſign, however, was ever ſeriouſly entertained, it was not carried into effect, and on the 26th of March the bill was read for the firſt time in the Houſe of Lords. Some of the opponents of the former bill now declared their adheſion to the new meaſure, their ſentiments having been changed partly by a fear of conſequences, and partly perhaps from a conviction that reform of ſome ſort was needed. Foremoſt amongſt theſe were Lords Harrowby and Wharncliffe, the leaders of the former oppoſition. The ſecond reading was moved on the 9th of April, and the debate was continued on the 10th, 11th, and 13th, having been ſuſpended on the 12th, in conſequence of its being a levee day. Fiercely did the tide of argument roll from one ſide of the Houſe to the other until ſeven o'clock in the morning of the 14th of April, when upon a diviſion the ſecond reading was carried by a narrow majority of nine.

And now the hopes of the reformers roſe high. The victory was theirs, for the bill was read a third time, and paſſed, on the 4th of June, and three days afterwards the Royal aſſent was given by commiſſion. The Biſhop of Exeter continued a ſtrenuous opponent of the bill to the very laft. A conviction of its in-expediency was fo firmly implanted in his mind, that neither the example of "the Waverers" (as his brother peers who having voted againft the firft bill, voted in favour of the fecond, were ftyled) nor the menace of popular indignation could move him. Seldom did he exhibit his characteriftic tenacity of purpofe more ftrikingly than upon this trying occafion. Painful as it was to incur public odium, efpecially in his own diocefe ; much as he might fhrink from being held up to fcorn as the type of a clafs, who, fo long as they could fill their own pockets, thought it a light matter to trample under foot the liberty of the people, he felt that his duty was imperative, and he did it.

Eafy enough would it have been to have earned a tranfient popularity by abandoning the caufe he had efpoufed, as the Bifhops of Bath and Wells, Lichfield, Lincoln, and Llandaff had done, and who could tell how high a reward might have awaited one fo gifted, if he had only thrown the weight of his talents into the minifterial fcale ? His fpeech upon this occafion was fingularly characteriftic, and is remarkable for having given rife to an angry difcuffion, which will be noticed further on. The *Morning Chronicle* of April 12th (a journal little friendly to the bifhop) defcribes it as *the beft fpeech on the oppofition fide* ; and fo it un-doubtedly was.

While difdaining to enter upon the details of a mea-fure which he believed to be fubverfive of the confti-tution, he fhowed, by comparing the Englifh Reform

Bill with the Irish, then under confideration in the Commons, that one effect of the meafure would be to diffolve
the few and infufficient fecurities which had been left
to the Eftablifhed Church by the Roman Catholic
Relief Bill. The aggreffions of later years have fhown
how thoroughly the bifhop underftood the temper of
the Roman Catholic hierarchy. It was to this part of
his fubject that he addreffed himfelf with fingular force
and energy,—elements which were fadly wanting in
moft of the other fpeeches. The wearifomenefs of
details which had been fo often difcuffed before, made
the debate for the moft part heavy and uninterefting.
But tedious as was the progrefs of the bill, the excitement infide and outfide the Houfe knew no bounds.
The *Spectator* fays:—

" A friend of ours defcribes the appearance of the Houfe
of Lords at five o'clock in the morning, when the horizontal
rays of the fun began to dafh through the windows, and
mingle with ' the petty mifty light ' of the decaying candles,
as hardly lefs interefting than the gay fcenes of the Abbey on
the morning of the Coronation Day. The body of the Houfe
was crowded with peers, eagerly bent forward to catch the
exordium of the premier, whofe tall and venerable figure
appeared on the floor. The eyes of the Chancellor flamed
like two diamonds ' in their native dew ' under his overwhelming wig. Lord Lyndhurft's lips were formed in their
ufual crafty fmile. ' The Duke ' looked as wooden as ever;
and nothing indicated the long, and heavy, and haraffing duty
in which the lifteners, more than the fpeakers, had for fo
many hours been engaged. The Peereffes had kept their
feats to the laft. They too fhowed no figns of fatigue ; and
one of them, confpicuous above the reft by the air of intereft
that ftill marked her countenance, feemed to fhow that fhe

was not unufed to late hours, and had perhaps perfonal or family advantages in contemplation. It was not until the moment when the divifion was called that the fair lady, and her gay bevy, reluctantly withdrew, refting however in the auguft precincts until the fate of the queftion was known."

Nor was this all. An impatient crowd thronged the ftreets. Coffee-houfes and taverns were full to choking. Popular orators were hoarfe with their de-nunciations of a pampered ariftocracy and a dominant Church. Eager lifteners were never tired, and every hour fwelled the crowd. Meffengers were in attend-ance to carry the firft news to the foreign embaffies, and couriers, already in the faddle, were ordered to fpare neither whip nor fpur till the tidings had been borne to the moft diftant corners of the land. The queftion ever in men's mouths was, " What will the lords do?" It was whifpered in the avenues of the palace, it was heard above the clamour of the exchange, it was the firft thing talked of when men left the Houfe of God. Woe to that auguft body, fo it was faid, if they fhould dare to crofs the people's will!

It was on April the 11th, the third night of the debate, when the tide of popular excitement was run-ning at the higheft, and the ftorm of indignation againft the Church was blowing its wildeft, that the Bifhop of Exeter rofe, immediately after the Bifhop of London, and fpoke as follows :*—

---

* Any one who reads this fpeech will not require an apology for its being inferted entire. As it was one of the earlieft of the bifhop's efforts in Parliament, fo will it ever rank among the beft.

" My Lords, it was my wiſh not to obtrude myſelf on the attention of your lordſhips during the preſent debate ; and I had reſolved to act on that wiſh, unleſs ſome of my right rev. brethren ſhould addreſs the Houſe in favour of the bill. My Lords, my two right rev. friends near me have thought it neceſſary ſo to addreſs your lordſhips. I truſt, therefore, that I ſhall be pardoned if, following them with equal openneſs and candour, but with very unequal ability, I ſhall endeavour to declare the reaſons which compel me to vote in oppoſition to them. My Lords, I feel that, of what theſe right rev. Prelates have ſaid, very little indeed calls for any obſervations from me. That they are ſincere ; that they are diſintereſted ; that they are perſuaded that the view they have taken of this ſubject, and the concluſions to which they have arrived, are juſt, I am perfectly ſatisfied. Whatever obſervations may have been anywhere made on them, I profeſs, my Lords, that I am at a loſs to diſcover any reaſonable ground of ſuſpicion againſt the purity of the motives which have actuated them on this occaſion. The firſt point, my Lords, to which I think it neceſſary to apply myſelf is, the obſervation which was made by the right rev. Prelate who ſpoke laſt, with reſpect to the notice given by the noble duke oppoſite laſt night. The noble duke (Buckingham), my Lords, gave notice that he would bring in a bill for a reform of Parliament, in caſe of the rejection of that which is now before the Houſe ; and it is moſt remarkable that this meaſure of reform promiſed by the noble duke coincides, in a very extraordinary manner, with the opinions and feelings expreſſed by the right rev. Prelate. Now, my Lords, I ſhould have thought that the natural courſe for him to have taken would have been to ſay, ' I rejoice to find that, after all the delay which has taken place—after all the diſappointment to which I have been ſubjected, in not having before had a meaſure ſubmitted to my conſideration which accorded with my views, I ſhall now have what I have ſo long wanted—a rival expedient will be propoſed, which falls in ſo peculiarly with my own feelings and my own notions, that I cannot hefitate to wait for it.' " [The Bifhop of London : " No, no !"] " The right rev. Prelate fays, ' No, no.' I do not know where I was wrong in the ftatement I have made of the opinions which he has expreffed ; but if I have mifreprefented him, I am fure he will believe that I have not done fo intentionally. At any rate, it muft be admitted that the reafon given by my right rev. friend coincides very remarkably with what I have ftated of his opinions ; for he finds no fault with the extent or purport of the noble duke's notice ; he only fays it has come too late for one who had found it neceffary to make up his mind fome time before. No doubt my right rev. friend had fo made up his mind, but why it was neceffary for him to do fo I cannot conceive ; and yet I am quite fure that the neceffity which is felt by fuch a mind as his is fome-thing very ftrong. Be this as it may, I fhould have thought it time enough for him to have made up his mind when the bill was before the Houfe, and when the queftion to be de-cided really preffed for decifion ; but he has anticipated that period—for very good reafons, I am quite fure, though I am at a lofs to perceive them. My Lords, I fhould not have been furprifed if any of the noble lords on this (the minifte-rial) fide of the Houfe had wifhed to get rid of this notice of the noble duke, which muft be felt by them as very incon-venient. But I fhould have thought that, to any one enter-taining the opinions expreffed by my right rev. friend, and who had read the bill which I hold in my hand, the noble duke's notice would have been the moft acceptable thing poffible, becaufe it affords the very beft means of getting out of all the difficulty which fuch a perfon muft feel. It en-fures the objeƈt he has in view, the real extent of reform which he thinks neceffary, and offers to deliver him from the dangers which he fees in this bill. But, my Lords, it is time for me to apply myfelf to the real queftion before the Houfe. And what is this queftion ? It is whether we will confent to the fecond reading of the bill ; in other words,

whether we will approve and adopt its principle.   Now, is
the principle of the bill fuch as is fit to be adopted by this
Houfe? efpecially is it fuch as can merit the approbation of
all the noble Lords and right reverend Prelates who have expreffed their opinions on the limits within which a fafe
meafure of reform muft be bounded?   Very far otherwife:
it is very true that we have not yet very clearly afcertained
what the real principle of the bill is, and to this point I will
now beg leave to addrefs my attention.   We have been told
by the noble earl who moved the fecond reading of the bill,
that the principle of it is declared in the preamble.   That
preamble ftates the expediency of taking ' effectual meafures
for correcting divers abufes that have long prevailed in the
choice of members to ferve in the Commons' Houfe of Parliament, to deprive many inconfiderable places of the right
of returning members, to grant fuch privileges to large, populous, and wealthy towns, to increafe the number of knights
of the fhire, to extend the elective franchife to many of His
Majefty's fubjects who have not heretofore enjoyed the fame,
and to diminifh the expenfe of elections.'   Now, I certainly
think it would be impoffible for any perfon not previoufly
aware of the fact to conceive from this preamble that the bill
itfelf would go not only to the abfolute extinction of many
rights of reprefentation, not only to the alteration of many
others, but to effect a complete and entire change in the
whole reprefentative fyftem, in the rights of election of every
county, city, and borough in England.   A change fuch as
this—a change fo enormous as was never before contemplated—is not to be expected from the preamble of the bill,
and if fo, then I fay that that preamble does not exprefs the
principle of the bill.   The real principle of the bill feems to
me to be a complete change in our reprefentative fyftem,
except with refpect to the Univerfities.   Such a change has,
I repeat, never before been contemplated ; in my opinion
fuch a change amounts to fomething very like revolution,
and therefore the principle of the bill feems to me to be

revolutionary. I am well aware that the account which I before ftated has been given of the principle of the bill, not only by the noble earl who introduced it, but alfo by a noble earl oppofite, who fpoke with fuch diftinguifhed ability and eloquence laft night (the Earl of Harrowby). That noble earl has likewife given you another principle of the bill; he has told your lordfhips that ' if you agree to the fecond reading of this bill'—in other words, if you acknowledge the principle of it—' you will admit that fome confiderable reform is required in the Commons' Houfe of Parliament.' But, my Lords, though we have this very high authority for the ftatement that fuch is the principle of the meafure, I cannot forget that we have had other principles attributed to it by the noble earl himfelf. I am far from wifhing to taunt that noble earl with inconfiftency in his views and conduct, in refpect to this queftion, at different times; for I do not think it matter of blame that man fhould be inconfiftent with himfelf with refpect to fo vaft a fubject. A queftion of this kind involves fo many confiderations, it muft appear at different times in fo many different lights to the fame man, that a change in his opinions is not to be wondered at. I fully believe that nothing but the conviction of the wifdom and neceffity of affenting now to this very fame meafure, which the noble earl fix months fince thought it wife and neceffary to oppofe, could have induced the noble earl to give it his fupport. But while I fully admit that voting differently at different times, with regard to queftions of this nature, does not neceffarily imply blameable inconfiftency, I am fure that the noble earl will, on his part, admit that (though a different line of action may be now neceffary in refpect to this bill, though he may now feel it his duty to fupport the fecond reading which he then oppofed), yet what he expreffed of the principle of the bill on the 4th of October laft, in oppofing it, cannot be lefs applicable to it this night, when he thinks it proper to give it his fupport. In fhort, my Lords, truth and reafon will ftand ftill even though the noble earl may have felt it neceſſary to turn round. Now, in opening this morning the ſpeech delivered by the noble earl laſt October, in oppoſition to this meaſure, the firſt ſentence that my eye fell upon was the following :—' The principle and object of this bill are to make the Conſtitution more democratic. Look to the conſequences of doing ſo.' Again, in another place :—' I am obliged to oppoſe this bill, as I conſider it a change which muſt inevitably lead to all other changes.' And, in a third inſtance, he ſays,—' I think that much of the power of a government may reſt in the confidence of the people ; and if that confidence be ſhaken, be the government in reality good or bad, it is the intereſt and the duty of the government to take ſuch reaſonable meaſures as ſuggeſt themſelves to recover that confidence, and to aſſure its continuance. That, however, is not to be done by changing at once the whole conſtitution of the Houſe of Commons.' Here, my Lords, is the deſcription given by the noble earl of the principle of the bill in October laſt : it is ' to make the Conſtitution more democratic ;' it is to effect ' a change which muſt neceſſarily lead to all other changes ;' it is ' to change at once the whole conſtitution of the Houſe of Commons.' And if this was its principle then, it is not leſs its principle now. I aſſent moſt completely to this view of the princi-ple, and therefore I ſhall vote againſt the ſecond reading of the bill. My Lords, I have already ſaid that I regard this meaſure as revolutionary. I know that the noble earl at the head of the Government has repelled this charge againſt the meaſure with indignation. I am glad that it was thought a charge, and that it was ſo anſwered ; for I ſhould think it very frightful if the noble earl thought lightly of producing a revolution : but the noble earl took a diſtinction which he thought juſtified himſelf. He ſaid that ' that was not a revo-lution which was not either a change of dynaſty or ſome other change that was wrought, not by the regular powers of the Conſtitution, but by the introduction of ſome force unknown to the Conſtitution.' From the ſilence of the noble earl I truft I have quoted his words correctly. But if fuch are the noble earl's notions of revolution, they are very different from mine.

" According to thofe notions it follows that no revolution occurred in France before the year 1792, and not until Louis XVI. fled from Paris ; for up to that period, vaft as were the changes that took place, all or almoft all were brought about under the forms of law, and by the regular powers of the Conftitution. ('No, no!') I truft that noble lords will have the goodnefs to correct me hereafter if I am wrong. Meanwhile I perfift in my affertion, and I believe that it will hardly be difputed that every portion of the French Revolution up to June, 1792—everything that was done before that period in the way of deftroying the ancient inftitutions of the country—was done under the forms of the Conftitution, and by the regularly conftituted powers of the Government of that country. Now, let us fuppofe for a moment that in this country a vaft change was introduced by both Houfes of Parliament, and fanctioned by the King—a change which went to deftroy the prefent exifting fyftem altogether. Let us fuppofe, for inftance, that the two Houfes of Parliament were bafe enough to pafs a bill to which the Sovereign gave his affent, making all the proclamations of the King equivalent to Acts of Parliament. Would it be faid, if fuch a thing as this fhould be done, that it would not amount to a revolution ? And yet it would be a change accomplifhed under the regular forms of the Conftitution, and fanctioned by the conftituted authorities of the State. We might fuppofe alfo a contrary cafe. Let us fuppofe that a Sovereign anxious for popularity, and thinking to gratify the wifhes of his fubjects, fhould defcend from his throne, and with the confent of Parliament, fo change all the forms of the Government as to eftablifh a republic, or a monarchy which would be one only in name and form, with all the effentials of a real republic—this would be a change brought about by the recog-

nized conftitutional authorities of the land ; and yet would
any one fay that fuch a change would not amount to a
complete revolution. But this, it may be faid, is putting extreme cafes. Well then, I would put another which a
twelvemonth ago we fhould all have thought an extreme
one too—but which after what we have recently heard
within thefe twenty-four hours, from a noble baron, may, I
fear, be fo regarded no longer. Let us fuppofe, my Lords,
that fome meafure were devifed the objeᶜt of which fhould
be to drown the voice of your lordfhips, and to extinguifh
for ever the independence of this Houfe—let us fuppofe
this to be done in all due form by the exercife of powers
fully recognized by law—and thus, my Lords, a third cafe
would occur, of which I apprehend moft of your lordfhips
would agree in opinion with me that it amounts to a revolution. (Interruption.) I muft fay that it is extremely
inconvenient to receive leffons in this way while I am
addreffing your lordfhips. I am well aware that fevere
leffons will be read to me by-and-bye — and then I fhall
bear them as I may. Meanwhile I entreat that I may not
be interrupted. After all, my Lords, however difagreeable
may be the mention of the word revolution to the ears polite
of the noble lords on the bench near me, I muft remind
them that fome of the chief fupporters of the bill glory in
it, becaufe it is a revolutionary meafure, and advocate it as
fuch. We all know that the public prefs has given
great fupport to this bill, and we are equally aware that by
the public prefs it is hailed as a revolution. In one of the
public journals—in a journal conduᶜted with great ability,
remarkable for its great information, and diftinguifhed for
the efficient fupport which it has given to this meafure—in
that journal I not long ago read the following words, as
characᵗerizing the conftitution of this land, ' That horrid
old mockery of a free government which we have hitherto
been enduring.' This is the defcription of the exifting
Conftitution given in that public journal which has rendered

the moft powerful fupport to this meafure, and which is believed by many to breathe the infpirations, if not of the
Treafury itfelf, at leaft of fome high office or offices of the
Government. I do not fay that this belief is well founded
—I do not fay that I believe it—I only fay that fuch a
charge has been made, and that it is believed by many to be
true. ('It is not true.') I have only faid what is believed
by many—not that I believe it. This, I repeat, is the defcription of a Conftitution—of which Englifhmen have been
wont to be proud—given by one of the ableft fupporters
of the prefent bill. I find no fault with it, on the contrary
I honour the franknefs of the avowal. To think and fpeak
thus is exactly what might be expected from an honeft and
intelligent advocate of the plan. My Lords, I will not inflict on your lordfhips any eulogy—or rather, I fear, I
fhould fay any elegy—of mine on our departing Conftitution,
but I will indulge myfelf with fpeaking of it in the lofty
language in which Milton defcribes a complete and generous
education. My Lords, for more ages than I fhall ftop to
number, the Britifh conftitution has 'fitted the people of this
land to perform juftly, fkilfully and magnanimoufly all the
duties both private and public of peace and war.' This in
my heart I believe to be true of our prefent conftitution.
Such in my heart I believe the Britifh conftitution to be;
and believing it to be fo, no earthly confideration fhall induce
me, by any vote of mine, to contribute to its deftruction. I
do not mean to go into the details of this bill; I fhall
rather look to its general character—and, looking at it thus,
I am fo forcibly ftruck by one of the things faid of it by the
noble earl oppofite, that I muft take the liberty of en-
larging a little upon it. I allude, my Lords, to that part
of the noble earl's former fpeech in which he fpoke of the
democratic tendency of this meafure. My Lords, I am
not difpofed to be making comparifons between the different
elements in the exifting conftitution; but I have no hefitation in faying that I confider the democratic element the

most glorious and the most valuable of all. I consider it
to be the perennial source of that spirit of liberty which is
the proudest distinction of our national character—the boast
and glory of our country; but while I feel it to be so valuable, I at the same time feel that it is a principle which peculiarly requires to be restrained. Like that element in the
physical world which it most resembles—the element of fire—
it is, while properly tempered and controlled, the most genial,
the most salutary, the most invigorating, the most productive
of all good; but like that element, also, when left to its own
unchecked and uncorrected workings, it becomes the most
destructive and the most devastating. In the constitution,
as it at present exists, I find that the democratic element
has such checks and corrections as reduce it to a due tem-
perament, and render it a safe and inestimable ingredient of
the whole. These checks and corrections are found in
parts of the Constitution which I fairly own at first sight
appear to be the least worthy of approbation, and the most
exposed to objection. I mean the nomination and close
boroughs. They have been called by a noble earl this
night—and I do not wish to quarrel with the expression—
'the rotten parts of the constitution.' A great man de-
ceased did not regard them in that light; he distinguished
them by a phrase certainly not of honour, but one which
recognizes their importance and necessity—he called them
the shameful parts of the Constitution.

 " Such parts of the Constitution are not the least necessary to the soundness of the whole; and if those boroughs
perform the distinctive functions which Mr. Burke says they
do perform, and for which he valued them; then I contend
that they ought not to be got rid of without some equivalent
check of a more seemly character. If that can be done, I
shall rejoice in their abolition, but, seeing no such correctives
in the present bill, I feel myself bound to adhere to the old
system, or at least not to go so far in innovation as is proposed in the measure before the House. In connection with
this part of the subject, there is one point to which I beg

leave to recall your lordſhips' attention. We have heard much of uſurpations on the rights of the people ; uſurpations that have been committed either by members of this Houſe, or by other wealthy proprietors. It is ſaid that ſome of your lordſhips have, in faƈt, uſurped a power over the repreſentation which particularly belonged to the people. That this has, in ſome inſtances, occurred, I readily admit : that it has occurred ſo often as is charged, I muſt beg leave reſpeƈtfully to deny. There is no period, I will venture to ſay, in the ancient hiſtory of the Parliament of this country in which it has not been the praƈtice of the Government to create boroughs which ſhould abſolutely be in the nomination of great proprietors. I believe I may ſay, with truth, that all thoſe boroughs, the franchiſe of which is burgage-tenure, are of this deſcription. Now when theſe uſurpations on the rights of the people are charged upon members of the Houſe and upon the great proprietors, I beg to be permitted to aſk, whether there has been no uſurpation on the part of the people on the rights of the Parliament ? There has been one gigantic uſurpation, in compariſon with which all others ſink into inſignificance,—I mean the publicity which is given to the proceedings of Parliament by the printing of the debates in both Houſes. This uſurpation upon the privileges of both Houſes of Parliament is far greater, and far more important in its operation, than all thoſe ten-times-told which have been charged againſt any of your lordſhips, or any other great proprietors, as regards any interference in the eleƈtion of repreſentatives of the Commons in Parliament. Nothing, I apprehend, can be more certain than that, by the letter and ſpirit of the Conſtitution of this country, the proceedings in the two Houſes of Parliament are to be free from all influence from without, and, therefore, it is that we are preſumed to be now difcuſſing this queſtion with cloſed doors. Do I lament that the praƈtice has been changed ? Far from it : I think that the publicity given to our proceedings is the moſt wholeſome measure that could have been adopted. I think it the best and most complete Reform of Parliament ever devised; because, I think that no greater security can be given for the purity of conduct of both Houses than that all we do, and all we say, should be known to the whole world. Thus it has happened, that while the people have not so large a direct influence on the proceedings of Parliament, as a less restrained system of representation might afford them, still everything is done to give them a real and efficient influence. But if in order to correct the excess of the power of the members of this House, or of other great proprietors, over the representation—if, in order to correct this excess, a new measure were introduced, which would abolish the balance hitherto maintained—which would destroy altogether the influence of peers and great proprietors over the Constitution of the other House, making all elections popular—but which, at the same time, would allow the publication of the proceedings of the Parliament to be continued—if, I say, to correct the excess complained of, such a course were adopted, then would the democratic element of the Constitution obtain so vast and overwhelming preponderance, that everything else must give way to it; and it would be impossible to carry on any regular system of government. In short, my Lords, thinking, as I do, that it is necessary, as the best protection of the purity of our own proceedings, and for the satisfaction of the people, that access should be had, not only to the votes, but to the debates of Parliament, I could never consent to any measure which could exclude the public from these walls. But then, I must insist on the necessity of bearing this important consideration in mind—when we are meditating Reform, when we are discussing what shall be the new Constitution of the country; and we should take care, while we permit the people irregularly to avail themselves of an advantage of the most important kind, not so to increase their regular power, as must positively overwhelm the monarchical and aristocratical elements of the Constitution. My Lords, there is one part of the ſubjeĉt to which I beg leave to thank the noble baron who ſpoke with ſuch extraordinary ability and eloquence two nights ago (Lord Ellenborough), and alſo the noble earl at the table (the Earl of Falmouth), for having direĉted our attention—I mean the conneĉtion of this bill with that for the reform of the re-preſentation of Ireland. As the noble earl well and truly ſaid, the preſent meaſure, and the two bills now before the other Houſe, muſt be conſidered as parts and parcels of the ſame meaſure. They are integral parts of one whole, and I am quite ſure that none of your lordſhips would aſk me to conſider them ſeparately, or would ſuppoſe that I am guilty of any irregularity in alluding to the Iriſh meaſure of Reform, although that meaſure is not yet before us, and in ſpeaking of it and of the Engliſh bill, as one and the ſame conjoint meaſure. I ſay this the more confidently, becauſe I have the example and the authority of the noble earl at the head of the Government for ſo doing ; for the noble earl, in ſubmitting this meaſure to the Houſe, ſpoke of the Iriſh bill, and told us what was the number of additional repreſentatives which it was propoſed to give to Ireland. Now, of courſe, the noble earl could only have done this from recognizing its conneĉtion with the preſent meaſure. Sanĉtioned then by this authority, and following the courſe of the noble earl, I ſhall not ſcruple to make one or two remarks upon the bill for Ireland, as taken in conneĉtion with that now before the Houſe. In the firſt place, then, if the Iriſh bill ſhould be carried, what will become of the repreſentation of the Iriſh boroughs ? It will be taken from the Proteſtant influence and conferred upon the Roman Catholic population. Can your lordſhips conceive a greater change—a more important change—a more fearful change ? It appears to me to be the more formidable, becauſe I can-not diſguiſe from myſelf that it is only one part of that ſyſtem, which, unhappily of late, has been too much prac-tiſed, of truckling to the Roman Catholics of Ireland   I see that, on every occasion, there is a readiness to yield the most high and sacred considerations connected with the religion of that country to temporal—nay, to temporary expediency. Expediency! My Lords: it is not expediency. The thing is as miserable in policy as it is indefensible in principle. It is a mere huckstering of pure religion for the brief, the hollow, the worthless support of men whom no concessions can win—who laugh at your bribes, and jeer at your elaborate and unwearied efforts to cocker, and soothe, and pamper them,—of men who no longer deign even to wear the mask of a decent hypocrisy, who proclaim their hopes—rather I should say their triumphs—of men who even now boast—and chuckle while they boast—that the oath they have taken, not to use the power which a too-confiding legislature gave them ' to weaken or disturb the Protestant government, or Protestant religion of the country' —admits of an explanation, which makes it a key—a pick-lock—with which they may open to themselves, at once, both the citadel and the temple of our Sion. My Lords, I speak not of visionary dangers, or matters of distant and doubtful speculation. Already the days of the Irish branch of the Protestant Church are numbered. The very month of its destruction has been openly, ostentatiously, authoritatively proclaimed. It has been declared that a general election will take place in November next, and at that general election the giant-spirit of democracy will rise in all its might, and crush the Protestant Church of Ireland to the dust. This high purpose has been proclaimed—not by some mad fanatic at the Rotunda in Dublin—not by some artful demagogue, or unprincipled agitator, seeking to inflame the passions of the mob, for the advancement of the sordid views of his own miserable ambition, or more miserable avarice. No! it has been proclaimed by a British senator, in a place second in dignity only to the assembly which I have now the honour of addressing, by a man of genius and of eloquence, by a man who was not long ago selected by the Lord-Lieu-

tenant of Ireland—aye, and not unworthy on many accounts
to be fo felected—to reprefent the principles of that noble
lord in Parliament. This gentleman, my Lords, whofe
fortunes and whofe principles alike place him above the
temptations of fordid lucre, and whofe high faculties—for he
has very high faculties—had found a full and adequate object
of their ambition in the peaceful honours of the fenate and
of the bar—this gentleman, after having laid down all hoftility to our Church—after having folemnly, and I doubt
not fincerely, pledged himfelf to promote with all his powers
the common peace and common fecurity of all his countrymen—has been forced and goaded by the meafure on which
we are this night to decide, to abandon that peaceful courfe
—to refume the poft and attitude of combat, to arm himfelf
in the caufe of his Church—his now, as it is fondly deemed,
triumphant Church. And while his better feelings recoil at
the work before him, while he vainly ftruggles againft the
chain which binds him, he is compelled again to take the
impulfe of all his public conduct from the mandate of his
fpiritual tafkmafter. In relation to this part of the queftion
—I mean the Irifh meafure of Reform—there is a matter
which I beg leave very earneftly to lay before your lordfhips—I mean the origin of the fyftem of reprefentation in
Ireland. I am perfuaded that it is not unknown to any of
your lordfhips that the reprefentative fyftem in Ireland
owes its origin to King James I. He eftablifhed that fyftem,
not as an equal fyftem, but avowedly as unequal. The
circumftances of Ireland—its condition—the relation in which
it ftood towards this country—forbade the introduction of an
impartial fyftem of reprefentation fimilar to our own. The
fyftem eftablifhed by King James I. was formed for a fmall
band of Englifhmen fettled in the midft of a hoftile population—a population oppofed to them in all that related to
civil rights, as well as to religious feelings. Under fuch
circumftances, King James I. felt that it was impoffible that
anything like a regular government could be kept up in that

country, unless either the Roman Catholic natives were treated as slaves, or the Protestant settler had a predominant power in Parliament.   For this reason he openly avowed in the proclamation which he set forth at the time, and by which he created a large number of boroughs in Ireland, and divided some of the provinces into new counties, that his object in doing so was to establish a system by which the Protestant interest and the Protestant Church of Ireland should be secured.   Such, my Lords, was the policy of James—such the foundation of the representative system of Ireland.   Within our recollection two epochs have occurred, at which the representation of that country has undergone considerable change.   I mean the Legislative Union of Ireland with this country, and the recent settlement of the question with respect to the disabilities of the Roman Catholics.   On both those occasions it was decided that the Protestant interest in the representation of boroughs should be retained.   In the words of the Treaty of Union, the maintenance of the Protestant Church was considered as an essential and fundamental principle in the government of the country.   For that reason, it was stipulated that certain boroughs should be retained, and the corporations of those boroughs were continued in the state in which they were, under their ancient charters, for the very purpose of securing the Protestant interest.   In the measure adopted three years ago—the measure for the emancipation of the Roman Catholics—that part of the Protestant security was left untouched.   It was stated by the noble duke, in bringing that measure forward, as a thing absolutely essential to the good faith of this country—to the good faith of a Protestant government dealing with Protestant interests—that in making the change which he proposed, the Protestant boroughs of Ireland should be continued in their existing state.   Is there, then, one of your lordships who, if told at that time, that within three years it would be proposed to do away with this security which was then so sedulously and carefully preferved—is there, I afk, one of your lordfhips who would not have fcouted the idea? And yet, it is fo propofed in the meafure now before us—a meafure, the principle of which has received the affent of many noble lords, who, I believe, are as firmly attached to the Proteftant interefts as myfelf—which has received the affent, too, of fome of my right rev. brethren. Now, I confefs, that this has fomewhat aftonifhed me, becaufe it is impoffible, I think, for any man not to be-aware of the connection between the Englifh and Irifh Reform bills, and, confequently, of the refults which muft follow the adoption of the firft. I do not wifh to ftate this too ftrongly, but, I fhould be wanting to the duty which I owe to the Church, in which I bear fo high an office, if I did not further ftate that there is fomething in this queftion of a very peculiar intereft as refpects the higheft individual in the realm. To the fecurity of the Proteftant interefts— to the fecurity of the Proteftant Church—it is not only our duty, as members of the Britifh Parliament, to pay particular attention, but it is alfo the particular duty of the Sovereign himfelf. In difcuffing this fubject we muft not forget that, by the oath which fealed the compact between the Sovereign and the people, and which we had all the happinefs of feeing his prefent gracious Majefty take with fuch interefting and impofing ceremonies, a few months ago—you muft not forget, I fay, that, by that oath, the Sovereign bound himfelf to maintain, to the utmoft of his power, the true profeffion of the Gofpel and the Proteftant reformed religion as by law eftablifhed within thefe realms. Looking upon the fubject in this light, I wifh to put it to the noble lords who fit on the bench near me— not in a tone of defiance (which would ill become me), nor in the fpirit of defiance (which I hope does not belong to me)—but calmly, and with a deep fenfe of its overwhelming importance, I wifh to afk thofe noble lords whether they can conceal from themfelves, on due confideration, that the plain, fimple, indifputable meaning of this oath, muft prevent the Sovereign from confenting to extinguifh the Proteftant power, which is retained in the exifting Corporations in Ireland.   I put this, I fay, to the confideration of thofe noble lords.   But I muft beg leave to remind the Houfe that Minifters are not the only refponfible perfons on this occafion, I muft be permitted to remind your lordfhips that each and every one of you is equally bound, not only not to lend himfelf to a meafure of this fort, but not to aid in forcing it upon the counfels of the Sovereign.   If I fay this to the Houfe at large, what muft I fay to my right rev. brethren in particular?   Will they—will any man among them, if he really thinks that I have fairly ftated the cafe—will he venture to fanction, by his vote this night, fuch a meafure as this before us?   I am fure that not one of my reverend brethren will do fo.   I am fure that, whatever pledges they may have given, they will fee that no pledge can relieve them from the folemn duty of protecting the Sovereign's oath, and the interefts of the Proteftant Church.   Having had this matter brought before their minds—even in the poor way in which it has been laid before them by myfelf— if, after this, they fupport the bill, they will do fo, I am fure, becaufe they do not fee the cafe, as I moft confcientioufly avow that it is feen by me.   Nothing, I am confident, could prevail on them to vote for this bill, if they thought as I think, that by voting for it they will facrifice one great fecurity of the Proteftant caufe in Ireland.   I have already trefpaffed at too great a length upon your lordfhips' time : I haften, therefore, to conclude.   My Lords, it is with no ordinary feeling that I find myfelf fpeaking upon this fubject in this the moft auguft affembly in the world—aye, I repeat it,—in this the moft auguft affembly in the world.   Such this Houfe for centuries has been—fuch it ftill is—fuch let us hope it may long continue to be.   God grant that it may: for if it fhould ever ceafe to be the moft auguft affembly in the world, it will become the moft degraded.   And why, my Lords, will this be ? becaufe, if this Houfe fhall fall from its proud eminence, it will fall, not by violence, from without ; for, notwithftanding all that has been faid or done, the people of this country will never be fo falfe to their own interefts as to be wanting in refpectful attachment to you, if you are not wanting to yourfelves and them. No, my Lords, if this Houfe fhall fall from its palmy ftate it will fall by corruption within. It will fall by the folly, or the guilt, by the cowardice or the treachery of fome, if there fhall be any fuch, of its own degenerate members. My Lords, it has been ordained by a fevere but moft merciful difpenfation, that thofe to whom great interefts are intrufted cannot be falfe to thofe interefts without drawing down a full meafure of righteous retribution on their own heads. My Lords, to you the guardianfhip of the Britifh Conftitution—that Conftitution which, for at leaft 800 years has foftered, nurfed, matured, and confolidated, the liberties and the happinefs of this much favoured people—to you the guardianfhip of that Conftitution has been mainly configned, to your fidelity, to your prudence, to your firmnefs. My Lords, if it fall, you will not only fall with it, but you will be ground to duft beneath its ruins. May He Who has appointed you to your high place enable you to fill it as you ought ! In this great crifis (for fo we all feel it to be), in this agony of our country's fate—may He give you wifdom to fee, and fortitude to purfue, fteadily and fearlefsly, that only path which can lead to honour or to fafety—the path of duty. True, my Lords, that path is befet with difficulties and with dangers ; clouds and thickeft darknefs reft upon it ; but one thing is clear, is right, and one thing only—to walk uprightly is within your own power. As for confequences, they are in the power of God. Will you diftruft that power ? My Lords, you will not."

It was felt on all fides that this fpeech was a mafterpiece of eloquence, and people were loud in its praife.

Not the leaſt remarkable part of it is the reſiſtleſs way in which the biſhop turned back the cry of invaſion of rights, ſo often raiſed by the lower againſt the higher orders againſt themſelves, when he ſhowed the importance of the publication of Parliamentary Debates, which had been tacitly ceded. This is a compenſating element in the Conſtitution which has not always received the attention which it deſerves. It has grown, however, with the growth of the country itſelf; and, upon the whole, its influence has been for good, for it muſt be admitted that in the communication of the tranſactions of the Houſes of Parliament the editors of public journals have uſually been guided by the ſtricteſt impartiality. The publicity given to all queſtions, and eſpecially to great meaſures of finance, has in modern times been the principal, if not the ſole means of reconciling the nation to a weight of taxes which might otherwiſe have excited it to diſcontent and even rebellion. Would it now be endured that the country ſhould be deprived of that information which it is moſt alive to be poſſeſſed of, and that it ſhould be kept in ignorance of what Parliament was doing at the moſt critical moments of its exiſtence? And yet, great as is the boon, people ſeem to have forgotten that it *is* a boon, and have come to look upon it as a right. The biſhop, therefore, deſerves our thanks for ſtating it as an element to be conſidered and weighed in ſettling any queſtion of repreſentative reform.

But admirable as was this ſpeech, it nevertheleſs afforded to the enemies of the biſhop an opportunity of indulging their fpleen at his expenfe. The *Times* in particular (13th of April) was at great pains to fhow that his argument drawn from the French Revolution was unfound, and commented with feverity on the rebuke adminiftered to Lord Harrowby for turning round on the queftion of reform while truth ftood immoveable.

" It came," fays the writer, " with an ill grace from this reverend perfonage, who ought to have remembered that on the Catholic queftion truth was no lefs ftationary than with regard to Reform, neverthelefs, there were thofe who at that period did not ftand ftill upon the pedeftal of truth. Dr. Phillpotts, for inftance, unlefs we are miftaken, fpun *completely* round, and never ceafed from turning until he fettled into a bifhop."

On the evening of the 13th the debate was refumed ; and it was upon this occafion that Lord Durham, the fon-in-law of the Premier, varied the monotony of the previous proceedings by taking violent exception to a remark which the bifhop had made in the courfe of his fpeech, to the effect that the *Times* breathed the infpiration of the Treafury. Lord Durham affumed that he was the perfon pointed at, and referring to the Bifhop of Exeter, expreffed himfelf with great vehemence, as follows :—

" If coarfe and virulent invective—malignant and falfe infinuations—the groffeft perverfion of hiftorical facts—decked out with all the choiceft flowers of his well-known pamphleteering flang "—

Lord Winchilfea here rofe to order, defiring that his lordfhip's words fhould be taken down ; and after fome difcuffion Lord Durham perfifted in maintaining that " pamphleteering flang " were the only words which he confidered could correctly defcribe the fpeech of the bifhop; a fomewhat forcible mode of expreffion, it muft be admitted, when it is remembered to what affembly it was addreffed, and the office of the perfon to whom it was intended to apply.

" As to the words ' malignant and falfe infinuations,' " the noble lord continued, " the rev. prelate in the courfe of his harangue infinuated that fome of his Majefty's minifters were unbecomingly connected with the prefs. From the terms in which that infinuation was couched, I could have no doubt that he alluded to me. It would be grofs affectation in me to deny it—the more efpecially as I had been previoufly told by thofe who had read thofe papers that the fame charge had been made againft me by name, in thofe weekly publications which are fo notorious for their fcurrility and indecency. When, therefore, I found that charge repeated, in this Houfe, in terms which neither I, nor any man living, could mifunderftand, I determined to take the earlieft opportunity of ftating to your lordfhips that it was as falfe as fcandalous. I now repeat that declaration, and paufe for the purpofe of giving any noble lord an opportunity of taking down my words."

After a fhort interval, Lord Durham proceeded to enlarge upon the merits of the Reform Bill. At the conclufion of his fpeech, Lord Carnarvon and the Bifhop of Exeter rofe at the fame time, but there was a general call for the latter to proceed; Lord Carnarvon therefore fat down, and the bifhop of Exeter faid,—

" I have been charged, my Lords, by the noble baron, with having made a malignant and falfe infinuation. I muft, therefore, beg permiſſion of your lordſhips to explain a part of what I ſaid on a former night. As well as I can remember, ſpeaking of the *Times* newſpaper, I ſaid that I ſuppoſed it was in ſome way or other connected with Government. The exact words I uſed are not preſent to my mind, but they were ſomething about certain articles, breathing the inſpiration— not of the Treaſury, becauſe I acquitted the noble lord at the head of it of any connection with the *Times*. (Laughter from the Miniſterial benches.) What I ſay ſeems ſport to noble lords near me, and I hope it will not be thought a very ſerious matter to myſelf When I gave utterance to what has been the ſubject of remark, I by no means meant to fix upon any individual in particular ; but in my own mind I did think that the rumours reſpecting the noble baron were not unlikely to be in ſome degree true. (Some noble lords here required the biſhop to ſpeak out.) I will endea- vour to ſpeak up, ſo as to be heard, but it is my misfortune not to have many friends near me, excepting the right rev. friends by whom I am ſurrounded. The noble marquis (Clanricarde, it was believed), if he has anything to ſay, ought to ſpeak ſo that I may anſwer him. I aſſure the noble baron that I was not anxious to preſs upon the notice of the Houſe the particular part of my ſpeech which he refers to. I ſpoke generally, becauſe, I fairly own, I had not evidence beyond apparent probability. But while I did not wiſh directly to charge the noble baron, give me leave to ſay, that what I alluded to was not the only occaſion on which there has been an apparent connection between the Government and the newſpapers. One inſtance weighs with me more ſtrongly than it may with the noble marquis. About five or ſix weeks ago—['order, order']—a charge has been made againſt me, and, if not irregular, I wiſh to advert to it. There was a ſtatement in the *Times* newſpaper regarding a correſpondence with the noble duke, whom I ſee oppoſite (the Duke of Buckingham)—I hope he will forgive my ſpeaking of it in this way in his preſence ; and it is my earneſt hope that he will contradict me if I state what is untrue, and correct me if I state what is improper. About the 23rd of January, or some such period, there was a direct allusion in the *Times* to a supposed correspondence between that noble duke and his Majesty, as well as between a noble duke and his Majesty's secretary. The nature of the correspondence appeared to be stated with such particularity, that, if it were at all true, it seemed to me that the information must have gone to the newspaper from some person who had had access to the correspondence. It seemed to me also more probable that it should have found its way to the public from some member of his Majesty's Government, than from the noble duke. Most certainly, I have no hesitation in saying that it does appear to me that it must have gone to the newspapers through some person who had access to the Government papers."

The Duke of Buckingham then rose, and fully confirmed the statement of the bishop, saying that in his capacity as a peer of the realm he had written the letter referred to, and had transmitted it to the King through his Majesty's secretary, in the usual and regular way. He further stated that he had given no one a copy of that letter, and had only read it to two members of his own family, to the Duke of Wellington, and to one other person, and that part of this letter was inserted *verbatim* in the *Times* newspaper. This announcement was received with loud and repeated cheers from the opposition benches. Earl Grey rose in the midst of the tumult—for it was scarcely less—and, after waiting a short time for a hearing, expressed his sorrow that the debate should have been interrupted by such a discussion. He then went on to say, in language which M. Guizot, when speaking of his treatment of Canning, has well characterized as "haughty and contemptuous violence," that the fact, as ftated by the Duke of Buckingham, was perfectly true. The King *had* received the letter, and, acting as a conftitutional monarch, had fent the letter to his minifter.

"I can fay, upon my honour as a peer," he continued, "that I gave no copy. I certainly did communicate it to my colleagues—it was my duty to do it; and I think I can fay for them, as I affert for myfelf, that it was not from them, nor from any perfon connected with them, that any part of the letter, any allufion to it, or abftract of it, found its way into the public papers. No perfon was more afto-nifhed than I was when I faw an allufion to it. I do not know whether it is neceffary for me to fay more upon this fubject; but I can fafely fay that what was printed did not proceed from his Majefty's advifers. As a perfon ftanding in an oftenfible fituation in the Government, I difclaim any connection with any one publication, and I moft diftinctly deny that I have done anything to influence a fingle newf-paper. But the right rev. prelate faid, on the former night, that he had heard thefe things, and he believed them; but if I am miftaken, I beg his pardon."

The Bifhop of Exeter.—"I did not fay that I believed them, but that they had been believed."

Earl Grey continued:—"That they have been believed. (Great confufion; cries of 'order' and 'fpoke.') I cer-tainly underftood the right rev. prelate to exprefs the impref-fion on his own mind that there was truth in the charge. He has undoubtedly faid that there were infinuations againft other members of the King's Government, and he added that he had heard a ftory of my noble friend near me (Lord Durham). Now, mark the charity of the right rev. prelate —I fay, mark his charity—mark what he does not think im-probable! That my noble friend near me, connected with me not only by the bonds of office, but by the neareft, deareft,

and clofeft ties of relationfhip, has been guilty not merely of
fraud, but falfehood, and has fecretly and infidioufly furnifhed
newfpapers with the means of attack upon the very Government of which he is a member. That this he was ready to
do, and actually did, at the expenfe of tearing afunder the
tendereft and deareft ties of affection. If this be charity—
if this be the charity of a Chriftian bifhop, I am much deceived in the true nature of that virtue."

The Bifhop of Exeter then faid :—

"I rife only to explain. I never meant to charge the
noble baron with communicating any particulars to the
Times; but I faid that there was an apparent general connection between that paper and the Miniftry. If a declaration of what was paffing in the inner mind be extorted from
it, it is a little too much to fay that I meant it for an infinuation. I declared from the firft that I did not mean to
charge the noble baron with any particulars. Some of my
right rev. friends did not even think that I alluded at all to
the noble baron."

The Radical portion of the prefs were elated beyond
meafure at what they were pleafed to confider the
overthrow of the unpopular Bifhop of Exeter. The
Morning Chronicle founded a note of triumph in this
way :—

"In the early part of the evening the Bifhop of Exeter
was humbled to the duft. Lord Durham treated him as a
calumniator of the firft magnitude ; and the doughty prelate
fared ftill worfe, after his awkward attempt at explanation,
from a fevere caftigation from Earl Grey. It is much more
fafe to flander in a Review, or anonymoufly, than in an
affembly where the injured can defend themfelves."

But, in fpite of all this, and much more, *there was
the letter*, or, at all events, portions of it, fo like the

original that Lord Grey himfelf could neither deny the fimilarity, nor account for its appearance in the *Times*. No parliamentary fkill could explain away this ugly fact, or even tone it down. There it was, and there it muft remain—a myftery. If the Minifters had been put upon their trial for the publication of the letter, it is certain that any jury would have convicted them; and far wifer would it have been if they had allowed the bifhop's well-merited rebuke to pafs in filence. They had much better not have accepted his challenge. Facts were againft them, and an ill-judged defire to clear up that which admitted of no clearing up only threw out their conduct in bolder relief. Every unprejudiced reader, looking at the affair as a queftion of evidence, will feel convinced that the bifhop had fufficient grounds for his affertion, and that nothing which was faid in way of explanation tended in the leaft degree to alleviate the fmart of the lafh which he had fo feverely, but juftly, adminiftered.

After the fecond reading of the Reform Bill had been carried, the Duke of Wellington entered a proteft againft it on the journals of the Houfe. It was fubfequently figned by the Bifhop of Exeter, and feventy-two peers, including the Royal Dukes of Cumberland and Gloucefter.

It may be well thought that the ftrenuous oppofition of the bifhop to the Government meafure of Reform did not increafe his popularity. Deep and ominous were the murmurs which were heard in his own diocese, while, in the county of Durham, his effigy was publicly burnt with every demonstration of contempt. But, bitter as was the feeling against him, the bishop was not to be driven from the path of duty by signs of popular displeasure, however menacing. He had not feared the angry peers, and he was not likely to fear a discontented people. Very shortly after the division upon the second reading of the Reform Bill he set out for Exeter, and arrived at his palace on the Wednesday in Holy Week, April the 18th, and, having administered the rite of Confirmation at Exmouth on the 21st, preached the next day (Easter Day) in the cathedral to an overflowing congregation. Even his enemies could find no fault with his preaching; and, if they were not conciliated towards the *man*, they could not deny the rare abilities of the *preacher*. Those who heard the bishop in his prime say that there was a quiet dignity about his eloquence which at once arrested attention, and claimed respect, where the highest efforts of a more florid orator would have fallen powerless. Be this as it may, certain it is that, in the later days of his life, there has ever been a charm about his public addresses against which it would be hopeless to struggle.

Immediately after this the bishop set out on a confirmation tour through the south of Devon, visiting in turn Dawlish, Teignmouth, Torre, Paignton, Brixham, Dartmouth, Harberton, Totnes, and Newton. On the 29th of April he held an ordination at Exeter, at which twelve deacons and thirteen priests were ordained; and on the following day he confirmed the large number of 852 perfons in the cathedral. A few days afterwards he left for London to attend Parliament, confirming at Sidmouth and Axminfter on his way.

CHAPTER XXIV.

Reform Meeting at Exeter. Three Groans for the Bishop.
Violent Conduct of the People of Exeter. Ministerial Plan
of Education in Ireland. Uncompromising Opposition of the
Bishop. Lord Belhaven's Petition. The Bishop's Remarks
upon it. Separation of Religious from Secular Instruction
denounced. Meaning of Moral Instruction. The Bishop
attacked by the Lord Chancellor on the subject of the Duke of
Buckingham's Letter to the King. Explanations by the
Bishop. Violent Language of Lord Grey. The Bishop en-
treats that the Discussion may not be continued. He revives
it himself two days later. Imprudence of the Step. He
repeats his former Statement, with further Explanations.
He maintains that Lord Grey understood the Matter in the
same way as himself. Returns to Exeter. Engages a Villa
at Teignmouth. Preaches at Wolborough.

HE bishop had scarcely reached London
when a large reform meeting was held at
Exeter, presided over by the mayor, at
which three hearty groans were given for
his lordship. This ebullition of feeling is to be ascribed
to the uncompromising opposition which he had shown
to " popular" measures, and is, upon the whole, to be
regarded as an honour. The conduct of the enlightened citizens of Exeter upon this occasion foreshadowed
their daring profanity in later days, when they scrupled
not publicly to burn the symbol of man's redemption
in front of the west door of the cathedral, amidst the
plaudits of not a few of the inhabitants whose wealth
had purchased for them the title of respectable. The

hiffes and groans of fuch a multitude would ever be more melodious to the ears of a good man than their heartieft cheers.

The minifterial plan of education in Ireland ftill continued to occupy as large a fhare of public attention as could be fpared from the all-abforbing quefton of reform. Numerous petitions were prefented to Parliament againft it, and the bifhop was ever in his place ready to refift the progrefs of the meafure, and to expofe its perilous charaéter.

On May the 24th and June the 2nd the prefentation of petitions afforded him the opportunity of making a few obfervations ; and on July the 3rd, when Lord Belhaven prefented a petition from the General Affembly of the Kirk of Scotland, ftating their approval of the national plan of education adopted by the Government for the inftruéion, as well religious as otherwife, of the poorer claffes of Ireland, both Proteftants and Roman Catholics, the bifhop rofe and made fome powerful remarks upon the unfatisfaétory way in which the petition had been drawn up, alleging that it had been adopted in error, and did not do juftice to the feelings of the General Affembly. Speaking of the propofal for feparating religious from fecular inftruétion, he denounced it as a tremendous fymptom of the times, when a national fyftem of education could be founded upon a plan of feparating the literary, and even the moral, inftruétion of the people from a knowledge of their religious obligations. In his eftimation, moral inftruétion not only ought to impart a knowledge of every man's duty to his fellow-beings in this world, but a deep feeling as well as a knowledge of his relation to the Supreme Being, and of his hopes of a future state. And could any such instruction be true, he demanded, which was not founded upon the basis of God's Word—upon the basis of the Will of the Supreme Being? And where could this be known if instructors would not look at the Word of God, with which He had inspired the holy men of old?

This debate was remarkable for an attack upon the bishop by the Lord Chancellor, who thought this a suitable opportunity for reviving the story of the Duke of Buckingham's Letter to the King.* What this had to do with the matter in hand it would be hard to say; but it is a plain evidence of the uncomfortable feelings which had taken possession of the ministers, and of their desire to clear themselves from an irritating imputation by heaping abuse upon an adversary who had proved too strong for them. Several peers took part in the discussion which followed, and the bishop repeated what he had previously stated, viz. that he had never said that he believed it himself, but he had said that it was believed by other persons that there was a connection between the *Times* and the Government, and that the belief gave to the opinions expressed in that paper a peculiar weight. So little was Lord Grey satisfied with this statement, that he immediately rose and said that " all the venom went

---

* See page 392.

forth with the thin veil which the right rev. Prelate cautioufly fpread over it." He concluded by faying that he felt only difguft at the time, and now he felt nothing but contempt. It muft be confeffed that this is ftrong language—ftronger indeed than is ufually applied to any member of the Epifcopal Bench— ftronger probably than Lord Grey would have thought it fafe to apply to a layman. But fome allowance muft be made for heated feelings, and the unfatisfactory pofition in which the Government was placed. The Marquis of Salifbury called upon the Houfe to take notice of the terms which had been ufed ; but the bifhop entreated that the difcuffion might not be purfued any further, expreffing his regret that he had been the caufe of raifing the excitement. Whether his public life had been fuch as to juftify the expreffion of contempt on the part of Lord Grey, he was contented to leave to thofe who had obferved his conduct. He would fay nothing further than that he trufted to his character to protect him againft fuch a remark.

This unfeemly difcuffion was then allowed to drop.

Two days afterwards, however (July the 5th), it was revived by the bifhop himfelf, who, on prefenting a petition from the archdeacon and clergy of the Archdeaconry of Totnes, againft the Government fyftem of education in Ireland, took occafion to refer to the proceedings of the recent debate, defiring, as he faid, to fet himfelf right with the Houfe on a matter of fact. Confidering the ftate of feeling fo recently exhibited by the prime minifter as well as by other members of

the Government on this irritating queftion, moft people
will think that it would have been prudent in the
bifhop not to have provoked further difcuffion, more
particularly as the matter was evidently beyond the
hope of amicable adjuftment. It feemed to him, however, that his character required that certain explanations fhould be made, and, therefore, in a manly and
ftraightforward way, he came forward to make them.
All muft admire his candour, though they may queftion his tafte. He denied that he had ever ftated that
the letter of the Duke of Buckingham to the King
had been publifhed in the *Times*. He merely ftated
that the letter in queftion had been alluded to in that
newfpaper. He underftood that his ftatement had
been publifhed, and had excited confiderable difcuffion
in the newfpapers at the time; but as he had, immediately after making it, gone into the country to attend
to the difcharge of his epifcopal duties, it fo happened
that he had not read any report of what he had then
faid, until within the laft few days, when, on referring
to the ordinary records, he found the following words
attributed to him on that occafion :—

" About the 23rd of January, or fome fuch period, there
was a direct allufion in the *Times* to a fuppofed correfpondence between the noble duke (Buckingham) whom I have
now the happinefs to fee in his place, and his Majefty,
as well as between a noble duke and his Majefty's fecre-
tary."

It appeared, therefore, he continued, that all he had
then faid was that there had been an allufion made in

the *Times* to the noble duke's letter. It would feem, indeed, from what then fell from the noble earl at the head of his Majefty's Government (Earl Grey), that the fame notion which he entertained was alfo paffing through his lordfhip's mind, for he was reported to have ufed the following words :—

" The noble duke gave no copy of it, and I can fay, upon my honour as a peer, that I gave none. I certainly did communicate it to my colleagues : it was my duty to do it ; and I think I can fay for them, as I affert for myfelf, that it was not from them, nor from any perfon connected with them, that any part of the letter, any allufion to it, or abftract of it, found its way into the public papers. No perfon was more aftonifhed than I was when I faw it. I do not know whether it is neceffary for me to fay more upon this fubject, but I can fafely fay that what was printed did not proceed from his Majefty's advifers."

It was plain from this, the bifhop argued, that Lord Grey underftood the matter in the fame way that he himfelf did at the time. From the noble earl's filence it is to be prefumed that he thought it difcreet not to enter into further controverfy with the bifhop, for, after fome remarks by the Marquis of Londonderry and Vifcount Melbourne, the fubject was allowed to drop.

A few days after this the bifhop returned to Exeter (July the 10th), confirming at Honiton on his way ; and a little later he proceeded to Teignmouth—an attractive watering-place on the fouth coaft of Devon, about fifteen miles from Exeter, where a pretty villa had been engaged for his reception. On the laft

Sunday in the month he preached at Wolborough, near
Newton Abbott, on behalf of the National School, and
a very impreffive fermon was refponded to by a liberal
collection.   While refiding at Teignmouth the living
of Pinhoe near Exeter fell to his gift, and he beftowed
it (20th of July) on the Rev. Dacres Adams.

405

CHAPTER XXV.

Appearance of the Cholera in Exeter. Diſgraceful Condition of the Principal Cemetery. The Order in Council for providing Special Burial-grounds not applicable to Exeter. Offer of a Field on S. David's Hill for Interment of Cholera Patients. DiſſatisfaЕtion of the Pariſhioners. Shocking Scene at a Funeral. Committee appointed to ſeleЕt a ſuitable Spot. The Biſhop applied to for his Licence. His Reply. Much Time loſt. The Biſhop unjuſtly blamed for the Delay. Bury Meadow appropriated as a Cholera Burying-ground. The Biſhop grants his Licence. A Day for Prayer and Humiliation appointed. Special Service at the Cathedral. The Cholera abates. A Day appointed for Thankſgiving. The Biſhop preaches at the Cathedral. Meeting at the Guildhall to preſent a Teſtimonial to the Medical Men. The Biſhop propoſes the Reſolutions. His high Praiſe of the ConduЕt of the Medical Men. Cenſured for having been abſent from Exeter during Ravages of the Cholera. His Abſence ex-plained.

HE cholera, which had been devaſtating other parts of England, broke out in Exeter on the 19th of July (1831). Its appearance found the good city unprepared to receive it, and great was the conſternation when it became known that the plague had aЕtually begun. The principal cemetery had long been a diſgrace to the municipal authorities, being in cloſe proximity to a crowded part of the town, and ſurrounded with houſes. It was totally incapable of anſwering the de-mands which were about to be made upon it. An Order in Council had empowered pariſhes to provide

private burial-grounds for thofe who died of cholera, but unfortunately this could not be made applicable to Exeter. Towards the end of July a remonftrance was addreffed to the Board of Health againft any further burials taking place in the cemetery (Bartholomew Yard). Meanwhile the corporation of the poor had generoufly offered a portion of Bury Meadow for the burial of cholera patients. This was a field fituate on S. David's Hill, and tolerably remote from any dwelling-houfe. But if the reft of the city were fatisfied with this arrangement, the parifhioners of S. David's were not difpofed fo eafily to acquiefce. It was bringing the peftilence too near to their own doors, they thought; and fo when a corpfe was about to be interred there they rofe in tumult and prevented the burial. The fexton took to his heels, and a ftrong party remained clofe at hand during the night to refift any further attempt at interment.

The feleftion of an appropriate fpot for burials then became a ferious queftion. A cemetery committee was appointed, and after examining various fites they came to the conclufion that no fpot was fo favourable as Bury Meadow. To enable the clergy to perform funerals there it was neceffary that it fhould be licenfed by the bifhop. A deputation was therefore appointed to wait upon his lordfhip; to which he returned the following reply:—

"Brideftowe, 12th Auguft, 1832.

"The Bifhop of Exeter having this day received a communication from the Mayor of Exeter, in perfon, as chairman of the Board of Health, attended by Mr. Pearfe, a member of the Board, and by Mr. Dymond, with a plan of the ground propofed to be affigned as a cemetery for the interment of the bodies of perfons who have died of cholera, has given immediate attention to the circumftances of the cafe, and has no difficulty or hefitation in faying that, fuppofing thefe circumftances to have been accurately reprefented in the plan and meafurements fubmitted to him, he will have real gratification in granting his licence for the purpofe.

" The circumftances which have induced him to come to this decifion are, that no footpath traverfes the piece of land propofed ; that, on the contrary, the path, at the neareft point, is diftant 180 or 200 feet, or thereabouts ; that only one houfe is in the neighbourhood, and that at a diftance of more than 500 feet ; that S. David's Church is at about the fame diftance ; that the land may be approached by a road of little traffic, and not actually contiguous to it, but nearly 100 feet diftant from it.

" If thefe particulars are as defcribed, the place feems to the bifhop as little liable to reafonable objection as can be hoped. He will, therefore, grant his licence, unlefs thefe particulars be difproved, or other objections of real weight ftated, which do not occur to his mind at prefent.

" His neceffary abfence from Exeter, and his frequent change of ftation in the courfe of the next few days,* will caufe delay in preparing the inftruments and fubmitting them for his fignature. Meanwhile, he cannot wifh the ufe of the ground to be delayed. Thofe, therefore, of the clergy of Exeter whofe parifhioners may need their fervice on this melancholy occafion, will not incur any cenfure from him if they immediately bury corpfes in this ground, unlefs they are fatisfied that the facts of the cafe are not fuch as have been ftated above.

" The bifhop depends on the mayor having the good-

* He was on a Confirmation tour.

nefs to make an immediate communication of the contents
of this paper to the minifter and churchwardens of S.
David's, in order that an immediate opportunity may be afforded to them to ftate any objeftions, or make any obfervations, which they may wifh, before the licence iffues.
The movements of the bifhop may be known by confulting
the paragraphs of the newfpapers, which ftate his route.
He purpofes being at Teignmouth on Thurfday evening
the 16th inftant."

A comparifon of the date of this letter with the
breaking out of the peftilence in Exeter (19th July)
will fhow that much valuable time had been loft.
Meanwhile, the ftate of the cemetery had become appalling. It was moft ungenerous and unjuftifiable,
however, to faften the blame of this delay upon the
bifhop, as a portion of the prefs endeavoured to do.
As foon as the application was made to him he refponded to it. And what more could he do? If the
inhabitants of Exeter were fo little alive to their own
interefts as to fpend a whole month in quarrelling
over the feleftion of a burial-ground, while the cholera
was raging with fearful violence among them, the
fault was all their own, and they had no right to
complain if they paid the penalty of their procrafti-
nation.

A few days after the receipt of the bifhop's letter
Bury Meadow was appropriated by the corporation of
the poor to be a cholera burying-ground for ten years
from the date of the laft interment. The parifhioners
of S. David's were ftill diffatisfied with the arrangement, and a deputation was appointed to wait upon

the bifhop, in the hope that he might be induced to withhold his licence. It was plain, however, that their complaints were frivolous, and that fimilar objections might be raifed againft nearly every other fpot of land in the neighbourhood of the town; the bifhop, therefore, caufed his licence to iffue on the 17th of Auguft.

Meanwhile the peftilence was increafing in violence; drunkennefs and the moft revolting profligacy among the poorer claffes only too furely preparing its way. It was under circumftances of almoft univerfal defolation, when men's hearts were failing them for fear, that Wednefday, Auguft the 22nd, was appointed for fpecial prayer and humiliation. The bifhop was abfent from the city, but he arrived the evening previoufly, and after attending the fpecial fervice at the cathedral in the morning, left Exeter to refume his Confirmation tour.

Never, within the memory of the oldeft inhabitant, had a Sunday been kept with greater ftrictnefs than the day appointed to fupplicate God to remove His plague from a repentant people. All worldly bufinefs was, as far as poffible, fufpended. The churches were open morning and evening, and were thronged with devout worfhippers. The mayor and chamber attended the fpecial fervice at the cathedral, when an appropriate and impreffive fermon was preached by the Rev. Dr. Barnes, Archdeacon of Barnftaple, from Ifaiah li. 12, 13.

About the middle of September the peftilence began

to abate, and, on the fuggeftion of the bifhop, Thurfday, October the 11th, was fet apart for the purpofe of
thanking God for removing it from Exeter.   The
day was obferved with great folemnity.   Bufinefs was
fufpended; public houfes were clofed; churches were
thrown open morning and evening, and a fpecial fervice was held in the cathedral, at which the mayor
and chamber were prefent, when the bifhop preached
from 2 Sam. xxiv. 14 and following.   Shortly after
this it was determined to offer to the medical gentlemen of the city a tribute of gratitude, in token of the
high value fet upon their fervices during this trying
emergency.   A public meeting was accordingly held
in the Guildhall, the 22nd of October, the mayor in
the chair, for the purpofe of taking the matter into
confideration.

The bifhop, it appears, had not been informed that
the meeting was convened, and only received intelligence of it half an hour before it affembled.   Determined, however, not to be wanting upon fuch an occafion he haftened to the Guildhall, and arrived in
time to propofe fome refolutions, which were unanimoufly adopted.   In the courfe of his fpeech he paid
the following well-deferved tribute to the zeal and
energy of the medical men :—

" It is well known that when the fearful difeafe firft
made its appearance in this city, the laudable exertions of
the medical practitioners were met, from the effect of unhappy prejudice, by the moft inveterate hoftility on the part of
the poorer clafes ; but this unfounded feeling they afterwards
deeply lamented, and they will now be enabled, as I am

fure they are moft eager to do, to add their teftimony to
that of their fellow-citizens, of the deep fenfe they entertain
of the fingular fkill, as well as great attention difplayed on
a moft trying occafion by our eftimable medical practitioners.
When the difeafe firft exhibited itfelf in this city, it found
us, from its new and formidable character, furrounded with
many difficulties, calculated to excite great fear and apprehenfion; but the medical gentlemen found the means at
once of oppofing, in a great degree, all the tremendoufly
perplexing circumftances with which we were encompaffed.
Such indeed was their perfevering devotion to the caufe of
fuffering humanity, that they did not leave their poft, by
day or night, fo that by their admirable arrangements, no
matter what might be the hour, or in what part of the city,
whenever an individual, however poor and deftitute might
be his or her condition, was attacked with the fymptoms of
the deftructive malady, a fkilful, able, and affectionate attendant was, in a very fhort fpace of time, at hand to render
all the affiftance which human aid could minifter; and it
muft be confidered, that, under the bleffing of Divine Providence, we owe to the fkill and ability difplayed in the fuccefsful treatment of the difeafe, and to the efficient plan
adopted for its fpeedy application, the happy ceffation of
the malady among us. If, then, this city has ever been
diftinguifhed for medical fcience, it is not now the lefs diftinguifhed by the talents of the members of that honourable
profeffion refiding within this city, who, without any hope,
in numberlefs cafes, of receiving even the miferable fees to
which they are by right entitled, have by overworking the
energies of their bodies, as well as the powers of their minds,
fucceeded in arrefting, under Providence, the progrefs of a
difeafe which threatened no one can tell what extent of deftruction; and although we cannot look for a perpetual
ceffation of the difeafe amongft us, we have the confolation
of knowing that, fhould it again appear within our city, it
will be met with the fame fkill and perfeverance, and with
the bleffing of Providence be again fubdued. I really feel

that I am doing great injuſtice to the cauſe I have taken in hand; but I truſt this will, in ſome meaſure, be attributed to the very ſhort period of time that has elapſed ſince I firſt became acquainted with your intention of meeting. At the ſame time I feel aſſured that no language I could have uſed would have done anything like juſtice to the ſkill and diſin-tereſted devotion of the medical gentlemen, or ·by any means adequately expreſſed the feelings of the public on this occa-ſion. I will not detain you longer, but beg at once to move the Reſolutions."

But while the biſhop was extolling the conduct of the medical men, his detractors were loud in cenſur-ing his own. Why had he quitted his cathedral city, they aſked, at a ſeaſon of ſuch unprecedented ſadneſs? Why had he not given the clergy the comfort of his preſence in the diſcharge of their trying and perilous duties? It is true enough that the biſhop was abſent from Exeter, with the exception of two or three hurried viſits, during the whole time in which the plague was raging, and thus a kind of colour was given to theſe complaints. But he was not conſulting for his own ſafety, or ſeeking his own convenience, much leſs was he flying from duty; and they who attribute fear to him can know little of thoſe iron nerves which the preſence of no danger has been ſtrong enough to ſhake. The truth is, he was abſent on a Confirmation tour, planned ſome time previouſly, the due completion of which was of paramount importance to the various pariſhes which he deſigned to viſit. No thought, therefore, of danger or perſonal inconvenience could induce him to change his plan. While his family, then, were in comparative ſafety in the pleaſant watering place of Teignmouth, the bifhop was traverfing his diocefe from parifh to parifh, confirming the younger members of his flock, and fhowing that the prefence even of the cholera itfelf was in his judgment no bar to their receiving the means of grace.

CHAPTER XXVI.

Confirmation Tour. Confecration of Bedford Chapel. The Bifhop's Letter to the Mayor on the Queftion of poftponing it. The Bifhop prefents to a Living by "lapfe." Remarks on it. The Precentorfhip of Exeter Cathedral. Further Promotion of the Bifhop's Son. The Bifhop and his Family return to Exeter from Teignmouth. Anniverfary of Society for Propagating the Gofpel in Foreign Parts. Ordination. Clofe of the Second Year of Epifcopate.

HE Confirmation tour referred to in the laft chapter commenced on Auguft the 6th, and continued until the 16th of the fame month. It was renewed on September the 1ft, and terminated on the 15th.

At intervals during this time the bifhop paid fhort vifits to Exeter; upon one occafion for the confecration of Bedford chapel, a hideous building which had recently been erected. It had been arranged that it fhould be confecrated on Auguft the 4th; but as the cholera was then raging in the city, the bifhop was doubtful about the propriety of proceeding with the ceremony, for reafons which are affigned by his lordfhip in the following letter to the mayor (William Kennaway, Efq.):—

"Dear Sir, "Teignmouth, 2 Auguft, 1832.
"Under the peculiar circumftances of the time, when it has pleafed God to fend the cholera into our city, I feel it my duty to communicate with you before I finally refolve on

performing a ceremony which may draw a large concourfe of people together, and fo may endanger the further propagation of the diforder. I allude to the intended confecration of the new church in Bedford Circus. If you, under the advice of the Medical Board, wifh that the ceremony fhould be deferred, I fhall certainly comply. In faying this, I affure you that I have no perfonal apprehenfion, nor do I myfelf forefee any greater danger than from a large congregation at church on an ordinary occafion, unlefs it be probable that there will be a confluence of perfons from the infected parts of the place. If there be not the probability of danger, I would greatly prefer letting the fervice proceed as was intended.

"Your faithful Servant,

"The Right Worfhipful   " H. Exeter.
the Mayor of Exeter."

The bifhop's letter was duly confidered; and it having been intimated that no rifk of a confluence of perfons from infected parts was to be anticipated, his lordfhip came to Exeter and confecrated the chapel on Auguft the 4th, and after the fervice immediately left for Teignmouth.

On the 17th of this month (Auguft), he prefented the Rev. Robert Gee to the vicarage of Paignton, near Torquay. This was by lapfe. It will be neceffary to explain the principle of "lapfe," and the ufe to which it has been turned by the bifhop. And this is the more imperative fince his conduct, in this particular, has been the fubject of fevere and very extenfive animadverfion. Inftead, however, of entering upon the queftion in this place it is thought more convenient to poftpone it till the cafe of a living comes under consideration which was the subject of protracted litigation, and which furnished occasion for bitter remark. The various instances in which the bishop has availed himself of a " lapse " to present to benefices will then be examined.

The Confirmation tour being ended, the bishop returned to Exeter, and immediately afterwards left for Teignmouth, where his family were still staying.

The precentorship of the cathedral having become vacant by the death of the Rev. Thomas Bartlam, the bishop conferred it on the Rev. Thomas Hill Lowe (afterwards Dean of Exeter), and at the same time collated him to a prebendal stall in the cathedral. This gentleman had hitherto held the vicarage of Grimley, with the chapel of Hallow annexed, in the diocese of Worcester ; a comfortable piece of preferment, which he resigned on being promoted to cathedral honours in Exeter, and to which the bishop's son, the Rev. John Phillpotts, of whom mention has been made already,* was collated.   The Rev. Uriah Tonkin was presented by the bishop to the living of Uny, vacated by his son, Mr. Phillpotts.

Early in October the bishop and his family returned to Exeter, where he continued in residence at the palace for several weeks.   On the 25th of that month the anniversary of the Society for Propagating the Gospel in Foreign Parts, and the Society for Promoting Christian Knowledge, was held.   The civic

---

* See page 325.

authorities walked in proceffion to the cathedral, and, after an impreffive fermon by the bifhop from Matt. xxiv. 14, a collection was made, amounting to 74*l.* After fervice there was the ufual meeting at the Guild-hall, the bifhop in the chair ; but the proceedings were of the ordinary character, and require no notice.

On the 28th of October—ftill in difregard of the Ember Seafon—an Ordination was held in the cathedral, at which nine deacons and fourteen priefts were ordained.

The next two months were fpent by the bifhop in the general work of fuperintending his diocefe. He frequently preached in the churches of Exeter and the neighbourhood, and his difcourfes were invariably liftened to by a reverent and refpectful congregation. Nothing worthy of record occurs to mark the clofe of the fecond year of his epifcopate ; but the year that was opening was deftined to be an eventful one.

APPENDIX.

A.

Chronological Lift of the Bifhops of Exeter.

A. D.

1050. Leofric.

1073. Ofbern, or Ofbert.

1107. William Warelwaft.

1138. Robert Chichefter.

1155. Robert Warelwaft—nephew to William, the third Bifhop.

1161. Bartholomew.

1186. John.

1194. Henry Marfhall.

1214. Simon de Apulia.

1224. William Briwere, or Bruere.

1245. Richard Blondy.

1258. Walter Bronefcombe.

1280. Peter Quivil.

1292. Thomas de Bytton.

1308. Walter de Stapledon.

1327. James Barkley.

1327. John de Grandiffon.

1370. Thomas de Brantyngham.

1395. Edmund Stafford.

1419. John Catterick.

1420. Edmund Lacy.

1458. George Nevylle.

1465. John Bothe.

1478. Peter Courtenay.

1487. Richard Fox.
1493. Oliver King.
1495. Richard Redmayne.
1502. John Arundell.
1504. Hugh Oldham.
1519. John Veyſey. (Deprived 1551.)
1551. Myles Coverdale.
1553. John Veyſey. (Reſtored.)
1555. James Turberville.
1560. William Alley.
1571. William Bradbridge.
1578. John Woolton.
1595. Gervaſe Babington.
1598. William Cotton.
1621. Valentine Cary.
1627. Joſeph Hall.
1642. Ralph Brownrigg.
1660. John Gauden.
1662. Seth Ward.
1667. Anthony Sparrow.
1676. Thomas Lamplugh.
1688. Jonathan Trelawney.
1707. Offspring Blackall.
1716. Lancelot Blackburn.
1724. Stephen Weſton.
1742. Nicholas Clagett.
1746. George Lavington.
1763. Frederick Keppel.
1778. John Roſs.
1792. William Buller.
1797. Henry Reginald Courtenay.
1803. John Fiſher.
1807. George Pelham.
1820. William Carey.
1830. Chriſtopher Bethell.
1831. Henry Phillpotts.

It occafionally happened that fome time elapfed between the death or tranflation of a bifhop and the appointment of a fucceffor. It cannot, therefore, always be afcertained with accuracy from the figures how long the epifcopate of each lafted.

It is worthy of remark that, of the fixty bifhops of Exeter, only three have filled the epifcopal chair for a longer period than the prefent occupant, viz :—John de Grandiffon, who was confecrated in 1327 and died in 1369, having been bifhop for forty-two years ; Edmund Lacy, who was tranflated from Hereford in 1420 and died in 1455, having been bifhop for thirty-five years ; and John Veyfey, who was confecrated in 1519, and was deprived in 1551, after an epifcopate of thirty-two years. He was reftored in 1553, and died the following year, having been bifhop for thirty-three years, not including the time during which he was deprived.

B.

Oath to the Pope taken by Roman Catholic Prelates.

" I, N. N., Archbifhop or Bifhop of the Church N., will henceforward be faithful and obedient to S. Peter the Apoftle, and the Holy Roman Catholic Church, and to our Lord N. Pope, and his fucceffors canonically inftituted. I will not in counfel, in confent, or in deed, be acceffory to their lofing life or limb : or that they be taken by wrongful caption ; or violent hands, in any fort, be laid upon them ; or any injuries inflicted, under any pretence whatever. Moreover, the counfel which they fhall entruft to me by themfelves, or by their Nuncios, or by letters, I will not difclofe to any one to their lofs knowingly. The Roman Papacy and the Royalties of S. Peter I will affift them to retain and defend (*falvo meo ordine*) againft every man. The Legate of the Apoftolic See, in his journeys to and fro, I will honourably entertain, and will affift in all his needs. The rights, the honors, privileges, and authority of the Holy Roman Church, of our Lord the Pope, and of his fucceffors aforefaid, I will take care to preferve, defend, augment, and promote. Neither will I be in counfel, nor in act, or enterprife, in which any things be devifed againft the fame our Lord, or the fame the Church, hurtful or pre-judicial to their perfons, right, honor, ftate, or power. And if I fhall know any fuch things treated of, or prepared, I will hinder it, to the beft of my power ; and, as foon as I can, will fignify it to the fame our Lord, or to fome other by whom it may come to his knowledge. The rules of the Holy Fathers, decrees, ordinances, or difpofitions, referva-tions, provifions, and mandates apoftolic, I will obferve with all my might, and will make to be obferved by others. When called to a Synod I will come, unlefs I fhall be pre-vented by a canonical impediment. The apoftolic refidence I will vifit myfelf in perfon every ten years; and to our Lord and his fucceffors aforefaid will render account con-cerning my paftoral office, and concerning all things to the ftate of my church, to the difcipline of my clergy and people, appertaining ; and the mandates Apoftolic given thereupon I will humbly receive, and with all diligence perform. But if by any legitimate impediment I fhall be detained, all the things aforefaid I will fulfil by a fure meffenger, having fpecial commiffion for that purpofe, out of the bofom of my chapter, or another placed in a dignity ecclefiaftical, or otherwife having a parfonage, or, in defect of thefe, by a diocefan prieft ; and if there be no clergy, by fome fecular or regular Prefbyter of tried probity and religion, fully in-ftructed concerning all the things aforefaid. But, refpecting the impediment aforefaid, I will give lawful proofs, to be tranfmitted through my faid meffenger to the Cardinal of the Holy Roman Church, prefect of the congregation *De propaganda Fide.* Moreover, the poffeffions to my table appertaining I will not fell, nor give, nor pledge, nor put

in feoffage anew, or in any way alienate, even under the
confent of the chapter of my church, without firft confulting
the Roman Pontiff. Thefe things all and feverally I will
the more inviolably obferve, the more affured I am that
nothing is contained therein which can conflict with my
due fidelity towards the moft ferene King of Great Britain
and Ireland, and the fucceffors to his throne. So help me
God, and thefe Holy Gofpels of God.

"So do I, N. N., Archbifhop or Bifhop of the Church
N., promife and engage."

C.

Oath to be taken by 3 James I. c. 4. s. 18.

" I, A. B., do truly and fincerely acknowledge, profefs,
teftify, and declare in my confcience before God and the
world, that our Sovereign Lord King James is lawful and
rightful King of this realm, and of all other His Majefty's
dominions and countries; and that the Pope, neither of
himfelf, nor by any authority of the Church or See of Rome,
or by any other means, with any other, hath any power or
authority to depofe the King, or to difpofe of any of his Majefty's kingdoms or dominions, or to authorize any foreign
prince to invade or annoy him or his countries, or to difcharge any of his fubjects of their allegiance and obedience
to his Majefty, or to give licence or leave to any of them to
bear arms, raife tumults, or to offer any violence or hurt to
His Majefty's royal perfon, ftate, or government, or to any
of His Majefty's fubjects within his dominions. And I do
fwear from my heart, that, notwithftanding any declaration
or fentence of excommunication or deprivation made or
granted, or to be made or granted, by the Pope or his fucceffors, or any authority derived or pretended to be derived
from him or his fee againft the faid King, his heirs or fucceffors, or any abfolution of the faid fubjects from their obe-

dience, I will bear faith and true allegiance to His Majefty, his heirs and fucceffors, and him and them will defend, to the uttermoft of my power, againft all confpiracies and attempts whatfoever which fhall be made againft his or their perfons, their Crown and dignity, by reafon or colour of any fuch fentence or declaration, or otherwife, and will do my beft endeavour to difclofe and make known to His Majefty, his heirs and fucceffors, all treafons and traitorous confpiracies, which I fhall know or hear of to be againft him or any of them. And I do further fwear that I do from my heart abhor, deteft, and abjure, as impious and heretical, this damnable doctrine and pofition, that Princes, which be excommunicated or deprived by the Pope, may be depofed or murdered by their fubjects, or any other whatfoever.

" And I do believe, and in my confcience am refolved, that neither the Pope, nor any other perfon whatfoever, hath power to abfolve me of this oath, or any part thereof, which I acknowledge by good and full authority to be lawfully miniftered unto me, and do renounce all pardons and difpenfations to the contrary.

" And all thefe things I do plainly and fincerely acknowledge and fwear, according to thefe exprefs words by me fpoken, and according to the plain and common fenfe and underftanding of the fame words, without any equivocation or mental evafion, or fecret refervation whatfoever ; and I do make this recognition and acknowledgment, heartily, willingly, and truly, upon the true faith of a Chriftian.

" So help me God."

END OF VOL. I.

CHISWICK PRESS : — PRINTED BY WHITTINGHAM AND WILKINS, TOOKS COURT, CHANCERY LANE.

www.ingramcontent.com/pod-product-compliance
Lightning Source LLC
Chambersburg PA
CBHW022028110726
47901CB00006B/1693